ABOUT 80 PERCENT LUCK

ABOUT 80 PERCENT LUCK

A Novel

Gene Wojciechowski

Kingston, New York  New York, New York

Copyright © 2001 Gene Wojciechowski

All rights reserved.

No part of this book may be reproduced or transmitted in any form or by any means, electronic or mechanical, including photocopying, recording, or by any information storage and retrieval system, without permission in writing from the publisher.

SPORTS ILLUSTRATED® and *Total*/SPORTS ILLUSTRATED are trademarks of Time Inc. Used under license.

For information about permission to reproduce selections from this book, please write to:
Permissions
Total Sports Publishing
100 Enterprise Drive
Kingston, NY 12401

www.TotalSportsPublishing.com

Cover design: Todd Radom
Interior design: Ann Sullivan

Library of Congress Cataloging-in-Publication Data

Wojciechowski, Gene.

    About 80 percent luck: a novel / Gene Wojciechowski.

      p. cm.

    ISBN 1-930844-08-5

     1. Sportswriters—Fiction. 2. Baseball—Fiction. I. Title: About eighty percent luck. II. Title.

PS3623.O53 A63 2001

813'.6—dc21

                                             00-054433

Printed in Canada

To Cheryl,

for saying yes to the blind date at Sox Park

ACKNOWLEDGMENTS

Assorted thanks to Chicago Cubs past and present, most notably Ed Lynch, whose baseball card will always occupy a place of honor; Jim Riggleman, Mark Grace, and Scott Servais—stand-up guys; seamheads extraordinaire Phil Rogers and Tim Kurkjian; Rick Reilly, who thinks 6-4-3 is the area code for Lake Forest; Janet Pawson; Ace Zablonski; Lara, Taylor, and the cat; T.L. Mann; Arlene Gill and Chuck Wasserstrom; Baich; Yosh Kawano; T.J. Simers, a beat man's nightmare; Kari Wojciechowski, translator; Buddy Lee; Daryl Van Schouwen; Barry Rozner; John Cherwa; and Jed Thorn.

ABOUT 80 PERCENT LUCK

One

THERE WAS A TIME WHEN JOE RILEY thought there was nothing better in the entire free world than working for the *Chicago Sentinel* sports department. Thought it was better than a square slice of Fox's pepperoni and sausage pizza, heavy on the sauce. Better than an Old Style in a frosted mug at Cork & Kerry. Even better than an afternoon at Wrigley Field, an early evening at Cubby Bear, and some pasta at Tuscany on Clark. But it was best to keep that a secret, what with Riley living on the South Side—Sox territory. He used to have a soft spot for the Sox, but all that ended when Jerry Reinsdorf bought the team, tore down old Comiskey, and replaced it with a concrete Wal-Mart with grass in the middle. You needed a pilot's license to reach your seat in the upper deck of new Comiskey. Bill Veeck, the beloved one-legged Sox owner of yesteryear, would have wept had he seen what they did to the place. The stadium was as sterile as a vasectomy clinic.

Of course, none of this meant much to Riley anymore. Sitting on his regular corner stool at the Cork, nursing a now lukewarm mug of Old Style, Riley barely glanced at his *Sentinel* sports section. Why bother? He had worked the copy rim 12 hours earlier, so he already knew what was in the 14-page, February 2 section: a Bulls game, a Bulls sider, a collection of pre-deadline Bulls notes, a Bulls "Who's Hot, Who's Not" filler piece, a Bulls scoring summary, some Bulls photo captions, a Bulls quote box, a Bulls column . . . everything Bulls. You would have thought Michael Jordan had never retired. There were also a couple of Hawks stories (big whoop), a pre-pre-NFL draft story on the

Bears' options with the number four pick, as well as another in a long line of mind-numbing pre-Olympic features, this one on some hormone-geeked, teenybopper ice skater from an obscure Eastern European police state posing as a republic. In protest, Riley had spell-checked *sequins* and then passed the story on without reading the remaining 71 inches of double lutzes and 5.9s. He did that all the time with stories he considered boring or unimportant—in other words, the MSL, XFL, Formula One, CBA, and anything that involved little girls twirling ribbons and throwing rubber balls into the air while Bach played over an arena loudspeaker. Rhythmic gymnastics, it was called, and it was an actual Olympic sport. *What's next?* thought Riley. *Grocery cart racing?*

There were some minor league notes about the Cubs and the Sox, an analysis on the continuing courtship of Colorado coach Gary Barnett by Southwest Missouri State (Barnett was quoted as saying he owed "the chance to see what the great state of Missouri had to say" to his family), a feature on the Northwestern basketball program, an advance on DePaul's upcoming game against South Florida, and an accompanying note about another heralded Blue Demons recruit who was sweating out the school's minimum admissions standards. There was a hunting column, a notes column, some wire stories, some high school stories (including a page-one account of the arrest of a local prep star who had allegedly moonlighted as a porn film extra), and the weekly Big Ten basketball preview. Standard early-February fare.

Riley had read the same stuff for years. Rather than relive it, he flipped open the business section, turned to the New York Stock Exchange agate, and ran his finger down the minuscule type until he reached the ticker symbol for *Sentinel* holdings: TSNE (The Sentinel Newspaper Empire). Up 25 cents to 52¼. He turned back to the front of the section, skimmed the stories above the fold, and then took a quick glance at the local market notes by Harding Owens, the *Sentinel*'s ancient business columnist. Owens used to write a twice-weekly stock column, but that was before his spectacular run of misinformed picks in the mid-1980s, when he shooed away would-be investors from Microsoft and Oracle and kept hyping any product from a certain electronic games producer ("I have seen the future, and it is Atari."). Now he rewrote press releases and was generally done in time to catch the 2:40 west line commuter back to Villa Park.

But the last item before the jump caught Riley's attention: "Sentinel, Union Set to Patch Differences." Riley turned the page and found the rest of Owens' column on page two. "Sources close to the stalled negotiations say the two sides are 'extremely optimistic' about finalizing a new deal between Sentinel management and the newspaper's union shop," wrote Owens. "As the Aussies say, 'No worries, mate!'"

Riley rolled his eyes at the forced writing style but was pleased with the news. Nobody wanted labor problems, especially a *Sentinel* near-lifer like himself. Riley wasn't anti-labor, per se, he just liked the idea of TSNE plodding along, making its money, throwing a little bit of it his way. Why bite the corporate hand that feeds you?

It had been about 11 tired years since Riley purchased his first share of TSNE stock. He was 25 at the time, fresh from three wonderful years covering small colleges and working the desk at the *Des Moines Register*. His roommate from Marquette (now a stockbroker at A.G. Edwards) had told him to join the company 401(k) plan, invest in TSNE, and watch the money grow. Riley wasn't rich, not by any stretch of the imagination; but he had a nice little nest egg, somewhere in the $80,000 range—though he couldn't touch it until he was 59½. That's all Riley cared about now: *Sentinel* stock, SIPs, ESOPs, mostly anything with an acronym. The sooner he could reach retirement, the better, too. That's why his late-morning routine (up at 11, walk the three blocks to the Cork by 12, first beer by 12:01) always included a careful look at the stock tables. It was what he lived for. That, Old Style, and his faithful pooch, Gil—named in honor of Gil Thorp, the sports section cartoon hero.

"Anything worth reading today, Joseph?" It was Connie, the Cork's afternoon bartender.

"Well," said Riley between sips, "the Fed isn't expected to tinker with the interest rates. Intel is nervous about a market glut of chips. And Paul Volcker is worried that Americans aren't saving enough."

"Volcker?" said Connie. "He play for the Sox?"

"No, Con. He used to play for the Federal Reserve Board. Now he starts for Bankers Trust of New York. He went free agent on us."

"I love when you talk high finance, Joseph."

Nobody ever called him Joseph, except his mother and his dean at Marquette. His father, who had worked the loading dock at the *Daily Times* for 32 years before dropping dead of Marlboro overdose, refused to acknowledge the name. He had pushed for "Zeke," but Gloria Riley wasn't about to name any son of hers after a former Green Bay Packers fullback. Gloria still sang "Bear Down, Chicago Bears" every Sunday.

"It will give the boy character," Sam Riley had argued.

"It will give him a complex, that's what it will do," Gloria had said, cradling the newborn in her arms. "I'm naming him Joseph James Riley, and if you don't like it, you can get pregnant on your own, carry eight pounds, six ounces of field-goal kicker around, go through fourteen hours of labor, have the nurses track down your spouse at the Billy Goat, and then, just when you think the little snapper is going to pop out, have the doctors say it's time for a cesarean."

"You know, this Joseph James name is growing on me," said Sam, pawing at the hospital floor with his battered steel-toed boots. "It's a beautiful thing."

But his dad never did call him Joseph. It was always J.J., or Riles, or Snapper. Or, in a tender moment, Joey. Sam died in 1983. He was 54. Riley was a week removed from graduation and only three weeks away from loading up his Chevy Impala and driving to Des Moines. The funeral mass was at St. Barnabas, the wake at St. Cork. Sam William Riley left behind a wife, a son, a paid-for bungalow on the outer reaches of Beverly, a company insurance policy, a savings account of $11,418, and a modest pension. All in all, the old man had done them proud. And, thanks to Sam, the Snapper knew everything there was to know about all things Chicago, especially when it came to Italian beef sandwiches, softball, and the Bears. By the time he spun in, sports was one of the few things father and son had in common.

Riley loved his dad, but not the way Roger Angell went on and on about *his* old man. Riley had just about had it with Angell's teary-eyed metaphors involving fatherhood and baseball. Enough already about the Brooklyn Dodgers. Sam Riley had taught his son how to fit a cup inside a jock, how to charge a ground ball, how to hook-slide, and how to carry five freshly poured ballpark beers with two hands. That was it. No fruited plains . . . no Ken Burns documentary . . . no inner meaning. It was baseball, for crissakes.

Sam had been partial to the Sox, but he'd had a soft spot for the Cubs. Softer than anyone ever knew. Sam played for the loading dock softball team and wore number 26, in honor of Billy Williams. He knew exactly how tall the Wrigley Field bleacher wall was (11½ feet high). He nearly cried when the Cubs gagged in 1969, and he never forgave Durocher. And it figured that the year after he died, the Cubs won 96 games and the National League Eastern Division.

"Freshen that up for you, Joseph?" Connie said.

"Not today," said Riley, snapped back to reality by the well-meaning bartender, who had a nice shape but was in dire need of orthodontics and a new bottle of peroxide. "Got to get to work early for another touchy-feely management seminar. Then comes the performance review session, followed by a brief lecture on synergy and the sobering news of my impending two percent raise."

"I didn't know you were the white-collar type," she said, the winter sunshine from the Western Avenue-side window doing an especially cruel number on her dark roots.

"All senior desk jockeys are considered union exempt," said Riley. "The *Sentinel* thinks it's a perk because this way we don't pay union dues. But on the management food chain, we're like pond scum."

"But you *are* management, right?" said Connie, edging closer, a smile beginning to emerge.

"Connie, I'm still just tipping you a buck, nothing more."

"Just checking, Joseph. Just checking."

The Dan Ryan was kind that day. Door to employee parking lot, the drive only took 25 minutes. Not bad for a Friday afternoon. Riley flashed his ID card at the security desk, walked up two flights of stairs, tapped the button on the cargo elevator, smiled happily for the security camera welded to the upper right-front corner, and then wondered how he was going to survive two hours of overhead projectors and pie charts without nodding off. He had fallen asleep in a similar seminar six months earlier, and Ileen Hollandsworth—the *Sentinel's* director of management services—was peeved enough to submit a written report to the Big Three: editor Thomas Jarrett, managing editor Robert "Hap" Storen, and assistant managing sports editor Terry Butler. Riley, who had a long-standing flirtation with Jarrett's secretary, arranged to have the editor's copy of the report "accidentally" disappear. Storen, who hated Hollandsworth and hated reports even more, tossed the memo as soon as he saw Ileen's name on the interoffice-mail envelope. But Butler, the ever efficient Butler, received and catalogued the report before Riley could soften the blow. It was sure to come up in the performance review.

While the others took notes on Hollandsworth's captivating account of the new cost-saving plans for editorial, Riley casually drew pictures of bunnies, pirates, Hornet F-17 fighter jets, houses with chimneys, and outlines of dead people. It would have made for a fascinating psychological study. Instead, it helped kill 90 minutes. Only 30 left.

"Okay," said Hollandsworth in that odd New England accent of hers, "I want to try a little exercise I learned at Wharton."

Riley rolled his eyes. Again with the Wharton School of Business? Hardly a sentence emerged from Hollandsworth's mouth that didn't include a reference to the nationally acclaimed business school at the University of Pennsylvania. Little did Ileen Hollandsworth know that her unofficial nickname at the *Sentinel* was "The Whoreton School of Horizontal Business," in honor of her remarkable corporate bedroom conquests. Riley could see why: The woman was built for a land-speed record. But Hollandsworth wasn't very discreet, a mortal sin in the gossipy world of newspapering. And it was a tie when it came to what was swelled more: her curvaceous upper body (some said enhanced by a smitten Beverly Hills cosmetic surgeon) or her head.

"Now then, I'd like each of you to pass your notes to the person directly to, let's say, your left," said Hollandsworth, as she flicked on the conference room lights. "That way we can exchange ideas, thoughts, suggestions. This worked wonders for me during my MBA work at Wharton."

Riley was busy staring at the Michigan Avenue traffic when the words began to take meaning. *Pass your notes to the left* . . .

"What the hell—" said Riley as he felt his "notes" being pulled from under his elbows. He reached for the papers, but it was too late.

"Let me guess," whispered his newly discovered classmate,

About 80 Percent Luck

"you're trying to win a scholarship to one of those art schools that you see advertised in *TV Guide*: 'Draw Pappy the Pirate and win free tuition.' Is that it?"

"Actually, it's *Readers Digest* . . . Bonny the Bunny . . . and it's free tuition, books, and all the number two pencils you can use. Now, can I have those back?"

"And disappoint Wonder Wharton? I don't think so. We must exchange ideas."

Riley hadn't noticed her before. He had arrived late, taken a seat in the near darkness, and then doodled by the light of the overhead projector. She was pretty—sort of a Princess Di cut, dirty-blond hair, dark green eyes, and a slightly crooked nose. No, not exactly crooked. More like a tiny S-curve in it.

"You're looking at my nose, aren't you?" she said.

"Huh?" said Riley, realizing that he had spent several full seconds staring at the thing. "I don't know what you're talking about."

"No, no, let's get this over with," she said, ignoring Riley's obvious lie. "Here's the deal with the nose: I played hoops at Wisconsin, caught an elbow from some butch at Purdue, and never got it fixed. Now it looks like a chicane, doesn't it?"

"A chicane?"

"I thought you were a sports guy," she said. "Daddy took me to the Monaco Grand Prix, that's the only reason I know what it's called. It's a real quick turn. A chicane."

"Monaco? I've barely been to Texaco. Anyway, there's not a lot of Formula One racing in Chicago," Riley said.

"Then you've never driven Lake Shore Drive during rush hour. Now *that's* competitive."

"Who exactly are you?"

"Megan Donahue," she said, pointing to the HELLO, I'M MEGAN DONAHUE sticker on her lapel. Riley hadn't bothered to wear his. "And you would be . . ."

"Damned."

"Tell me, or I pass your bunny rabbits to Fraulein Hollandsworth."

"Joe Riley. I'm associate assistant sports editor. One of a cast of thousands."

7

"Sounds exciting."

"Only if you like to eat Hormel beef stew dinners from a vending machine. By the look of your suit, you're not in maintenance services."

"Advertising. I'm the reason you had a Bulls special section."

"No, you're the reason I had to work seventy hours that week. No overtime, by the way."

"That's too bad. I made one hell of a commission."

"Congratulations. I'll make sure to nominate you for employee of the month."

"Already got it, plus the five free shares of *Sentinel* stock."

Riley had never been employee of the month, week, day, or nanosecond. And he certainly hadn't received any free stock. Most of all, he'd never met anyone like Megan Donahue in sports. Megan Donahue looked like someone who worked in advertising. Manicured nails. The Ann Taylor ensemble. A healthy, but not overbearing, amount of tasteful Tiffany's pickings. One of her diamond-stud earrings probably cost more than a new set of titanium Pings. Why hadn't he tried the advertising gig? That's where the real money was. After all, he had seen the account execs' private spaces in the covered parking area, the one right next to the historic *Sentinel* building, the one three blocks closer than the dimly lit yet $120-per-month lot where *Sentinel* serfs such as himself were required to park. The account execs lived well. Mercedeses. Lexuses. Beemers. Lincoln Navigators. All of them polished, Armor-Alled to death, and only moments removed from their respective car showrooms. Riley's Corolla had 111,847 miles on it and counting. Those things in the exec lot were road virgins. The odometers hadn't even worked up a sweat.

"By the way, how'd you know I worked in sports?"

"The Fraulein called roll before you snuck in. She wasn't pleased by your absence."

"I wasn't absent. I was tardy. There's a difference."

"Not to her, there isn't. She said it was 'typical of sports people'—and she said that with lots of disdain—and 'symptomatic of all members of the Toy Department.' That's what she called it, 'the Toy Department.'"

"She's not the first one to say that."

"So you're not worried?"

"What can I say—she's a Pisces queen and I'm a Taurus."

"Well, whatever you are, you're not much of an artist," she said, glancing at the drawings. "I wouldn't quit your day job."

"I work nights."

"Too bad; I don't. I was free tomorrow evening."

Riley hadn't had a Saturday night off in a thousand years. The *Sentinel*'s Sunday sports section was thick enough to crush a chihuahua. It was the department's pride and joy, an annual award winner in the Associated Press Sports Editors competition (the results usually fixed beforehand), and, most important, the *Sentinel*'s number one money-making section of the paper. It was filled with ads—tire ads, penile-implant ads, stereo ads, computer ads, more penile-implant ads, tout-sheet ads, car ads, golf-equipment ads—some of them sold by the somewhat alluring woman with the chicane nose.

"Are you asking me out?" Riley said.

"Daddy would never approve of such a thing," she said. "I was merely—"

"Ms. Donahue"—it was a peeved Hollandsworth, her New England prep-school accent at full power—"if you're done with your, uh . . . mild flirting, would you mind providing us with a thumbnail sketch of Mr. Riley's lecture notes?"

Megan's eyebrows formed an inverted V. All conversations ceased. It was as quiet as a confessional.

"Why Fra— I mean, Miss Hollandsworth," said Megan, rising from her seat, "I think 'sketch' is a perfect description of Mr. Riley's efforts."

Riley squirmed uneasily in his chair. Hollandsworth stood at the front of the conference room, arms crossed, clearly enjoying the moment. She would put Riley and his new little friend in their respective places.

"Continue, Ms. Donahue."

"In short, Mr. Riley proposes a three-part strategic economic plan to reduce company costs by further emphasizing synergy between our broadcast and publishing units," said Megan, pretending to read from Riley's doodling, when in fact she was staring at an F-17 with a spiffy jungle camouflage motif. "One, we should experiment with a hybrid reporter, someone capable of writing for the paper but also able to serve as an available on-air talent. Two, we cross-promote more effectively and aggressively. The *Sentinel*, in Mr. Riley's opinion, doesn't do enough to push our radio and television product. And three, in light of our recent gains in circulation and broadcast ratings, Mr. Riley thinks a two percent increase in advertising rates would be accepted with minimal complaint by our client base. In summation, I wish I would have thought of it myself."

Hollandsworth was speechless. So was Riley.

"Mr. Riley, perhaps I misjudged you," said Hollandsworth, her voice filled with newfound respect. "Two of those proposals are already under consideration by Mr. Lawrence himself, and I'd be most grateful if you'd allow me to submit your third proposal to my superiors."

"Uh, that would be fine. Whatever's best for the company. You know me . . . Mr. Team Player."

"Of course, I'd attach your name to the memo. That was SOP at Wharton."

"That's AOK with me."

"Well, then, I think that concludes today's session," said Hollandsworth, her smile lingering a few extra moments. "Thank you so much for coming, everybody. And again, Mr. Riley, thank you for your many insights."

"Just trying to make the Toy Department proud."

Riley made a beeline from his seat to the doorway, where Megan stood waiting with a smug smile on her face.

"Those are your proposals on Lawrence's desk, aren't they?"

"Maybe."

"Then why bail me out?"

"I liked your bunnies."

Across the hall, one of the rare working elevators arrived. Megan sprinted to the contraption, slipping in just before the gold doors came together. Riley couldn't help but notice her legs. Athletic, but zero chop. The woman had definitely played some hoops.

Riley glanced at his battered Bulova, a freebie given to him years ago during a pre-tournament day at Medinah. The *Sentinel*'s golf writer had called in sick, so Riley had taken his place, collected the complimentary goody bag (against company policy), shot a 97, tried to hit on the beer-cart girls, had three too many shots of free Macallan, and then ralphed on the club pro during the awards ceremony photo session. He wasn't invited back the following year.

"Shit, my performance review," muttered Riley, looking for the closest stairwell. "Butler will kill me."

Terry Butler was a fanatic about deadlines. Breaking deadline, preached Butler, cost time and money. He wouldn't stand for it. Not in deadline writing, deadline editing, or deadline appointments.

Riley sprinted down the stairs, gobbling up two, three steps at a time. Down six flights he went, until he reached the fourth floor—editorial. He hurriedly slapped his ID card against the security sensor, pushed the heavy glass door open, and then streaked past the business and metro departments before finally reaching sports. It was 3:58.

Sheila was at her desk just outside Butler's vacant office. She had a skin-colored earphone in place and a Casio mini-TV tucked inside a partially open desk drawer. *Oprah* was on in two minutes. Sheila never missed *Oprah*.

"Sheila, where's our fearless leader?"

"Taking a fearless dump," said Sheila in her rich, obnoxious nasal voice, the result of 60 years in Oak Lawn. "Anyway, what do I look like, his parole officer?"

The phone rang. Sheila glared at the offending instrument, waited until it was apparent no one else in the department was going to pick up, and then grabbed the receiver from its cradle.

"Sports," she said, not hiding the disgust in her voice.

Riley grabbed a copy of *USA Today* off her desk and began browsing. Sheila jotted down a quick note.

"Yes, sir," she said to the caller. "If you'll just hold on a moment I'm going to transfer you to someone on the copy desk. They'll be able to help you better."

She pressed the hold button.

"Somebody calling in a score?" Riley said.

"Not exactly," Sheila said.

Then she yelled to the copy rim. "I've got a death threat on line two! Says he has a packet of C-4! Says he'll use it if we don't start covering soccer! Who wants it?"

"I'll take it," said Greer, one of the layout editors. "Is it that guy from Bolivia again?"

"Do I look like Rand McNally to you?" Sheila said. "How the hell do I know?"

She turned her attention back to Riley, but only for a moment. "Oprah's on with Carol Burnett," she said. "So whatever you want, say it fast. I'm not going to miss a minute of the First Lady of Comedy."

"I thought Lucille Ball was the First Lady of Comedy."

"Who told you that? Whoever told you that don't know squat about comedy. Lucille Ball? I'll take my Carol and Harvey Korman over Lucy and Ethel any old day." Sheila tweaked the channel dial ever so slightly. Then she pulled a tissue from her Kleenex box, removed her earpiece, and wiped away what seemed to be a pea-sized lump of wax.

"What?" said Sheila. "You got some of those special ears that don't make wax? What is it you want? I'm less than a minute from *Oprah*."

"I've got a performance review at four," Riley said.

"Tell me about it. I had to type up everybody's review, all fifty-eight of them. You know what that does to fake nails? It ain't pretty, mister."

"So you know what my review says?"

"I know what mine says. I couldn't care less about yours or the rest of them."

That wasn't exactly true. According to Sheila's third husband, Barney . . . Bennie . . . Bobby—Riley couldn't remember for sure—the sports department secretary made duplicates of every Butler memo and performance review. "She thinks Butler wants to fire her because of her age, so she keeps everything," husband number three had said at the annual Christmas party. "The woman can be a class-A bitch, but she's a fireball in bed. You should see her."

Riley's stomach did a backflip at the memory of that conversation.

At exactly 4 P.M., Butler appeared from around the corner. His fly was open.

"C'mon in," he said without saying hello. "I've done seven of these today. Got two more left."

"So I can expect some quality job analysis?"

Butler shot him a death glance.

"I think you know how this is going to go," he said, pulling Riley's manila file from a stack atop his desk. "Here's your copy, with space reserved for any rebuttal comments you'd like to make."

Riley looked at the categories and Butler's accompanying remarks.

Management skills: *Below average. Not a go-getter.*
Leadership: *Below average. Rarely takes the initiative in deadline situations.*
Editing skills: *Average. Has trouble with ice skating stories.*
Attitude: *Below average. Not a team player. Seems bored with duties.*

Under "General Comments," Butler had written:

I had hoped that your promotion to associate assistant sports editor would result in a higher level of enthusiasm, productivity, and Sentinel spirit. Instead, you remain a marginally competent, but hardly inspired, member of our staff. In order for this section to achieve its ultimate goal—to be the best darn sports department in America—we need junior management personnel willing to do whatever it takes. The reality of the situation is this: You simply have no inclination to do so on a consistent basis. Therefore, I cannot recommend that you receive even a perfunctory raise of one percent.

Best wishes and have a super great day,
Butler

Riley stared at the final paragraph in disbelief.
"Nothing?"
"I've got a budget," Butler said. "I'm not going to waste it on people who think this is a nine-to-five job. I need people with passion."
"Then hire starving actors," Riley said. "I'm supposed to edit the section and make sure it meets deadline. I've done that."
"Hardly. Your night shift crew had the highest number of replates and missed deadlines."
"I missed two in three months."
"I rest my case."
Riley grabbed a pen off Butler's desk, signed the review, and tossed both toward his boss. It was useless to fight.
"By the way," said Riley, as he left the office, "your fly's open. Bet you were a big hit in the afternoon news meeting."

The image-conscious Butler nearly had a convulsion as he fumbled for his zipper. Sheila saw and heard the whole thing.

"Nice touch, honey," she said, snapping her wad of gum as Riley walked out of Butler's office. "I knew you could be an asshole if you put your mind to it."

"I thought you were getting your *Oprah* fix?"

"She's talking diet with Carol. Been there, done that. Anyway, has the woman looked at my Carol? She's a hundred pounds, fifty of it teeth. The last person she needs to be talking weight loss with is Carol Burnett."

"Nothing personal, Sheila," said Riley, glancing back at Butler, "but I better leave the vicinity before I do something silly, like get a gun permit."

"Get two, will ya?"

Riley stomped down the hall to the department mailboxes. He had 15 minutes to kill before his desk shift started. Considering what had just happened, he wasn't about to give the *Sentinel* any bonus work.

Mike Ratowski, the *Sentinel*'s Blackhawks beat reporter, was sifting through a stack of reader mail. The Hawks were one of the NHL's original six franchises, and their fans were as passionate as any in the country. They were never shy in their criticism or praise of Ratowski's coverage.

"What do you know, the great Riley," said Ratowski, otherwise known as "Rat." "I didn't know you desk guys got mail."

"We don't. We mostly steal free books and magazines sent to hockey writers."

"Thief."

"I like to think of it as inventive borrowing."

"By the way, thanks for going light on my copy these days. Some of those other guys are performing major surgery on my gamers. They must be on commission."

"Oh, you know me. I'm just trying to go oot and play the good 'ockey for the 'ockey club."

Rat shook his head. "There it is, ladies and gentlemen: the single worst Canadian accent in the lower forty-eight."

"But done with heart, Rat. Anyway, don't our kids play the Broad Street Billies tonight?"

"It's 'Bullies,' Bobby Hull. Yeah, I'm going there as soon as I get done meeting with Butler. In fact, I was supposed to follow you. You're done already?"

"Yep."

"That didn't take long. How'd it go?"

"About as well as Pamela Anderson doing Shakespeare."

"In the park? Or in the nude?"

"The park."

"That bad?"

"Put it this way: Connie is not going to be happy. I might have to reduce my tip allowance."

"Well, I'm hoping for five percent this year. I broke some stories. Didn't miss deadline. Made sure to call Butler 'Your Holy Eminence' every time I talked to him."

Rat had had a hell of a run. He scooped everyone with his story on Hawks owner Gerald Gustafson, who actually planned to require season ticket holders to purchase commemorative two-inch chunks of United Center ice for $150 each. *"A great way to own a piece of America's most beloved hockey franchise,"* read the brochure, which was secretly obtained by Rat weeks before the first scheduled mailing. *"Keep a chunk or two in your freezer. The gift that can last forever.* (*The Chicago Blackhawks are not responsible for any electrical malfunctions that may cause said chunk of ice to experience meltage in non-working freezer unit.)"*

Gustafson, who squeezed pennies so hard that Lincoln gasped for breath, was so upset by the story that he revoked Rat's media credentials. To Butler's credit, he simply quit covering the Hawks altogether. Gustafson finally relented, but Rat's press-row seat was curiously relocated to a spot directly behind a two-foot-wide support column. Rat responded by breaking another story, this one detailing an internal memo where Gustafson ordered team locker-room attendants to stop using detergent when washing Hawks sweaters. Instead, he suggested that attendants hoard hotel-room shampoo on road trips and then use the bottles for makeshift detergent. "This will save the organization tens of dollars per season and allow us to put a better hockey club on the ice," said the memo as reprinted in the *Sentinel*. "Thank you for your cooperation. Any mention of this memo to the press will result in immediate dismissal. Thank you, G.G."

Gustafson ordered an internal investigation to uncover the *Sentinel*'s source, going so far as to hire a private security agency (at $750 a day) to look into the matter. Rat never had the heart to tell Gustafson that he found the memo mistakenly placed in a media-release packet for "Hawks Fan Appreciation Night." The other reporters had tossed the packet. Rat, who read everything, discovered the mistake and made it his lead story the next day. Then he pulled the team media relations director aside and told her about the packet mistake but promised not to tell any club officials. The grateful media director quietly had Rat's press box position moved to a better vantage point.

"I'm sure you'll do just fine," Riley said. "Butler likes you. Better yet, he likes your work. You're good for five percent, maybe more."

"I hope so. Linda and I are expecting in June. I could use the money."

"Not me. I'm more into the minimum-wage experience."

"You are so full of shit, Riley," said Rat, as he placed his mail in his computer bag. "By the way, you read that thing in Owens' column today? Looks like we're okay on this labor thing."

"I take everything Harding says with a lump of salt."

"But he's usually right with the *Sentinel* sources," Rat said. "I mean, we're family, right?"

"Yeah, I'll give the geezer that much," Riley said. "He hasn't botched the *Sentinel* company line in years."

"Well," said Rat, nodding toward Butler's office, "I've got a review session."

"Yeah, you run along now," Riley said. "Don't worry about Grandma and me. We'll be fine. You kids just go oot and cover the 'ockey club."

Riley watched Rat as he walked to the sports editor's office. Butler greeted Rat at the doorway with a warm handshake and a smile as wide as a puck. There was even a backslap. Riley never got a backslap. Rat, only 25, was a rising star. The *Sentinel* would take care of him as if he were a newborn, wrapping him in the best assignments and presenting him with the occasional wink-wink, don't-tell-anybody-we-gave-you-an-eight-percent-bump-in-salary. He deserved it.

It was 4:30. Time for Riley to start editing high school basketball copy. Instead, he stared out the mailroom window into another Chicago dusk, wondering why nothing mattered to him.

Two

E. BENSON LAWRENCE, publisher of the great and powerful *Chicago Sentinel*, steered the kelly green Range Rover onto Lower Wacker Drive, his thoughts not on the little Honda he nearly broadsided while merging but on how he was about to bring a union and its supposedly bulletproof members to its knees. E. Benson Lawrence didn't like unions, though for appearances' sake he was a registered Democrat and was never shy about telling interviewers that his grandfather had been in Samuel Gompers' "army of blue collars"—whatever that meant. Lawrence's grandfather never actually knew the legendary labor leader, but since it was impossible for the magazine fact checkers to confirm the outlandish claim, the line almost always made it into yet another flattering story on the *Sentinel* publisher. If it were an especially gullible magazine writer, Lawrence would occasionally mention something about secretly funding Cesar Chavez's protest efforts in California during the mid-'60s. Of course, the only thing Lawrence and Chavez had in common was a fondness for grapes, though Lawrence preferred his from the private cellar of his sprawling new faux Tudor in Lake Forest.

The Guild leaders considered the handsome 46-year-old a loyal friend of labor—a severe miscalculation on their part. He had a newspaper to run, or, more correctly, a profit margin to maintain. During his 11 years as publisher of the *Sentinel* and chairman of the board of TSNE, the profit margin had gone from nine percent to 13, then to 16, then to an industry-best 31 before leveling off nicely at 27. The *Sentinel* made money. Lots of it. But not enough for TSNE shareholders, who thought the printing presses should be spitting out newspapers *and* dividend checks on a daily basis. Lawrence despised the shareholders almost as much as the union. He had a plan for both.

The speed limit was 30 miles per hour on Lower Wacker, but it was more of a suggestion than a law. Yellow taxis weaved between lanes like garter snakes between grass blades, their drivers leaning on their horns, their fares looking out the rear side windows with bored, superior faces. Lawrence pressed the gas pedal and the Range Rover's British-made V-8 responded immediately, leaving a Camry in his exhaust and almost forcing a blue-hair in her Dodge Dart to veer into the frozen Chicago River.

Glancing to his right, Lawrence could see the rows of cardboard refrigerator boxes propped against the outer basement walls of office buildings. Battered shopping carts, filled with beer and soda cans, stood guard outside the makeshift dwellings. His wife, the liposuction queen of the Midwest, laughingly called them "homeless subdivisions." Typical Veronica.

Lawrence had a strange fondness for the subterranean Lower Wacker. It was every bit as Chicago as Michigan Avenue, but in a grimier, grittier way. He liked playing a little game while driving the narrow four-lane road, which had more curves than his very private administrative assistant, the Stanford-educated and overqualified Miss Claire Beecher. First, could he miss the two puddles of grayish ooze that sat near the first turn of Lower Wacker? The ooze twins were the result of some indeterminate half-solid gunk that dripped from the tunnel's ancient ceiling. And second, could he reach Lower Michigan Avenue without having to stop for a red light and an unwanted visit from Charley, the toothless panhandler who spit-shined windshields for a buck?

So far, so good. Lawrence cut off one of the kamikaze Checkers, slipped into the left lane, and then—as the ooze pond appeared on the potholed-asphalt horizon—he straddled the center line, just missing the gunk with his brand new Bridgestones. Horns honked behind him, but Lawrence didn't care. The speedometer hit 53 as he gunned the great limey machine through a yellow light. He cleared the second light with no problem and was on his way past the third when a delivery truck appeared from behind a row of concrete columns on the south side of the street. Lawrence's freshly shined Bally wing tips pressed hard against the brake pedal. There was a screech, the smell of rubber, the gentle thud of Lawrence's alligator-skin briefcase doing a Nestea plunge from the passenger's seat to the floor mat. "Son of a bitch!" yelled Lawrence as the truck pulled slowly away, ignoring the red light in front of it.

Lawrence put the Rover in Park, unfastened his seat belt, and leaned down to retrieve the briefcase. That's when he heard the sound.

Hhhhhhhrrrrrriiiiinnnnkkk.

It was Charley. Actually, it was Charley's hawker. The green glob cascaded down the windshield like a fast-moving glacier and then, exhausted from its glass dance, slowly solidified on one of the wiper blades. Lawrence pressed the electric window opener just enough to slip a dollar bill through the crack and into Charley's outstretched hand.

"Bless y—" said Charley as the fast-closing window nearly snipped off his bare fingertips.

Lawrence stared straight ahead. He was tired of this daily-dollar commute. Someone would pay, beginning with John MacCauley, Guild leader and general *Sentinel* pain in the ass. It was time for a new world order, and Lawrence was just the guy to do the ordering.

He angrily stabbed a finger on the fast-dial button of his dashboard-mounted cellular. It rang twice.

"Mr. Lawrence's office," came the voice. Lawrence loved that voice. Actually, Lawrence loved Claire Beecher. But as long as the Countess of Collagen was around, he wasn't about to take a run at his lovely assistant. Illinois divorce statutes weren't fond of infidelity, even with someone as spectacularly proportioned as Miss Beecher. And since Lawrence valued money more than anything, the thought of Veronica living happily ever after on his vast array of zero-coupon bonds was incentive enough to remain relatively true to his second wife of 11 years.

"Claire, Lawrence here," his voice softening at the thought of what tight-fitting business suit his assistant might be wearing today.

"Yes, Mr. Lawrence. I take it you're on your way in?"

By now, Lawrence had taken a left onto Michigan Avenue, a quick right at that dreadful little Billy Goat Tavern that the paper's pressmen favored, and a quicker left into the *Sentinel*'s gated executive lot. He could have waited to make the call, but what was the use of being a powerful publisher if you couldn't abuse your cell phone allowance?

"I'm here. Look, what time is my appointment with MacCauley?"

"Mr. MacCauley is meeting you in the private dining room at Harry Caray's at 2:45, Mr. Lawrence. I've blocked out two hours for the lunch."

"Well, cancel it. Tell MacCauley that the *Sentinel* is ceasing its collective bargaining schedule. Wait. Don't cancel it. Let the son of a bitch cool his heels at the restaurant for a couple of hours. I hope they seat him near my eight-by-ten glossy."

"Uh, yes, sir, whatever you say. So you won't be joining Mr. MacCauley?"

"Joining him? Claire, we are declaring negotiating war today. Now, cancel the appointment, get our crack negotiating team on the phone, and tell them to be in my office at two o'clock. We have a big day in front of us. We're going to bust a union."

"I'll take care of it, sir."

Lawrence clicked off the speakerphone, grabbed his briefcase, locked the green beast, and made his way toward the back entrance. A few feet from the steel door he was met by a panhandler selling newspapers.

"Hey, mister," said the small, ill-kept man. "Buy a copy of *StreetSmarts*?"

"Certainly," said Lawrence, smiling as he flipped the man a quarter and then grabbed an issue of the paper, which was written on behalf of the city's homeless and funded with the help of the *Sentinel*. As the door shut, Lawrence glanced around in time to see the homeless man trying to pick up the quarter while wearing a pair of tattered mittens. Then he summoned the security officer on duty.

"See that man?" said Lawrence, pointing to one of the closed-circuit-television monitors mounted on the security-office wall.

"Why, yes I do, sir," said the security officer, whose crooked badge said SIMMONS—25 YEARS OF SERVICE. "That's ol' Bobby J. He's gentle as a summer breeze. Comes by here every so often. Used to be a cashier at the parking lot across the street until they went automated on him.

Now he can't find a job, so he sells those papers. We do what we can for him."

Lawrence glared. "If I wanted a Lifetime Channel biography, I would have asked for one . . . Simmons," said Lawrence, fumbling to remember the security officer's name. "Have him removed from the premises or I'll make sure you join him by day's end. Understand?"

"Uh-huh."

"Pardon me?"

"Yes, Mr. Lawrence. Right away."

"That's more like it," Lawrence said.

Lawrence stuffed his copy of *StreetSmarts* into a trash can, climbed a short flight of stairs, pressed the button for his private elevator, and then pulled out his pocket cellular.

"I'm a mere twenty-four stories away. By the time I walk off this elevator, I want to know if our security force is union. Thank you."

A smile crossed Lawrence's freshly shaven face. What a wonderful day to be management.

Three

MacCauley poked at the remnants of what had been two very good pork chops. All that was left now was bone and gristle, not that it mattered to MacCauley, who had a legendary appetite (and gut to go along with it). He picked up one of the bones and began gnawing at it as if it were an ear of corn. MacCauley liked Harry Caray's, especially when someone else was paying for a considerable lunch that included oysters, minestrone soup, a large salad, a half-loaf of sourdough bread, a pair of chops as thick as an overstuffed wallet, garlic mashed potatoes and gravy, a fudge sundae, and now a snifter of Courvoisier XO.

"Sir, may I take your plates?" said the busboy, his eyes wide in disbelief as he surveyed the remarkable array of empty dishes in front of MacCauley.

"Son, when you hear me belch, then you can clear my plates. Until then, get lost."

"Pardon me, sir?"

"You've got an inner ear infection, or something? I said, I'll let you know when I'm done."

The busboy nodded his head and quickly disappeared behind a partition. The waiter had warned him about John Patrick MacCauley, but the busboy, new to the job, was persistent. Now he knew.

MacCauley wore a Burberry double-breasted suit that did its best to hide his 280 pounds. But a good suit and tailor can only do so much. MacCauley was a large man and used his size—six foot six—to his advantage. Many an opposing negotiator had felt a table shudder under the considerable force of MacCauley's pounding fist.

"Time," said MacCauley, not bothering to look at his assistant, the ever faithful Fred Moss.

"Exactly 4:44. He's two hours late."

"He's not late, Fred. He's exactly where he wants to be. This isn't an accident. E. Benson Lawrence doesn't do anything by accident. The Yalie probably plans his trips to the crapper."

"I thought he was a Princeton man."

"Princeton, Yale . . . what does it matter? He's just another preppy who knows how to tie a Windsor knot and spell *candelabra*. But he still doesn't realize that this is Chicago, not the Ivy League. Still hasn't figured out that I'm John fuckin' MacCauley and I'm not taking his 'final' offer."

"The membership supports you wholeheartedly."

"Damn right, they do. Lawrence will understand that soon enough."

"If he ever shows up."

"Oh, he'll be here. He can't publish without my people. And if he can't publish, he can't make his precious profit margin. And if he can't make his profit margin, he'll be working for a shopper in Salina, Kansas."

"True enough, sir. But he is rather late."

"This is nothing. Making me wait two hours? Big fuckin' deal. The Mayor Richard Daley, God bless his lionhearted soul, used to make me wait twice as long. Tough son of a bitch, that Daley. Ruthless. But fair, mind you. Twice the man this Lawrence is."

"What do you think his intentions are, sir?"

"Not to look like a whimpering prick to his shareholders. He'll talk big, but when it comes nut-crunching time, he'll fold like the rest of them, like he did before. And if he doesn't piss me off too much, I won't de-nut him in the press. I almost feel sorry for His Bow Tie–ness."

"Sir, I think that's him coming up the steps."

"So it is. Busboy! Get these damn plates off here. Can't you see I've got company?"

The waiter moved first, not waiting for the busboy and not wanting to risk what could be a very substantial tip. Instead, waiter and busboy collided, sending the busboy face-first into MacCauley's lap. That's when Lawrence arrived.

"Why, MacCauley, those bread crumbs fall in the most peculiar places, don't they?" said Lawrence, clearly enjoying the chaos. "I prefer the usual fifteen percent tip, but you union boys have different ways of negotiating."

MacCauley pushed the busboy backwards, angrily stared at the waiter, and then steadied his gaze on Lawrence.

"Apparently, you don't prefer a watch," MacCauley said. "If you did, you would have been here two hours ago."

"Didn't my assistant call about the scheduling revision? I'm so sorry. I'll talk to her about the oversight first thing in the morning."

"I'm sure you will."

There was a moment of awkward silence as MacCauley tried to cover the busboy's saliva marks, which, unfortunately, were located near the union boss's crotch.

"I believe Martha Stewart recommends tonic water to clean those messy busboy stains," Lawrence said. "Or is it distilled water? I can never remember."

"You can kiss my ass."

"And ruin your budding relationship with the Harry Caray's support staff?" said Lawrence. "I wouldn't think of it."

The three men sat down. There was no shaking of hands, no hint of civility. MacCauley considered Lawrence no more of an adversary than Nixon did Pat Paulsen. Lawrence considered MacCauley a mutt, part Doberman, part terrier, part German shepherd. Dangerous, but trainable with firm, disciplined commands.

"Just so there isn't any misunderstanding, Lawrence, the Guild considers your most recent offer an insult," said MacCauley, back to his blustery self.

"An insult," chimed Moss.

"And, just so you also know, we're prepared to go public with your lame proposal, as well as expose old man Owens as the company mouthpiece that he is," MacCauley said. "Did you really think anyone would fall for that 'optimistic' bullshit you planted in his column? We've already contacted the local TV stations, including the one owned by your company. That should go over real well with the people who still remember the last time you tried busting the union. Your circulation dipped, what, twenty-eight thousand in a single week?"

"Since regained and doubled, I believe," said Lawrence, ignoring MacCauley's mocking tone.

"I went easy on you that time," MacCauley said. "If you're smart, there won't be a next time."

"I didn't attempt to bust the union six years ago, nor am I attempting to do so now," Lawrence lied with practiced ease. "We simply cannot sustain the financial demands of your membership and satisfy the needs of our shareholders."

"That's your problem, sonny boy. Your empire crumbles without my people. Didn't you learn that lesson already?"

Yes, I did, thought Lawrence. *And I'm about to show you exactly how well I learned it.*

"So, you find the final offer unsatisfactory?" Lawrence asked calmly.

"Jesus Christ," MacCauley grumbled. "Unsatisfactory. Unacceptable. Untenable. That clear enough for you?"

"As Waterford," said Lawrence.

"Now if you're done jerking off, maybe you can pay my lunch bill and we'll go find a bar where they serve hard liquor," said MacCauley as he waved the waiter to the table. "Then we'll work out a deal that makes my membership happy and lets you spend a month in the company condo at Steamboat."

"I'm afraid not," said Lawrence.

"Afraid not about what, sonny boy? The bill? Hell, I'll pay the damn thing. It was worth it just to see you squirm for a while."

"No, I'll pay the bill. But there will be no more negotiating. The final offer is hereby withdrawn. At midnight, your membership will be asked to leave the *Sentinel* premises. The *Sentinel* will release a detailed explanation of its offer, as well as a transcript of your comments during this meeting. As a personal favor, I'll delete all references to your dalliance with the busboy. The *Sentinel* will also make it clear that it was you who initiated this situation by your unwillingness to discuss our final offer in good faith. Now then, if you'll excuse me."

MacCauley's face turned the color of a Malibu sunset, all reds and purples and splotches of orange.

"You're walking out on me?! You're as ignorant as a Polack!" MacCauley screeched.

"A moment, please," said Lawrence, fumbling with his lapel. "I just wanted to make sure the recorder was still on voice activation. Why, yes, it is. Go on. You were talking about the Poles, of which there are a good many in your union."

"Give me that tape recorder," said MacCauley, reaching for Lawrence's suit coat.

"I don't think so," said Lawrence, stepping nimbly away. "I'd hate to add assault-and-battery charges to your already miserable day."

This wasn't what MacCauley had expected at all. A lockout at the *Sentinel*? What would he tell the membership, which had been working without a contract for months? He had assured the Guild at last month's meeting that he would take care of everything, that Lawrence would agree to the union's proposed contract demands. He had even scoffed at the idea of *Sentinel* repercussions. Now this.

"We're not backing down," MacCauley said. "If this is a bluff, you're the world's worst poker player."

"I don't believe in gambling," said Lawrence, conveniently ignoring his annual week-long stays at Bellagio in Vegas, where he was something of a stud-poker celebrity legend. "You had your chance to sign a fair offer. Now we must act accordingly."

"Fair? It was a shit offer and you know it."

"Specious, in the truest sense of the word," chirped Moss.

"It was fair by our standards," said Lawrence. "Good day."

MacCauley met him at the stairwell. He swelled to his full size, like a peacock, looking down on the *Sentinel* publisher with a rage not seen since his days fighting Daley.

"You're messing with the wrong fucking Irishman, sonny boy. Force us out and your paper won't last a month. This might not be a two-paper town anymore, but by God, I'll make sure it's a no-paper town if you go through with this!"

Lawrence pointed the recorder at MacCauley. "Could you please speak into the microphone, just in case the audio people at WTSE have trouble converting this to a digital sound format for the six P.M. broadcast?"

"Why you son of a bitch," said the union boss, again lunging toward Lawrence. Lawrence sidestepped the lumbering man, tossed a trio of $100 bills at the waiter, and made his way down the steps, through the lobby, out the double doors, and into the winter air. He was five blocks from the gothic landmark that housed the *Sentinel*. He would walk the distance with a silly grin on his face. Lawrence felt free.

Six years earlier MacCauley had nearly cost Lawrence his job. Lawrence had underestimated MacCauley, underestimated his nerve. MacCauley had orchestrated a strike vote that left Lawrence and the *Sentinel* unprepared for a massive walkout. Sure, there had been contingency plans for a strike, but they were more theoretical than practical. What had looked so comforting in leather-bound *Sentinel* management books simply didn't translate when the strike hit. It was like service academy cadets studying at the War College, only to find the lessons useless on an actual battlefield.

MacCauley had clearly been in his element, while Lawrence had struggled to keep the empire intact. From his massive office at Sentinel Tower, Lawrence had been forced to react to every MacCauley move. It was a defensive war and it cost the *Sentinel* dearly. Advertising plummeted. Circulation took a nosedive. The pro-union city naturally sided with the underdog Guild. Lawrence eventually agreed to almost every major Guild demand but privately vowed it would never happen again.

It was a matter of economics. To maintain its profit margin, the *Sentinel* couldn't continue to improve its employee health-care package, and institute cost-of-living raises, and increase the ESOP plan, and safeguard the pension program—as MacCauley and the 450-member Editorial Guild demanded. Actually, the *Sentinel* could do all of this, but only if it were willing to take a hit on the quarterly dividends. And the shareholders wouldn't stand for that. So Lawrence had plotted and planned. He quietly approved the hiring of more than 115 intern reporters during the previous two years and had them placed in key editorial departments and suburban circulation zones. The interns received reduced benefits, a modest stipend, and no promises of future employment. They were nicknamed "three-years," a reference to the pre-agreed length of their stay with the paper. There was a waiting list of 800.

The three-years included recent journalism school grads, as well as leftovers from the *Daily Times* collapse (another Lawrence production). There was quality and, best of all, it was cheap, legal, and the perfect safety net. The interns couldn't sign fast enough. Three years guaranteed? What a deal. These were people willing to compromise their conscience in exchange for a steady paycheck. Labor unrest—strike, lockout . . . whatever—meant the possibility of full-time employment. And in Chicago. On famous Michigan Avenue. At the well-respected *Sentinel*. Only a handful of prospective intern reporters questioned the details of the offer, and they were quickly replaced by names on the bulging national waiting list.

Lawrence had also begun reducing the number of FTEs, as they were called: full-time equivalents. An FTE cost more money than a part-timer working 30 hours with no benefits. Counting salary and medical benefits, an FTE could cost the company about 40 percent more per year than a non-FTE.

Under normal circumstances, there were 600 budgeted management and non-management editorial positions at the *Sentinel*. But because of attrition—retirements, deaths, job changes, etc.—the number was actually 579. That meant 21 openings.

But these weren't normal circumstances. Lawrence had adjusted the "float," which was management-speak for the number of positions that went unfilled at any one time. At the *Sentinel*, the number was usually 17, meaning the newspaper should have an editorial work force of at least 583. Lawrence raised the float from 17 to 30, thus saving the company even more money in FTEs. Lawrence also eliminated overtime pay, lowered the travel per diems, and closed the company-subsidized cafeteria.

MacCauley knew nothing of this. He thought he was fighting a media conglomerate, with all the media conglomerate weaknesses. But what he was really fighting was a secretly stockpiled work force with no union allegiances, as well as a valuable army of former Daily Timers who had felt the sting of unemployment and, in some cases, welfare. This was what Lawrence was banking on, this and a bloated junior management roster that had purposely been expanded for this very moment. In short, Lawrence had at his disposal an emergency work force that could, with little difficulty, do everything that his soon-to-be-stunned Guild employees could do. It was a brilliant, devious plan, and Lawrence was sure he could sustain it for weeks, months, however long it took for MacCauley to come crawling back on knee pads, begging for half of what the *Sentinel*'s final offer had been.

Lawrence pulled out his Nokia.

"Claire, I want you to do three things, in this exact order."

"Yes, sir. Three things."

"One, alert our security personnel that all Guild members are to be escorted out of the offices at the conclusion of their individual work shifts. I want photo ID badges collected and all *Sentinel*-related materials confiscated. There will be no repeat of the previous strike, when several of their members snuck into the building and altered, among other items, the statue of Nathan Hale and the official portraits of prominent *Sentinel* executives."

"Sir, I thought the codpiece on Nathan Hale was extremely tasteful, and I thought you looked quite striking with an eye patch."

"The Hathaway Man isn't my idea of a joke— You thought I looked striking?"

"Of course, sir."

"Why, thank you, Claire."

"Certainly, sir."

"Secondly, I want all personal effects to be removed from each work cubicle and carefully packaged for retrieval by our, uh . . . former employees. I don't want to be accused of callousness regarding personal items. We'll be the corporate monolith with a heart."

"I understand, sir."

"Thirdly, I want you to arrange for someone in the Monet Room to bring me roasted duck in a nice orange glaze, some sort of green vegetable, an appropriate salad, and a bottle of Dom Perignon."

The Monet Room, located in the upper reaches of Sentinel Tower, was so named because an original sketch of the artist's masterpiece, *Terrace at Sainte-Adresse,* adorned a small but prominently lighted portion of the corporate dining room. Only a select few of the Sentinel hierarchy were granted regular eating privileges within the plush, walnut-paneled walls. Everyone else was on an invitation-only basis, with Lawrence having final approval of all guests.

"Very well, sir," said his assistant. "Sir, I think it's necessary that I make you aware of a certain personal conflict that might require your attention."

Miss Beecher heard a scream over her speakerphone, the muffled sound of her boss cursing somebody, and then the rattle of the cellular as it apparently hit the ground. A car horn blared and in the distance, she heard the faint sound of an ambulance.

"Sir. Are you there, sir?"

Several seconds went by. No answer.

"Sir, are you still on the line?"

"Yes, yes, I'm here," said Lawrence, seemingly more annoyed than anything else.

"What happened? Are you okay, sir?"

"I'm fine now, though I can't say the same for a certain street saxophonist," Lawrence said.

"A saxophonist?"

"Yes, Claire. A saxophonist, though only because he happened to be holding a saxophone. He was to music what Beefaroni is to Italian cuisine."

"I don't follow you, sir."

"A panhandler, Claire. I tried walking around him on the sidewalk, but there wasn't enough room. He began playing some sort of Captain and Tenille song and when I wouldn't drop any money into his saxophone case, he turned cruel."

"How so, sir?"

"He played 'It's a Small World,' that dreadful tune from that ride at Disney World. Do you know which tune I'm talking about? Probably written by CIA operatives to coerce political prisoners into confessing."

"I'm lost, sir."

"It doesn't matter. When the panhandler wouldn't stop, I accidentally bumped into his saxophone as I walked by. It must have chipped a tooth, if he had any to begin with. There was a slight struggle, at which point he was struck by a bicycle."

"Oh."

"Now, what were you saying about a personal conflict?"

"Well, sir, I'm technically a member of the Guild. My employee-designation status considers me part of the editorial department. There's a handful of us in corporate."

"Well," said Lawrence, "there's only one way to handle this situation. Miss Beecher, you're fired."

"What, sir?"

"Fired and immediately rehired as an assistant managing editor in charge of administrative assistants. How does that sound?"

"Wonderful, sir."

"I'll see you in a few minutes. No need for me to stick around the accident scene and have to fill out any messy police reports."

"Fine, sir."

It didn't take long before word of the spectacularly pyrotechnic meeting between MacCauley and Lawrence reached the *Sentinel* newsroom. It was the waiter who called the NewsTip line first. It was the easiest $50 he had ever made.

Margaret Hatcher, whose job it was to check the NewsTip answering machine every 15 minutes, could scarcely believe the waiter's story. She called Harry Caray's, spoke to the waiter, then to the busboy, then to the maitre d', all of whom verified the events. That done, Hatcher took the microcassette tape and her notes to metro editor Howard Williams.

"Howard, you're not going to believe this," she said.

She loaded the cassette into her recorder, pressed the Play button, and watched Williams' face contort in various shades of disbelief. Then she read him her detailed notes.

"Holy shit," Williams said.

"Howard, I'd love to write this story, but I think I'm on the streets as soon as our security force assembles for duty," Hatcher said.

"Like bloody hell."

Williams had spent a summer studying at Oxford 30 years ago. He also said "smashing," "quite right," "righto," "splendid," and every other word you'd expect to hear on PBS Mystery Theatre. He picked up the phone and dialed Hap Storen, the managing editor, who was in a closed-door meeting with the graphics director.

"Hap, I don't know what you're bloody doing in there, but it can't be any more important than what's going on in here."

"I'll be right over," Storen said.

Storen listened to the tape, swooped up the recorder and Hatcher's notes, took them to Thomas Jarrett's office, played them for the stunned editor, and then disappeared for a few minutes. He returned with a bottle of bourbon under his arm.

"Gentlemen," he said, "let's drink to the last sane day at the *Sentinel*."

Four

A LIST OF EDITORIAL PERSONNEL was posted in each department. Calls were made to every foreign-based reporter to tell him to expect a one-way ticket back to O'Hare. Washington and national reporters were given the option to sit tight, at their own expense, or return to Chicago. Butler pulled his columnists and Bulls, NFL, and college writers off the road. Rat was paged at the United Center and told not to worry about the Hawks. So much for the big raise. The *Sentinel* would make do with wire stories, evergreen pieces, and freelance and stringer work until a lockout plan could be finalized and instituted.

There were hugs and tears as the Guild members were herded toward the elevators. There were also obscenities and a small amount of vandalism. Someone managed to draw another eye patch on Lawrence's lobby portrait. Told of the act, a giddy Lawrence, lubricated nicely by the bottle of Dom, asked, "Which one, right or left?"

By 12:30 A.M., all union personnel had been escorted out of the building. Those not working were informed by phone of the lockout. The war had begun.

An emergency Guild meeting was held at a downtown auditorium, where MacCauley was accused of thoroughly botching the negotiations. MacCauley denied it all, imploring his "union brothers and sisters" to "stay together as we fight these bastards." It didn't work. Lawrence had seen to it that MacCauley's remarks at Harry Caray's were fed to the local affiliates for the six, nine, and ten o'clock news cycles. MacCauley didn't have a chance.

Meanwhile, non-Guild members were sent home after the paper

was put to bed and told to report for a 9 A.M. meeting to discuss "altered assignments." This was bureaucratese for "You'll do what we tell you to do, and you'll like it."

Riley, numbed by the news, drove to the Cork, ordered an Old Style, and took account of his life. He was 36. He worked the desk. He lived alone. He dated about once every autumnal equinox. The best friend in his life was a cocker spaniel. He rented. His car was a pothole away from a snapped chassis. His wardrobe was so out it was almost back in. He had money—none of which he could touch for another 23½ years, lest the feds get 30 percent of it. He couldn't do a sit-up, chin-up, or push-up without an oxygen tent. His eyes lingered on the women's-underwear ads in the Sears promotional section. He was management, but only because it was convenient for the *Sentinel*. Otherwise, he was considered a has-been. He wasn't getting a raise. And in all likelihood, he was about to be told that in addition to his usual desk duties he was going to have to pick up at least another shift, maybe two. In other words, a seven-day work week.

Riley pushed his empty glass toward Bernie, the Marquette Park lifer who promptly dunked it in soapy water, shoved it onto a stationary sink brush, submerged it in a tub of semi-clean lukewarm water and placed it on a worn rubber counter mat to dry. Such precision.

"Thank you, sir, may I have another," Riley said.

"I know that one," said Bernie, who worked the night shift. "That's from *Animal House*. Kevin Bacon getting his ass whacked by one of those frat boys. I saw it on 'GN a couple of nights ago."

"Quick," said Riley, "was he wearing boxers or briefs?"

"What, I look like some kind of homo to you? What the hell do I know what he was wearing? He was getting his ass whacked, that's all I know."

"I'm not making a lifestyle judgment, Bernie. It's a trivia question."

"Well, you never know these days, you know what I'm saying? It ain't like the old days, when men were men and homos were homos."

"Bernie, I'm sorry I asked. Can you give me change for a ten-spot? I need some ones for the jukebox."

"Yeah, yeah, yeah," he said, heading toward the cash register.

Riley leaned against the bar as he waited for Bernie. Not too bad of a crowd for a weeknight. The Six O'Clock Club—about a half-dozen losers who drank themselves into oblivion on a daily basis—had come and staggered home. A softball team named the Gadflies took up most of the bar. One of the players, a cigarette dangling from his lips, his beer belly straining for freedom against his jersey, was trying to close a deal with one of the waitresses.

"I'll tell you what I'll do," he said, his Sox cap turned backwards, ashes falling from his Winston as he spoke. "I promise not to remember you in the morning. How's that?"

"That's okay, babe," said the waitress, a new one Riley had yet to meet. "I don't remember any of 'em anyway."

"I'll wear a bag," said the player, begging.

"Only if there's a noose around it," she said, slipping past the bar stool. She didn't look back.

The Gadfly turned to yell something, giving Riley just enough time to see the back of the jersey. BIG LARRY, it read. The player caught Riley's glance.

"Can you believe that bitch? What, she too good for a working stiff?"

"Hard to believe, Big Larry," Riley said. "Especially with you sprinkling all that charm dust around."

"Don't see no women hanging on your arm, buddy," said Big Larry, lighting up a new cigarette.

"That's because I'm a priest over at St. Barnabas," said Riley. "Just got transferred by the diocese about six days ago. It's a nice rectory they have here, and so close for an evening sip of something cold. Are you a parishioner?"

Big Larry turned as red as a Budweiser label. "Shit, Father, I had no idea. I mean . . . you know what I mean. Christ . . . I don't know what to say. Can I buy you a beer?"

Bernie arrived with the dollar bills.

"Thanks, Bernie."

"Yeah, sure," Bernie said. "Hey, why don't you ask me something about Bogart or Mitchum? Now those were men's men. Nobody ever whacked their asses."

"What?" said Big Larry, entirely confused.

"Bernie, I've got to return to the planet Earth now, but do me a favor and give this fine young man here another beverage—my treat," said Riley, pushing three of the dollar bills back toward the bartender.

"Gotcha, Joe."

"Thank *you*, Father," said Big Larry.

"You're welcome, my son," Riley said. "Now if you'll excuse me . . ."

"Yeah, sure," said Big Larry, as Riley walked toward an open table next to the CD jukebox.

Riley had spent the last four years feeding this jukebox. He slipped in a buck and punched the numbers by heart: 104, 233, 152—his three favorites. "Layla," by Derek and the Dominos; "Peace, Love and Understanding," by Elvis Costello; and "Willin'," by Little Feat. He took a long swig of beer, leaned back in his chair, and closed his eyes as Clapton made his nightly appearance.

"He was wearing briefs."

It was a woman's voice. Riley opened his eyes, and there stood Megan Donahue of *Sentinel* advertising and bullshitting-your-way-through-seminar fame. She wore a black beret and full-length camel-hair coat. She looked at him with those piercing green eyes, that S-curve of a nose, and a promising smile.

"I'd say something urbane and witty, but all I can think of is Champaign-Urbana," Riley said. "That doesn't really work in this situation."

"A 'hello' will do."

"Hello," said Riley, trying to get his bearings, "and what's a nice girl with five shares of Sentinel empire stock doing in a place—at 1:18, I might add—where the bartender is a homophobe and all the TVs are stuck on ESPN?"

"I'm their account exec," Megan said. "Don't you ever read the weekend section?"

"Not on purpose," Riley said. "Plus, that would mean I actually have a weekend, which I don't."

"You work two jobs?"

"Seems like it," Riley said, motioning for Megan to take a seat. "So you heard the thing about Kevin Bacon?"

"Sorry," she said. "I was in the corner. I'm dropping off a contract."

"I didn't know this place could afford advertising."

"That's what they thought," said Megan, tugging at her beret. Her hair fell neatly into place. "I convinced them to take out a happy-hour ad for Friday and Saturday. Nothing elaborate. Business has increased nineteen percent thanks to those ads."

"So you're the reason I can't find a parking space whenever I drive here on the weekends?"

"Something like that," she said, draping her coat over the back of the chair.

"Let me get this straight," said Riley. "You sell ads to the Cork. You've increased their weekend traffic. And you service the client with the traditional post-midnight business visit? Whatever they're paying you, it isn't enough."

"It was plenty until the Guild walked."

"Walked?" Riley said. "They were shown the door. I just came from the *Sentinel*. Lawrence signed the memo himself. The Guild turned down his offer, so Lawrence took his printing presses and went home."

"He can do that?"

"The union was working without a contract," Riley said. "I guess he can do anything he wants when there isn't a contract."

"I guess I got the management version of the news," said Megan. "Whatever happened, it's going to be the law of the jungle when it comes to ad sales."

"Yeah," said Riley. "I'm sure that's what the Guild members and their middle-income families are thinking at this very moment: 'How is this going to affect Megan?'"

"That came out wrong," she said. "You know, I could really use a beer."

"Say no more. Bernie!" said Riley, holding up his own beer bottle. "Another Old Style."

Megan scrunched her nose. "Think they have Beck's?"

"Probably," said Riley. "But it's not worth the trouble."

"How come?" she said. "It's beer. I'm not asking him to fly to Munich to get it."

"Okay, but I warned you," he said, before turning toward the bar. "Hey, Bernie! Give me the Old Style, frosted mug, please. And get the lady a Beck's."

Bernie stared at the table, angrily pulled a Beck's from the glass refrigerator case, tugged at the Old Style tap lever, and then deposited the beers on Riley's table with a thud.

"That'll be three seventy-five," said Bernie, refusing to look at Riley or Megan.

Megan reached for her purse. Riley put five ones on Bernie's tray.

"Keep it, Bernie," Riley said. "And be polite. She didn't know any better."

"Fucking Krauts," said the bartender.

"Bernie, she's not a regular," Riley said. "Cut her some slack."

Megan leaned toward Riley.

"What'd I do?" she said, lowering her voice. "Is he mad because I didn't order American?"

"Bernie is a World War Two veteran," Riley said. "A member of the Big Red One—that's army infantry. He hates the Germans."

"That was, like, fifty-five years ago," she said. "He hates all Germans?"

"Mozart, Beethoven, Wagner, Kant, Nietzsche, Porsche, Becker, even Oktoberfest," Riley said. "If it's German, Bernie despises it. He even hates blind people."

"Blind people?" said Megan. "How can he hate blind people?"

"German shepherds," Riley said.

"They killed my buddies," said Bernie, still pouting near the table. "A night ambush. Battle of the Bulge."

"I'm so sorry, Bernie," said Megan. "I had no idea. Tell you what. Take this back and bring me your finest Budweiser."

"Another Kraut," muttered Bernie, as he left the table.

"Maybe I should be leaving," Megan said.

"He'll be okay," Riley said. "It's late, so his medication is beginning to wear off. Now, you still haven't told me why you're here."

"I'm wondering the same thing," she said, looking at Bernie as he walked toward the bar.

"Maybe this will help."

Riley scooted his chair closer and began to lean forward. Megan recoiled.

"Whoa, bunny boy," she said.

Riley held up a dollar bill.

"I wasn't going to kiss you. I was going to stick a buck in the jukebox and give you your choice between 'Nothingman' and 'Better Man.' I think I know which one to play now."

"Oh," said Megan. "I guess this is where I apologize."

"Don't worry about it," he said, shoving the dollar in his shirt pocket. "I would have needed instructions anyway."

"To play a CD?"

"No, to kiss," he said. "Not counting Gil, it's been a while."

"Gil?"

"Man's best friend. Cocker spaniel. Pooch deluxe."

"Oh, again."

Megan stared at her loafers.

"You know what?" she said, grabbing her coat off the back of the chair. "This was a bad idea from the start. I think I'll ask Bernie about Volkswagens and BMWs and then go on the Death Walk."

Riley did a double take.

"Wait a second," he said. "Since when does Miss Wisconsin know about the Western Avenue Death Walk? That's local knowledge."

"I went to school at Madison, but I wasn't born there," she said. "I'm *from* Beverly. Went to St. Barnabas, then St. Ignatius, then On Wisconsin. I spent my prom night throwing up on Western after the Walk and a half-dozen sliders at Whitey's. And I'm Irish Catholic enough to know that Cork & Kerry is named after two counties in Ireland."

"Which bar did you lose it at?"

"Coaches. Tequila did me in. And if it didn't, White Castle did."

"How old are you?"

"Old enough to know that you were an all-state wrestler at St. Iggy, that you had a full ride at Marquette, that you quit the team after your sophomore season, that you worked at the *Milwaukee Journal* to help pay for school, that you went to Des Moines, were wooed by the *Sentinel*, and later became the poster child for journalistic depression," Megan said. "Did I miss anything?"

"How the hell do you know all that?" said Riley, stunned on the same level that Big Larry had been with the priest gag.

"My mom knows your mom."

"This is amazing."

"Not really," Megan said. "My folks divorced when I was in eighth grade. My dad moved to the North Side, my mom moved in with her sister here in Beverly. I lived with my dad, went to St. Iggy because my mom insisted. You were leaving when I was starting. Our volleyball coach was your assistant wrestling coach. He talked about you all the time. Said you never got pinned during your entire high school career. He thought you were the cat's meow."

"Coach Benson said that? I think he's done one too many neck bridges."

"He said it. And can I help it if your mom plays bridge with my mom? They talk about you all the time. See, simple."

Riley yelled to the bar. "Bernie, something that requires a shot glass, please."

"I'm not a stalker or anything," said Megan. "I never called you at work because it seemed too complicated. So when I saw you at the seminar, I decided to have a little fun. I'm crashing at my mom's house tonight, so I thought I'd test her information."

"Which was?"

"Your mom told my mom that this is your favorite hangout. I've seen you here a couple times myself, but that was a few years ago, when I'd come home from Madison on break."

"Great," Riley said. "I've got the Golden Girls running a tail on me, and Miss Wisconsin thinking I'm trying to hit on her."

"Like I said, I made a mistake."

"No, I'm flattered," Riley said. "I guess I'm just not very good company these days."

"That's what your mom told my mom, too."

"Super. Anything else my mom said?"

"Something about you taking the road less traveled," Megan said. "Didn't quite get that one."

"Mom loves her Robert Frost."

"What does that mean?"

"You don't read Frost?" said Riley. He cleared his throat. "'How my horse must think it queer, with your Audi parked so near.'"

"Kraut car!" yelled Bernie.

"War's over, we won!" Riley yelled back.

"I have no idea what you're talking about," said Megan, adjusting her beret.

"Literary license," Riley said. "Look, why don't we try this some other night. I'm zero fun to be around right now. Nothing against your ad sales, but some very good people are unemployed tonight. Plus, my boss told me I suck. And I just found out that the oral history of my quiet life of desperation is available on Moms-on-Tape. What I really wish is that I could be born again and start all over. You know what I mean?"

"No, not really," she said. "Then again, I didn't major in self-pity."

"Bernie, make it a double!" Riley yelled.

Megan took two steps toward the door, stopped, and looked directly at Riley. She was every bit of six feet, maybe a tad taller.

"You don't know me, I don't know you," she said. "But you're not the loser you think you are . . . though, after seeing you tonight, you're close. You're borderline cute and pathetic, a rare combination. Had you asked me out, I might have said yes. You could use some new clothes, something that didn't have a Members Only label on it. You could use a personal trainer, and a haircut by someone not affiliated with the local barber college would be nice. And you might want to think about an Altoid every now and then."

"Is that all?" Riley said. "Teeth okay, or do you think orthodontics?" Riley took a gulp of his beer, trying to pretend as if the words had just grazed him. He attempted his best smirk, all for her benefit.

"No," she said. "That's it for now."

Riley summoned the proper indignation. No way was he going to let some six-figure ad saleswoman with—*Damn, is that her new A6 parked outside the door?* He was just kidding about the Audi.—an admittedly fine shape and promising sense of humor give Joseph Riley the third, fourth, and fifth degree. So he jabbed back. And immediately regretted it.

"Look, Miss Bucky Badger, just because you took a freshman psych class doesn't make you Sigmund Freud."

"Another fucking German!" yelled Bernie.

"Bernie, will you shut the hell up?" said Riley, before continuing with the former honorable mention all–Big Ten small forward. "Anyway, the only thing you were right about is that you don't know me."

"Likewise," she said. "But the stuff about self-pity, the clothes, the personal trainer, and the haircut?"

"Yeah?" said Riley.

"I'm not the one who said it first," Megan said.

"Who did?" he said.

"Your mom."

Riley's smirk disappeared. So did Megan, but not before she paused at the doorway.

"Oh, Bernie," she said sweetly.

Bernie turned suspiciously.

"*Achtung*, baby!" she said.

Bernie threw a dishrag at her, but the door had already squeezed shut. Riley unfolded the dollar, pressed 247—"Nothingman"—and listened to his new anthem. "Megan frickin' Donahue," he said, as he saw the A6 pull away.

Five

U<small>H, JOE, CAN I TALK TO YOU FOR A SECOND?</small>
It was Butler. The Saturday-morning staff meeting had just ended. There were a lot of new faces in the room, most of them with acne. The 16 interns (12 men, four women) looked exactly how interns should look: annoyingly energetic, quixotic, still on a Woodward-Bernstein high from rereading *All the President's Men*. They wore ties, button-down J. Crews, wide-wale corduroys, Banana Republic outfits, or freshly pressed Gap khakis. They said "yes, sir" or "no, sir." Some of them said, without prompting, "Yes, sir, but at Medill, we were told . . ." or, "No, sir, at Missouri the professors said . . ." as if Northwestern and Missouri had all of journalism's answers. They were mostly kids, but they didn't realize it, didn't realize that life was about 80 percent luck. They thought a summer of fact checking at *Sports Illustrated* made them the next Jim Murray. Fat chance. They thought they could out-write, out-report, out-hustle, out-party anybody in the business. They would learn the hard way.

Riley used to be just like them. He had had a timetable: a Big Five paper (the *Sentinel, Washington Post, Los Angeles Times, New York Times,* or *Boston Globe*) before he was 25. A major beat before he was 26. An APSE award before he was 27. A Pulitzer nomination before he was 33. A move to the editor's track before he was 35. An assistant managing editor's job before he was 38. ME by 42. Editor by 45.

What arrogance, thought Riley. Yes, the *Sentinel* had hired him in accordance with his silly master plan. But there would be no major beat, only a forgettable attempt to cover DePaul. The low moment came during the NCAA West Regionals at the Huntsman Center in

Salt Lake City. DePaul had just made it into the big dance as a 12 seed, one of the last at-large bids given. Playing in the night's final game, the Blue Demons had lost to 5 seed Tennessee on a buzzer beater. Afterward, Riley worked the DePaul locker room almost entirely by himself, with the exception of a couple of Salt Lake City writers for the *Deseret News* and the *Tribune*.

"Don't you need to get up there and start hacking?" the *Deseret News* guy asked.

"Nah," said Riley, casually checking his watch. "I've got plenty of time. It's only 10:06. I've got till 10:45 to file for the final."

"Pretty good deadlines for a Chicago paper," the *Deseret News* hack said. "We've got to be in by 10:30 local. You've got till 11:45 back home. Not bad at all."

"Whattaya mean?" said Riley, surveying the near-empty locker room. An attendant pushed wet, used towels into a small pile. Another attendant started sweeping up Gatorade cups and empty postgame box dinners.

"You said 10:45," the *News* reporter said. "That's 11:45 Chicago time, isn't it? You're an hour ahead, aren't you?"

And that's when it had hit Riley. Even now his stomach did back flips as he remembered the chain of events that had made him a laughingstock for months thereafter. He had set his cheap Swatch an hour back when he landed at Salt Lake. The flight attendant had said something about setting your watch to local time, so Riley, the lemming that he was, did exactly that. But in the postgame excitement of the NCAAs, Riley had forgotten about the time difference. That's why nobody else from Chicago was in the locker room. They were on press row, hacking like crazy, stuffing a lead atop their running game stories. It wouldn't be anything fancy, just the score, the hurried sequence of those final seconds when the Tennessee kid heaved the game winner just inside the half-court line, and then maybe a quote or two from DePaul's coach and the jubilant kid from Cookeville, Tennessee.

Meanwhile, there was Riley really *working* the locker room, all the time figuring he was going to kick some serious butt with the stuff he was getting. Scene-setter stuff: crying, kicking of doors, wonderful quotes. The only problem was that deadline had come and gone.

Riley had sprinted to his phone at press row and called the office. He got Gary Sherman on the fourth ring. Sherman was the layout guy for the night. When he wasn't tooling with the Power Mac G3 (one of the few decent pieces of hardware the department had at its disposal), he was thumbing through golf magazines and boring people to death with talk of his swing. "Look at this grip," he'd say. "You think I've got a weak left hand?"

That night, as he rushed to get the section out, there was no such talk about grips. Riley had told him there was a "time management problem."

"No shit, Sherlock," said Sherman. "We tried calling the number you left us, but they said you were in the locker room. We ran an AP story instead. What the fuck happened?"

"My watch stopped," Riley said.

"Yeah, well, Butler's down in composing, but he wants a piece of you when you get back in town."

That wouldn't be pleasant. "I've got some great stuff," Riley said. "Want me to write through?"

"Yeah, why don't you write through," Sherman said. "I'll print out a copy and leave it for the cleaning people. 'Cause it ain't making it in this rag."

"Maybe I can use it in the follow?" Riley said.

"Sherlock, I think your writing days are over," Sherman said. "Butler's so mad he wants to transfer you to paperboy. Hey, look, I've got to go. Thanks for zip. And you might want to learn the difference between time zones, Ace."

There was a click. And then a dial tone. And then that feeling of utter dread. A week later he was transferred to the copy rim. There would be no APSE writing award. There definitely would be no Pulitzer, no fast track, no nothing. Editor by 45? Riley couldn't get a two percent raise at 36.

Riley knew the Associated Press style book, the bible of newspaper editing, by heart. He knew how to work the *Sentinel*'s antiquated computer system. He knew how to sweet-talk the back-shop people. But he didn't get a woody anymore if the *Sentinel* broke a story about the hiring of the Bears' special-teams coach. He didn't particularly care if circulation reached a new high. Check that—he cared, but only because it might bump up the price of TSNE stock. And he certainly didn't care if the section won another Chicago Press Club award. Maybe Butler was right. Maybe Riley *was* marginally competent.

Riley watched the new staff file out of the room. The interns tried to look as if they weren't nervous. They were. The former Daily Timers, of which there were four, seemed uncomfortable with the idea of working for the enemy. They glanced nervously around the room, as if they were afraid to be seen by anybody. Loyalties ran thick in Chicago and nobody wanted to be called a traitor. But the need for a regular paycheck made strange bedfellows.

There were freelancers. Stringers. The rest of the associate assistant sports editors. The part-time agate clerks. All in all, this was some bunch. It needed Lee Marvin and six weeks of basic training. Instead, it got the anal-retentive Butler, a neatnik who would wipe down the sink in the newsroom bathroom if he thought it was dirty. What he needed, thought Riley, was someone who could serve as a buffer and help with the awkward transition. What he needed, Riley decided, was . . . well, Joseph Riley. It was obvious, wasn't it?

Riley considered the best way to handle Butler's approach. An apology would probably come first, followed by a sheepish offer to increase his salary by three percent. Riley would act slightly offended but then accept immediately. No use trying to bargain for more.

Butler closed the door to the conference room.

"Joe, needless to say, this is going to be a difficult time for this newspaper, but especially for this sports section," said Butler, carefully choosing his words as he fiddled with his blue clip-on tie. "We were understaffed to begin with, and the, uh . . . sudden departure of assorted co-workers has left us in a major bind."

Butler was such a company man. He couldn't bring himself to utter the word *lockout*.

"Terry, you don't have to say anything else," Riley said. "I know what you want and I'll be happy to do it."

Riley was proud of himself. He had given Butler the perfect opportunity to grovel but also to save face. Riley, who was feeling very Oriental at the moment, had read about saving face in *Shogun*. By launching a pre-emptive kindness strike, Riley had disarmed an opponent and improved his own standing. Toranaga would have been proud.

"You will?" said Butler.

"Absolutely," Riley said. "Think of yesterday's performance review as a shanked shot off the hosel. This is your mulligan."

Here comes the apology, thought Riley.

"I've got to admit, Joe, you've floored me with your flexibility," Butler said. "I didn't think this was going to be a pleasant session. Not pleasant at all."

"We're grown men, Terry. I'm not crazy about the situation. I think the lockout is a bunch of corporate posturing, but there's not a whole lot I can do about it. Let's just hope it doesn't last long."

Butler knew otherwise, but he wasn't about to divulge the specifics of an earlier meeting with *Sentinel* upper management.

"Of course, we're hoping for the best," Butler said vaguely. "In the meantime, I guess I should apologize for what happened yesterday during the performance review. It had been a long day and I let that affect our meeting. But gosh darnit, Joe, you have a knack for frustrating me. That's one of the reasons I've decided to make this move."

Riley bit his tongue at the minor insult. No reason to disrupt the goodwill festival.

"I know I've disappointed you in the past, but maybe we can start fresh," said Riley, pleased with his calm demeanor. "I know you probably need me to work an extra shift, so I'll do it. We can figure out the overtime at a later date."

Butler flinched.

"Okay, no overtime for now," Riley said quickly. "Maybe some sort of comp time arrangement. Anyway, I'm ready to help with these interns, work with them on their copy and keep the 'What a difference a year makes' leads down to a minimum. I'll set up a meeting with them later today and we can go over the writing do's and don'ts."

Butler was obviously confused. Riley could see the confusion on the sports editor's face and responded by talking faster.

"You're stunned, aren't you?" said Riley. "I guess so am I. Something about those interns got me thinking. Hell, maybe I love this business more than I thought I did. Maybe I can help them become special. Maybe—"

"Joe, I don't want you on the copy rim."

"Oh, well, I suppose I can do this in some sort of supervisory role."

"Joe, you're not listening to me," Butler said. "I'm moving you off the rim. I'm rescinding your associate assistant sports editor title. I'm sorry."

"You're what?" said Riley, who suddenly felt as if he'd fallen crotch-first onto a bicycle crossbar.

"I don't have much choice," said Butler, organizing his pencil tray. "The staff is utterly depleted. I had to make some hard decisions. Your name came up."

"So I'm fired?" Riley said.

"Not fired," Butler said. " Reassigned."

Riley couldn't think straight. How had he miscalculated this moment? None of it made sense. "This is a living, breathing nightmare," Riley said. "Reassigned to what?"

Butler paused for a full 10 seconds and then let out a long sigh. "The Cubs," he said.

"Say again?"

"The Cubs. I need people with writing experience. You have some, albeit of questionable quality."

"Don't sugarcoat it, Terry. Tell me exactly how you feel."

"It's not an ideal situation for either one of us, but I don't have much of a choice." Now Butler was indexing his file folders.

Riley refused to believe the turn of events. "The Chicago Cubs?" he said. "The Major League Baseball Cubs? Balls? Bats? Testicle scratching? Are you mad? I've never covered baseball. I'll die."

"Like I said, it's not an ideal situation," Butler said.

"Getting caught picking your nose qualifies as 'not an ideal situation,'" Riley said. "This is a *Poseidon Adventure* waiting to happen. This is Shelley Winters doing the frog kick in twenty-foot-deep water. I can't do this. I won't do this."

"Then I've been instructed to terminate your employment," Butler said.

"You can't do that," Riley said, his voice at a near shriek. "I'm management."

"Not if you don't agree to in-house employment relocation," said Butler, pulling out a sheet of paper with the appropriate legalese. "It's a standard requirement for junior management. It's in the manual."

"Which you know by heart."

"Afraid so."

"Christ, if you've got to put me on a beat, why not something I've covered before?" Riley pleaded. "What about college hoops? At least I've done that."

"I'm going to use wire copy for the DePaul, Northwestern, UIC, Loyola, and Illinois away games, and use two of the interns for the home games," Butler said. "I need somebody with a little more seasoning for the pro beats."

"Seasoning?" Riley said. "I'm as unseasoned as boiled water. There has to be a way I can talk you out of this."

"Sorry. Take it or leave it."

Riley slumped in his chair. The Cubs. The National League's perennial loser. In a recent writers' poll that moved across the wire, the Cubs were named the least-coverable team in the big leagues. Riley remembered Phil Mitchell, the *Sentinel's* longtime Cubs beat guy, saying team management was in year 90 of its 100-year plan. He also said the players were as enjoyable as canker sores. Mitchell wasn't known for his tact.

"So you're saying you don't want me on the desk?" Riley said.

"That's what I'm saying," said Butler, using a Handi-wipe to dab the bottom of his trash can.

"And you're saying that if I don't take the Cubs beat, I'm out of a job?"

"That's right."

"I could hire a lawyer, you know," Riley said. "I might have a case here."

"Legal already checked it out. It's ironclad," Butler said.

"Figures."

"This wasn't my idea, Joe. To be completely honest with you, I proposed something altogether different."

"Well, I know it wasn't a raise," Riley said.

"It was a buyout," Butler said. "Considering your work ethic during the last few years, I thought it might be the best solution for everybody. But the situation changed with the most recent labor developments."

"Are you saying what I think you're saying?"

"Joe, this is difficult. I hired you. I tried working with you. I covered for you. But do you really think nobody sees you doing the crossword puzzles when you're supposed to be checking the first-edition proofs? Do you think nobody can smell the beer on your breath after one of your quickie trips to the Goat? Do you think I don't have someone reread each of the stories you *sort of* edit? I know about the sequins. You've changed, Joe. You've quit giving a damn. Your cynicism is off the charts. Yes, I wanted you out. These latest union difficulties saved your job. For now."

"And after the lockout?" Riley said.

"I'm recommending they offer you a buyout package," Butler said. "And I'm also recommending that you take it. If you want, I'll even make some calls about finding you another job. I hear there's some desk openings in Ogden."

"Utah?" Riley said.

"It's the best I can do," said Butler.

"Is that a state or a territory?"

"I need an answer, Joe. You want the Cubs or not?"

Riley took a deep breath. Toranaga was dead.

"When do pitchers and catchers report to Mesa?" he said, his voice a monotone.

"February fourteenth," said Butler, checking his desk calendar (encased in plastic) as if it were a play sheet on a quarterback's wristband. Every Chicago sporting event was noted by date.

Riley dropped his head in despair. "I'll be there."

Six

THE MONDAY FLIGHT FROM MIDWAY to Phoenix's Sky Harbor Airport took three and a half of the longest hours of Riley's life. Thanks to the *Sentinel*'s notoriously cheap travel agency, Riley found himself in row 38 of a 39-row MD-80, wedged in the middle seat between a Bob's Big Boy look-alike and a woman with an apparent fetish for garlic, curry, and onion.

In the seat in front of him was a 3-year-old boy whose nose hadn't been wiped since birth. Phlegm stalactites hung from the child's nostrils. Ten minutes into the flight the boy reached around the seat and unhooked the plastic snap to Riley's tray table. The tray fell flush on Riley's kneecaps.

"That's not a very nice kid," Riley said sweetly, his knees still throbbing.

The boy flicked one of his stalactites at Riley. "Booger," the boy said.

Then there was the meal. The Budget Air flight attendant had tossed the small box on Riley's lap and kept walking. Inside the box was a lug nut–sized sandwichette, which featured a brownish green piece of indeterminate meat. The bun was as soggy as a South Carolina marsh. The lettuce was nothing more than a nearly indistinguishable strip of green, hardly enough to attract a starving rabbit. The minuscule bag of chips required the jaws of life to open. Riley had never heard of the chips brand, nor had he ever tasted such artificial flavoring: marshmallow-barbecue. The fruit-juice box was no better. There was no miniature straw attached, so Riley had to punch a hole through the container with his forefinger. The drink cart arrived 40 minutes later, with nothing more to choose from than warm tomato juice and four cans of daiquiri mix. Riley asked for a cup of ice.

"Three dollars, please," said the attendant, whose wing-shaped ID tag revealed his name as Ken. Ken wore a diamond-stud earring, and his left wrist featured a tattoo that read, "Vincent, with Love."

"Three bucks for ice?" Riley said.

"Sir, we have a full flight," said the attendant. "It's three dollars." Ken didn't hide his exasperation. He couldn't wait to be done with these Priceline.com cheapskates who paid $73 for a round-trip ticket and then wondered why filet mignon wasn't being served. What he wouldn't give to be working first class, where the passengers didn't wear jean cutoffs and knew the difference between Colt 45 and a nice Cab Sav from wine country. Better yet, there were only 10 passengers to serve in first, compared to the endless rows of coach vermin.

"How much is a Dewars on ice?" Riley said.

"Two dollars," Ken answered. This was taking too much time. Ken had a new *CondeNast Traveler* stashed away in the aft galley he wanted to read.

"Then I'll have that," Riley said.

"We're out of Dewars, sir," Ken said.

"Then I'll have an ice with no Dewars for two dollars," Riley said, pleased with himself.

"You're delightful, sir. Do you want the ice or what?" Ken was getting impatient.

"I want the ice, but not for three dollars," Riley said. "That's ridiculous."

"Sir, it's company policy. It discourages passengers from bringing aboard their own soft drinks or alcohol. It encourages passengers to purchase Budget Air beverages."

"But you don't *have* any beverages," Riley said.

"That doesn't mean you might not have some under your seat, sir."

"Even if I did, I don't have enough room to reach them," Riley said. "This is like being in the Mercury space capsule."

"Very funny, sir," Ken said. "I'll check back with you near the end of the flight."

"Hold on," said Riley, handing him the cash. "Give me the damn ice. I'm already dehydrated from the marsha-cue chips."

Ken looked annoyingly at the five-dollar bill.

"I'll have to bring back the change," he said, not bothering to hide the disgust in his voice.

"You do that, Ken," Riley said. "Knowing this airline, I'll probably need it to use the lavatory."

"You are soooo funny, sir," said Ken as he pushed his cart toward the galley.

At that exact moment, the sleeping giant rammed one of his massive elbows into Riley's chin, knocking the cup of ice onto the filthy floor. That was followed by the garlic-curry queen having a small gaseous experience.

Riley considered weeping.

The plane landed at 2 P.M. Riley took a shuttle to the car-rental lot, where he discovered he had no reservation. After 45 minutes of haggling, Riley settled on a Volvo S80 Turbo—$62 a day. There would no doubt be a confrontation with the *Sentinel*'s expense-account people when he returned to Chicago, but that was seven weeks from now. Until then, he was going to suffer in luxury.

Compared to his Corolla, the Volvo was like driving a motorized cloud. He flicked on the air conditioning—in February!—and glanced at the directions to the Cubs' HoHoKam Park in Mesa. Easy stuff. Route 143 south to University Drive, east to Center Street, north to HoHoKam. The whole thing took about 25 minutes.

Riley pulled into the parking lot of the Cubs' newly refurbished 10,000-seat stadium, which also housed a remodeled clubhouse and team offices. Four blocks away was Fitch Park, the team's minor league facility. That's where most of the early workouts and intrasquad games would be played. Riley knew this only because Phil Mitchell had been nice enough to give him the bare essentials.

Mitchell had covered baseball for nearly 35 years. He had some of the best sources in the business, a prized list of home phone numbers for almost every agent, player, umpire, manager, general manager, owner, and league official. He had near-immediate access to the commissioner, as well as long-cultivated minor league connections and a vast network of other beat reporters who were willing to trade Mitchell prized information. Riley had zilch.

That wasn't exactly true. He had directions to HoHoKam, the

name of the media relations director, and a few mercy names and numbers given to him by Mitchell. Riley had called Mitchell shortly after being demoted.

"Hoss," said Mitchell, who was born and raised in College Station and still had a Texas accent as thick as five-alarm chili, "you are one unlucky sumbitch. They done neutered you as management and now you got to cover these peckerheads. Ain't no rosary long enough to handle the prayers you gonna need."

"Hail, Mary, full of infield fly rules," said Riley.

"Ain't no joking matter, Hoss," said Mitchell, his voice turning serious. "These boys are going to munch on you like Red Man. It's like those prison movies, when the new meat is led to his cell and all those crazies are banging their metal cups against the iron bars, and the fellas in solitary are poking their hand-held mirrors out the doors, and everyone is hootin' and hollerin' and looking like they can't wait to introduce you to a bar of Ivory in the shower room."

"Thanks, Mitchell. Just the imagery I was hoping for: *Escape from HoHoKam*."

"Hoss, I'm just telling it like it is. The players don't know you from Adam. They ain't gonna cut you a break. And the other beat guys are gonna hate you because you're a management scab, plus you work at the *Sentinel*, which is where all those suburban newspaper fellas want to work, though they'll never admit it. They're going to try to kick your ass every day. Make you look bad. Hell, if I wasn't such a softy, I wouldn't be helping you myself. But we go back a little ways, so you hold on to those names and numbers. Don't call 'em unless you have to. Those are emergency numbers. You can only use them once. Tell 'em Big Mitch said it was okay."

"Gotcha," said Riley.

"Lookee here, Riley. Keep your mouth shut, but don't back down from nothing. Ballplayers are like dogs; they can smell fear. Me and the missus will probably come to Arizona in a couple of weeks. Lockout or no lockout, I ain't missing spring training."

Mitchell could afford it. Unlike most of the other reporters on staff, he made a killing in freelance work during the offseason. There was hardly a preseason baseball magazine or sports website that didn't include a Mitchell byline and some remarkably well written prose. In addition, Mitchell did some work for ESPN. Nothing regular, but enough to keep him visible and put some decent jack in his Janus fund.

"Anybody you recommend I talk to first?" Riley asked. "Got a favorite player?"

"They're all pricks, Hoss. At least, most of them are. The only guy who might help you out is Strickland. He's a pro's pro and a lot smarter than he lets on. He's always been a good talker and if he thinks he can trust you, you might get lucky. Otherwise, you're screwed. Most of these guys—well, the only time they act civil is right before they negotiate their contracts. Then they're all lovey-dovey because they want you to get their side of the story to the public. The rest of the time they'd be just as happy to see us fed to a school of piranha. The sumbitches ought to have triple sixes carved in their scalps. No, sir, I don't think much of your chances."

"You're kidding," Riley said. "Someone has to talk to me."

"Hoss, you have to understand something. You're the Black Plague to these fellas. You're an intruder. You come into their house every day, asking questions, probing, stirring the shit up, digging for dirt. You know how much they make, how long they'll make it, and why they're making it. But what they got over you is them big gajillion-dollar paydays. Remember, their per diem is more than you earn in six months. They don't need you. They don't want you. *Comprende?*"

"So you're saying I'm probably not going to be invited to the team picnic?"

"You ain't gonna be invited anywhere," Mitchell said. "It ain't part of the Code."

"The Code?"

"Ballplayers and writers don't mix," Mitchell said. "At least, they shouldn't. Now, you'll still find some Rudolph the Brown-Nose Reindeers around, the beat guys who suck up to one of the pricks . . . play poker with 'em, go out drinking with 'em. But I'd never do it. Get yourself in trouble that way."

"Tell you the truth, Mitch, I'm not planning to cover the team all that long," Riley said. "As soon as the lockout is settled, I'm taking the first flight home."

"Don't matter," Mitchell said. "One day, one month, one season.

If you want to survive, you do what I say. Bust your ass. Don't take shit from nobody. You hear?"

"*Comprende*," Riley said.

"One other thing, Hoss. I want you to find Max Dewitt. He's the equipment guy. Been there longer than some of the ivy at Wrigley. Bring him a bottle of Absolut and a box of cigars—the more expensive, the better. Do that and he might take pity on you, though I doubt it."

"Mitch, thanks for the help. I'll buy you dinner at Rosebud when I get back."

"Don't worry about dinner," Mitchell said. "Just don't embarrass me. And don't mess with the Code."

According to the itinerary faxed to him by the Cubs' media relations department, the pitchers and catchers didn't have to report until Wednesday. The rest of the invitees would arrive the following Monday. In all, there would be 57 players—40 roster and 17 non-roster. The non-roster players had next to no chance of making the team. By the time the Cubs broke camp and headed to San Diego for the April 1 opener, only 25 players would be on the active roster.

Riley locked the Volvo, nodded to the lumpy security guard stationed outside the main entrance of the Fitch Park offices, took a deep breath, and walked inside.

"May I help you?" asked the receptionist, not quite sure what to make of Riley. He wasn't one of the regulars. Too young to be a HoHo.

"Yes, I'm looking for Gary Hoffman," Riley said.

"Third door on the right," she said.

Riley found Hoffman on all fours, surrounded by boxes of media guides. The office could have qualified for national disaster relief. On his desk was a very worn Rawlings infielder's glove.

"Knock, knock," said Riley, standing in the doorway.

"Who's there?" said Hoffman, not bothering to look up. "If you're delivering more boxes, I hope you burn in God's fiery hell."

"No boxes, just me. I'm Joe Riley. I'm the replacement player for the *Sentinel*."

"Oh," said Hoffman, now in a catcher's squat. "Gary Hoffman. I guess you got the faxes and all the other information we sent. Welcome to Mesa, pearl of the west."

"Good to be here, I think," said Riley as he leaned over to shake hands.

"You'll be fine," Hoffman said. "Think of it as the worst seven weeks of your life. That way, if anything good happens, it will be a pleasant surprise. That's my philosophy."

Hoffman removed some boxes from a chair and pointed Riley toward the seat.

"So, how long will you be with us?" Hoffman said.

"I'm not sure," Riley said, "but I hope just long enough that nobody notices I've left."

"How serious is the *Sentinel* about the lockout?" Hoffman asked. "Our marketing people say it's for real. Word is that Lawrence wants to bust the union."

"I'm not exactly in the inner loop," Riley said, "but I can't believe that's the deal. The last time they had a stare-down with labor it cost the paper huge bucks. Maybe Lawrence is just trying to put the fear of God into MacCauley, get some union concessions, and then everybody can go back to despising one another."

"You'd know better than me," Hoffman said.

"You'd be surprised."

"Well, while you're here, I might as well give you your goodies," said Hoffman, reaching behind his desk for an oversized manila envelope. "Okay, here's your Cubs spring training credential. Guard it with your life. It gives you access to just about anyplace around HoHoKam and the minor league facility. If you're still around here at the end of camp, I'll issue you your season media pass and parking pass for Wrigley."

"Let's hope that day never occurs."

"Here's your BBWAA card," said Hoffman. "Your chapter rep asked me to give it to you. He must know something you don't."

"My what?" Riley asked, examining the laminated wallet-sized card.

"Your Baseball Writers' Association of America card," Hoffman said. "It says here that you're . . . 'a duly qualified member, and entitled to press courtesies of the clubs of the National and American Leagues of professional baseball clubs, subject to the conditions set forth on the back hereof.' Basically, this gets you into any big league press box and clubhouse. Wear it around your neck whenever you're at the ball yard. The players tend to cooperate a little more with the BBWAA guys than they do with some yahoo with a day pass."

"About the players . . ."

"Not now," Hoffman interrupted. "Enjoy the moment. Okay, here's your spring training roster, which I'll update whenever we make a move. Here's some pre-camp notes. Here's a set of NL and AL press guides. I'm missing the Reds—surprise!—and the Marlins from the National, and Oakland from the AL. Here's a HoHoKam parking pass. Here's a spring training guide to the Cactus League. Here's a list of local restaurants. Here's our spring playing schedule. Here's a Cubs refrigerator magnet. Here's a card with all of our office numbers."

Riley struggled to hold everything.

"Any heavy farm machinery you want to toss on?" Riley said. "I've got a few more inches of room."

"No, that should do it for now," Hoffman said. "I don't know what Mitchell told you, but I suggest you show up early Wednesday. The other beat guys will."

"What's early?"

"Seven."

"In the morning?" Riley said. "I'm more of an eleven-ish kind of guy."

"Suit yourself."

"They don't actually play games that early, do they?" Riley said. "It's mostly stretching, fungoes, and bunting drills, that sort of thing, right?"

"Oh, boy," said Hoffman. "Joe, I'll try to help you when I can, but it's pretty much every seamhead for himself. I don't have time to hold your hand. By the way, have you ever done this before—I mean, cover baseball?"

"I wrote the newsletter for our *Sentinel* fantasy league."

"Sure, same thing," said Hoffman, rolling his eyes.

"That your glove?" Riley asked with a nod toward the desk.

"This?" said Hoffman, picking the glove up off the desk. "I was a walk-on second baseman at Arizona State in the mid-eighties. The groundskeepers got on the field more than I did."

"Still . . . ASU baseball," Riley said. "Pretty impressive."

"If you say so," he said.

The receptionist walked into Hoffman's office. "Mr. Hightower is looking for you," she said.

Hoffman nodded. Riley nudged a statistics packet with his nose.

"I'll let you go talk to your general manager," said Riley, staggering toward the hallway. "See you Wednesday."

"I'll be here."

Riley made his way down the hall but didn't have a free hand to open the door.

"Let me get that for you."

Riley recognized the voice. It was R.J. Morris, Cubs beat reporter for the *Arlington Standard* and a regular on SportsCom's weekly cable show *Sportswriters Roundtable*. Though he worked for the smallest of the suburban papers, Morris had clout. He was good for a scoop every two weeks and wasn't shy in bragging about it, either.

"Thanks," said Riley, pausing at the door, his sight lines obscured by the media guides. "I'm Joe Riley of the *Sentinel*. I'd shake your hand, but I'm a little overwhelmed right now."

"You're from the *Sentinel*?" Morris asked suspiciously.

"Yeah, I'm taking Phil Mitchell's place."

"Then open your own damn door," said Morris, releasing the doorknob and brushing past Riley.

Riley tried poking the door with his foot but lost his balance and dropped everything. Morris didn't bother to turn around.

Down the hallway, Hoffman and the receptionist watched with pity.

"Do you think he'll make it through camp?" asked the receptionist.

Hoffman shook his head. "I'm not sure he'll make it through the door."

Seven

THE ALARM RANG AT 8:30. Riley had thought about setting the clock for 6 but figured Hoffman was just trying to scare him with the 7 A.M. thing. *Hell*, he thought, *a can of Folgers doesn't get up that early.* Riley showered, shaved, picked out a pair of khaki shorts, a freebie golf shirt (courtesy of the good folks at Olympia Fields), ate a bowl of stale cereal, brushed his teeth, and then ran a comb across his receding hairline. Maybe it was time to take the Rogaine plunge. As best as Riley could tell, his ear hair was growing faster than anything on his head.

The Volvo purred like a Swedish starlet. He took a left out of the condo complex and another left onto Center Street, and drove a quarter mile before he felt his heart do a sprint for his throat. There on the practice fields were dozens of Cubs players. And standing in the middle of the diamond was Cubs manager Barry Braswell. And forming a half circle around Braswell were Morris and several other reporters.

Riley gunned the car into the lot, locked the doors, waved his pass as he ran past the security guard, and then, upon reaching the bleacher seats, settled into a brisk walk. He didn't want to look panicked. He arrived just as Braswell said, "Goddamn, R.J., where do you dig up this shit? Gotta go, gentlemen."

Fungo bat in hand, Braswell jogged to an adjacent field and started hitting grounders to pitchers. Riley, out of breath from his walk-sprint, wiped a bead of sweat from his forehead.

"Joe, you made it," said Hoffman, who noticed Riley first. The small herd of reporters turned toward Riley.

"Overslept. Must be the jet lag," Riley said.

"Or laziness," said Morris.

Someone laughed. Riley tried to fake a carefree chuckle.

"I might as well introduce you to everybody," said Hoffman. "Everybody, this is Joe Riley. He's taking Mitchell's place until the lockout is over. Joe, I guess you already know R.J. Morris."

"I'm learning," said Riley, extending his hand to the *Standard* reporter. Morris, on the hard side of 50, ignored it.

"This is Andy Blair of the *Herald-Democrat*."

The younger Blair, who had eyebrows the size of carpet swatches, looked at Morris for approval. Morris shook his head ever so slightly. Blair stuck his hands in his pockets.

"This is Paul Hill of Post News Services."

"Nice to meet you, Joseph Riley," said Hill, skinny as a foul pole and, by Riley's guess, in his early thirties.

"Joseph is what my mom calls me," said Riley. "Joe is fine. So is J.J. Or even Snapper."

"Snapper," sneered Morris. "More like Flounder."

Blair giggled. Riley ignored the remark. Hoffman pressed on.

"This is Greg Armour of WMVP."

"One thousand on your dial," said Armour in a perfect radio voice. Armour was in his late twenties, dressed in a pair of black linen slacks, stylish loafers, and a mock turtleneck.

"And this is Alan Nadel of WGN-TV. He's a producer and does a lot of 'GN's preseason work."

"Welcome," said Nadel, who looked to be about the same age as Armour—maybe 26, 27—but not nearly as well dressed.

"Thanks," Riley said. "I've got a small case of first-day jitters. It's been a while since I've done this."

"Really?" said Morris. "Except for the fact that you showed up two hours late, didn't bring a notebook, a tape recorder, or a pen, I would have never guessed this was new to you."

Blair laughed again.

"I've got a photographic memory," said Riley weakly.

"That's not what I hear," Morris said. "I heard you were a disaster on the DePaul beat, a junior-management flop, and a burnout on the desk. Now you're scabbing it just to keep your job."

"Knock it off, Morris," Hoffman said.

"You knock it off," said Morris, whose hair part started somewhere around his left armpit. "This guy shouldn't even have a credential. There are beer vendors who've been to Wrigley more than he's ever been—and they probably know more about baseball than he does. And when's the last time he covered a beat? Ten years ago? I talked to some *Sentinel* people last night and they said he can't even remember what time zone he's in. And from what I hear, if you sent Riley to cover the Crucifixion, he'd write about the other two guys."

"Give it a rest," Armour said.

"Hey, I'm just telling it like it is," Morris said. "He doesn't belong here. How he got a BBWAA card, I'll never know. But I'm not going to pretend I like him or the situation."

With that, Morris turned and walked toward the clubhouse. Blair was right behind him.

"I'm sorry about that, Joe," Hoffman said. "R.J. can be on the pompous side."

"Hell, he's probably right," Riley said. "I *don't* belong here."

"Shit," said Armour, "you should have seen what happened to me my first day covering this team."

"I've never heard this one," Hoffman said.

"I'll tell the story," said Armour, "but only if what's said here stays here. Agreed?"

"Agreed," they said.

"Okay, there's a whole table of gum and candy in the clubhouse, so I decided to sneak one of those malted balls. You know the ones I'm talking about?"

"The chocolate malted things," Riley said. "They come in those fat milk-carton containers."

"Yeah, the chocolate malted things," Armour said. "I know it's sort of forbidden for writers to scarf down the munchies, but I was hungry. And anyway, I've got a soft spot for those malted balls."

"Is this going to be a long story?" asked Nadel. "If it is, I can get some work done in the truck and then come back for the finish."

"Patience," said Armour. "So I'm munching on a couple of malted balls when Travis Campbell, that dickhead pitcher, calls me over to his locker stall. I'm thinking he's going to jump down my shirt for taking a piece of candy, but instead he's all smiles and warmth. He's a got a whole carton of those malted balls and pours me out a handful of the things. He's yukking it up with me, being like my best friend. I don't even know the guy. I'm thinking these big league boys aren't so bad. All-star pitcher giving me malted balls. I'm loving it."

"How come I never heard this?" Hoffman asked.

"Because I'm still considering a lawsuit," said Armour.

"What for, gummy bear discrimination?" Hoffman said.

"No, because the malted balls weren't malted balls."

"Whattaya mean, they weren't malted balls?" Hoffman asked.

"Because they were dried deer turds dipped in cheap chocolate," Armour said. "I was sick for a week."

Hill gagged. Nadel doubled over in laughter. Riley didn't quite know what to do.

"Pardon the pun," Hoffman said, "but you're shitting me?"

"I wish," Armour said. "The whole time I was eating those things, I kept hearing some of the players giggling. I should have known something was wrong. Campbell set me up."

"Why didn't you tell me?" Hoffman asked. "Not that I could have done much about it."

"And get freezed out after one day on the job?" Armour said. "That would have gone over real well back at the station."

"How do you know they were deer turds?" Riley asked. "Maybe they were just really stale malted balls."

"No, they were deer turds, all right," Armour said. "One of the clubhouse boys told me later that Campbell paid him ten bucks to go buy a carton of the real stuff at the Osco down the street. Then he poured out the candy, substituted the deer turds, and then waited for a sucker."

"You're sure about this?" Hoffman asked.

"I talked to the clubby myself," Armour said. "The kid said that Campbell came to camp straight from a bow-hunting trip in Montana."

"How sick were you?" Riley asked.

"Had diarrhea for four days, nausea for three more."

"What about Campbell?" Hill asked.

"Don't worry about our friend Travis," Armour said. "I don't get mad. I get even."

A whistle blew from a two-story observation tower located near the base of the clubhouse. Time for a new set of drills to begin. The pitchers and catchers, now in seven groups of five, rotated to another practice field.

"That's enough fun for one morning," Nadel said. "I've got to get back to the truck and edit some stuff for the noon feed."

"I'm out of here, too," Hill said. "Transcribe some notes. Get a head start on a thrilling first-day feature."

"Give me a ride back to the hotel?" Armour asked.

"You got money for gas?" Hill said.

"What?"

"Just kidding," said Hill, shaking his head. "Let's go."

As Hill and Armour walked away, Hill turned around, pointed at Armour, placed his forefinger in his mouth and gently pulled. Hooked another fish.

"That's quite a double play combination you got there," Riley said to the Cubs' PR man.

"Armour is a piece of work," Hoffman said. "He paid his dues before he got to Chicago. He worked at a handful of dinky stations in the South, the kind of stations so small they announce what's being served for lunch at the local elementary school. He was the voice of mystery meat in Starkville, Mississippi. He was married, but his wife died in an auto accident just before he got the offer from MVP."

"I don't even know what to say to that," Riley said.

"What can you say? She was thirty-one. An attorney. From what I understand, they were talking about starting a family."

"Well, that's a real pick-me-upper story," said Riley. "How about Hill?"

"A career hack, but a professional," Hoffman said. "You've read his stuff. A solid reporter. A decent writer, nothing fancy. Last year the *Houston Chronicle* asked him to interview for their Astros opening, but he wasn't interested."

"You're kidding?" Riley said. "That's a pretty solid newspaper."

"I know, but Hill has spent his whole life in Chicago."

"I know the feeling."

"You, too?" Hoffman said. "Where?"

"Beverly. You?"

"Glencoe."

"Wooo, fashionable Glencoe," said Riley. "A hated North Sider."

"And you're a hated South Sider," said Hoffman, used to trading insults with anyone who used the Dan Ryan. "By the way, is it true South Siders don't cut their toenails or use fluoride?"

"Nah," Riley said. "We're too busy putting our Ford Pintos on blocks."

"That's what I thought," Hoffman said.

"I feel so worthless," Riley said.

"You should," Hoffman said. "So as a public service to you, Mr. Worthless, I'll give you a quickie tour of the clubhouse. We'll be here for the first three weeks, until we start trimming the roster and playing exhibition games. Then we'll move over to HoHoKam for—"

"WATCH OUT!"

Riley covered his head, fell to the ground in the fetal position, and waited to hear the sound of ball striking flesh. Instead, he heard nothing but belly laughs. Lots of them.

"Uh, Riley, get up," whispered Hoffman, who hadn't budged.

"There's no foul ball, is there?" said Riley, uncurling himself.

"No," said Hoffman. "Rookie mistake."

"What a day I'm having," said Riley, rising to his feet.

There was more laughter, even some clapping, most of it coming from Travis Campbell. Riley looked up in time to see Hightower on the observation perch. He wasn't smiling.

"What's the deal with your GM?" Riley said.

"Hightower? I wouldn't count on many breaking stories with him as your source. The guy has more secrets than John Ehrlichman," said Hoffman. "I shouldn't be telling you this, but I've got to get clearance from him just to include the day's weather in the pregame notes. A control nut."

"Decent guy?" Riley asked.

"Got me," said Hoffman. "I barely know him, but I've only been working for the Cubs eight years."

"He must be doing something right."

"We'll see. This is only his second year as GM. But I can definitely tell you there won't be any inside leaks. Hightower is a leak freak. He canned a secretary because she didn't run a salary sheet through the shredder twice."

"Really?"

"No," said Hoffman. "But let's just say that we, as Cubs support staff, have a healthy respect for him. Hell, he's probably looking at us right now, wondering what I'm telling you."

Riley pretended to glance at one of the nearby drills: catchers blocking wild pitches. Then he slowly angled his head toward the tower. And there was the Cubs' general manager, wearing a pair of highway patrol reflector sunglasses, looking down at Hoffman and Riley.

"Christ, you're right," said Riley, turning away. "He was looking straight at me. Can he lip-read from fifty yards?"

"Probably," Hoffman said. "Let's get inside."

As Riley and Hoffman walked toward the clubhouse, Hightower pulled a legal pad and his Mountblanc from a leather briefcase. The other Cubs officials thought he was jotting a note about one of the players. But Hightower, who considered no detail too small, was busy with a checklist.

Who is he? he wrote. *What media organization? Personality profile? Experience level? Threat to organization? Weak points? Strengths?* Information was power. The more information Hightower had at his disposal, the more power he possessed. He would make some calls about Riley after the morning session.

By 11:45 the players were back in the clubhouse for showers and then lunch. A meeting was scheduled for 1:30. Afternoon drills would start at two and end at 3:30. It was just early enough for some of the catchers and pitchers to squeeze in a quick nine holes at Mesa Country Club.

Riley called the office for instructions. Butler said the section was tight. No notes unless somebody tore a rotator cuff or something. "But we're going to want an eighteen-inch feature and ten inches of notes for Friday," Butler said. "The same amount of notes for Saturday. A feature for Sunday. An advance on the full team reporting for Monday. Questions?"

"How do I turn on my laptop?" Riley asked.

"Very funny," said Butler before hanging up.

"No, I'm serious," said Riley, staring at the receiver.

That night Riley bought $100 worth of groceries and $25 worth of Old Style, which worked out to two 24-packs. He drank five cans before he thought about trying to call Chicago directory assistance to get Megan Donahue's number. Instead, he popped open another can of beer and turned on *SportsCenter*. He passed out on the rattan couch an hour later.

The phone rang just as the morning sun was beginning to sneak through the crack in the living room curtains. Riley didn't know what time it was, but it was early. Too damn early for anyone to be calling.

"Hello, and this better be good," he said after staggering to the receiver in the kitchen.

"Sorry," said a muffled voice. "Wrong number." Dial tone.

Riley slammed the phone on the hook, but the sound quickly reminded him of his beer-induced hangover. He looked at the time on the microwave clock. It was 6:11.

"Jesus," he said.

According to the usual itinerary, which Riley had neglected to read, players were available in the clubhouse between seven and eight o'clock. Braswell, it said, also would be available in his office. So that's what Hoffman meant by getting there early.

Riley took account of himself in front of the bathroom mirror. He still had the remnants of cottonmouth. Worse yet, his T-shirt, pants, and shoes were still on, and his arms and face were covered with imprints of the rattan. He looked like a grid pattern. Riley had left the TV on. He could hear Kenny Mayne's voice, which meant an ESPN rebroadcast of the previous late-night *SportsCenter*.

Determined not to subject his eyes to light until the last possible moment, Riley showered in the dark. He nicked himself three times while shaving, shoveled down a bowl of Frosted Flakes, and then grabbed his car keys.

"Almost forgot," he said, digging into his computer bag for a fresh notepad and pen. The little Olympus microcassette recorder was already in his shirt pocket.

The parking lot was three-quarters full by the time he pulled in at 7:03. Every luxury car in the world was in that lot. If Riley hadn't known any better, he would have thought it was a meeting of the international oil cartel. Rolls-Royces. Mercedeses. Jaguars. Beemers. Lexuses. Corvettes. Some vintage hot rods. A pair of Harleys. Off to the side were three monster trucks with wheels the size of those found on corn harvesters. One of them had a huge set of deer horns in the back. The Montana license plate read: SXYCUB.

"Oh, God," said Riley. "Campbell."

Riley walked through the entranceway, down a hall past Braswell's closed office door, past the weight room, and into the maze-like clubhouse. There were name tags above each locker stall, but Riley hardly recognized any of the names. Morris and Blair were in an opposite corner of the room, talking to Casey Harris, the newly acquired relief pitcher from the Seattle Mariners. Harris had saved 31 games the previous season. The Cubs signed him to a huge free agent deal and handed him the closer's job.

Riley pulled his notebook from the back pocket of his Levis and walked over to Harris's locker. Riley needed a feature for Sunday.

Harris had on a T-shirt from the Cheetah IV strip joint in Atlanta and a pair of sanitary socks. He sipped from a steaming cup of coffee and flicked a Winston with his other hand.

"So I tell the bitch that she ain't never gonna make any money table-dancing like that," Harris said, hardly noticing Riley. "I got up on the table and started grinding away. Some of the bitches in the place started putting dollar bills in my pants. It was wild."

"What a great story," Blair said excitedly.

"We're in Atlanta in late May," Morris said. "We'll go there then."

"Cool," said Harris. "You won't believe how fine they are."

Harris took a drag from his Winston, blew a pair of halos, and then looked at Riley.

"Who the fuck are you?" he said.

"Joe Riley. I'm with the *Sentinel*," said Riley, attempting a handshake.

"This the scab?" said Harris, glancing at Morris.

"The one and only," said Morris, pulling a tin of Kodiak from his back pocket and sticking a pinch in his mouth.

"Well, then, I've got nothing to say to you, pardner," said Harris.

"I'm not a scab," said Riley, glancing at Morris. "There was a management-imposed lockout. I got assigned this beat. I didn't ask for it."

"You management?" Harris said.

"In a pawn sort of way, I guess," Riley said.

"Then I got nothing to say to you," Harris said.

"Hey, I'm just trying to do my job," Riley said. "Why don't you give me a chance before you decide anything?"

Harris took a step forward.

"You want me to accidentally spill this coffee on you?" Harris said. "Now get your management ass out of here. I tried to be polite with you. Don't make me do something else."

Riley backed away. Morris turned around and smiled.

"Shoo, now," said Morris, before spitting a tiny stream of tobacco juice into a small Styrofoam cup.

Riley took two more steps backward, turned, and ran into somebody built like a bank safe. He dropped his notepad. As he bent over to pick it up, the Olympus fell out of his shirt pocket. The recorder bounced noisily on the floor, causing the back latch to open and sending a pair of double-A batteries rolling out of reach.

"Sorry about that," Riley said, without looking up.

"*Quizás la próxima vez ten cuidado adonde vas,*" said the voice.

Maybe you'll watch where you're going next time.

"I'm sorry, what?" said Riley, looking up to match voice with face.

Riley watched in amazement as the player, wearing only a pair of Cubs-issued blue shorts, ambled away. From the back, the player was a single slab of sculpted granite. His shoulders were the width of a dugout. His thighs were as thick as ceiling beams. He had the physique of one of those Saturday morning cartoon superheroes.

"See you met our Dominican rookie catcher."

It was Hoffman.

"Met him?" said Riley. "I nearly got a concussion from him."

"Never lifted a weight, either," Hoffman said. "Born that way. Even more amazing: Not only is he the strongest guy in the organization, but he tested number one in flexibility."

"You're kidding?" Riley said. "Does he speak English?"

"Not a word. Doesn't want too, either. We've hired tutors . . . the works, but he says he isn't interested."

"He said something to me," Riley said. "But I'm not real fluid with the *español.*"

"Yeah, I caught the tail end of it," Hoffman said. "If my high school Spanish still works, he said you should watch where you're going."

"If the Human Eclipse says so, that's what I'll do."

"English or no English, I think there's a good chance you'll see Mr. Omar Hernandez in the starting lineup on Opening Day," said Hoffman.

"That good?"

"We signed him when he was sixteen. He spent a half season in rookie ball, a half season in Double A. He could have started for about a dozen big league teams last year, including ours. We brought him up in September, but he never played because of the Wild Card race. Braswell didn't want to take any chances. Rather than pretend he needed more time in the minors, Hightower invited him to camp. I'm guessing he's here to stay."

"I don't think you'll be saying the same about me."

"Well, at least you got here on time."

"How did you know— Wait a minute, that was you who called this morning, wasn't it?"

"I've got no idea what you're talking about," said Hoffman, trying hard to hide a grin. "I'll see you out on the field."

Riley decided it was time to introduce himself to Braswell, who had come to the Cubs from the Atlanta Braves organization two seasons earlier. Braswell was as plump as a spring tomato, with a temper as hot as the tip of a lit cigarette. Mitchell had said Braswell didn't suffer fools gladly.

This time the office door was open. Riley knocked and stuck his head inside the entrance. Braswell was on the phone.

"C'mon in," he said, covering the receiver with his hand. There was an open Diet Coke on his desk, a schedule of the day's drills, an injury report, and a carton of Kents. "Have to do some goddamn radio thing, then I'll be right with you."

Riley sat down. Braswell was a baseball lifer. Came up in the Dodgers organization when being a Dodger still meant something. Played nine years in the big leagues—Dodgers, Phillies, Padres, Brewers, and finally the Braves—as a no-hit backup catcher (.211 career batting average) before he was given a choice by the Braves: try to squeeze another big league season out of diminishing skills, or become a manager in Atlanta's minor league system. He took the minor league gig, starting in short-season rookie ball and eventually working his way up to Triple-A Richmond. Impressed with his record, but more so with his ability to connect with his players, the Braves moved him to bench coach on the big league team. The Cubs, after interviewing a half-dozen retreads, invited Braswell to the O'Hare Hilton for a secret meeting. Braswell, figuring he had nothing to lose, decided honesty was the best policy. He told Cubs management that it seemed more interested in making Wrigley a tourist attraction than in making it a place to be feared by visiting teams. He said the minor league organization was for shit and that, if given the job, he'd want to nuke at least half the roster. He said he didn't believe in three-run homers and two-dimensional players. He said if the team really wanted to win, it was going to cost money. Some for him. A lot for free agents. Even more for the farm system. Then he waited for the Cubs to kick him out of the room.

Instead, they asked him to wait in a nearby suite. Exactly 32 minutes later, Hightower—whose own future was in serious jeopardy—asked Braswell one question: "You made your point. Want to do something about it?"

"Goddamn right I do," Braswell said. Hightower and Braswell shook hands, and that was that.

As expected, the first year was painful, as Braswell and Hightower overhauled the roster. Year two was an unexpected surprise, with the Cubs making a late run at the playoffs before a thin and tired bullpen collapsed with 11 days to go. The Cubs finished 4½ out of the Wild Card spot.

Braswell's no-nonsense style had earned him admirers. He was 52 with a farmer's tan, and his fingernails and fingertips were brown with tobacco stains. He wasn't afraid to take chances, and few managers could finesse a starting staff the way Braswell could. Rather than treat the game as if it were some type of physics equation, Braswell reduced everything to its simplest form and then made a decision. In fact, he thought it was hilarious when some managers were referred to as geniuses, as if only a select few could figure out the double switch. To Braswell, managing baseball was intuitive, a question of feel more than anything else. Stats and tendency charts were nice to have, but Braswell managed with his heart and his mind. He loved trying to find the perfect mix of both. As for the media, Braswell didn't share the same passion.

"Yeah, I'm still here," said Braswell to what Riley guessed was a producer on the other end of the line. "How many more goddamn commercials you gonna play before we talk some baseball? I'm gonna die of old age waiting here."

Braswell winked at Riley. Then, with his segment apparently ready to begin, Braswell cleared his throat.

"Nice to be with you, too, and all your listeners in Davenport," said Braswell, now on the air. "Uh-huh . . . uh-huh . . . uh-huh, well, like I always say: I'll win with assholes, but I won't lose with them. You can bleep that, can't you? Oh, this is live. Goddamn, why didn't you tell me? Anyway, like I was saying, I think we've got a real good blend of youth and experience on this ballclub. I like our chances to do some damage."

There was a long pause.

"Uh-huh, well, I never looked at it that way before," Braswell said. "This is a new season, a new start, and we feel real good about the potential of this particular ballclub."

Another pause.

"Well, that's your opinion, but to be honest with you, you don't sound like the sharpest knife in the drawer, if you know what I mean," said Braswell, leaning forward in his chair, a neck vein beginning to protrude. "Baseball is what I do for a living. I don't sit in a radio booth and punch buttons and become an expert by reading what Hal Bodley writes in *USA Today*. You ever play baseball professionally? I didn't think so. Uh-oh, my cellular battery is beeping. You're fading out. You're fading . . ."

Braswell gently hung up the phone.

"Take that, you little piece of Davenport chickenshit," Braswell said to the phone. "Asking me if I had the 'pedigree' to manage a team like the Cubs. Goddamn, the Cubs haven't won a World Series since Teddy Roosevelt was president. It's not like I could do much worse."

Braswell reached for the carton of Kents, pulled out a pack, tore off the wrapper, and tapped on the bottom until a cigarette poked its head out. "Hoffman makes me do these goddamn shows. The call-in shows are the worst. Every call starts out, 'I've been a Cubs fan since 1958 and I love the team, but I hate your guts and I wish you would die.'"

Braswell looked up. "Okay, now that I've ranted and raved, just tell me you aren't a reporter who takes good notes," he said as he snapped shut his silver Zippo and took a deep drag on the Kent.

"I'm Joe Riley, a reporter who barely knows how to work a Bic."

"My favorite kind of journalist: dumb and technologically challenged," Braswell said. "Who you write for?"

"The *Sentinel*," Riley said.

Braswell pushed the pack of Kents toward Riley. Riley shook his head no. "The *Sentinel*, huh?" said Braswell. "What happened to Mitchell? Find those pictures of him with those farm animals?"

"Lockout," Riley said. "Management locked out the Guild. I'm filling in."

"I'd heard something about that," Braswell said. "How long?"

"Don't know. A few days, weeks, months. There isn't a lot of dialogue going on between the union and my paper right now."

"I'll be goddamned," Braswell said. "What other teams have you covered?"

"None," said Riley, embarrassed by the admission. "I'm new to this."

"Goddamn, this is one hell of an indoctrination," Braswell said. "I'm guessing that was you they pulled the fake foul-ball trick on yesterday?"

"Yeah. I've always been a talented flincher."

Braswell started laughing. "I'd say. You looked like a goddamn roly-poly all curled up. I nearly swallowed my chaw on that one."

"I do what I can," said Riley.

"Don't you worry about it," said Braswell. "Some of my players are so stupid they don't know when the War of 1812 was fought. But here's the deal. I'm gonna give you some ground rules. Follow them, and you and me won't ever have any trouble. I gave the same rules to Li'l Bit when he came on the beat."

"Who's Li'l Bit?"

"That's my nickname for Mitchell. Every time I see him, I tell him he's a li'l bit fatter."

"Not bad," Riley said. "Okay, your ground rules. I'm taking notes."

"One," said Braswell, in between pulls on the Kent. "You can ask one stupid question a week. I determine what's stupid, what isn't. For instance, you can second-guess me on something, but you better have a good reason to do it. If not, I'm going to mulch you like a Toro.

Two, I don't like cynicism and I don't like sarcasm. It's a cheap laugh. I can't stop you from writing like that—hell, I don't read the goddamn papers anyway—but I sure as hell don't have to listen to it. Three, I don't do off-the-record interviews. You ask me a question, I'll answer it. If I can't or don't want to, I'll tell you so. We all square on this?"

"Except the part about mulching," Riley said.

"You'll be all right," said Braswell, grinding his cigarette into a glass ashtray.

Riley went over the roster with Braswell, who broke down each position and talked about which jobs might be open. Then Hill and Nadel came in. Nadel tried some hypotheticals on Braswell, but the Cubs manager wasn't biting.

"Here me good on this, Nadel," said Braswell to the WGN producer. "There are two things I don't give a rat's ass about: tits on a man and your goddamn hypotheticals. That's what we've got spring training for, fellas. I mean, why bother with what-ifs when we get to play the goddamn exhibition games?"

"But let's just say that Henderson's arm isn't a hundred percent," Nadel persisted. "Who takes his spot in the rotation?"

"You know," said Braswell, standing up, "I was just telling the rookie here about his stupid-question allotment. Nadel, you're coming dangerously close to using yours up. And now, fellas, if you'll excuse me. I've got an appointment with Mr. Commode. End of session, unless you want to hear what I had for dinner last night."

Later that morning, Riley filed his notes, as well as a story on a non-roster pitcher from Belgium. More worthless notes were written for Saturday. Then Riley made another run at Casey Harris for the Sunday feature.

"You wait right here," said Harris. "I'll be right back."

Harris ducked out a side door. As Riley waited on a bench in front of Harris's locker, someone hung a clothes hanger on his belt loop. As a last resort, Riley wrote a story about the four-seam fastball. Pitching coach Ernie Gesser had taken pity on him and patiently explained why the four-seamer was a required pitch for Cubs pitchers. The office wasn't as excited.

"Can you write about actual baseball players the next time?" said one of the interns working the rim. "It sounded like something George Will would write."

"And you are . . .?" said Riley, unfamiliar with the voice.

"Ronald M. Bartlett," said the voice.

"Of the Singing Von Bartlett Family?" Riley said.

"Oh, I get it," the intern said. "Now I can see why you didn't get a merit raise."

"How the hell do you know about merit raises?" said Riley, suddenly on the defensive. "Someone publish them?"

"Not exactly," said the smarmy intern. "One of the Guild members stole a copy of the raise list and e-mailed it to the entire company. Another copy got sent to the TV stations, to show how cheap management is."

Riley sagged. "Any questions on the story?" he asked tiredly.

"Yeah, why'd you write it?" said the intern, no doubt smirking.

At Hoffman's urging, Riley made an appearance at a Mexican restaurant called Casa Del Sol, known to the locals and a handful of Cubs players and officials. It was located next to an auto-body repair shop, and Riley had driven past the building three times before spying the tiny sign in the restaurant window.

"You're late again," said Nadel, holding a glass of sangria.

"But fashionably so," said Riley. "What, no Morris and Blair? I thought we had a real bond."

"They canceled out when I told them you might be coming," said Hoffman.

"What'd I ever do to them?" Riley said.

"It's not you, it's the lockout," Hoffman said. "And the *Sentinel*. Not to mention that Morris is wound tighter than a Hair Club for Men weave. His whole life revolves around getting the story first."

"That's comforting," said Riley.

"You'll get used to it, in a year or two," said Hill of Post News. "I remember during my first season I used to fear that daily walk down my driveway to pick up the paper and see if Morris had scooped me. Now I never feel that way."

"So you worked through it?" Riley asked.

"Not really," said Hill. "I just canceled the subscription."

"So what's his secret?" Riley asked.

"He sucks up to the players, I know that," Armour said. "Gets Christmas cards from some of them. Goes out drinking with them. Runs beef. The works."

"Runs beef?" Riley said.

"Chases women. The players call it 'running beef.'" Armour said.

"Nice," Riley said. "And Morris isn't worried how this looks?"

"He's not married," Nadel said.

"No, I mean how it looks journalistically," Riley said. "Doesn't he sort of compromise himself by getting so close to these guys?"

"I guess he figures it's worth the trade-off," Nadel said. "All I know is that I thought I had a couple stories cold, was going to kick everybody's ass, and he either beat me to them or we tied."

"Same here," said Hill, who suddenly sprang to life, as if timer activated. "I don't know how the hell he does it, but I don't think I've ever beaten him on a spring training story. The guy has some sort of supernatural sixth sense. He's probably beating us on a story right now."

"Or jogging with Braswell," Hoffman said.

"What?" said Nadel.

"Just kidding," Hoffman said.

"If he's so good, why is he still at the *Standard*?"

"I hear he's had his chances," Hill said. "Your paper even made a run at him. So did the *LA Times*. He went out to LA for an interview, but turned them down."

"Why?" Riley said. "The money had to be better than what he gets now."

"He got pissed when they wouldn't let him string for *Baseball America*," Hill said.

"I didn't know he covered the NL for them," Riley said.

"He doesn't," said Hoffman. "He covers the Pacific Coast League. That's where the Iowa Cubs play, in the Central Division of the PCL."

"And that's why he turned down LA?" Riley said.

"You got it," Hoffman said.

"That, and he likes being the big fish in his small pond," Hill said. "And as much as I hate to admit it, he must have some hellacious sources on the Cubs . . . hmmm, Mr. Hoffman?"

"Don't look at me," Hoffman said. "I treat you all the same, like the pond scum you really are. I don't have any idea who Morris's go-to guys are."

The dinner conversation drifted from Morris to the Cubs' chances in the NL Central to the merits of the designated hitter. Hoffman and Armour were clearly the baseball traditionalists, while Nadel and

Riley supported continued league expansion, a true World Series, and the inclusion of Shoeless Joe Jackson in the Hall of Fame.

Hill offered no opinion.

"You're awfully quiet, Paul," Hoffman said.

"I know that look," Nadel said.

"Yeah, here we go," Armour said. "Mount Hill is about to erupt."

Hill waited several seconds before speaking. The others leaned back in their chairs and waited. Riley looked around the table, not quite sure what was about to happen.

"I want to know something," Hill said, the remnants of a fourth frozen margarita on his bushy mustache.

"He speaks!" Hoffman said.

"I want to know," continued Hill, "why Aunt Bee doesn't have a southern accent."

"Who?" said Armour.

"Aunt Bee," Hill said. "Mayberry RFD. *The Andy Griffith Show*. It's on TBS about every eleven minutes."

"Yeah, okay, Aunt Bee," Hoffman said. "So, what about her?"

Undeterred, Hill pressed on. "Here's this sixty-something-year-old woman. She lives in the heart of North Carolina and she doesn't have a southern accent? How is that possible? Listen to her. She sounds like she's from Montpelier, Vermont. And Barney sure as hell doesn't sound like he's from around there, either."

The waiter arrived. "Will there be anything else?"

"Yes, a stomach pump for my friend, here," Hoffman said.

"A stomach pump?" the waiter said.

"Just kidding," Hoffman said. "I'll have another Corona. No, make it three Coronas all together."

"*Tres*," blurted Hill. "And uno margarita grande, hold the el salto."

"You're drunk," Nadel said.

"If I were drunk, would I be able to ask this: Why doesn't Ford build the '67 Mustang again? Just update the thing. Put in the safety stuff, some new electrical systems, whatever, but build it the same shape and size of the '67. They should do the same thing with the '62 Corvette."

"That's a Chevy, not a Ford," Riley said.

"I know it's a Chevy," Hill said. "You're missing my point. Quit trying to improve the car. You had it right in '67. Just update it."

"Anybody know the area code for Detroit?" Hoffman said. "Paul has an important phone call to make."

"They mocked Alexander Graham Bell, too," Hill said.

"Of course they did," Riley said. "Did you see those lamb-chop sideburns?"

The drinks arrived a few minutes later. Armour raised his beer bottle for a toast.

"To another season of hell. God help us," he said.

"To hell," they said.

"And making it back alive," Riley added.

Eight

There could have been a better start to his Monday morning, but Lawrence couldn't think of one.

It had begun with the spectacular sight of Claire Beecher in some little Neiman Marcus number that nearly caused him to hyperventilate. When she said hello, Lawrence fumbled about like Niles Crane during a Daphne encounter. Next came a phone call from MacCauley. The union boss was surprisingly calm, but Lawrence could sense the tiniest hint of panic and desperation in his voice. MacCauley hid it well, but not well enough.

"Against my recommendation, the Guild has instructed me to discuss a handful of revisions regarding the *Sentinel*'s final offer," MacCauley said pleasantly enough. Lawrence guessed it was a bluff. According to his spies, the Guild membership had been outraged by MacCauley's mishandling of the initial negotiations. There was even a movement to replace him, but MacCauley had quelled the uprising with a promise to be more conciliatory. Lawrence had calculated all of this beforehand. Now the planning was beginning to pay off.

"I'm afraid there won't be any revisions," Lawrence told him. "The final offer has been revoked."

"This is bullsh— This is highly unusual," said MacCauley, catching himself. Then he softened his voice even more, in a fatherly, Irish-cop way. "Son, I'm sure we can find some common ground to reopen negotiations. It makes sense for both parties."

"Not to this party, it doesn't," Lawrence said. "Thank you for your interest, but I have a paper to publish. Good day."

Next, Lawrence called his secret contact at Danielson & Sons, Inc., the New York firm that specialized in leveraged buyouts.

"We're quite pleased with your course of action to date," the contact said. "When might we discuss the specifics of the takeover?"

"Not now," Lawrence cautioned, "but soon. I'm trying to trim as much fat off the bone as possible. Plus, there's the matter of our CEO and several other high-ranking voices."

"Yes, yes," said the contact, bored with the response. "Anyway, the less fat, the more profit for you and your shareholders."

"I'm keenly aware of the rewards," Lawrence said, not at all pleased with the obvious economics lecture.

"Of course you are," the contact replied.

Both men knew exactly how much Lawrence stood to earn from a successful takeover. The figures were staggering. Only a handful of people was privy to the projection sheets.

"I'll keep you informed," Lawrence said before ending the call.

Miss Beecher was summoned.

"Claire, by the end of the business day, I want a detailed account from each editorial department head of ways to further reduce costs," Lawrence said. "Word it any way you choose, but make it clear that the lockout will force us to make some painful decisions. Keep it vague, but ominous."

"Yes, sir."

"And Claire . . ."

"Yes, sir?"

"Have we discussed an appropriate raise for you?"

"Why, no, sir. But in light of your comments regarding cost cutting . . ."

"Uh, that's for junior management," said Lawrence. "Conditions for executive-level employees remain very favorable."

"Whatever you think is proper, sir," said Claire. "You've always been most generous."

"And you most deserving, Claire."

"Thank you, sir," said Claire, slightly flustered herself. "I'll start on the memo immediately. It should be ready for your approval within the hour."

"That's fine," said Lawrence, knowing he had been too overt. "Thank you."

About 80 Percent Luck

Lawrence watched Claire leave the office, the last hint of Chanel hanging in the air. If only there were some way to dispose of the Collagen Queen that wouldn't cost him a few zeroes before the decimal point. *Then* it would be a perfect day.

The first real day of spring training, when the entire roster fills the clubhouse, was like nothing Riley had ever witnessed. He arrived at 6:30 instead of the usual 7. His wasn't the first car in the lot, but the twelfth. A handful of Cubs fans were already stationed outside the entrance gate.

Riley found an empty clubhouse corner and watched as the position players trickled in for their nine o'clock physicals. They looked bigger and, for the most part, stronger than what he had seen on TV. There were a few prodigious beer guts but, all things considered, these Cubs seemed in admirable shape. And that didn't include the massive Omar Hernandez, who counted as two Cubs.

Whether by coincidence or actual plan, the Latin players' locker stalls were all generally located in the same area. It was a neighborhood rich in noise, laughter, gold crucifixes, and the sometimes excitable sounds of Spanish. There were Dominicans. Puerto Ricans. Venezuelans. Mexicans. Arubans. Colombians. Cubans. Nicaraguans. Panamanians. Somehow the lone Belgian had been assigned a cubicle there, which meant someone had a wicked sense of humor or couldn't read a map. Riley didn't understand a word any of them said.

Veteran all-star third baseman Brett Strickland, born and raised near the Missouri–Arkansas border and as white as a Holiday Inn shower curtain, walked toward the group with a country grin on his face. Strickland was something of a clubhouse politician but had few enemies and was generally regarded as the team leader. So said Mitchell, who added that Strickland led the league in dating the most beautiful women on the planet.

Strickland had a backslap or a handshake for each of the players. Pedro Gonzalez, the Cubs' star center fielder and highest-paid player, received a warm bear hug. Strickland took a step back, soaked in the sounds, and announced, "Fellas, if I didn't know any better I'd say I'm in Little San Juan."

"*Mejor que* Poplar Bluff, Missouri," said Gonzalez.

Strickland wheeled around. "I heard that, Petey. Don't you think

I didn't. I still remember some *español* from winter ball. I didn't hear you complaining too much when I took you home to Poplar Bluff and you had some of my momma's cooking. You didn't say it was better then."

"The woman is a saint," said Gonzalez, switching easily to accented English. "Not only she raise you, but she have to live in Missouri."

"Aw, go say a novena, Petey," said Strickland.

Gonzalez, wearing a tight-fitting golf shirt, clenched his fists and made a muscle man pose. "Look at me, Streekland," he said. "Pure steel. I lose twenty-five pounds during the offseason."

"Petey, the only way you'd lose twenty-five pounds is if you took off those gold chains," said Strickland.

"No, Streekland," said Gonzalez. "The gold gives me my strength."

A handful of other players walked in, probably minor league invitees, followed by second baseman Tim LeMott, shortstop Hector Valdez, and another half-dozen no-names. Then came right fielder Bob Lake, who had a cellular phone glued to his ear and a Taylor Made golf bag the size of a casket slung across his shoulder. Not far behind was left fielder Mike Delagotti and, later, 19-year-old rookie first baseman Lance Kasparovich, who had hit 51 homers at Triple-A Des Moines the previous season and was expected to challenge for a starting job. Kasparovich arrived wearing a lime green tank top, battle fatigues, black high-top Doc Martens, and a pair of sunglasses that wrapped halfway around his crew cut. His long, thin sideburns looked like hairy ant trails.

"Hey, Kaspie, what's with the shades?" said Strickland from across the room. "You waiting for a supernova?"

"Nah, I'm allergic to gamma rays," said Kasparovich, completely serious.

"Rook, I'm allergic to unpacking my bag," said Strickland. "Get your two-ton ass over here and unpack it for me. Do it right and maybe I won't make you wax and buff my Prowler this afternoon."

"Shit, tradition is a bitch," said Kasparovich, who dropped his own bags and lumbered toward Strickland's locker.

Riley could hear bits and pieces of conversation. LeMott was telling someone named Manny Olta (that's what it said on the piece of tape above Olta's locker) a string of bad jokes.

"Whattaya call a hundred twenty white guys chasing a black guy?" LeMott asked.

"Oh, Christ," said Olta, who was black. "I don't know."

"The PGA Tour," said LeMott excitedly. "Get it? Tiger Woods. Get it? It's funny, man."

"Yeah, man, you ought to be on Comedy Central," said Olta, who turned his back.

A trio of other players—Riley couldn't tell who they were—was discussing some sort of real-estate venture in Las Vegas. Meanwhile, Lake was recounting his visit to the Cubs Convention in mid-January.

"Banged these three Annies in the same night," said Lake, whose diamond-studded wedding band glistened in the morning light. "Didn't even have to talk to them."

"You have protection during those things, don't you?" said another player.

"Hell, yes," said Lake indignantly. "I disconnect the SpectraVision before they come up. I don't want anybody watching those pay movies if I fall asleep. Damn things are $8.99 apiece."

"No, man, I meant a rubber, a jimmy cap, a glove," said the player.

Lake looked aghast. "Buddy, the only glove I wear is a Rawlings."

"What if one of those Annies gets pregnant, man?" said another player. "Remember what Tidewater Tammy did? Or Shreveport Sue? You ready to be a daddy and pay child support?"

"They can do that?" said Lake.

One of the coaches, former Cubs great Boomer Hayes, walked into the clubhouse holding a copy of the day's schedule. He posted it on the oversized bulletin board near the training-room wall.

9 A.M.–noon: *Physicals with Dr. Walker*
noon–12:45 P.M.: *Lunch*
1 P.M.: *Team meeting (No media in clubhouse)*
1:15 P.M.: *Stretching, Field 2*
1:35–5 P.M.: *Individual Groups (See sheets in your welcome packet for hitting group assignments)*
5:30 P.M.: *Team meeting*

By now, Morris, Armour, Blair, Nadel, and Hill had begun circulating among the players. There were a handful of local hacks, too, as well as a couple of magazine bigfoots, Tom Verducci of *Sports Illustrated* and Tim Kurkjian of *ESPN: The Magazine*. Hoffman was busy dealing with the sudden influx of radio and TV reporters, each of whom wanted Strickland, Campbell, or Braswell for a live shot or for a guest appearance on some morning show.

Riley wandered into Little San Juan.

"Excuse me, Omar?" Riley said to the rookie catcher.

Hernandez didn't acknowledge him.

"Hey, whoever you are," said Valdez, whose locker was across from Hernandez's, "Omar don't speak English."

"That's what I heard," said Riley. "It's just that I ran into him yesterday, and I just wanted to apologize."

"Omar, *el reportero*—" said Valdez, before turning to Riley—"What's your name again, man?"

"Joe Riley. I'm with the *Sentinel*."

"Yeah, okay," said Valdez, turning back to Hernandez. "Joe Riley del Sentinel *dice que se siente mal al darse de cara contigo ayer. Si me preguntas, parece que el tiene algo para ti.*"

Joe Riley of the Sentinel *says he's sorry about running into you yesterday. If you ask me, he looks like he's got a thing for you.*

Hernandez slowly turned to face Riley.

"*Dile que yo no hablo a los reporteros,*" the catcher said. "*Dile que estoy aquí para jugar el béisbol.*"

Tell him I don't talk to reporters. Tell him I'm here to play baseball.

Riley waited for the translation.

"He told me to tell you that if you keep bothering him, he'll kick your ass, man," said Valdez. "You don't want to mess with Omar, man."

"Oh," said Riley. "But I was just trying—"

"Hey, man, Omar don't want to be bothered," said Valdez, his voice rising. "Understand?"

"I guess," Riley said.

"Sorry, man."

"Thanks for the help," Riley said. "I mean, the translating."

"You got it," Valdez said.

Riley walked away. Valdez laughed. "*Vendejo.*"

Dumbass.

Hernandez glanced at Valdez and then at Riley as the reporter returned to his place near a clubhouse wall. Hill was already back from a quick round of interviews.

"Congratulations," said the Post News Services reporter. "You just conducted the longest-running conversation with our soon-to-be rookie catcher."

"Is he always like that?"

"Like, mute?" said Hill. "At least you got something out of him. That's like the Gettysburg Address for Omar. He brings new meaning to the phrase *tools of ignorance*."

"That's a little harsh, isn't it?"

"Probably, but we have a little more history with him than you do," Hill said. "Last September we had a pool. Morris even popped for twenty bucks, that's how confident he was. The first guy to get a comment out of Omar won the pot."

"What happened?"

"Nothing. It was useless. We all made runs at him, but Omar never said a word. Not one."

"Valdez says he doesn't speak English."

"Hell, he barely speaks Spanish," Hill said. "We don't even try anymore. Not worth the trouble."

Riley nodded in the direction of Valdez, who was entertaining the rest of Little San Juan with some sort of imitation of a hitter. Riley was struck by how much fun they were having. "What about an interpreter?" said Riley. "Valdez seems willing."

"Valdez cares about Valdez," Hill said. "I don't know how he walks, what with that chip on his shoulder. He's a hell of a defensive shortstop, but a pain in the ass to deal with. He'd never put himself in that position, helping us out."

"Have you talked to Hoffman about Omar?" Riley asked.

"Sure, we did," Hill said. "I asked him about it late last season, but he said the club can't force a player to talk. So we're stuck with the Spanish version of George Hendrick."

When the players returned from their physicals they were measured for game and practice uniforms. The clubhouse attendants, known as "clubbies" by the players, were making shuttle runs from the equipment room to each player's locker. Riley marveled at the amount of clothing placed in each cubicle: a half-dozen T-shirts—long-sleeve and short-sleeve—two pairs of practice pants, protective sliding pants, jocks, sanitary socks, stirrups, athletic socks, warm-up jackets, pullover windbreakers, caps, and a sweater. Lurking nearby were the shoe, glove, and bat reps, who showered their contract players with dozens of freebies. Riley saw the Nike rep personally deliver four pairs of metal cleats, four pairs of hard-plastic cleats, three pairs of running shoes, and a pair of the newest Air Jordans to Strickland. As always, there was a clubby available to pre-stretch the shoes and caps for the players on a small metal instrument that worked like a reverse vise.

The Mizuno glove rep was there to present Strickland with three new gloves—all fitted to the third baseman's exact measurement specifications—to go along with his broken-in game glove. The Louisville Slugger rep gave Strickland a box of ash bats, model S359—the S for "Strickland" and the 359 for what he hit in 1996, the year he led the league in batting average.

Strickland pulled one of the two-tone bats out of the box and carefully turned it in his hands. Then he closely inspected the barrel of the cupped bat.

"Feels heavy," Strickland said.

"It's thirty-one ounces, just like you ordered," said the rep.

Strickland wasn't easily convinced. "This isn't the same shitty wood you gave me last September, is it?" said the third baseman. "Big Unit jammed me in Phoenix and the bat disintegrated. Ever try to hit propane with a handful of mulch? I was kicking rocks all the way back to the dugout."

"This is the best we have at the Jeffersonville plant, Brett. I personally oversaw your order from start to finish. Still got the original form," said the rep, pulling the tattered yellow sheet from his short-sleeve shirt pocket and adjusting his reading glasses. "Says here, 'Thirty-one-ounce, narrow grain, knot in the barrel (if possible), cone knob, Walker finish.' You've got a lot of hits in this box. I've got one of the clubbies storing six more boxes in the coolest part of the storage room. I'll have some sent to San Diego in time for Opening Day and the rest of them delivered to Wrigley."

"Handle is a little thick, isn't it?" said Strickland.

"You said you like to shave the handle, so we gave you a little room to play with," said the rep.

"I'll try 'em, but it better not be that shitty wood." Strickland was serious about his bats.

"Look at that barrel," said the rep, running his hand along the top of the bat. "Nothing's been juiced up. Narrow grain, so you know it aged naturally."

"Yeah, I suppose it looks okay," said Strickland, who began wrapping trainer's tape around the barrel. "I'll let you know. What about my box of in-betweens?"

"Should be done any day now," said the rep, looking again at his order sheet. "You said to save the first shipment for Opening Day."

"Don't forget those," said Strickland.

Strickland, Seattle's Edgar Martinez, and maybe a dozen or so other players were so meticulous when it came to the art of hitting that they occasionally used "in-betweens," or bats whose weight varied only fractions of ounces. In Strickland's case, he liked to have a small supply of supplementary bats that weighed a little less and little more than his favored 31 ounces. He started at 30.4 ounces, moving to 30.6, to 30.8, to 31.2, to 31.4, to 31.6. Martinez, the great designated hitter of the Mariners, had convinced him to try it in 1996, which turned out to be the best season of his career. In most cases he used the 31-ounce bat. But if he felt a little tired, he might drop down in weight; a little strong, he'd bump up. He might also switch bat weight depending on the pitcher, the pitcher's best pitch, even the day's weather. Strickland even adopted Martinez's pregame routine and was known to take batting practice with the weighted "doughnut" still on the bat.

"Have I ever let you down, Brett?" said the rep. "Just to be on the safe side, I put in an extra order."

"Good man," said Strickland, placing the bat back in the cardboard box. "Sorry to bust your ass about it, but I get nervous about my babies."

Done with Strickland, the rep made his way to LeMott's locker. Riley could hear LeMott ask the rep, "Hey, you know what they call a hundred twenty white guys chasing one black guy?"

Riley needed something for his daily notes package. A glutton for punishment, he tried Casey Harris again. Harris ducked into the trainer's room—off-limits to the media—before Riley could catch him. Strickland was nowhere to be found. The San Juan crowd was chattering away. Kasparovich was being interviewed by the tag team of Morris and Blair. Hill was in with Braswell.

Riley stuck his head outside the clubhouse door. There was Nadel coordinating interviews with WGN sports anchor Gary Danger. Danger spent the first week of every spring training with the Cubs before flying to Florida for a week with the White Sox. A Chicago fixture, Danger was a blowhard who got lots of access because of 'GN's clout, but also because the players knew he was no journalistic threat. He lobbed questions as if they were 16-inch softballs at Grant Park. When the dim-witted Lake had been arrested and later pleaded guilty to a misdemeanor DUI two years earlier, Danger was the only one to be granted an interview. He used the exclusive to ask the Cubs' right fielder why the American League still used the DH, and if the ivy at Wrigley was real or a clever silk substitute. It wasn't until the segment's producer screamed in his earpiece to ask Lake about the DUI that Danger actually broached the subject. Needless to say, the question didn't earn him a local Emmy.

"Robert," he had said benevolently, "do you think we in the media have spent too much time focusing on your recent, uh . . . youthful indiscretions than on the really important matters, such as the Cubs winning the pennant?"

A sound technician who was at the shoot later told Nadel that Lake's agent, who was positioned off camera, pumped his fist with glee when Danger finished with the question. Not even Lake could miss hitting that one out of the park. The controversy subsided and Lake eventually signed a three-year extension worth $12 million. So grateful was the agent that he arranged for an all-expenses-paid trip to Kapalula for Danger and Danger's mistress. It was no coincidence that Danger's nickname was "CompUSA," because he led the country in freebies accepted.

Today he wore a blue blazer, a Hawaiian shirt, and a pair of cherry red Bermuda shorts. The cord leading from his microphone to the sound man's machine was duct-taped to the back of the anchor's sport coat. His dyed brown hair was lacquer stiff.

"Can somebody get me my makeup kit?" said the preening

Danger. "This sun is killing my foundation." He turned to the lighting guy, who was aiming a round reflective shield called a flex fill at Danger's face, the better to direct the sunlight. "Could you *please* not do that until the interview begins? I feel like I'm on the face of the sun when you point that at me. Do you want me to have permanent retina damage? Do you think the station wants their number one sports talent, who just happens to draw the highest ratings in the eighteen-to-forty-nine demos, to require pupil replacement?"

"No," said the lighting assistant.

"Then fold that fucking thing up, find me my makeup kit, get me a Diet Coke—caffeine free—and tell Cecil B. DeMille, here," he said, gesturing toward Nadel, "that I need a warm body to interview!"

Nadel saw Riley peeking through the clubhouse's side door. Nadel rolled his eyes and mouthed the word *prick*. Riley nodded.

Desperate for a lead note, Riley approached Jason Hammler, who had the misfortune of being the odd man out at first base, all thanks to the phenom Kasparovich. Riley introduced himself and had hardly begun his first question when Hammler, eyes darting nervously about, interrupted.

"Whattaya hearing?" he asked quickly.

"Pardon me?" Riley said.

"Whattaya hearing around the league?" said Hammler. "Am I gonna get traded? What's Hightower saying? I'm hearing Boston as a DH. Maybe San Diego in the six spot."

"I'm not hearing a whole lot," said Riley, which was true enough.

"Chickenshit organization," Hammler said. "I give them four good years and what the hell do they do? They bring in the golden child over there."

Riley glanced at Kasparovich and then at his tape recorder to make sure it was on. He furiously took notes as Hammler railed against the Cubs management. A scoop. Already.

The interview lasted about 15 minutes. Riley got a quote from Kasparovich, who said he thought Hammler was a swell guy, and a quote from Braswell, who said the first base position was "wide open." Then he stopped by Hightower's office. Hammler's tirade would require a management response.

"Mr. Hightower is unavailable at the moment," said his secretary,

Alice Hodge. "Can I tell him what this pertains to?"

"Could you just tell him that I need to discuss a story with him?" Riley asked.

The secretary wasn't satisfied.

"I'll need a little more information than that, Mr. Riley," she said.

"It's about your first base situation," Riley said, trying to contain his excitement.

"I see," said Hodge, jotting down notes. "I'll make sure he gets your message."

Riley walked down to the far end of the hall, where a small, makeshift media room was located. There were six seats, two phones, and three folding tables. Riley took out his Mac and began his story.

By Joe Riley
Sentinel Staff Writer
> *Veteran Cubs first baseman Jason Hammler, upset over the apparent loss of his starting job to unproven rookie Lance Kasparovich, told the Sentinel in an exclusive interview that he will demand a trade.*

Riley finished the story by noon, leaving a space to insert any comments from Hightower. At two o'clock, just before the daily sports department planning meeting, Riley called Butler. Butler would no doubt want to congratulate him on the Hammler coup.

"You get the Hammler story?" asked Riley, trying not to sound overly proud. "I sent it a little while ago."

"Oh, we got it, all right," Butler said.

"Good," said Riley. "I don't know what else you've got running on page one for tomorrow, but I figure Hammler would be worth considering."

"Under normal circumstances, I'd say you're right," Butler said.

"Under normal circumstances? What happened . . . the Bulls announce a change in sock colors?"

"I wish," Butler said. "No, Morris had the Hammler story in today's *Standard*. You got beat."

"Hell, Hammler just got to camp today," said Riley.

"It's called the phone," Butler said. "Morris must have reached him at home."

"Shit," said Riley, whose own little-used black book contained the numbers of his softball teammates, his automated banking exchange, his uncle's condo in Pompano Beach, and a woman named something-Baich, whose first name and phone number had been blotted out by a beer spill that night at the Cork. He still had Mitchell's bailout numbers, but it wasn't desperation time—yet.

"It wasn't a total scoop," said Butler. "Hill had it, too."

"That doesn't make me feel a lot better."

"It wasn't meant to."

Riley had to rewrite the story, this time inserting the dreaded "According to published reports" clause. Everyone would know that Riley had been scooped. Butler had said Nadel and Armour were leading their afternoon reports with the story. Worse yet, Riley had failed to check the small table behind the receptionist's desk at the Cubs' main facility. It was there that one of Hoffman's interns had delivered a comprehensive clips package of the day's Cubs news from the three Chicago-area daily publications. Had Riley simply looked, he would have saved himself the embarrassment of sending in a "scoop" a day late.

It was 6:30 before Riley finally called it a day. Once again, Morris gave him the ice shoulder, and Blair managed a smirk. Hill was almost apologetic.

"Don't worry about it," Hill said. "I've been doing this awhile. What I can't figure out is how Morris got it. Hammler hates Morris. They nearly got in a brawl after a game last season. There's no way Hammler would have told Morris anything, except to fuck off."

"I would have taken a tie," Riley said. "I'm dying."

"Like I said, I've got a few years on you," Hill said. "It happens to everyone. Morris has kicked my ass plenty."

"It's not Morris so much," Riley said. "It's just that I'm way out of my depth here."

"For what it's worth, you're doing a hell of a lot better than we thought you would," said Hill.

"Here's the phone," said Riley, handing him the receiver. "Can you call and tell my boss that? I'll dial, you talk."

"You know what Scarlett said," said Hill as he loaded up his laptop. "'Tomorrow is another day.'"

"And as God is my witness, I'll never go scoopless again."

"See? You've got your health and your sense of humor," Hill said. "Talk to you tomorrow morning."

The light on his message machine was blinking when Riley got back to the condo. He ignored it and instead pulled a chilled Old Style from the fridge. What he wouldn't give for a pizza from Fox's, or even a beef sandwich from Pop's. Instead, he opened a can of Spaghettios and plopped it into a pan.

"The dinner of losers," he said to himself.

Riley unbuttoned the clasp on his shorts. He was averaging three or four beers each night and it showed in his waistline. Sansabelts were becoming a possibility. He was lonely. He was tired. And then there was something Butler had said at the end of their conversation, something about "a possible new management mandate," and "increased financial pressures." Riley had asked what that meant, but Butler wouldn't say. "It's already hard enough around here," Butler had said. "Don't make it harder by getting beat."

There wasn't much on TV: a couple of college basketball games, a Suns game, some miserable sitcoms. It wasn't until he made another trip to the fridge that he decided to put the blinking light on the message machine out of its misery.

Beep. Phil Mitchell was first. "Well, Hoss, you done won me twenty dollars. I had the two-week under on how long it would take for Morris to beat you. He's a piece of work, ain't he? You ain't the first he's done it to and you won't be the last. Now then, me and the missus will be there next week. We'll be at the Biltmore. You call, you hear?"

Beep. "Joseph, honey, this is your mother. I'm sending a little care package to you. There's some sunscreen and your father's Bears fishing cap—I want you to wear both. There's some fudge, too, though there might be some teeth marks from Gil. He got up on the kitchen table again. And in case you're interested, I asked Carol Donahue for Megan's home number. It's 312-555-5170. Nice girl, that Megan. Take care, honey."

Beep. "This is Butler. Don't forget the major league notes for Sunday. We'll need them Friday by two."

Riley began to reach for another beer but then checked himself. Desperate times required desperate measures, especially now that he had Megan's number.

Nine

THE SHOPPING SPREE COST HIM $163—money he'd have to make up on his modest *Sentinel* expense account by eating macaroni and cheese for 10 days—but Riley wanted to make the right impression. He had the box gift wrapped and stuck a bow on the other present. Then he forced himself to be in bed, lights off, by 9:30. *SportsCenter* would have to do without him.

The next morning Riley was at the clubhouse at 5:10. The office entrance was locked, but the side door was open. Riley walked inside.

"Hello?" he said.

Riley heard a slight rustle, like a handful of leaves grazing the ground, but then nothing. The room was nearly pitch black. A lone ray of light sneaked in from the adjoining weight room. Riley was forced to navigate his way across the clubhouse by memory.

Carrying the two packages in both arms, Riley poked at the floor with his toes. He ran into Lake's chair near the door, shuffled through Little San Juan with little difficulty, hit his knee flush on the corner of what should have been LeMott's locker, and was about to reach the weight room when he tripped over an unseen lump on the clubhouse floor. Riley fell backwards, the packages pulled tight to his chest, and hoped for the best.

He caromed off the side of a locker stall, bounced sideways, and then landed on the lump. There was a loud *ummpphhff*, an anguished cry of pain, and an equally loud "Jesus Christ!"—none of which came from Riley.

"Whoever you are," said the voice, "you better have a gun. Because as soon as I turn on this light, I'm gonna kill you."

The lump moved. Riley didn't.

The fluorescent lights came to life, blinding Riley for a moment. When his eyes finally adjusted, Riley could see the old man hovering over him. He was holding one of Strickland's newly taped Louisville Sluggers.

"Who the hell are you?" said the old man. "What the hell are you doing in the clubhouse? And why shouldn't I go to right field with that side of your skull?"

"I'm Joe Riley of the *Sentinel*," he said, looking up from the cold tile floor. "I was looking for Max Dewitt. And by the look of your grip, I'd say you're a pull hitter, not someone who goes to the opposite field."

"What?" said the old man.

"Bad joke," said Riley.

"Get up," he snarled.

Riley struggled to his feet, still gripping his two packages.

"How'd you get in here?" said the old man.

"Side door," Riley said, rubbing the sore spot on his knee. "I wanted to get here before Max."

"Nobody gets here before Max."

"You did."

"Never mind that," said the old man, wearing a pair of wrinkled painter's pants, a T-shirt with brown sweat stains, and a white pair of worn Keds. He looked like an elderly Gilligan. "Who told you about Max? Nobody talks to Max."

"Phil Mitchell did," Riley said. "I'm temporarily taking his place covering the team."

"Never heard of him," said the old man.

"Look, can you do me a favor? Can you just point me toward Max's office, or his cubicle, or his bunker, or wherever he is? I'll only be a minute."

"What for?"

"I need to drop off these presents," said Riley, adjusting one of the ribbons.

"Give 'em to me," said the old man. "I'll make sure he gets them."

"No," said Riley, tightening his grip on the packages. "I really need to talk to him myself."

About 80 Percent Luck

The old man leaned the bat against a locker. Nearby was a cot with a small inflatable mattress, a pillow with no pillowcase, and a navy blue wool blanket.

"Come back later," said the old man. "You'll see him then."

"This is only going to take a couple of minutes," Riley said.

"You want me to swing away?" said the old man, grabbing the bat again.

"You don't understand, sir," said Riley, gauging whether he could slip by the muscular geezer without getting hit in the back of the neck with 31 ounces of white ash. "I've got to talk to him. I need his help."

"Not now," said the old man, poking Riley toward the door with the bat head. "Leave those things on that chair and I'll find you later today."

"Who are you?" said Riley.

"Doesn't matter who I am."

"I've been here almost two weeks," Riley said. "I've never seen you."

"Maybe you haven't been looking hard enough," said the codger. "Now go."

Riley reluctantly left the clubhouse. He heard the sound of the deadbolt. And through the window slits, Riley saw the clubhouse go dark. On the horizon was a sliver of the morning sun.

The old man waited until he heard Riley's Volvo leave the gravel parking lot. Then he carefully unwrapped the gifts. And there they were: a bottle of Absolut and a box of 10 Macanudos.

"Not bad," said the old man, running one of the expensive cigars under his nose. He poked a hole in the cigar tip with a toothpick, struck a match, and puffed away in the darkness. Nothing like a Macanudo, even at dawn. He sat back in the rickety cot, pulled the blanket to his chest, and watched the orange glow of fine tobacco.

"Joe Riley," said Max Dewitt with a satisfied smile, "it was very nice to meet you. Very nice, indeed."

It rained a few hours later. Riley—back after a quick hour nap—and the other reporters worked the clubhouse as the players and coaches waited for the clouds to break. Riley had asked one of the clubbies about Max Dewitt but was told he was busy "and he never talks to you guys anyway." LeMott interrupted.

"Hey, Sparky," said LeMott indifferently.

"It's Andrew," said the clubby, a Northwestern sophomore taking the semester off to work in Arizona.

"Yeah, whatever," said LeMott. "Here's the keys to my ride. Go out and get me some Cocoa Puffs. I mean, you call that a breakfast spread? Seriously, you gotta be kidding me."

The clubby and Riley looked at the food table. There were five different kinds of cereal. There was orange, grapefruit, and cranberry juice; fat-free, one percent, two percent, and whole milk. Pastries. Yogurt. Cottage cheese. Bananas and sliced oranges. It was a mini-Denny's. The only thing missing was the French Slam.

"Nothing there you like?" the clubby said.

"Hey, you want me to talk to somebody about demoting you?" LeMott said. "Maybe we can get you switched to the guy who scrapes the fungus off our shower sandals. How's that sound?"

"Cocoa Puffs, right away," said the clubby as he sprinted into the rain and toward LeMott's metallic gold Lexus.

"Put a ding in my car and I'm using your head to pound it out!" LeMott yelled toward the parking lot. He turned to Riley.

"Kids," he said.

"Yeah, slave labor isn't what it used to be," Riley said.

"You got that right," said LeMott, as he squeezed an ingrown hair on his forearm. He wiped the tiny bead of pus on his T-shirt and walked away.

"He's Mr. Class, isn't he?" said Nadel, stationed a few feet away.

"The kind of guy you'd like your daughter to marry . . . and shove face-first into a wood-chip machine," Riley said.

"Whatcha got working for tomorrow?" Nadel said.

"Well," said Riley, opening his notebook as if he were running down a checklist, "I've got Braswell talking about his rehab at Betty Ford. Lots of tears and all on the record."

"Not bad," said Nadel. "Anything else?"

"Not too much," said Riley. "Hightower admitted to me—again on the record—that he vacuums his office in the nude and enjoys the Spice Channel. Is that any good?"

"Decent lead note, nothing more," Nadel said. "I wouldn't build your day around it. Any chance you could revive your series on the four-seamer?"

"Funny."

"Seriously, you working on anything interesting?" Nadel said. "You can tell me. I'm a TV guy. I'm 'GN. We're the place that gives you twelve minutes of Tom Skilling and the weather, and two minutes of sports."

"Nah," said Riley, who wasn't about to tell anybody anything. He liked Nadel enough, but the guy had a reputation as a news hound, even if he did work at a place that was happy to run highlight after highlight. "I've got nothing. But it's early. I'm trolling for notes and I'll have to manufacture a feature at some point today."

"Uh-oh," said Nadel.

"That didn't sound like a good 'Uh-oh,'" Riley said.

"It isn't," said Nadel. "Blair just walked in, but no Morris. Blair usually doesn't go anywhere without Morris. Something's up."

"Shit," said Riley. "I saw him lingering near Hightower's office when I came in. That was forty-five minutes ago."

"Then we're toast," Nadel said. "He must have something. Damn! The guy's a cyborg. He's like Schwarzenegger in *The Terminator*. Relentless. Needs no sleep or food. Runs on chaw. The ultimate seamhead. He loves the road. His epitaph will read, "Marriott Platinum Member." His favorite song is the national anthem. You know what he does on his vacation?"

"Memorize the baseball encyclopedia?" Riley said.

"Worse," said Nadel. "He goes to winter ball in Venezuela and keeps a file on every prospect."

"On purpose?"

"Says it relaxes him."

"I can't imagine Morris ever relaxed," Riley said. "Why the hard-ass routine?"

"He's ultra-competitive. It doesn't happen very often, but you should see him when somebody else breaks a story. He goes apeshit. Then he'll spend the rest of the week trying to knock down your scoop. He's like the Tin Man—no heart."

"And what's with Blair?" Riley said. "Why are him and Morris attached at the hip?"

"Here's the short version," Nadel said. "Blair got fired from Morris's paper a few years ago. Nobody knows why. Morris knows the sports editor at the *Herald Democrat* and put in a big word for Blair. Blair can't do enough for Morris."

"How much do I owe you for the history lesson?"

"Nothing if you'll find out what Morris is working on and, while you're at it, stick a very sharp fork in Danger's heart," Nadel said. "You should have seen him yesterday. He wouldn't do a live shot until he moussed his hair just so. You could have served tea on that hair, it was so hard."

"You TV guys," Riley said. "All the glamour."

Riley noticed the scowling Omar Hernandez was at his locker. Better yet, Little San Juan was deserted. "Gotta go," he told Nadel and then pulled a small paperback book from his pocket.

"Uh, Señor Hernandez," said Riley, nervously thumbing through the marked pages of his Spanish phrase book. "*Qué buen tiempo hace!*"

What pleasant weather we are having.

The sound of thunder resonated in the distance. Rain pounded the gravel roof. Hernandez stared at Riley, his face totally blank.

"Wrong page," said Riley. "Uh, *cómo está usted?*"

How are you?

"*Chingate.*"

Fuck you.

"*Chingate . . . chingate,*" said Riley, failing to find the word in his book. "I'm guessing that must be in the Spanish obscenity phrase book. Uh, *Podemos ser amigos? Quiero conocerte mejor.*"

Can we be friends? I would like to get to know you.

"*Chingate.*"

"There's that word again," said Riley, running his finger down the *C*'s in his book. "Look, I'm dying here, Omar. Okay, how about, *Cómo podemos construir mejor los puentes de entender?*"

How can we best build bridges of understanding?

Hernandez took the book out of Riley's hands and, with the ease with which someone would tear a Kleenex, the hulking Dominican ripped the 225 pages in half.

"*Ahora, hables español no más.*"

About 80 Percent Luck

Now you speak Spanish no more.

"I've got a pretty good idea of what you just said," Riley said.

As Riley picked up the remnants of the book, Valdez arrived. He carried a cellular phone. In fact, Riley couldn't think of a single time when he had seen Valdez in the clubhouse without a phone attached to his hand or ear.

"What's that, reporter?" said Valdez, pointing toward the floor.

"Nothing," said Riley, furiously picking up the pages in clumps.

"Don't look like nothing," said Valdez, snapping a page out of Riley's fist. "No, it looks like—"

Valdez doubled over in laughter. In between breaths, he managed to call several other Latino players to the locker.

"*Yo hablo español?*" he said mockingly.

Riley stared at his shoes.

"Man, Omar don't like you," said Valdez, dropping the page back on the clubhouse floor. "Omar don't like English. Omar don't like complications."

"Just thought I'd try," Riley said.

"Omar," said Valdez, lowering his voice, "is as dumb as a catcher's mask. You know what I'm saying, man?"

Riley peeked at Hernandez.

"Don't bother looking at him, man," Valdez said. "He doesn't understand a word we're saying."

"But he could," Riley said. "*You* speak English."

"Omar ain't that kind of smart, man," Valdez said. "Anyway, you think the team wants Omar to speak English, to learn the ways of baseball management? No way. They like him dumb. They need him dumb. Yeah, they want him to know enough English so he can talk to the pitchers, but that's it. The less he knows about everything else, the more the organization can screw him. That's how it is with the Latino players. They treat us different. We're second-class citizens, man."

"I've seen the salary lists," Riley said. "There are lots of Latino players making amazing amounts of money. Look at what Boston gave Pedro Martinez. Look at Pudge. Look at Ramirez."

"The exceptions, man, the exceptions," Valdez said. "For every Manny Ramirez there are fifty Omars. And even if we do get the money, we're still third in line."

"Third in line," Riley said. "Behind who?"

"The white players, man," said Valdez. "Then the black players. See, that's the problem, man. Nobody even thinks there's a problem."

"You really believe that?" Riley said. "That's pretty cynical, considering the average player salary is about $1.8 million. I saw the figures in *USA Today*."

"Believe it, man?" Valdez said. "I've lived it. I've seen it. I've heard it. You ain't going to find any of it in your little book there, but it's around. Every day, man. You're too hung up on money numbers. Just because you pay us don't mean you're not a racist."

Riley's story antenna finally came to life. Racism was a buzzword, the kind that could make up for the four-seamer debacle.

"Maybe this is something you and I can talk about," Riley said. "Sounds like a pretty good story."

"No fucking way, man," said Valdez. "Hightower see my name and I'm in hot water. This is last year of my contract, so I ain't saying anything to fuck that up."

"What about any of the other players?" Riley said. "Think they'll talk?"

"Man, give it up," Valdez said. "Gonzo over there makes a lot of money, but he's too scared to talk. He's a company man and anyway, he's got too many endorsement deals. Omar can't talk. I'm not going to talk. The rest of them think it's okay to look the other way."

"But you're doing the same thing," Riley said. "You're looking the other way."

"Fuck you, man," said Valdez, becoming more agitated. "I got family who depend on me. I got family in the States. I got family in Rio Piedras. I ain't going to ruin that so you can write a story, be a big newspaper hero."

Valdez's Nokia rang. The shortstop waved him off. Riley edged away, but not before knocking over a stack of fan mail in front of Campbell's locker.

"Hey, watch it!" Campbell said.

"Sorry about that," Riley said.

"You're going to pick them up, aren't you?" Campbell said.

"Oh, yeah . . . right," said Riley, trying to look composed. "Sorry."

Riley stacked the envelopes and slinked away.

The rest of the day didn't go much better. He had accidentally left the passenger-side window of the Volvo half open. The leather seat was drenched from the morning downpour, as were his notebooks from the two previous weeks. In the notebooks were several interviews that Riley had planned to turn into features. Now the notes looked like Rorschach drawings; Riley would have to conduct the interviews all over again.

Even more disturbing was the continued absence of Morris. There was the earlier sighting and then *poof*, he disappeared. He wasn't the only one flying under the radar. Max Dewitt still couldn't be found, and Hightower had stiffed Riley for a two o'clock interview. Something was going on. Even Hill, Nadel, Blair, and Armour had left the media workroom earlier than usual.

Riley filed his usual 16 inches of notes. The office would cut them to 11 inches. Riley would complain. The office would tell him an ad (probably something about breast augmentation) had been stuck on the page at the last minute. Or that the Bulls coverage needed more space. Or there would be no explanation at all, just a determined silence on the other end of the phone.

Dinner was a Red Baron cheese pizza from the grocery store. While walking to the frozen-foods section Riley had noticed one of the Cubs players—a minor leaguer from Double-A ball—loitering around the deli counter. His name was Dwight Willingham, or something like that. A pitcher with no chance to make the 25-man roster. A kid, really.

Willingham was ordering lunchmeat. At least, that's what Riley thought he was doing. Then he noticed that the minor leaguer never seemed quite satisfied with his choice. He'd ask for a sample slice of honey-baked ham, eat it, and then shake his head no. Then he'd ask for a thick slice of roasted turkey. Of roast beef. Of bologna. Of summer sausage. Of tavern ham. Each time he would shake his head no and choose another chunk of meat for sampling. And, each time, the deli worker, an elderly woman with a faded name tag, would smile and cut him another piece.

This went on for almost 10 minutes until Willingham left the counter without buying anything. Riley couldn't resist.

"Excuse me, ma'am?" Riley said.

"Yes, sir, what can I get you?" said the woman.

"How about a half pound of the honey-cured." Riley said. "The stuff on sale."

"Thin, sandwich, or thick slice?" she said.

"Thin's fine."

The woman plopped the ham on the metal carver. She cut 13 slices, weighed them, stuck a label on the plastic bag, and handed it to Riley. "Anything else?"

"Well, now that you ask . . . Was that a Cubs player here a few moments ago?"

"Yeah, the poor thing," said the woman. "They come in here every spring. Mostly the real young ones."

"I don't get it."

"They always ask for samples, sliced thick, too," she said, tugging the disposable cellophane gloves off her hands. "If my manager isn't around, I go ahead and do it. Little babies."

"It's deli meat, ma'am," Riley said.

"Sweetie, that's dinner for those minor leaguers," she said. "I asked one of them. He said he was trying to save his allowance . . ."

"You mean, per diem money?"

"Yeah, that's right," she said. "Per diem money. Anyway, he said some of the minor leaguers save their allowance and try to live off the free food the team gives them in the morning and at lunch. Then some of them come here after their afternoon workouts and use the deli samples as dinner."

"Dinner?"

"Oh, yeah, sweetie. Sometimes I'll cut up a bunch of cheeses and meats and put them in baskets on the counter. Those boys go through those baskets like locusts."

"How often you seen this one?"

"Him?" she said. "He's new. Gave me his autograph, though. Wrote it on some deli wrap. Looks like . . . Randy Willingham. Now, isn't that funny?"

"His autograph?"

"No, sweetie. The fact that his name is Willingham, but he kept asking to taste the roast beef. You know, Willing-*ham*."

"I see what you mean," said Riley. "Thanks for your help."

"Anytime, sweetie. Stop by Wednesday. The store will be crawling with those minor leaguers."

"Why Wednesday?"

"That's the day the big food companies usually send over their sampler people."

"You had me, you lost me, ma'am."

"You know, those people who set up their little tables near the end of the aisles and offer free samples," she said. "This week we got somebody coming from Jimmy Dean sausage, from Tostitos, from Hamburger Helper, and from Minute Maid. Those minor leaguers clean those sampler people out quick."

"That's amazing," Riley said. "I had no idea these guys were this poor."

"I noticed something else about that nice Willingham boy," she said.

"What was that?" said Riley, sounding more like Joe Friday with each passing minute.

"He was wearing a wedding band," she said.

Riley finished his grocery shopping and did it without making his customary swing through the liquor wing of the store. Old Style was on sale, but a vow was a vow. Riley had even started doing push-ups and sit-ups in the morning. Not many—a painful 10 apiece that first day—but enough to realize he was exponentially out of shape.

As he loaded the plastic grocery bags into the car trunk, Riley noticed Willingham. He was 23, maybe 24. About six-foot-two, 185 pounds. A righthanded pitcher, Riley seemed to remember. A non-roster invitee. Was in the San Diego Padres organization? Or was it the Colorado Rockies? Riley would have to check his spring training media guide when he got back to the condo.

Willingham didn't drive a luxury car. Riley couldn't tell for sure, but it looked like a Ford Tempo. Whatever it was, it had a rust spot on the rear side panel as wide as home plate. The miles hadn't been kind to it. Willingham carried one bag. He got into his battered vehicle, pulled out of the parking lot, and sputtered away.

There was a note on Riley's front door when he returned home.

It was on Cubs letterhead.

I left a message on your machine. But just in case—
We're going to have a major announcement at 10 o'clock
tomorrow morning. You should be there.
                                Hoffman

"Shit," said Riley.

He dumped the groceries in the fridge and checked his machine. There was a long, babbling pitch from a salesman at MCI. A hang-up. Someone asking for the parts department. Another hang-up. Hoffman. A frantic call from the *Sentinel* office.

Riley called Butler.

"We just got the fax from the Cubs," the *Sentinel* sports editor said. "What's it about?"

"I'm not sure."

"You're not sure, or you don't know?" Butler said.

"I don't know if I'm not sure."

"Well, you better find out real fast," Butler said. "The Cubs don't schedule major news conferences to announce a switch in stadium hot dogs. Something serious is going on."

Riley's mind was racing. He had no more idea about the news conference topic than the deli lady. His palms became sweaty. He could hear his heart thumping like a bass drum.

"Terry, what do you want me to do?"

Butler lost it.

"What do I want you to do?!" he said. "I want you to get off your ass and break a story during some part of your Arizona vacation. I don't need any more notes about the mistral winds of Mesa, or how many ground balls Strickland took. I need news. So far, you're getting your South Side butt kicked from one end of the Cactus League to the next. Is that clear enough for you?"

"I'm doing my best," Riley said weakly.

"That's marvelous, Riley," said Butler. "From now on, when the *Sentinel* gets beat on another Cubs story, I'll have the desk insert a disclaimer above your byline. Something like, 'The Sentinel apologizes for getting its ass handed to it again on the Cubs. But our beat reporter, Joe Riley, assures us all that he is doing his best. Thank you.' How's that sound?"

"A little wordy," said Riley, instantly regretting the response.

"Damnit, Riley, you have no idea what's going on there or here," Butler said. "This is serious stuff. I'm telling you, for your own good, that you can't take many more hits on the Cubs. I don't know how long . . ."

"How long what?" Riley said.

"Nothing," Butler said quickly. "Call me back if you get something worth running on the front page. You remember where that is, don't you?"

Riley called Hoffman. It was a desperation call, pure and simple.

"Can you tell me anything?" Riley pleaded.

"Wish I could," said the Cubs' PR man. "I've never leaked a story before and I'm not going to start now. Nothing personal."

"Don't worry about it," said Riley, knowing time was running out. "Maybe you can help me with one thing, though."

"Like what?" Hoffman said.

"Know the address of the nearest gun store?" Riley said. "How about access to a pharmacy? I might want to end things tomorrow at 10:01."

"You catching heat from the office?"

"Like the Apollo space capsule tiles during re-entry."

"Well, all I can say for the record is that we're having a major announcement," Hoffman said. "I wish I could throw you a crumb, but that wouldn't be fair to everyone else."

"And off the record?" said Riley, the desperation in his voice as clear as distilled water.

Hoffman sighed. "That we're having a major announcement tomorrow at ten o'clock," he said. "It's the same thing I'm telling everybody. Sorry."

"Don't apologize," Riley said. "If I get something, can I call you later to confirm?"

"You can call, but I'll only give you some vague, useless answers," Hoffman said.

"So, the usual, then?"

"You got it."

Riley tried Mitchell, but he kept getting his answering machine. Riley didn't have a number for Braswell or Hightower, so he drove to Fitch Park. The doors were locked, including the side clubhouse entrance.

"Stick a toe tag on me," Riley muttered to himself.

Then came the sound of bat on ball. *Thwack!* A five-second gap. Then *Thwack!* Another five seconds. *Thwack!* Somebody was still working out, and doing it to music.

Riley broke into a half jog. Whoever was hitting was doing it in the auxiliary set of batting cages, located about 50 yards from the clubhouse. That's strange, thought Riley. Hoffman had told him during his first-day tour that none of the batting cages had lights. Maybe a couple of the clubbies were sneaking in a few swings.

About 20 yards from the huge wire cage, Riley could see a red Jeep parked at the front end of the structure. Its headlights sent two beams toward the batter and illuminated almost the entire cage and beyond. Salsa blared from the Jeep's stereo.

The player had his back turned, but Riley knew instantly it was Hernandez. There was no mistaking those shoulders. Hernandez had a garbage can of baseballs set close to a weighted black hitting tee. The rookie catcher was bathed in sweat, his Popeye arms defined by sharp shadows and halogen light. He'd place a ball on the tee, pause for a moment, and then swing with a ferocity that made Riley feel sorry for rawhide and stitching.

Riley moved closer. Each of Hernandez's line drives sailed hard into a giant fisherman's net that was draped over the side and back of the cage. Soon the garbage can was half empty, and Hernandez stopped to take a swig of water from a nearby cooler. He closed his eyes and let the music wash over him. Riley watched in amazement as the massive catcher began dancing as lithely as a willow sways in the wind. It was as pure a moment as Riley had ever witnessed.

At song's end, Hernandez ducked out of the cage and walked toward the Jeep. He leaned through the passenger-side window and began sifting through a collection of CDs. Riley took a chance.

"Señor Hernandez?"

Hernandez poked his head out of the Jeep. Riley smiled and gave a small wave.

"*Cómo está usted?*" Riley ventured.

Hernandez glared at him, dropped the CDs, and returned to the cage. Riley tried again.

"Señor Hernandez?"

Thwack! . . . Thwack! . . . Thwack!

"Sure, what the hell do you care?" Riley said, raising his voice to be heard over the music. Hernandez ignored him. "Go ahead and hit the goddamn baseball. I'll just stand here and talk to myself. It's about the same as talking to you anyway."

Hernandez paused long enough to wipe his forehead with the back of a white wristband.

"That's right, wipe the sweat," said Riley, pacing from one end of the Jeep to the other. "Don't worry about me. I'll be fine. Just a small career crisis to contend with. Of course, you wouldn't know about a career crisis. Your biggest problem is which muscle group to flex. Well, I'm not going to have a shitty night by myself. Just so you know, Valdez thinks you're moron material. So take that, *muchacho*."

Hernandez turned and stared.

"What, am I bothering you?" Riley said. "Omar upset? Jesus, listen to me. I'm talking to the Spanish Marcel Marceau, and I haven't even had a beer. You know, Omar—and you don't mind if I call you Omar, do you?—I've got a lump in my stomach the size of a canned ham. Tomorrow morning I'm predicting that somebody, probably Morris, will have the scoop on the big news announcement. He'll have the scoop and I'll know how to count to ten in Spanish. That's because I spent my precious off hours thumbing through that translator book so I could talk to you. *Tú*. And by the way, you owe me $9.99 for ripping it up. I want cash."

Hernandez said nothing.

"I thought so," Riley said. "Okay, I'm leaving now. But you remember what I said, even if you can't understand a word I said. You and me, we could have been contenduhs. We could have been the beans and rice of the Cubs. The tamales and tacos. The whatever-the-hell-it-is-you-eat-in-the-Dominican."

Hernandez reached into the can and pulled a ball out.

"Godspeed, Omar," Riley said. "If you need me tomorrow, I'll be the small sweat puddle in the media room. Jesus, I'm losing my mind."

Morris had the story. So did Blair and Hill.

Morris's lead from the morning clip sheet:

> *Romanced and mesmerized by a $100 million title-sponsor fee, the Cubs will announce today that storied Wrigley Field will be renamed Sears Stadium, the Standard has learned.*
>
> *The Chicagoland-based retailing giant will officially agree to the landmark deal in a morning news conference. The unprecedented deal . . .*

Riley was too numb to read on.

"Butler is giving birth to a very large cow at this very moment," said Riley to himself.

Riley steered clear of the media room. The last person he wanted to see was Morris. Blair wouldn't be much of a treat, either. Hill, he could live with.

Forty minutes until the news conference. Riley needed to advance the stadium story. He needed a drop-dead follow-up that would break new ground, keep Butler off his back, and have Morris, Blair, and company chasing *him* for once.

Hightower would tell him nothing. The man might as well have had his lips sewn shut. Riley didn't know any league officials. The closest source he had at Sears was Jerry, who worked in the lawn-and-garden department.

"You're that guy from the *Sentinel*, right?" said a clubby.

"For the next hour or so, yeah," said Riley. "Did I win the Publishers Clearinghouse?"

"No, but Max wants to see you."

"Max who?"

"Max Dewitt."

"You're kidding," said Riley, who had all but given up on getting an audience with Dewitt.

"I'm just passing on the message," said the clubby. "I can't believe it myself. The last time Max talked to a reporter was four years ago."

"Phil Mitchell?"

"I think so," said the clubby. "Is he from Arkansas?"

"Texas," Riley said.

"That's the guy. Max says he's a baseball man. Anyway, you ready?"

The clubby led Riley through the clubhouse, out the side door, and around to the back of the building. There was a door marked ELECTRICAL WIRING—HIGH VOLTAGE. KEEP OUT! No wonder Riley had never been able to locate Dewitt. The clubby knocked twice, then three times, then twice more. You needed a secret decoder ring to keep track.

Several seconds passed. Then came four knocks from the inside. The clubby knocked once. Moments later, the door swung open.

The room was the size of the presidential suite at the Drake. There were rows of neatly stacked Cubs uniforms. There were bats catalogued by player name. There were boxes of baseballs, caps, candy, tobacco, and a two-foot-high stack of *Playboys*, *Penthouses*, and *Hustlers*. It was a storage room fantasy camp.

There were framed autographed jerseys on the wall, all with fawning inscriptions to Dewitt. There were framed autographed photos, all with similar notations.

Max,
If you ever need anything (and I mean anything), you let me know.
—Ernie Banks

And . . .

Maxie,
Your advice was invaluable. Baseball is forever indebted to you.
—Bart Giamatti

And . . .

You saw the hitch before anybody. I couldn't have hit No. 715 without you. Thanks.
—Hank

Riley couldn't help staring.
"You done gawking?"

Riley looked up. It was the old man from the locker room.

"These can't be for real," said Riley, looking back at the Giamatti photo. "Dewitt gave the commissioner of baseball advice?"

"Helped prevent a renegade league from forming," said the old man.

"He's an equipment manager, not Yoda," Riley said.

"It's not the title that makes the man, it's the smarts," said the codger.

"Uh-huh. Sure," Riley said. "And what about this Aaron thing? He doesn't expect anybody to really think he fixed Hammerin' Hank's home run swing, does he?"

"It wasn't a matter of fixing it," said the old man. "Hank was forty years old in '74. He was using his arms a little too much, instead of those magic wrists of his. And he was pissed about Bartholomay. And then there were the death threats."

"What about Bartholomay?" Riley said.

"You know anything about baseball?" said the old man. "Bill Bartholomay was the owner of the Atlanta Braves. He wanted Hank to skip the opening three-game series at Cincinnati and try to break the record at old Fulton County Stadium. Of course, what he really wanted was a bunch of full houses in Atlanta, which I can't say I blame him for. But Bowie Kuhn, in one of the few smart things he ever did as commissioner, told Bartholomay that Hank had to play against the Reds. So Hank walked up to the plate and hit number 714. First swing. First at bat. Gone."

"And he couldn't have done it without Dewitt?" Riley said. "Please."

"That's what the man said."

"He folds T-shirts for a living," Riley said, now staring at a signed photo of Mickey Mantle.

"He knows baseball."

"You make him sound like the Wizard of Oz."

"Nah, the wizard hid behind a curtain," said the old man. "What you see with Max is what you get."

The old man reached into his back pocket, pulled out a small metal case, opened it, and offered the contents to Riley.

"Macanudo?"

"Nah," said Riley, before stopping in mid-wave.

"Wait a second," he said. "These were for Dewitt!"

"That's what you told me," said the old man, smiling.

"Which means," said Riley, finally understanding, "that I'm an idiot. You're Max."

"The one and only T-shirt folder," he said.

Riley's eyes darted down in embarrassment. "Sorry about that," Riley said. "But why didn't you tell me at the clubhouse that morning?"

"Because you woke me up," said Dewitt. "I keep a shotgun under that cot, you know. I coulda blown your head off."

"You might have done me a favor," Riley said. "So you knew who I was?"

"I know *everything* when it comes to this team."

"Then you know why I've been looking for you?"

"Mitchell sent you."

"He said you were a good person to know."

"He's right," said Dewitt, lighting up one of the cigars.

"But can you help me?"

"Depends on what you want," said Dewitt, spitting out a sliver of tobacco. "Depends how much I can trust you. Depends on what's in it for me."

"Well, I'm tapped out on money, so you better smoke those things real slow," Riley said. "On the trust issue, I can still recite the Boy Scout oath by heart, and I've never been caught with a White House intern. As far as what I want, I'm not really sure. Guidance, mostly. Advice."

"What kind of advice?"

"Well, I'm getting beat on stories like an orchestra percussion section," Riley said. "Morris and Blair break everything. Hill's damn good. So are Armour and Nadel, especially for radio/TV guys."

"Then work harder," Dewitt said.

"I'm trying, but my paper keeps forgetting that I'm new at this," Riley said. "I can't seem to connect with any of the players. Most of them treat me like boil pus. And Hightower gives me zero access and Braswell is a pure company man."

"Well," said Dewitt, puffing hard on the cigar, "I'll make a deal with you. I'll run a reconnaissance mission for you. I'm not making any promises, but if something interesting comes up, I'll pass it on to you."

"Like Deep Throat?" Riley said.

"Like hell," Dewitt said. "You want information on the players or management, then you find it out yourself. I love this organization and I don't believe in gossip. But if I think there's something worth you knowing about, I'll let one of the clubbies come get you."

"Where do I sign?"

"A handshake will do."

Dewitt's weathered hand enveloped Riley's. Riley figured Dewitt was in his late sixties, maybe early seventies. But his viselike handshake nearly cut off Riley's circulation.

"I've got to ask you something," Riley said.

"Don't push your luck, kid."

"No, this isn't a favor," Riley said. "I was just wondering why you're helping me."

"Because I repay my debts," he said. "Mitchell did me a good turn a few years ago."

"What happened?"

"None of your business," Dewitt replied. "Now, shoo." He pointed toward the door.

"So that's the only reason . . . Mitchell?" said Riley, stalling for time.

"Not the only reason, but one of them."

"What's the other?"

Dewitt folded his arms and cocked his head toward Riley. He took a long puff on his cigar, exhaled, and flicked away the ash. He was deciding how much he wanted to say. "I like what you've been doing with the Dominican kid," Dewitt finally said.

"Hernandez?"

"Yeah, Omar. He's a good kid, but the rest of them treat him like shit."

"I haven't exactly made a cultural breakthrough. I'm pretty sure he told me to kiss off."

"But you try," Dewitt said. "I heard about your translator book. And I saw you at the batting cage."

"You saw that?" said Riley, now beginning to realize that maybe this Dewitt guy was Yoda after all.

"I told you, kid, nothing happens without me knowing about it. Exactly 1,679 players have worn a Cubs uniform through the years, and I've probably seen half of them—from the time I was bat boy, to clubby, to assistant equipment manager, to now."

"I'm convinced."

Riley gestured toward Dewitt's battered desk and a photograph of Roberto Clemente. "What'd you do for Clemente?"

"Roberto," said Dewitt, picking up the dusty picture frame. "All I did was convince Rawlings to send a few boxes of uniforms down to the Dominican for Roberto's Little League teams. Compared to what Roberto did for those kids, I did nothing."

"He was one of my dad's favorite opposing players," Riley said.

"He should be," Dewitt said. "Only two players have ever come close to hitting the center field scoreboard at Wrigley. One was—"

"Bill Nicholson . . . 1948," interrupted Riley. "The other was Clemente . . . 1959. Clemente's homer was hit to left-center. My dad was there."

"Okay, so you do know a little baseball," Dewitt said. "There might be hope for you yet."

"I know just enough to be dangerous in Trivial Pursuit."

Dewitt led him to the door. Riley stepped outside, where the morning sun was in full baking mode.

"Thanks," Riley said.

"Ain't done nothing yet," said Dewitt, closing the door.

The news conference was orchestrated for full corporate effect. There were Sears logos everywhere, as well as an architect's rendering of Wrigley Field with obscenely large signage located on the front stadium facade and on the famed center field scoreboard. The Sears emblem had also replaced the Torco sign beyond the right field wall and Sheffield Avenue. Riley weaved his way through the crowd. He found a seat next to Hill.

"Good story today," Riley complimented the Post News Service reporter. "This is a recording."

"Thanks," Hill said. "I thought I was flying solo with that one."

"Instead you got Morris and Blair as copilots?" Riley said.

"I wish I knew how they do it," Hill said. He nodded to the array of logos. "So, what do you think of the new and improved Wrigley?"

"I think my dad just did a two-and-a-half flip in the tuck position in his grave," Riley said.

"Cubs fan, huh?"

"Huge," Riley said. "He knew more about this franchise than most of the players who wore the uniform."

"Yeah, this is too strange," Hill said. "Next thing you know, McDonald's will buy the rights to the Masters and open a franchise at Amen Corner."

"Or, 'Jiffy Lube presents Wimbledon,'" Riley said.

"Scary."

Hoffman was at the lectern, testing the sound system. TV crews had set up their cameras and tripods on a low riser at the back of the room. The print and radio reporters were seated in front. It was a packed house.

At exactly ten o'clock, Hightower, some corporate suit named Victor Gregory, and Cubs president Harris Domlin took their seats on the makeshift dais. Hoffman introduced the group. Leaning against a wall near the back of the room was Morris. Riley nodded. Morris pointed at Riley and then snapped his fingers in mock chagrin, as if to say, "Darnit, you missed another story." Then Morris laughed. Red-faced, Riley turned around.

"I'm beginning to hate that son of a bitch," Riley whispered.

Hill turned around and saw Morris. Morris did a little salute and nudged Blair, his *Herald Democrat* toady. Hill had seen enough. "I'm surprised it took you this long," Hill whispered back to Riley.

The news conference lasted about 40 minutes, 30 of which were monopolized by Gregory, the Sears stooge. For $100 million, Gregory must have figured he needed to get his money's worth. There was a lot of talk of the Sears–Cubs "family," and of future efforts to maintain the "integrity" of Wrigley Field. Asked by WMVP's Armour if the Sears signage didn't compromise that integrity, Gregory mumbled something about this being "a celebration, not an inquisition." Domlin quickly replaced Gregory at the lectern. Hill had a question.

"Will the $100 million be used to improve a franchise that hasn't competed for a World Series in a generation?"

"Paul, that is a fair question," said Domlin, who liked to disarm reporters by using their first names early and often. "It is an appropriate question. It is a question worthy of a long and thoughtful response. Since we are short on time, Paul, I will only say that the

Cubs will continue to do whatever is necessary to ensure that our fans continue to receive the best baseball value for their hard-earned dollars. Thank you again, Paul, for your insightful inquiry."

Riley raised his hand.

"You have a question?" Domlin said.

"Yes, I was wondering if you could answer Mr. Hill's question?" Riley said.

Domlin motioned for Hoffman. The two huddled momentarily. Domlin returned to his place behind the microphone.

"Joe," said Domlin, who had never spoken to Riley before, "I'm sure you can appreciate the sensitive nature of the decision-making process regarding the outlay of said monies. At this point in time, I'm simply not prepared to comment on the specific nature of our intentions. But while I have the opportunity and the forum, I'd like everybody to please give Joe a nice round of applause. This is his first training camp with us and we're glad the *Sentinel* saw fit to assign such a fine, capable young journalist to our team. Welcome to the family."

There was a small smattering of applause. Riley sank to his seat.

"Congratulations," said Hill. "You were just Domlin-ized. You can shower off later."

"He's good," Riley said. "I didn't even have to drop my pants for that one."

"If he were a hooker, he'd be a millionaire," Hill said.

"Instead, he's a club president and a multimillionaire," Riley said. "I knew I should have gone to business school."

The news conference ended shortly after Gary Danger—wearing more makeup than a rodeo clown—accused Sears of false advertising. "Isn't it true, Mr. Gregory," Danger had said in his deepest broadcast voice, "that the slogan 'Sears: Where America Shops' is not only misleading but a blatant lie? I, for one, have never set foot in a Sears, nor would I wear anything from the Johnny Miller collection."

Gregory looked at Domlin for help. Domlin shrugged his shoulders. Gregory said, "I'm not sure I understand your question, Mr."—

"Mr. Gary Danger," said Danger dramatically, "lead sports anchor, WGN-TV, Chicago, Illinois. I'm sure you've heard of us."

Riley wheeled around. On the low riser was Nadel, head buried in his hands. Whatever they were paying Nadel at 'GN, it wasn't enough.

Afterward, the reporters surged forward for failed attempts at some one-on-one interviews. Riley heard someone ask Hightower if the $100 million infusion of money would mean more free agent signings.

"I've got no comment," he snapped. "And that's off the record."

Morris and Riley bumped into each other.

"Great question," said Morris sarcastically. "Now I can see why they stuck you on the desk."

"I didn't hear you ask anything," Riley said.

"Didn't have to," said Morris. "I had the story."

"It's a long season."

"Not for you, it won't be. I hear you're already in deep shit at the *Sentinel*. You've got 'short-timer' written all over you."

"I've got an idea," Riley said. "Why don't you go to the parking lot and see if the car exhausts work?"

"I'm getting to you."

"Don't flatter yourself."

"No, I'm getting to you," said Morris with a smirk. "I can tell. At least Mitchell had some fight in him. Hill gave me a small run for the money. Nadel and Armour were pests. But you don't even qualify as a nuisance."

"How about if I let you discuss it with my fist?" Riley said.

"Go ahead," said Morris, moving closer. "I'd love a nice court settlement. Maybe I could get something out of the *Sentinel*, too. Here, try this jaw."

Riley was a shade of crimson. Morris was right; he had gotten to him.

"So sad," Morris said. "The short-timer is speechless."

"You're going to be toothless," said Riley, tossing his notebook and tape recorder to the floor. Morris blanched as Riley raised his fist. Hoffman stepped between them.

"Gentlemen, not the place, not the time," said the Cubs' PR man evenly.

"No, let him try," said Morris. "Hey, Joe, you going to hit me with your two-seam punch or your four-seamer?"

"How about my *knuckleball*?"

"That's enough," Hoffman said. "Morris, Hightower wants to see you. Now might be a good time."

"It's a perfect time," Morris said. "In fact, why don't you stick around, Joe? I'll introduce you to the general manager. I hear you and him haven't talked yet."

Hoffman waited until Morris was gone and then looked hard at Riley.

"What?" Riley said.

"First, that was totally unprofessional," Hoffman said.

"Guilty. But he's such a prick."

"So?" said Hoffman. "And how in the hell did you expect to cover this team without talking to the general manager?"

"I *didn't* expect to cover this team, that's the whole point," Riley said. "I thought this would be like invading Grenada: you're in, you're out. I keep waiting for Butler to call and say the lockout is over, come on home."

"That still doesn't explain why no Hightower," Hoffman said.

"I've tried. We were supposed to talk, but his secretary canceled it at the last minute. I don't have his condo number, and anyway, you heard him after this thing. Even when he does say something, he doesn't say anything."

"Look, if you need to arrange something with Hightower, you ask me," Hoffman said. "Alice probably wadded up your message and threw it in the circular file the second you walked away. She thinks she's doing Hightower a favor by protecting him from the media. I'll give you Hightower's condo number, but I wouldn't call there unless you've got a story down cold and only need confirmation. Otherwise, it's going to be a short conversation."

"Thanks."

"It's my job. I give the same speech and the same numbers to all the writers. All you have to do is ask. I'll set something up when I get back to the office."

"Okay," Riley said.

"And just so you know, I think Domlin got a kick out of your question."

"Great," Riley said. "I'll make it the lead to my notes: 'Sentinel Writer Scores Brownie Points with Cubs Prez.'"

"I wouldn't go overboard with it," Hoffman said. "Twenty-four-point type, nothing more."

"I hear you," Riley said.

The morning workouts were almost finished by the time Riley was ready to leave the media room. He had tried to call Butler, but all he got was a painfully long phone-mail message describing *Sentinel* policy regarding faxes (couldn't be confirmed), story ideas (call one of the assistant sports editors), and complaints (send a letter). Riley didn't bother to leave a message after the beep.

Out of habit, Riley plugged in his laptop—might as well let the battery charge up. When he moved the power adapter toward the back of the computer, he noticed it was hot to the touch. He'd have to get that checked when he returned to Chicago.

Morris and Blair were already on the field talking to Braswell. Nadel was in the WGN truck, doing whatever producer-reporters do after a news conference. Armour was in the media room, doing a 10-minute gig for the noon show in Chicago. The signage issue was sure to be a big topic of conversation for the radio talk-show hosts that day. Hill was at Field One, standing behind the portable batting cage.

"Heard you and Morris almost had a fist-a-thon in there," Hill said.

"Who told you that?"

"Morris. He said you were this close to crying."

"He's lucky I didn't rearrange his jaw structure."

"Take it for what it's worth, but can I give you two pieces of advice?"

"Sure," said Riley, leaning forward on the metal railing behind the cage, the netting brushing up against his knees. "It's not like I can have a worse day."

"One," said Hill, "don't get caught up in Morris's mind games. The best thing to do is ignore him."

"And two?" Riley said.

The batting-practice pitcher, a local high school baseball coach who earned $25 a day for throwing 65 mile-per-hour fastballs and hanging curves, let loose with a belt-high dinger-to-be. But LeMott, just a little too anxious, mistimed the swing. The ball nicked the taped wood barrel, creating enough backspin to send the newly muddied Rawlings directly toward the back netting, and directly into Riley's crotch.

Riley dropped to his knees. He hadn't felt pain like this since he was nine, when he slipped off his bicycle seat and onto the metal support bar of his Schwinn Stingray. One of the Cubs' assistant trainers, a bemused smile on his face, knelt down next to Riley.

"Catch you flush?" he asked.

Riley couldn't speak.

"Thought so," said the trainer. "I'm gonna roll you over on your back. Try to relax and we'll get some ice on it."

Through the pain, Riley could hear a child's voice from the nearby bleachers.

"Daddy," said the child, "why are they putting an ice bag on that man's pee-wee?"

Hill brought a towel from the bench and placed it under Riley's head.

"You gonna be okay?" Hill asked.

"I hope so," Riley said slowly, "or else it's going to be one hell of an obit."

"I'll get you some water," Hill said.

"Better not. I'm feeling a bit queasy right now."

Hill turned to the assistant trainer. "Should I call an ambulance or something?"

"Not worth the effort," he said. "Just give him a few minutes. He's gonna have a nasty dick bruise, but he'll be fine."

"See?" said Hill. "The day isn't a total waste. You're going to be the proud owner of a dick bruise. You're lucky they didn't spray that liquid freeze stuff on it."

"You didn't finish," Riley said through gritted teeth.

"Finish what?" Hill said.

"One and two. What's number two on your advice list?"

"You don't really want to know."

"How bad can it be?" said Riley, the pain slowly subsiding.

"Well," said Hill, "I was going to tell you not to lean so close to the batting cage."

Ten

THE FIRST ROUND OF CUTS AND REASSIGNMENTS came three and a half weeks into camp. One by one, the unlucky seven players were quietly asked to report to Braswell's office. Boomer Hayes served as the Grim Reaper. He would put a hand on the player's shoulder, whisper the news, and then solemnly shake his hand. It was all very fatherly.

Near the corner of the clubhouse, left fielder Delagotti pulled out a harmonica and began playing with surprising confidence. There was a suggestion of Muddy Waters in his melody.

"There he goes again," said Strickland, who knew the music wasn't meant for him. As usual, there wasn't any competition for his third base position.

Delagotti held the harmonica with his left palm and cupped his right hand over the top. He was committed to the music. His right foot pounded the tile floor, the rubber cleats creating a crackling noise.

"Play it!" Strickland said. "Play those 'Minor League Blues'!"

And that's where six of the seven players were going: designated for reassignment. The other player, a veteran to whom Riley hadn't even bothered to say hello, had been given his outright release. It was note filler, nothing more.

The NCAA Tournament was fast approaching—a fact not lost on Tyler Hurlock. Hurlock was a starter who had pitched well during his five seasons in the Cubs minor league system, but could never quite make the big club. He had come close last spring, but a strained right shoulder with a week remaining in camp cost him a chance in the rotation. Hurlock won 17 games in Iowa, got called up twice during the season, but only saw spot duty out of the bullpen. Under normal circumstances, 17 victories would be cause for celebration. But to win 17 games at Des Moines meant you had to *be* in Des Moines long enough to put up those kind of numbers. Hurlock didn't want to be known as the best 30-year-old starter in Triple A. That's why this was considered a make-or-break camp for him. After all, righthanders were expendable, especially old ones.

Hurlock wore a green plastic visor, the kind you might see in an old-time newspaper room or at a poker table. He carried a blue bank pouch, its zipper open wide enough to reveal lots of green stuff. Riley craned his neck to see the contents.

"Don't even bother, Scoop," said Hurlock. "You can't afford it."

Hurlock called all the reporters "Scoop."

"You're probably right," Riley said.

"Not probably—I am," he said. "Anyway, it's for players only."

Hurlock was running the clubhouse tournament pool. It cost $100 per team for the blind draft. There was a two-team limit. The winner would collect 80 percent of the $6,400 pot, with the runner-up getting 15 percent and the third-place finisher getting five percent. Technically speaking, it was illegal and expressly prohibited by Major League Baseball rules. No gambling allowed. But, realistically speaking, it was a rite of spring in every big league clubhouse from Arizona to Florida.

"Whattaya say, Petey, you in?" said Hurlock to Gonzalez.

"No way, man," said the center fielder. "Last year I get Fairfield. I never seen Fairfield, and I own dish."

"They put a scare into Carolina, Petey," said Hurlock. "Almost the upset of the century."

"The year before I get Crest University," Gonzalez said. "You pat me on back for that pick. Remember?"

"That's Colgate, Petey," said Hurlock, "and it was a very good long-shot pick. I wanted them bad that year." Hurlock could keep a straight face as well as anyone.

"Doesn't matter," Gonzalez said. "I'm out."

"Petey, you make more money than Oprah," Hurlock said. "It's a hundred bucks. God willing, it will go to a deserving charity."

"What charity?" Gonzalez said.

"Me," Hurlock said. "If I don't make this team, I'm gonna need all the money I can get."

Gonzalez laughed. "Okay," he said, pulling out two fifty-dollar bills from his wallet, "here's your money. I want to pick first, though. I want the round man from Utah."

"Petey, I personally will guarantee you first pick, but the laws of chance take over when it comes to teams," said Hurlock, checking Gonzalez's name off his master list and placing the money in the blue pouch. "But I like your instincts. Rick Majerus is a hell of a coach. Hardly any brothers on his team, but a hell of a coach."

Hurlock surveyed the room. He found LeMott, Harris, and Campbell huddled in conversation.

"Fellas?" Hurlock said.

"Can't you see we're talking?" LeMott snapped. "Keep going, Case. This is unbelievable."

"Well," said Harris, glancing suspiciously at Hurlock, who had inched forward, "I get to my buddy's wedding and he tells me he has a big surprise planned at the reception. I'm not a wedding sort of a guy, so I don't have a clue. I figure I'll scope out some bitches and be on my way."

"What a romantic," Campbell said.

"Hey," said Harris, "you want to hear the story or not?"

"I do," Hurlock said. "Get it? 'I do.' It's a wedding joke."

"Hey, you're the fucking joke," Harris said. "Who is this guy?"

"Doesn't matter," Campbell said. "He'll be gone in two weeks anyway."

"That is Antarctica cold, man," Hurlock said.

"I'm just fucking with you," Campbell said.

"Tell the story," LeMott persisted.

"So I go to the rehearsal dinner," said the reliever. "It's at Vivere—you know, over at the Italian Village."

"On Madison, right?" said Campbell.

"Monroe," Harris said. "Anyway, it must have cost a fortune. Booze everywhere. Magnums of champagne. A feast."

"Who pays for that?" LeMott asked.

About 80 Percent Luck

"Whattaya mean, who pays for that?" Campbell said. "You've been married."

"Twice," LeMott said. "Eloped the first time. Got married at City Hall the second time."

"You're a cheap son of a bitch," Campbell said.

"Didn't want to spoil them," said LeMott, who had movie-star looks but was considered dumber than a rock.

"Will you shut the fuck up?" said Harris, glaring at Campbell and LeMott. "Anyway, the bride's family was picking up the tab for this, okay? And for being in the wedding party, I got a Coach wallet. I mean, they were doing this thing up big."

"What next?" LeMott said.

"The wedding is at some huge Presbyterian church in Evanston," said Harris. "Must have been five hundred people at this thing. I'm surprised there wasn't TV coverage. There were more people there than what we'd get playing in Beloit."

"That's for damn sure," LeMott said.

"The wedding's done, so now we pile into these stretch limos the length of the Panama Canal and head to the Four Seasons," Harris said. "One of the bridesmaids, with a swing on her back porch you wouldn't believe, is telling me my buddy's new wife is wearing a fifty-thousand-dollar wedding dress. That's more than my signing bonus out of high school."

"Ten times mine," LeMott said.

"Figures," Campbell said.

"Hey, my agent screwed me," LeMott said.

"Whatever," Campbell said.

"We get to the Four Seasons and it's like Fantasyland in the ballroom," Harris said. "I've never seen such a spread. The best of the best. The waiters wore gloves. There were two bottles of Dom on every table."

"How many tables?" LeMott said.

"What, you studying for a quiz show?" Harris said.

"I'm naturally curious."

"You're naturally a pain in the ass," Campbell said.

"I'm guessing eighty tables, six to a table," Harris said.

"Jesus," Hurlock said.

"You got that right," Harris said. "Okay, so it's another feast. My buddy and his new wife finally get there. Everyone's drinking. There's a great band. We're all dancing. It's like the party of the century. The best man—I don't know the dude—gets up and gives this big teary-eyed speech about how my buddy is like a brother to him, and how Betsy—that's my buddy's new wife—is like the sister he never had. This guy's crying, and the family is crying, and people at their tables are crying, and the goddamn waiters are dabbing away some tears. I even got a little misty."

"Then what?" LeMott said.

"Then my buddy gets up to give a speech," Harris said. "He thanks everyone for coming to the big wedding. He toasts his parents. He toasts his friends. He hates his new father- and mother-in-law because they're always bragging about how much money they have, but he toasts them, too. But I can tell my buddy is up to something. He gets this look. Real intense. The kind of look you get right before a bar fight."

"And?" Campbell said.

"So he says he has a presentation," Harris continued. "One of the hotel workers flicks a couple of switches and the ballroom lights dim and a big screen comes down from the ceiling. There's a projector, one of those things you see in sports bars or big meeting rooms, that pops out of the wall. It's amazing. My buddy starts narrating this slide show. You know . . . stuff like, 'Here's a picture of the bride when she was a baby.' There's lots of oohs and aahs. 'Here's a picture of the bride as a high school cheerleader.' More 'Ain't she precious' oohs and aahs. 'As student body president.' 'As prom queen.' 'As a Tri-Delt at Michigan State.' 'As an associate at some big law firm in Chicago.' My buddy's bride is loving it. She's beaming. The family is loving it."

"Anybody have a Kleenex?" said Campbell, sniffling.

Hurlock handed him a freshly laundered sanitary sock.

"Thanks," Campbell said, wiping his nose.

Harris stared at Campbell.

"What can I say?" Campbell said. "I've got a soft spot for love."

"Okay, so the touchy-feely photo show goes on for a few more minutes," Harris said. "Then my buddy says, 'Now I'd like to show you some very special photos of Betsy, photos that I'm sure you'll never forget. I know I never will.'

About 80 Percent Luck

"Everybody in the place is on the edge of their chairs. My buddy looks at Betsy, blows her a kiss, and then hits the projector button. On comes this black-and-white photo of Betsy with the best man . . . in the sack . . . doing some serious parallel parking."

"You gotta be kidding," Hurlock said.

"Swear to God," Harris said. "I nearly fell on my ass, I was laughing so hard. Then my buddy hits the button again. And again. And again. Photo after photo of Betsy and his best man in, uh, love's warm embrace. Turns out one of Betsy's friends ratted on her. My buddy hired a private investigator and the guy caught them at the Hyatt on Wacker during a nooner. They left the drapes open. Oh, the power of a telephoto lens."

"What'd Betsy do?" LeMott said.

"She was shrieking a lot," Harris said. "So were her parents. The best man tried to apologize, but my buddy sent him flying with a right cross. Then Betsy's old man, who probably spent two hundred large for everything, climbed over the table on the dais and did a swan dive on the best man. Started beating the hell out of him. Damnedest reception I've ever been to."

"What about the marriage?" Hurlock said.

"My buddy got it annulled the next day," Harris said. "Said the only reason he went through with the ceremony is that he wanted to stick it to Betsy and her snobby folks."

"He stuck it to them, all right," Campbell said.

There was a pause. Harris looked at Hurlock the intruder.

"Now what the fuck do you want?" said Harris.

"Your money," Hurlock said. "A hundred bucks for the NCAA pool. Blind draft. Two-team maximum."

"Why didn't you say so?" said Harris, pulling out his Coach wallet and handing Hurlock a couple of Ben Franklins. "I won this thing two years ago when I was with the Astros. Used it for strip clubs the whole season."

Hurlock made his rounds until all but one of the 64 NCAA entrants were accounted for. Riley saw him approach Willingham, of grocery-store fame. Riley pretended not to hear.

"It's only a hundred bucks, man," Hurlock said. "So you skip a few dinners."

"Can't do it," Willingham answered.

"Hey, if it's a matter of credit, I'm sure we can work out something," Hurlock said. "Think of me as Jim Palmer of the Money Store."

Willingham looked up from his seat. "Ty, I don't have a hundred bucks to spare," he half whispered. "I ate dinner last night at the deli counter of the Piggly-Wiggly. My wife and kids are coming in tomorrow night. I've been trying to stockpile food from the breakfast spread. Got about thirty of those blueberry muffins stashed in my equipment bag. I wish I could, but I can't, man."

Hurlock rubbed his forehead.

"Here's what I'm gonna do," Hurlock said. "I'm gonna bankroll your hundred for the pool. I don't normally do this, but I've got a good feeling about you. You win, I get fifty percent of your winnings. You lose, you only owe me fifty dollars."

"Sad thing is, I don't even have fifty bucks to spare," Willingham said. "But hey, Ty, you're all right, man. I mean it."

"Don't go mushy on me," Hurlock said. "It's just that us minor league phenoms have to stick together."

"Yeah, right. Phenom, that's me."

"Sure you don't want the once-in-a-lifetime offer?"

"Better not, Ty," Willingham said. "But thanks."

Hurlock patted Willingham on the shoulder. "Hang in there, baby," he said.

Riley couldn't help himself. He waited a few minutes and then tracked down Hurlock near the front desk, where the pitcher had just sweet-talked the part-time receptionist into giving him poster board and Magic Markers. He didn't tell her it was for an oversized scoring sheet and brackets to be taped on the training-room wall.

"Mr. Hurlock?" Riley said.

Hurlock wheeled around. "Scoop, I already told you, no reporters in the pool. The last time I let one of you guys in, the son of a bitch wrote about it, the commissioner got sent a copy of the story, and I had to shut things down for a year."

"I don't want in the pool," Riley said. "I just wanted to tell you that was a real nice thing you tried to do for Willingham."

"You did, did you?"

"Yeah, I was impressed."

"Do me a favor," Hurlock said. "Don't tell anyone."

"I won't," Riley said.

"And do me one other thing."

"Sure."

"Mind your own business, Scoop," Hurlock said. "That was a private conversation."

Hurlock brushed past him and returned to the clubhouse. Riley slumped against the painted cinderblock wall.

"And then," said Riley, repeating his favorite Bill Murray line, "depression set in."

Hoffman walked past.

"More trouble?" he said.

"Nothing a six-pack of Old Style wouldn't solve," Riley said.

"Don't drink too much," Hoffman said. "The Hacks are going to need you for the annual hoops game."

"The Hacks?"

"Hacks versus the Fronties," Hoffman said. "Media versus front-office types."

"In basketball?"

"No, in rhythmic gymnastics," Hoffman said. "Don't forget to bring your ball and ribbon."

"I haven't played basketball in years," Riley said. "I've got the vertical jump of Drew Carey. Can't we go bowling or something? I'm a hell of a kegler."

"Sorry, it's a Mesa tradition," Hoffman said. "I'm just the keeper of the basketball flame. Losers buy dinner and a pony keg."

"You'll kill us," Riley said. "Armour needs a step ladder just to be called short. Nadel is in worse shape than me. Hill thinks the act of wearing jogging shoes is the same as the actual act of jogging."

"What about Danger?" Hoffman said. "He looks like he's in shape."

"You're right," Riley said. "Nadel says he ran in the Chicago Marathon last year. Nadel also says he won't go Christmas shopping because he's afraid of large crowds."

"I don't get it," Hoffman said.

"He's paranoid about getting hit in the face," Riley said. "You think he'll risk getting his TV nose ruined by an errant elbow in hoops? No way."

"What about the Chicago Marathon?" Hoffman said. "The starting line is packed."

"Nadel says Danger wears a modified Bears helmet and doesn't take it off until the eight-mile mark," Riley said.

"Don't worry, we'll find you a fifth."

"Who?"

"I might have a ringer for you," Hoffman said. "I'll let you know."

"Tell him to bring friends. And make sure he can dunk."

"Uh, yeah, I'll do that."

The exhibition season began two days later. The opening game of the Cubs' Cactus League schedule was played at HoHoKam Park, with the mayor of Mesa, the president of the HoHos, Hightower, and Domlin all taking part in the pregame ceremony. The mayor spent much too long recounting his days as an American Legion shortstop, while Hightower and Domlin kept their remarks brief. That was mostly because the partisan Cubs fans—many of whom were unhappy with the present management regime and this latest corporate intrusion at beloved Wrigley—began showering Hightower and Domlin with boos. Riley would have to ask both men about the reception.

The HoHoKam president was a 50-ish man named Francis Baldwin. According to the short bio in the pregame notes, Baldwin was a native Chicagoan who had moved to Phoenix 20 years earlier, made a fortune in real estate, and now devoted much of his time to charitable causes. As Baldwin stepped to the microphone near home plate, someone shouted from the stands, "No more speeches! Let's play some baseball!"

Baldwin pawed at the infield dirt with his Cole-Hahns. "Yes, yes, I know you didn't come here on such a glorious day to listen to a broken-down real-estate broker," Baldwin said.

"You're darn tootin' about that!" yelled a codger from behind the Cubs' dugout.

"But if you'll let me finish," said Baldwin, shooting a glance at the old man, "what I have to say here today is important, at least, to the rest of us HoHoKams. I'm proud to announce . . . in fact, honored to announce—that from this moment forward, HoHoKam Park will no longer exist. It's done. Finished. A memory."

There was a murmur from the crowd. Hightower and Domlin conferred, tactfully of course. The mayor appeared perplexed.

"From this moment on, HoHoKam Park will have a new name," Baldwin said. "We should have done this years ago, but better late than never."

Baldwin turned to face the covered scoreboard in center field. Two stadium workers were positioned on each side of the electronic structure. Baldwin raised his arm, like the starter at the Daytona Speedway. Then he turned again to the crowd.

"Please, ladies and gentlemen, join me in the countdown," he said.

So the sellout crowd, suddenly mesmerized by the mystery, began the subtraction. "Ten, nine, eight, seven, six, five, four, three, two . . . one." Baldwin dropped his arm. The workers removed a metal plate that featured the name *HoHoKam Park* in huge black lettering. Behind it was the stadium's new name.

"Well, I'll be a son of a bitch," said Hoffman in the press box.

Riley looked at the scoreboard and felt a lump forming in his throat. The crowd was cheering wildly. Even the Cubs players, as well as the Seattle Mariners, had emerged clapping from their dugouts. Some of the veterans were pinching the bridges of their noses, trying to squeeze back the tears.

"Ladies and gentlemen," said Baldwin, "welcome to Harry Caray Stadium! It could be! It might be! It is!"

Nobody—not Domlin, not Hightower, not the mayor—had been told about the change. Because the HoHoKams operated the stadium, they technically had the right to alter its name. Baldwin had sworn each member to secrecy, threatening expulsion from the HoHoKams if there was a leak of any kind. As an added incentive to keep their lips zipped, Baldwin, it would later be revealed, had arranged for each of the members to enjoy a three-day stay at one of his many time-share condos with the nation's most desirable resort addresses. The HoHoKams didn't disappoint him.

A 360-degree photograph of the newly named ballpark was produced and framed and would be presented to Caray's widow, the loving Dutchie, before the home opener in Chicago. Meanwhile, there wasn't a dry eye in the house as Baldwin thanked the Mesa crowd, shook hands with the mayor, and then took his seat behind the first base dugout. The old codger was the first to greet him, giving the surprised real-estate magnate a bear hug and offering him a gulp of his freshly poured Bud. Baldwin, a party animal in his day, chugged the beer in less than 10 seconds.

The inspirational pregame festivities didn't help the Cubs. They lost, 8–4. Campbell started the game, pitched three innings, and gave up six runs, including a line-drive homer to John Olerud. Willingham made an appearance and got nicked for an unearned run in the fifth. Hurlock pitched a scoreless sixth. Harris later entered the game in the ninth and promptly gave up a leadoff home run to Edgar Martinez. Hernandez had a pair of RBI doubles, Strickland singled in the third run, and Hammler had a one-out homer in the ninth.

Riley and the other reporters trudged down the stadium stairs after the fifth inning. By then, Campbell had done his running and was sitting in front of his locker with an oversized ice-pack wrap on his left elbow. It was a precautionary measure, done by trainers around the league.

Hill spoke first.

"Interesting day," he said.

"Shit, I was throwing tossed salad out there," said Campbell, lighting a cigarette. "Was there anybody who didn't get a knock or two against me?"

"No, I meant the Harry Caray thing," Hill said.

"Oh, yeah," Campbell said. "The pisser is, I think that ceremony lasted too long. I was loose and then I tightened up. But don't write that. Then I come off sounding like I'm blaming a dead man for three horseshit innings."

"Horseshit questions aside," said Morris, glancing at Hill, "what was working for you today?"

"Slider wasn't too bad," said Campbell between drags on his Winston. "I didn't try too many curveballs. No reason to this early. Olerud left a bruise on that one he hit. Other than that, I looked like a guy without a fucking clue. Next question."

"You think three innings was too much the first time out there?" Nadel said.

"You asking me to second-guess my skipper?" Campbell said.

"No way."

"I didn't mean it like that," Nadel said.

"Sounded that way to me," Campbell said.

"I just meant—"

"I know what you meant," Campbell said. "They pay me to pitch, I pitch. Jesus, Nadel, I don't expect those kind of horseshit questions from you. I'm going to take a shower. Try to do better tomorrow, will you?"

Campbell flicked his cigarette with his right hand into a half-empty cup of Gatorade and then turned his back on the writers.

Riley was slow to leave.

"What, you waiting for an exclusive or something?" Campbell said. "I'm done. But I'll tell you what: You let me know who made you wear that shirt and I'll find the guy and beat the shit out of him for you."

"What's wrong with the shirt?" Riley said.

"Are you kidding me?" Campbell said. "Munsingwear? That's so Dow Finsterwald."

"You know who Dow Finsterwald is?"

"ESPN Classic Sports," Campbell said. "What, you think we don't have cable where I come from? Now get the fuck out of here."

Riley caught up with the rest of the writers. Morris was chiding Nadel.

"Nice effort," Morris said.

"How would you know?" Nadel said. "Your head was so far up Campbell's ass, I'm surprised you could hear the question."

"All I know is that I kick your ass about once a week," Morris said.

"And the other six days you're kissing some player's ass," Nadel said. "You're the only writer I know who should have a Handi-wipes endorsement."

"Blow me."

"And what, ruin a wonderful relationship between you and Campbell?"

If Braswell was upset about his team's performance, he didn't show it. After all, it was only the first of 31 exhibition games, followed by a 162-game regular-season schedule, followed by—Harry Caray willing—the postseason.

"How'd you think Campbell looked?" Armour asked.

"Shit, fellas, he looked like someone facing big league hitters for the first time this spring," he said. "I ain't reading too much into it. I'm more pissed about Delagotti getting thrown out at home on what should have been a sacrifice fly."

"You mean, in the fourth?" Riley asked tentatively.

"Was there another one?" Braswell said.

Riley started thumbing through his scorebook.

"Son, there wasn't another play at home," Braswell said soothingly.

"It was a close play," Nadel said.

"Close play, my ass," Braswell said. "Goddamn Ironside could have scored from third. Gonzalez hit that ball a ton."

"Anybody impress you today?" Morris said.

"Now that you ask, yes, there were a few impressive performances," said Braswell, popping open a can of Bud. "Hernandez nearly vaporized that one ball, and I liked what Hurlock and that other kid—what's his name?—did out there."

"Willingham," Riley said.

"Yeah, Willingham. He showed me a little something."

"Anything else?" Nadel said.

"Nah, we'll just go out there tomorrow and try to get a little bit better," Braswell said. "I ain't gonna win the World Series in March."

"Thanks," said Armour, the first to leave the office. The others followed.

"Hey, Riley-whatever-your-name-is," Braswell said.

Riley peeled back into the office.

"You called?"

"I guess congratulations are in order, son."

"Congratulations, for what?"

"You being the full-time Cubs guy."

"I'm not following you," Riley said.

"Well, son, I got a call a little while ago from Mitchell," Braswell said. "Said he was taking a job with ESPN. Going to work with Gammons and Kurkjian."

"He what?"

"Said the money was too good and that the *Sentinel*'s lockout situation wasn't worth the bullshit. He's got a face for radio, but I guess if someone's willing to stick you on TV, you might as well take the money and run."

"He what?"

"Son, don't tell me you didn't know about this," Braswell said. "I'm gonna feel like horseshit if I'm the first to tell you."

Riley just stared blankly.

"Aw, damn," Braswell said. "Well, then, you probably need this more than I do."

Braswell pushed the sweating can of beer toward Riley. Without thinking, Riley took a big swig, and then another. The can was half empty.

"I can't believe this," he said.

"Son, it wouldn't be life without a little birdshit on our shoulders," said Braswell, reaching into his office fridge and pulling out another can of Bud.

"Nothing personal, but this was supposed to be a temporary thing," said Riley, slumping against the cinderblock wall. "I only pre-paid my bills for six weeks."

"Look at it this way, son," said Braswell, "at least you got a job. A lot of them union folks are walking the picket line and the unemployment line."

"I know," Riley said. "I feel like Dracula. The only reason I've got this job is because of the lockout. Otherwise . . ."

"Otherwise what, son?"

"Ah, nothing," Riley said. "Thanks for the beer."

Riley left the room, but reappeared moments later. "Forgot my notebook," he said.

"Don't want to do that, son," Braswell said. "Might forget some of my postgame pearls of wisdom."

Riley managed a grin.

"Thanks for trying," Riley said.

"You hang in there. Shit, all you got to do is cover the Cubs. I've got to manage the sumbitches."

"I'll remember that."

Riley left the clubhouse without talking to any other players. He hoped he got beat on a story. Then maybe the nightmare would be finished. No more Omar Hernandez, the brooding Latino. No more R.J. Morris, the human nightmare. No more Casey Harris and Bob Lake, the morally reprehensible twins. No more Jim Hightower, as mysterious as the Shroud of Turin. No more groin bruises. No more migraines, lumps in the stomach, and road-warrior status.

No more job.

"Shit," Riley said to himself.

There was a message taped to his laptop. *Call your office.* Riley dialed Butler's extension. Sheila answered.

"Hold on," she said. "I'll get the little fartwad for you."

Riley could hear her in the background. Rather than put people on hold, Sheila liked to drop the phone on her desk and then summon Butler to his office.

"He's pissed and I don't blame him," Riley heard her say to Butler.

Well, come to think of it, Riley *was* pissed. Damn that Mitchell.

"I'm transferring you, honey," said Sheila, an actual softness in her voice. "Between you, me, and the lamppost, I think you're getting it right up the pooper shooter."

"Thanks, Sheila," Riley said.

There was a pause as she sent the call to the sports editor's office.

"Butler, here."

"Riley, here."

"You're upset," said Butler.

"Numb is more like it."

"I didn't have a clue he was talking to ESPN," Butler said. "Apparently the money was too good to turn down."

"So what happens to me?"

"In what sense?"

"Whattaya mean, 'What sense?'" Riley said, his voice rising. "In the sense that I wasn't figuring on doing the Cubs indefinitely."

"I have no choice," Butler said. "You want a paycheck, don't you?"

"What does that mean?"

"You know exactly what it means. The ground rules haven't changed. You can stay on the Cubs or have your employment terminated."

"Right, how could I forget? Corporate man," Riley said.

"Be careful, Riley," said Butler, who leaned forward in his chair, opened the bottom right-hand desk drawer, and pulled out a small rag and a can of Pledge. He lightly sprayed the rag and then dragged it over the desktop. Butler loved a clean desk, to say nothing of the lemony smell of the dust cleaner. "Now then, what will it be?"

Silence.

"Riley?"

"Okay, if I do this, can you guarantee me that I'll have my old job back, without conditions, when you find a replacement?"

"Of course not. But what I can tell you is this: You'll have the gratitude of this company and I'll do everything in my power to see that your record in the permanent file reflects your team play."

"But what about my job?"

"Again, you have my word that I'll discuss your standing with Mr. Jarrett, Mr. Storen, and Ms. Hollandsworth."

"Hollandsworth?" Riley said. "What does she have to do with this?"

"Ms. Hollandsworth is taking a more active role in the day-to-day operations of the editorial side," Butler said. "She's a huge fan of sports."

"She doesn't know a widget from a bases-loaded walk."

"And your point is . . ."

"Never mind," Riley said. "I'll do it. I'm trusting you on this, Butler."

"Of course you are," Butler said. "I know this is a very difficult time for you. We want to be understanding of that, sensitive to these latest developments. By the way, I'm going to need you to file a feature to go along with your gamer and notes. Oops. Have to run."

Riley placed the receiver on the phone cradle. By now, Nadel was back in the press box. He had an update to do at the top of the hour.

"You okay?" Nadel asked.

"I guess so," Riley said. "I still have a job. So I have that going for me."

"Which is good," said Nadel, completing the line from *Caddyshack*.

Butler reached Jarrett's office in less than two minutes.

"Mitchell's gone, but Riley is staying on," Butler told the paper's editor.

"How much did Mitchell make?" said Jarrett, grabbing a notepad.

"About $102,000," said the sports editor.

"That much?" Jarrett said. "And Riley?"

"Half that."

Jarrett's eyebrows shot up. "That's all?" Jarrett said. "He's been here for years."

"We've done a nice job with cost containment," said Butler, fishing for a compliment.

"Our publisher wants more cuts," Jarrett said. "I thought you said Riley would never last this long."

Butler tugged nervously at his "Save the Whales" tie.

"I thought so, too," Butler said. "I've loaded him down with assignments and from what I understand, he isn't popular among most of the players or the other writers. It's only a matter of time. But we can't fire him unless he refuses to accept any reasonable assignment. So far, he's done everything we've asked."

"What about the quality of his work?" Jarrett said. "Anything we can do there?"

"He has gotten beat on several stories, one of them substantial," Butler said. "But R.J. Morris, the beat guy for the *Standard*, does that to everyone. And to be fair to Riley, he has been thrown into the deep end without swim lessons."

"I don't care about fairness, nor am I concerned about aquatics," Jarrett said. "Every day, every penny counts. I can't go into any more detail than that, only to say that the more you trim, the fatter your reward will be. How did you leave it with Riley?"

"I promised I would discuss his situation with you."

"You're a bit of a weasel, aren't you, Butler?"

"I like to think of myself as a pragmatist, sir."

"Under the current climate, aren't we all?" Jarrett said. "Look, I'm not entirely comfortable with what we're doing here, but this is survival-of-the-fittest time. We can't afford to confuse compassion with commitment. We don't have that luxury."

"I understand," said Butler, as the editor led him to the door.

"For your sake and maybe mine, I hope you do," said Jarrett, whose icy comment sent a chill down where Butler's spine should have been.

Eleven

THE SECOND INNING HAD JUST BEGUN when Armour squeezed a chair between Nadel and Riley. Hill was seated to Riley's left.

"Gentlemen, you are about to witness sweet revenge," Armour said.

"Oh, Christ," said Nadel, "I didn't do anything to you."

"You're safe," Armour said. "But don't think I've forgotten about the time you put that piece of tin foil over the phone tab."

Nadel feigned any knowledge of the incident.

"Tin foil?" Riley said.

"Oh, yes," said Armour. "A certain unnamed party—unnamed only because I haven't completely confirmed who was responsible—unscrewed the phone cap, you know, the part you speak into. Then the unnamed party put a piece of tin foil between the connection pad and the metal tab that activates your voice. I had a live spot to do, but little did I know that the station wasn't able to hear me. They kept telling me to speak up. I was practically screaming into the phone, and that's when I noticed our friend here almost doubled over in laughter. He denies responsibility, but I have serious doubts about his honesty."

"I'm like Sergeant Schultz," said Nadel. "I know noth-ing. Absolutely noth-ing."

"Uh-huh," Armour said.

"So you could hear them through the receiver, but they couldn't hear you?" Riley said.

Armour had a look of disappointment on his face. "You know, Riley, a mind is a terrible thing to waste," he said. "I actually thought you were like Kate Jackson, the smart one. Now I'm not so sure.

But to answer your ridiculously dumb question, yes, I could hear them, but they couldn't hear me."

"Sorry," Riley said. "I'm still recovering from my one-man drinking party."

"Yeah, sorry to hear about the news," Armour said. "That was a shitty way to find out. You ever hear from Mitchell?"

"Nope," Riley said. "He's in Arizona, but I haven't talked to him yet."

"But once the lockout ends, you'll get your old job back, right?" Hill said. "I mean, they're not going to keep you on the Cubs?"

"Good question," Riley said. "Who knows how long this thing is going to last."

"Gentlemen, while I have great empathy for Mr. Riley, here, there are matters of far greater importance on our agenda," Armour said.

"Such as . . .?" Nadel said.

"One Mr. Travis Campbell," said Armour, pointing to the bullpen area.

Campbell, who had pitched the day before, was scheduled to do little more than sit on his butt for the afternoon. You could see him next to Harris, stuffing his cheeks with sunflower seeds and casually checking out the crowd for anyone wearing a bikini top.

"What about him?" Nadel said.

"Remember the aforementioned malted-balls caper? Today is payback," Armour said.

"Oh, good," said Riley. "I can finally watch somebody else have a shitty day."

"Oh, you will," Armour said. "You definitely will."

"Okay, let's hear it," Nadel said.

"You're sworn to secrecy, of course," Armour said.

Riley and Nadel nodded their heads.

"After careful scouting, I noticed that Campbell likes to bring a small personal container of Gatorade with him to the bullpen," Armour said. "Unfortunately for our friend Campbell, he made the mistake of leaving the squeeze bottle near his locker during pregame workouts. So I casually dropped a dozen tablets into the Gatorade. By now they've dissolved quite nicely."

"What kind of tablets?" Riley said.

"Ex-Lax," Armour said. "Extra-strength."

"Oh, shit," Nadel said.

"Let's hope so," Armour said.

The three men watched Campbell's every move. He drank the lime-flavored stuff during the third inning and again at the top of the fourth.

"Oh, how the hot Arizona sun makes a man thirsty," said Armour.

"What's going on?" asked Morris, noticing the huddle.

"Nothing at all," Armour said. "Just watching the game."

"Sure doesn't look like you're watching the same game I am," he muttered. Morris hated to be left out of anything.

"Run along, R.J.," Armour said. "Don't you have some license-plate numbers that need to be run?"

"You're a real stitch," said Morris, stomping away.

Midway through the fifth inning, Campbell began to move uneasily on the bullpen bench. His intestines were doing the watusi. The first hints of discomfort began to appear.

"You okay?" Harris said to him.

"Do I look okay?" Campbell snapped.

"Hey, fuck you," the reliever said. "I was only trying to help."

Braswell had a rule. Once an inning was underway, you couldn't leave the bullpen for the dugout or the clubhouse. Campbell was stuck.

Another seismic surge swept through Campbell's midsection.

"Jeezus Christ!" Campbell said.

"What?" Harris said.

"Nothing."

But it was too late. There was only so much the sphincter muscle was designed to do, and holding back the tidal wave created by 12 extra-strength tablets of Ex-Lax wasn't on the list.

"I gotta go," said Campbell.

"Go where?" Harris said. "We're up. If Braswell sees you, he'll fine you five hundred dollars."

"No, I mean I really got to go," said Campbell, his face the color of skim milk. "I must have had some bad fish or something."

"Yeah, you don't look so good," Harris said. "Want me to call one of the trainers?"

"No," Campbell winced. "I'm going to try to sneak out of here for a few minutes. I think I can—"

Campbell had waited too long to act. There was a noise and then came what can only be described as a bowel movement for the ages. Intestine tectonics. Carnage.

"What the hell is that smell?" Harris said. "Is that you?"

The other relievers and starters caught a full whiff of Campbell's situation. It was a near-windless day, so the stench stayed put.

"Is your ass rotting, or what?" said bullpen coach Oscar Wulf. "You have a gallon of beans last night?"

Soon the entire bullpen corps was standing in disbelief. The pitchers waved their arms and hands, as if a hive of bumblebees had been dropped in the bullpen. Some began fanning towels. Others took to covering their faces with their gloves. Back in the dugout Ernie Gesser, the pitching coach, noticed the disturbance first.

"Brazzy," he said to the Cubs manager, "what the hell do you think is going on down there?"

Braswell looked up in time to see Harris fall to his knees, the smell nearly rendering the reliever unconscious. He had been the closest. The other pitchers and bullpen catchers had retreated toward the right field corner, as far away from Campbell as possible. Campbell hadn't moved, but every few minutes he grimaced in pain.

"Stevie D," said Braswell to the Cubs trainer, "get your ass out there and see what the hell is wrong."

By now every fan at Harry Caray Stadium was mesmerized by the bullpen mystery. So was Hurlock, who kept sneaking peeks at his teammate from the mound. Even the visiting Colorado Rockies were peering out of the dugout. Up in the press box, Riley heard the Rockies' radio play-by-play announcer say, "Well, it appears that Travis Campbell is suffering from some sort of strange paralysis. We can see him talking to long-time Cubs trainer Steve Davidson, but Campbell seems reluctant to leave the bullpen bench. Wait, Davidson is putting on some sort of surgical mask and calling for something out of the dugout. I must say, this is one of the most bizarre scenes I have witnessed in twenty-one years of broadcasting.

"Okay, several towels have been handed to Davidson, who is gingerly wrapping them around Campbell's midsection," said the Rockies announcer. "Ladies and gentlemen, I can't be sure, but it appears that Campbell—what's the best way of putting this?—soiled himself."

ABOUT 80 PERCENT LUCK

Armour subtly pumped his fist. Nadel swore silently to himself that he would never pull another practical joke on Armour. Riley glanced at Morris, who was staring at Armour.

Down on the field, Campbell's face was pasty. Dehydration would arrive soon.

"Get me inside, goddamnit!" he hissed.

"I'm trying," Davidson said, "but you've got shit dripping down your legs."

"Get some guys to carry me off," he said. "I can't leave like this."

"I need some volunteers," said Davidson, turning to the rest of the bullpen.

"No way," said Harris. "Not till you hose him down and sprinkle baby powder on his perky little bottom."

"Fuck you!" Campbell said.

"Did leetle-weetle Travis go poopy over himself?" Harris said.

Davidson taped the towels around Campbell's waist as if they were diapers, but it was apparent to everyone what had happened. The crowd roared with laughter. Braswell walked down the dugout runway, ducked into the adjacent bathroom and laughed until his rib cage hurt.

One of the local newspaper photographers clicked away with his high-powered telephoto lens. A CNN crew taped everything.

"I'm gonna stick that thing up your ass if you keep taking pictures," said Campbell as he neared the photographers' well.

"I'd worry about my own ass, if I were you," said the cameraman, who resumed his shooting.

The Rockies won the game, not that anyone was talking about the score that day. Braswell told the reporters that Campbell had an intestinal "bug" and was expected back at practice the next day. Until then, he would be unavailable for comment.

"Where is he?" Riley asked.

"In the training room getting an IV," Braswell said.

Meanwhile, maintenance workers used a pressure hose to clean off the bullpen bench. They wore knee-high wading boots and huge rubber-coated coats, as if they were dealing with some sort of radioactive material. Later, a fresh coat of green paint was applied. And when Campbell finally emerged from a long shower, he found a large box of Depends in his locker.

"You can all kiss my ass!" he yelled.

"Not until you wipe it," someone yelled back.

After filing his story and notes, Riley decided to treat himself to a decent meal. He drove to Don & Charlie's, a Cactus League institution. Good food. Lots of atmosphere. A baseball man's hangout.

He was seated near a corner of the restaurant, a few yards away from a waiters' station. It was a two-top and it gave Riley a surprisingly good view of the entire dining room. Riley ordered an Old Style, a dinner salad, a Porterhouse—medium well—and a side dish of scalloped potatoes.

He noticed Rockies manager Buddy Bell sitting with some Colorado scouts and front-office types. Against the far wall was Milwaukee announcer Bob Uecker. And in a booth was the Cubs' Strickland with some unidentified blonde. The woman had her back to Riley.

As he sipped at his beer, Riley began to form a plan. First, he would start using some of those phone numbers Mitchell had given him. They weren't doing him any good sitting in his notebook. Next, he would make another run at Hightower. Nobody could be that secretive. And then he would . . .

"Hey, Pappy the Pirate."

He looked up.

"Surprise," said Megan Donahue. "It's me. I see you're still buddies with Old Style."

"You can take the South Sider out of Chicago, but you can't take the Chicago out of the South Sider," he said, surprised but happy to see her. She looked good. She had the beginnings of a nice tan and the expensive jacket-and-slacks combo hugged her just right.

"That is so deep," she said, smiling.

"You know, I had your number and I was going to call. And . . . wait a second—what are you doing in Arizona?" Riley said. "Don't tell me you're selling Don & Charlie's a happy hour ad for the *Sentinel* weekend section."

"No, I'm here for a business dinner," she said.

"Really," said Riley, who tried not to look disappointed. He had thought about asking her to join him. "With who? And I hope you're getting gas mileage."

"Brett Strickland," she said. "He saw you sitting in the corner, mentioned there was a writer here, and boom, here I am."

Riley leaned around Megan and caught a glimpse of Strickland, who was chatting up one of the waiters. Strickland looked as if he'd just walked off the cover of *GQ*. Riley was wearing a sun-bleached Izod from three Christmases ago. "What sort of business are you and Strickland in?" said Riley, trying not to sound suspicious. Or jealous.

"The details haven't been worked out yet, but we're trying to sign him and maybe one other player as a TSNE spokesman," she said. "That's why they flew me out here. Me and one of the lawyer types."

"Strickland?" Riley said. "Is he that popular?"

"His focus-group numbers are through the roof," she said. "Women love him."

"I bet," said Riley. There was an awkward pause as Riley ran his finger across the top of his frosted glass.

"So . . ." said Megan.

"So," said Riley, trying to restart the conversation. "How'd you get this gig? I thought you were in advertising, not marketing."

"Remember, I was employee of the month," she said.

"That's right, I forgot," Riley said. "Special privileges."

"Actually, I pitched the idea to TSNE months ago and they finally went for it," she said. "What about you? Any big stories you working on?"

"You don't expect me to talk, do you?"

"No, Mr. Bond," she said dramatically. "I expect you to *die*."

"You know *Goldfinger*?"

"It's only on TBS every other week," she said. "Plus, Sean Connery is a major babe magnet, especially back then. Look, I better get back. I just wanted to say hello. I'll probably see you at the ballpark. I'm here for as long as this takes."

"Me, too," Riley said unconvincingly.

"But you're doing okay, right?"

"Oh, yeah," he said. "I'm *this* close to a Pulitzer nomination. One more good note about a pulled groin and I think I've got it locked up."

"Nice to see your sarcasm is in fine working order," Megan said, glancing back at Strickland. "Anyway, maybe I'll see you around. I'm staying at the Phoenician, so don't be a stranger."

Donahue returned to her table, but took her time doing so. She looked better than Riley had remembered. Smelled nice, too. Riley sneaked a peek at their table. Strickland was leaning forward, his finger tracing something in her palm. They were giggling like fourth graders.

Riley finished his meal, paid the bill, and briefly thought about circling toward Strickland's table. Then he saw the waiter delivering a bottle of champagne and decided Strickland and Megan were well on their way to some sort of bubbly delight. Just his luck.

On the way home Riley put 10 bucks of unleaded in the S80. What he wouldn't give to bring the beauty back to Chicago. Once at the condo, Riley parked the car and checked his mail—nothing. He turned on the living-room lights, and that's when he saw the envelope. It had been slipped under the front door.

"Again with the condo association?" Riley said as he reached for the envelope. A week earlier he had left the garbage can long after the pickup. It had rolled into the street and later been retrieved by a member of the condo board. That night there was a warning letter left on his door. Now this.

Riley tore open the envelope and found a small note.

Watch Morris. Also Blair. They cheat.

Morris? R.J. Morris? And his faithful sidekick, Andy Blair? Why? And who the hell was sending him secret notes? And what did it mean, "They cheat"?

It had to be Armour. Another practical joke. No, Riley hadn't done anything to Armour. Anyway, it wasn't Armour's style.

What about Hoffman? Or maybe it was Dewitt. Dewitt said he'd help point him in the right direction. Mitchell? Maybe Mitchell had some pangs of guilt and was trying to set things straight. Whoever it was, he didn't want his name attached.

Riley tossed the note away. Okay, Morris and Blair would become surveillance targets. Why, he wasn't exactly sure.

There was one other thing to be done. Riley picked up the cordless, dialed the 1-800 catalog number he had circled in a magazine, and waited for an operator at the company's headquarters in Riverside, New Jersey. He pulled out his Visa card, double-checked the expiration date (he had two more months), and then placed his $225 order with someone named Marcia.

The *Sentinel* wanted a Cubs beat reporter. They were going to get one.

Twelve

WHENEVER THERE WAS A HOME GAME, Kasparovich was sent out to catch the ceremonial first pitch. It was grunt duty, but the rookie did it with a smile on his face. And despite the hazing, Kasparovich handled every indignation with calm and grace. There was the time when Valdez put his arm around him moments before the team took the field against the San Diego Padres.

"Keed," said Valdez, "I like your style. You lead us out today."

"You sure?" Kasparovich asked the shortstop. "Doesn't Strickland always go first?"

"I talked to Streekland about it," Valdez said. "He's all for it. You've earned it."

"Really?" Kasparovich said. His parents, watching the game back in Pittsburgh on WGN, would be thrilled.

"Absolutely, positively," Valdez said. "Streekland told me you're the best rook he's ever seen."

Kasparovich beamed. He put a paw around Valdez's shoulder and pulled the shortstop close. "Dude, you don't know what this means to me," the rookie said. "Thanks, man."

"No problem, man," Valdez said uncomfortably. He looked over to the end of the bench where Strickland and Delagotti had their faces buried in their gloves. Valdez rolled his eyes.

The public address announcer did his part. "Ladies and gentlemen, here's yourrrrrrrrrr Chicago Cubs!"

Valdez tapped Kasparovich on the back. "You ready?" Valdez said.

"Damn straight I am, dude," he said. And off the rookie went.

Kasparovich needed only two steps to bounce out of the dugout, and only three more after that to sprint to first base. What an honor. What an adrenaline rush. Imagine, a rookie leading the Chicago Cubs. Who cared if it was only an exhibition game? Kasparovich wasn't too proud to admit he had goosebumps. Who wouldn't?

And then he turned around, ball in hand, waiting to throw a few grounders to Strickland and the rest of the infield during warm-ups. Problem was, the rest of the Cubs' lineup was still in the dugout. Strickland and Valdez were crumpled on the bench laughing. All of Little San Juan was howling. Braswell waited a few moments and then ordered them out to the field.

"You got me good," yelled Kasparovich to Valdez.

"It's because I love you, Rook."

Kasparovich laughed, which was the only way to take it. Take it personally, throw a fit as some rookies had done in the past, and the veterans would eat you alive. A few seasons earlier Valdez had orchestrated a postgame prank on one of the Cubs' rookie pitchers, a high-strung South Korean who had nasty stuff but thought his huge signing bonus protected him from any first-year hazing. The Cubs were on their first road trip of that season and had just beaten the Dodgers to take the three-game series. The South Korean had pitched the seventh inning, struck out two, and helped keep the Cubs close until a ninth-inning rally won it for Chicago. Afterward, with the Cubs rushing to catch a Sunday-night flight to San Francisco, the rookie emerged from the shower and found his $1,100 suit cut off at the knees and elbows. His shoes had been stolen and the buttons on his dress shirt had been snipped off.

The South Korean stormed through the clubhouse, screaming at his interpreter to retrieve his shoes and find the culprit. The interpreter, an employee of the Cubs, was going to do no such thing. Valdez had told him if he said a peep they would remove his leg hairs with ankle tape. That was more than enough to keep him quiet.

The South Korean had no choice. His traveling bag had been taken while he was in the shower and hidden on the team charter bus by a clubby. His uniform had also been packed away, leaving the rookie with his ruined suit and shirt and a pair of shower sandals. Cursing in Korean, the pitcher angrily got dressed and made his way to the bus. When he opened the clubhouse door, he was greeted by the entire team, as well as 50 or so autograph seekers. White towels had been placed on the ground, creating a cotton path to the first step of the bus.

This is where most rookies would have broken into a good-natured smile. Instead, the South Korean kicked the towels away and made his way inside the bus. He pouted all the way to LAX, and could barely contain his temper as he was forced to walk through the long terminal in his Huck Finn pants. The rookie lasted until July, when he demanded a release from his contract and a one-way ticket to South Korea.

Kasparovich had no such ego problems. He was the son of a Pittsburgh grocer and wasn't motivated by money. He would sit in the dugout between innings, close his eyes, and let the sounds and smells of the stadium wash over him. "Is this the greatest thing, or what?" he'd say to the other players. They'd roll their eyes, but the rookie didn't care. He was loving every minute of it.

Though he hadn't hit any home runs yet, Kasparovich had shown surprisingly good defensive skills at first. His spring training average was at .311, thanks to a half-dozen line drives that left pock marks in the wooden outfield advertisement boards. He was a lock to make the team.

The silent Omar Hernandez also was well on his way to securing a roster spot. He was a four-tool player, which was one tool short of a general manager's wet dream. Hernandez could hit for average and power. He was a gifted fielder, and his arm was considered the strongest in the organization. A few days earlier he had picked off Miguel Tejada at first, even though the Oakland shortstop had only taken three baby steps off the bag. Tejada stared in disbelief when Kasparovich tagged him. And on the way back to the dugout, the Athletics' young star shouted something to Hernandez in Spanish. One of the Cubs batboys remembered the phrase.

"*Brazo de dios*."

Riley looked it up in what was left of his translation book.

Arm of God.

Like most catchers, the only thing Hernandez lacked was leg speed. But the Cubs didn't seem to mind. Braswell played him during the early innings, when most of the regulars were in. It was obvious the Cubs wanted to see how Hernandez responded to the pressure. So far, so good.

Of course, Barry Garrison wasn't thrilled with the situation. The veteran catcher—released during the offseason by the Pittsburgh Pirates—thought he had a chance to win the job, Omar or no Omar. Invited as a non-roster player, Garrison was hitting .289 with a homer and four RBIs. He cornered Riley in the clubhouse before the morning workout.

"You got something against a man trying to put food on his family's table?" said Garrison, who at five-foot-ten, 220 pounds was built like a phone booth.

"Should I?" squeaked Riley.

"You keep writing that chickenshit about the rook having the job to himself," he said. "Maybe you ought to look at the fucking stats, paperboy."

Riley suddenly remembered what Mitchell had said: never back down from a ballplayer. Ballplayers can smell fear. How, Riley had no idea. But here was the perfect opportunity to establish some media turf. Riley took a small breath.

"I did read the stats," said Riley, his voice quivering only slightly. "Hernandez is hitting almost thirty points higher than you, has double your RBIs, and two homers to your one."

"Hey, dickwad, I didn't say I was hitting better than him," said Garrison. "I said it was too early to hand him the job."

"And I didn't say the Cubs had handed him the job," said Riley. "Did you read the story?"

"I read enough of it to know you don't know dick about baseball," Garrison said. "I've been in this game twelve years. I've forgotten more about the game than you'll ever know. There's more to it than hitting .319 in spring training . . . in Arizona, where the infield dirt is so hard you can't help but torque up your average with some hard-hit grounders. Hit the same ball at Wrigley, and that cow pasture of an infield soaks it up for an easy out. But you wouldn't know that. You wouldn't know how to call a game, or work a staff, or hold a rookie's hand so he doesn't throw up all over himself when the game is on the line."

Garrison was right. In fact, Riley was still learning how to keep a proper scorebook.

"Look, Barry, I didn't write that Hernandez had the job wrapped up," Riley said. "I wrote that he was off to a fast start and that Cubs management loved his upside."

"That's great," said Garrison, who moved closer to Riley, close enough that Riley could see flecks of cream cheese and bagel crumbs on the catcher's reddish-gray mustache. "I guess all you need to get ahead on this team is a green card, an accent, and some chickenshit reporter writing sweet things about you."

"You're kidding, right?"

"I don't kid about me making a living," Garrison said. "Now get out of my face."

Riley started to say something, but didn't. No use risking bodily harm.

"Hey, Barry!"

It was Strickland, whose locker was three cubicles away. Strickland was sitting on a metal stool, browsing through the *Arizona Republic* sports section.

"You know that dinger you hit off Eldred a couple of days ago?" Strickland said.

"Yeah," Garrison said.

"Wouldn't have made it to the warning track in some of those minor league ballparks you played in," Strickland said.

"Sure as hell would have," Garrison said indignantly.

"How about Old Memorial in Buffalo?" Strickland said.

"Never played in that one," said Garrison, taking the bait.

"Oh, that's right," said Strickland, grinning at Riley, "you played in the one *before* Old Memorial."

Garrison tried to defend himself, but Strickland was already on his way out the clubhouse door. A few rookies soon to be designated for assignment were clearly enjoying Garrison's plight. So was Riley.

"What's so funny, paperboy?" Garrison said. "You better wipe that smirk off your face or I'm gonna—"

"You're gonna do what, son?" said Braswell, who had walked into the clubhouse to get a fresh cup of coffee.

"Nothing, Skip," Garrison said nervously. "Just shitting around with the media guys."

"That's what I thought," said Braswell, pouring some cream into his mug. "Do me a favor, will you, and tell Coach Hayes that we're gonna start fifteen minutes later today. I think he's already out on Field Two."

"Sure thing, Skip," said Garrison, who grabbed his glove and bat and darted out the door.

Braswell didn't look up. Instead, he swirled the cup until the cream had melted into the coffee.

"Thanks," Riley said.

"Didn't do a thing," Braswell said. "There's always a peckerwood trying to pick a fight. Happens every year."

"Can I ask you a question?" Riley said.

"Shoot," the manager said.

"How do you know when a player is really pissed at you?"

"Oh, you'll just know," Braswell said. "Like Garrison there. What he say to you about Omar?"

"He said I was trying to take food off his table," Riley said.

"But what adjective did he use, son?" Braswell said impatiently. "I mean, goddamn, I need the adjective."

"He said I was writing chickenshit stories."

"Well, then, you got nothing to worry about," said Braswell, peeling the wrapping off a blueberry muffin.

"How do you know?"

"Because 'chickenshit' is a low-grade baseball cuss word. Now, if the boy had used *horseshit*, then I would have been mildly concerned. And if he would have used the word *brutal*, then you got some problems."

"*Brutal* is bad," Riley said.

"*Brutal* is very bad. A player says you've done something 'brutal,' then you're in deep shit."

"I understand," Riley said.

"Glad I could help," said Braswell. "Son, you've got to remember that some of these pricks have been spoiled rotten by money. Not me. I used to manage in the Cape Cod League, that's how desperate I was. They told me I could manage, and they said they'd also get me a job at the Holiday Inn. I figured I'd be a part-time waiter or work as a pool lifeguard. I didn't know they meant *building* the goddamn Holiday Inn."

"I get your point," Riley said.

"Garrison is okay, just a former bonus baby," Braswell said. "He don't know no better."

"I'll remember that."

"You do that," Braswell said. "See you out there."

There was a chill to the early morning air, enough so that the clubbies were instructed to deliver warm-up sweaters to the players. Lake tossed the blue button-up sweater onto the damp grass.

"I'm not wearing that thing," he said. "I'll look like Beaver Cleaver."

Riley stood off to the side as the players stretched for the morning workout. The conversations constantly amazed him. None of it could go into a family newspaper, which was probably why the players didn't care if Riley was within listening distance.

"So was that your daughter who was out here yesterday?" said Harris to Ernie Gesser, the pitching coach.

"That was her, and don't you get any ideas," Gesser said. "She's only a junior in high school. She's out here looking at Arizona State and Arizona. Wants to study drama. In fact, she's got a school play coming up in two weeks. I'm gonna miss it."

"Hey, Ernie," said a fully recovered Campbell. "Any nudity in your daughter's play?"

"I swear, Campbell, you've got shit for brains," said Gesser.

"By the looks of his game pants, he don't have any shit left," Hurlock said.

"Laugh now," Campbell said, "but I'll find out what happened."

"Sure you will," Hurlock said. "But quit asking about the man's daughter. Like what, 'Immaculate Conception High School presents *Oh, Calcutta*'?"

"*Oh* who?" said Campbell.

"Forget it," Hurlock said.

A Fox TV crew, led by a producer who should have been in front of the camera instead of behind it, walked past the players. Hurlock let out a long, low whistle.

"Will you look at that woman?" Hurlock said. "I'd pay a year's salary to see what she's like in bed."

"She'd never do it for four hundred dollars," said Campbell, stretching his hamstrings.

"Hilarious," said Hurlock. "Just once I'd like to go up to a woman like that and say, 'Excuse me, I'm Tyler Hurlock, and I'm a man who appreciates a woman of your physical stature. That's not to say you don't possess a robust mind, but that's for another time. For now, though, I'd like to spend the next few minutes simply staring at your breasts. It's purely an aesthetic exercise. Then I'll be moving on to your buttocks area, where I anticipate staring at that beautiful ass of yours for, say, five to seven minutes. From there, I'll settle on your legs. Again, consider me no threat. I simply want to stare, but with no guilt.'"

"I'll give you four hundred dollars if you do that right now with the Fox babe," Campbell said.

"Gentlemen," said Stevie D in his sternest tone, "we're stretching here. Let's concentrate, please."

"Spoilsport," said Hurlock.

Riley walked to the dugout, poured himself a cup of ice water, and then returned to the field. This time Delagotti was talking to Carl Stephens, a non-roster middle reliever, about a tee time he had planned on a rare upcoming off day.

"Got it all arranged," Delagotti said.

"Need a fourth?" asked Stephens.

"No, but I need somebody to carry my clubs," Delagotti said. "You interested?"

"Kiss my ass."

"Oh, sensitive?" said Delagotti. "Anyway, this Fazio course is supposed to be outstanding. The best in the Valley."

"How much are the greens fees?" Stephens said.

"How the hell do I know? I'm on full scholly with a sleeve."

"Full scholly with a sleeve?"

"Kid, I'm predicting a long and worthless minor league career for you," said Delagotti, as he rolled over on his back and pulled his knees to his chest. "'Full scholly' . . . full scholarship. Free. Pay nothing. Understand? And the club pro better throw in a sleeve of free balls, too. Professional. Balata. Titleists. Ninety compression."

"They do that?" Stephens said.

"Hey, I scratch their back, they scratch mine. I leave free tickets for the pro and his girl. He looks like a big shot and I get a free round of golf. It's not like it costs him anything to send out another foursome."

"Well, if someone cancels out, let me know," Stephens said. "I play to a twelve."

"Yeah, if I'm ever in the Florida State League again, I'll be sure to look you up," Delagotti said.

"You're brutal, man," said Stephens.

"Got to be in this business," said Delagotti, who purposely never became close friends with his teammates. Too much competition. Too many trades.

Riley heard a half squeal, half laugh in the middle of the infielders' group. Number 14 . . . that would be the one and only Varsity Mormoa, a second baseman who had been traded from the Minnesota Twins during the offseason. Riley remembered a feature on him from the previous year: how his real first name was Victor, but then he'd had it legally changed to Varsity—Mormoa had refused to explain why. Mormoa had a reputation for being a bit eccentric. This was his third team in five seasons. He was an accomplished utility player but always seemed to grate on a manager's nerves.

"Hector, I had a dream about you last night," Mormoa said to Valdez.

"What you dream, that you weren't loco?" Valdez said.

"No, man," said Mormoa. "I dreamed you were going to kill me. You were charging right at me with a pair of shearing scissors, but since I liked you so much, I shot you in the leg. That way you didn't die."

"Man, you a crazy son of a bitch, you know that?" Valdez said.

"Hey, Varsy," said Strickland, who was stretching two rows behind Mormoa. "You're an Ivy Leaguer, right?"

"A Harvard man," said Mormoa.

"That's the Doonesbury guy, right?" Strickland said.

"No," Mormoa said, "that was done by Gary Trudeau, from Yale."

"But you can relate to Doonesbury, right, with the drug stuff?" Strickland said. "'Cause, man, you are out there."

"Never taken a puff, a pill, a snort, a whiff, a chug of anything illegal in my life, and that's God's truth," Mormoa said. "Majored in psychology, minored in philosophy."

"Psychology, huh?" Valdez said. "You must have studied yourself."

"I'm stunned, Valdez," Mormoa said. "That was borderline funny."

"What kind of philosophy?" Strickland asked.

"You know, the biggies," Mormoa said. "Kierkegaard, Schopenhauer, Spinoza, Locke, Descartes, Plato, Aristotle, Dewey. I was into Structuralism for a while, but it was so Left Bank. Know what I mean?"

"Not exactly," Strickland said. "Cal State–Fullerton isn't exactly the Harvard of the West Coast."

"I brought some books if you're interested," Mormoa said.

"Yeah, I'll be over tonight to pick them up," Strickland said. "Right after I split the atom in my hotel supercollider."

Riley didn't know Strickland well enough to ask about his dinner with Megan. He could only imagine: a bottle or two of Dom; a ride in his Mercedes convertible; the cool desert air; a visit to his rented condo; Strickland's disarming, soothing Missouri twang; his perfect smile. And Riley had to admit that Megan looked beautiful that night. Damn her. Why couldn't she have stayed at her own table? Why couldn't she have stayed in her own city? And what right did she have to be so friendly? Didn't she see that Riley *liked* self-pity?

Riley didn't hold a grudge against Strickland. Unlike Harris or some of the others, Strickland didn't treat women as conquests. If anything, Strickland almost never talked about any of his legendary dates. Several players asked him about his reported romances with Meg Ryan and later Jennifer Aniston. Strickland would just smile and say, "A Missouri gentleman never comments on the ladies of his life." And it wasn't an act. Riley had called up a few stories from the Nexus directory—stories from Strickland's early days as a pro—and it was obvious the star third baseman had remained true to himself. He almost always complimented his teammates. And if the Cubs lost, Strickland usually found a way to blame himself, even when it was obvious that someone else had been responsible. He was a rarity: a team leader without really trying to be one.

Riley wandered back to the media room. Morris looked surprised to see him and began typing furiously on his battered Tandy 200. Hill said hello and then began thumbing through the newly issued Major League Baseball media information directory. The 235-page spiral-bound book included names, numbers, and addresses of every media member who covered a major league team. Beat writers. National writers. Columnists. Sports editors. Backup beat writers. Television sportscasters. Radio broadcasters. Play-by-play announcers. Wire service reporters. The prized blue book also featured names and numbers for the commissioner's office, the National and American leagues, the Players Relations Committee, MLB Properties, Enterprises, International, the MLB Players Association, the National Baseball Hall of Fame, the Professional Baseball Umpire Corporation, the MLB Umpires Association, the Society for American Baseball Research, MLB Players Alumni, STATS Inc., the Elias Sports Bureau, and Baseball Chapel, among others. The book listed each team's hotel headquarters on the road and also provided a list of restaurants for visiting writers. Riley had been amazed by the amount of information crammed into the pocket-sized book.

"Just looking to see how many Marriotts we're staying at this season," Hill said. "So far I'm counting—"

"Three," Morris snapped. "Fort Lauderdale Marina Marriott for the Florida trip. The downtown Marriott for the Los Angeles trip. The Marriott Pavilion for the St. Louis trip."

"Very good, Mr. Morris," Hill said. "No wonder Marriott is thinking about retiring your platinum number."

"I can give you reviews of the nearby restaurants, tell you what the weather will probably be that day, advise you on traffic patterns, give you every flight schedule you need for our trip in and out," Morris said. "I'm so organized, it's scary."

"You got half of it right," Armour said.

"If you're smart, you'll do what I did," said Morris, obviously pleased with himself. "I'm already booked at an Athletic VIP rate at Marriotts in Atlanta, Denver, Houston, Detroit, Kansas City, Minnesota, New York, San Diego, and San Francisco. I'll have enough points to go see some offseason ball in Mexico City and also spend a couple of weeks at the Caribbean World Series."

"Don't you ever get tired of baseball?" Hill said. "Thirty exhibition games. One hundred and sixty-two regular-season games. The Division Series. The League Championship Series. The World Series. The offseason trades and signings. You're like a mutant seamhead."

"You don't become the premier baseball writer in the country by taking time off," Morris said.

"I'll pass along your humble advice to Murray Chass, Tracy Ringolsby, Phil Rogers, and the rest of those slackers the next time I see them," Hill said.

"You have no idea about baseball writing excellence," Morris said.

"Maybe not, but I notice you're still working for the *Standard*, hotshot," Hill said.

"By choice. By choice," Morris said.

"Whose choice? Yours or theirs?" Hill said.

"This conversation is over," Morris said. "We'll chat again after I scoop your ass on another story."

Morris gathered his notebook and his Tandy, grabbed his rental car keys, and headed toward the door. He didn't acknowledge Riley.

"There he goes, ladies and gentlemen," said Hill as Morris departed. "He'll be back, though. He has a matinee at one P.M."

"How do you put up with that ego?" Riley said.

"I don't," Hill said. "But let's be honest. The guy is a hell of a reporter and probably headed to the media wing of the Hall of Fame. Now there's a scary thought."

"Can you imagine that bust?" Riley said. "They'll have to remove a wall to fit his head into the building."

"The prick," Hill said. "I despise him with every sinewy fiber of my body."

"You don't have any sinewy fibers," Riley said. "You have a beer gut."

"Speaking of which, where's yours?" Hill said. "I could have sworn you were four months pregnant not long ago. What happened?"

"The art of the sit-up," Riley said, patting his tummy. "I'm doing the commit-to-get-fit thing."

"I'm very disappointed," Hill said. "What right do you have to be healthier than the rest of us? You'll make me look bad in front of my girls."

"How old?" Riley asked.

"Gracie is seventeen," Hill said. "Sadie May is twelve. Complete pains in the ass, but I love them to death."

"How do they feel about you being on the road so much?"

"They're used to it. It was hard at first, but now they barely notice I'm gone. I called a couple nights ago and Gracie was on her way out. She said she was going over to a friend's house to dye his hair blue.

I heard her mom in the background tell her to wear something less revealing. So she says, 'Daddy, why doesn't Mom realize that bras are prisons for breasts?'"

"So she takes after you?" Riley said.

"It's a push," Hill said. "Sadie May goes to St. Mike's in Wheaton. After Mass one day she asked one of the priests about one of the readings, something about Paul's letter to the Corinthians."

"Yeah, standard Mass fare."

"Standard," Hill said, "except that Sadie May wanted to know if the Corinthians ever wrote Paul back."

"How proud you must be," said Riley, pulling up a chair. "By the way, who keeps moving my computer bag in the morning?"

"Got me," said Hill. "It was there when I walked in. Morris was already here, but he had his headphones on. And one of the interns was using your table to staple some press releases."

"An intern?"

"Hey, they figure you're a rookie, too."

Gonzalez hit two home runs and Mormoa had a bases-clearing triple and a two-run double as the Cubs defeated the Padres 11–6. Mormoa was a late replacement for LeMott, who pulled a hamstring while walking down the dugout steps.

"Goddamn," fumed Braswell, "just our luck. Win a game, lose a starting second baseman." Afterward, Mormoa offered LeMott some homemade herbal tea. Said it had natural healing powers. Surprisingly enough, LeMott drank the rancid-smelling liquid.

Gonzalez, who had had a slow spring, couldn't contain his postgame excitement. As the reporters crowded around his locker, Gonzalez burst out, "I just thank God for the opportunity to thank God." Morris actually wrote it down.

Hurlock got dinged for two runs in two innings of relief, but Willingham threw well again. One hit in $1\frac{2}{3}$ innings. Afterward, Riley introduced himself.

"Feeling better about your chances?" Riley asked.

"I'm just glad I still have my name taped above this locker," he said. "There are a lot of other guys—good players, too—who weren't so lucky."

"It's not all luck," Riley said.

"Agh, I hung too many curves and my slider was all over the place," he said. "You can't do that and win in the big leagues."

"Hey, Rook," yelled Strickland from across the clubhouse. "Not bad today. You Earl Scheib–ed poor little Phil Nevin on the two-two pitch."

"Thanks," said Willingham, embarrassed by the attention.

"Keep it up, Rook," said Strickland.

Willingham adjusted the ice pack on his elbow.

"What does 'Earl Scheib–ed' mean?" Riley asked. "He's the car-paint guy from those commercials, right?"

"Yeah, you know, 'paint' the plate," Willingham said.

"I'm still learning the language," said Riley. "By the way, when does your family get in?"

"How'd you know about my family?"

"I'm sorry. I heard you telling Hurlock a few days ago. I wasn't trying to eavesdrop."

"Don't worry about it," Willingham said. "They got in late last night. We're all crammed into a little efficiency at the Mesa Motel. But it beats the alternative."

"I bet it does," Riley said. "Anyway, thanks for the time."

"Hey," said Willingham, "treat me right in your paper. I don't want to come off sounding like I've made the team."

"It's a deal," Riley said.

The FedEx package was stuck behind a potted plant near the front door of the condo. Riley had left a note with his signature authorizing delivery. He opened the box and spread the contents across the dining-room table. Then, after making himself an iced tea, Riley began reading from the first manual. He would be up until 2 A.M.

Thirteen

"Hey, Hoss, get your ass over here!"

Riley knew that voice. It was Mitchell.

"Hoss, I told you I'd come to the rescue," said the Texan, waving to Riley from behind the batting cage. "Here I am."

Riley didn't know how to react. Mitchell had promised to call days ago but never did. And his arrival at Cubs camp was expected the previous weekend. Now this. Mitchell was wearing a blue double-breasted suit, a Falconnable tie, some very expensive-looking loafers, and a new hairstyle. Compared to his previous clothing choices, Mitchell looked like an Armani ad.

"You clean up real good, Mr. Mitchell," Riley said. "Now where the hell have you been?"

"I'm sorry about that, Hoss, I truly am," said Mitchell. "These ESPN folks had me going to a broadcasting consultant so I could learn how to hold a microphone and pick out a tie. In case you're curious, they're big on red. Then I had to meet with my producer, who is a royal pain in the ass. Worst of all, I had to go to Bristol, Connecticut, which is every bit as bad as Olbermann said it was. Hoss, Dunkin Donuts is the best restaurant in that town, I kid you not."

"Pete, I'm scuffling a bit here," Riley said.

"So I hear," Mitchell said. "You use any of those phone numbers I gave you?"

"Not yet," Riley said. "You said for emergencies only."

"Hoss, from what I'm hearing, you're past emergency and headed directly to dire crisis," Mitchell said. "The word is that you're on your way to unemployment."

"It's not that bad," Riley said.

"You're right . . . it's worse," said Mitchell, tugging at his shirt collar. "Why the hell do you think I left? The corporate bigwigs are blowing out all the editorial folks they can. They don't want to settle the lockout. They've got all these temps and part-timers working for peanuts. Circulation is holding firm, profits are actually up, so why settle? And the more full-timers they can bust, the leaner their operation is."

"How do you know so much?" Riley said.

"Sources, Hoss. Sources."

"But I don't make shit," Riley said. "Anyway, I'm management. They can't fire me."

"Is that what they're telling you?" Mitchell said. "Hoss, you're laundry lint to them. They're going to keep piling the work on you, just hoping you make some noise. Then they'll cite you for insubordination or some sort of nonsense and cut you loose with some cheap severance package."

"I'm keeping up."

"Barely," said Mitchell. "I've been reading your stuff on the Internet. You're hanging in there, but you can't take many more hits on scoops."

"I'm trying, but Morris has this team wired for sound," Riley said. "He's omnipresent."

"Yeah, he can be that way. I'm damn good, but he still got me a few times, too."

Riley remembered the mystery note. "Uh, Pete, you didn't happen to drop me a line during your travels, did you?"

"Hoss, I haven't had time to blow my nose, much less write you a letter," Mitchell said. "ESPN has me going from one place to another. And Martin Scorsese over there—my *producer*, if you can believe it—has me doing all sorts of crazy things during my TV interviews. A couple of days ago we were in Phoenix shooting some video of the Diamondbacks' Bank One Ballpark. You must have seen the thing when you were flying in. The place is huge."

"I've driven by it," Riley said.

"Well, Scorsese decides he wants me to do my stand-up thing-a-ma-jig from the top of the retractable roof," Mitchell said. "I had to sign some special release, and it was so windy up there that they had to duct-tape my feet to the roof. I was scared shitless."

"I didn't see that one, Pete, and all I do is watch *Baseball Tonight* or *SportsCenter*."

"Nobody saw it. Scorsese never sent it on the satellite because he didn't like 'the aesthetic and ethereal quality of the scene.' That's what he said. It's bad enough they've got me dressed up like a Nordstrom mannequin, but the least they could do is use the frickin' video. I felt like Waldo Pepper."

"So you hate it?"

"I hate it, Hoss, until I get the paycheck."

"Well, what should I do?" Riley said. "Morris is kicking butt and taking my name as a prisoner. I can't get through to Hightower. I'm going nowhere with half the players on the roster. Braswell and Strickland are giving me some mercy interviews, but otherwise I'm semi-obsolete."

"You talk to Max yet?" Mitchell asked.

"A little. He said he'd help if he could, whatever that means."

"If Max says he'll help, he'll help. Anybody else?"

"Well, like I was saying, I got this strange envelope a couple of days ago," Riley said. "There was a note with some advice, and I thought maybe you sent it—you know, trying to be my guardian angel."

"Weren't me, Hoss. What sort of advice?"

"It said to watch out for Morris and Blair," Riley said. "The exact quote was, 'They cheat.'"

"That's it?" Mitchell said. "Hell, I could have told you to watch out for those fellers and saved somebody some envelope money. Those two boys are strange agents. Not sure, though, what that cheating stuff means."

"Me either," Riley said. "But why would somebody go through that kind of trouble?"

"Got no earthly idea. But if I were you, I'd arrange an interview with Hightower. He's got to talk to you sometime."

"And ask him what? I hear he's more secretive than Jerry Krause. Hoffman told me he has the offices screened for listening devices once a month."

"That's our Jimbo. I walked in one time and he was shredding a Papa John's takeout menu."

"My point exactly," Riley said.

"Just make it as innocent as possible," Mitchell said. "Don't even bring a notepad. Barely ask him a question about the team. Make yourself harmless. You're Bambi."

"Anything else?"

"Break a story, Hoss."

"I'll get right on it. What about you?"

"Oh, Scorsese has me doing some sort of historical piece on the Cubs," Mitchell said. "He wants me to sit out in the bleachers and pretend I'm talking to Harry. I told him I'd need two things to make it work: a case of Bud . . . and all the frickin' money ESPN has. Scorsese wasn't pleased. He said the setup would have been a perfect metaphor for 'man's struggle with immortality.' What any of that has to do with baseball . . . Anyway, Hoss, call me at the Biltmore later tonight."

Riley took the number and then found Hoffman to request an interview with Hightower. An hour later Hoffman had an answer: report to Hightower's office at 6 P.M. That would give Riley just enough time to do his daily notes, cover the afternoon game, file a second story, and then meet the great man.

First the notes. He walked down the dugout stairs, into the long runway that ran below the first base-side seats, and into the clubhouse. LeMott—who was having a very good spring—had tweaked his ankle the day before, and Riley wanted to check on the second baseman's condition.

"Got a couple of minutes?" Riley asked.

LeMott, his back to Riley, said nothing.

"Uh, Tim?"

"I hear you," said LeMott, who pulled out a tin of dip and carefully shoved half his hand into his mouth for the perfect placement of the dreadful tobacco. "Little busy here."

"Well, it's just that I'm going to be on a slightly tighter deadline after the game, so I was hoping I could ask you a couple of questions before you got started today."

LeMott turned slowly around. "Let me tell you something. Tim LeMott has Tim LeMott to think about first, second, and third. When I'm ready to talk, I'll talk."

"I'll be out of your hair in less than five minutes, Tim," Riley said.

"You ain't gonna be *in* Tim LeMott's hair, that's what I'm trying to tell you."

"Three questions, tops. Promise."

"You're hearing, but you're not listening," LeMott said. "Your questions, they for a Tim LeMott feature profile, or for or a Tim LeMott note for your inside package?"

"I'm impressed," Riley said. "You read the paper."

"Just the sports and the stock quotes," LeMott said matter-of-factly. "And your answer is . . ."

"It's for my notes."

"That's what I thought," said LeMott. "Come back when you want to talk feature. Tim LeMott doesn't waste valuable pregame preparation time on a notes package."

With that, LeMott pulled out a copy of *Hustler* and began thumbing through the pages.

"I'm leaving," said Riley, "but can I ask you a personal question, not for print or anything?"

"What?" said LeMott, preceded by an exasperated sigh.

"Why do you refer to yourself in the third person? It seems like a lot of players do that these days."

LeMott spit a trail of juice into a Styrofoam cup. "Tim LeMott doesn't feel he's obligated to answer those kind of Tim LeMott questions," said the second baseman. "Understand?"

"No," said Riley.

"Doesn't matter," said LeMott, again turning his back on the reporter.

This was what it had come to. Every day another compromise, another insult swallowed, another layer of skin separating Riley from the sports and profession he once loved. Everything had become more cynical, more unforgiving. You walked into a clubhouse and hoped for the most elementary of civilities. A simple hello. A firm handshake. A nod of polite recognition. Braswell was good that way, but he was old school. Same went for Strickland. Kasparovich still had an innocence about him, but that would probably change as he got older. What was it that Braswell said? Every player in the big leagues ought to take a lesson in professionalism from Tony Gwynn. "That son of a bitch can pick out a blade of grass in left, center, or right and hit it there," Braswell had said. "Then afterward, he'll be the most accommodating guy in the clubhouse. I'd love to manage him. He treats everybody with class."

But Braswell, Strickland, and Kasparovich were usually the exceptions in the Cubs clubhouse. More often than not, you were greeted with an annoyed glance, a dismissive grunt, an exasperated sigh. Riley could partly understand the players' attitudes. The clubhouse—now, *there* was a juvenile term—was their sacred place, their refuge. Riley and the rest of the reporters were paid to pry and question, but that didn't mean the players had to like it. At best, the beat reporters were tolerated. But no matter how many hours, days, months, or years they spent covering the team, they would always be considered outsiders.

Hill stuck his head into the clubhouse.

"Anything going on?" he said.

"Just a lot of third-person stuff," Riley said.

"Ah-ha, you talked to LeMott," Hill said. "I should have warned you."

"Joe Riley isn't about warnings," Riley said.

"LeMott's quirky that way," Hill said. "And, just so you know, he'll only do interviews for feature pieces. Try asking him something for a note, and he'll tune you out. It's like trying to tell someone about 10K split times, or your WNBA fantasy league draft."

"Late again," Riley said. "I got the brush-off a few minutes ago."

As usual, the game was a sellout at Harry Caray Stadium. It didn't matter that the regulars only played five innings, or that the quality of pitching was usually uninspired, or that a cup of beer went for $4.50, or that the no-name Padres were in town again. The Cubs were the Cubs, which meant a near-fanatical following by sunbirds and transplants. Riley couldn't fully explain the appeal, only that it was never duplicated by any other team except maybe the Yankees, possibly the Red Sox, but most definitely not the White Sox. The last time Riley had ventured to new Comiskey was during the first year of interleague play, when the Cubs visited Reinsdorf's folly. Sitting in the right field bleachers that night, Riley the fan had almost gotten into a fight with six drunken Sox fans, who kept F-bombing everything in sight. A father with his two young boys had politely asked the drunks to tone down their language. The drunks, two of them wearing their beers on their shirts, responded by dropping more F-bombs.

Riley had stepped in, only to have one of the other drunks flick a cigarette at him.

Afterward, as Riley was leaving the game (Cubs win! Cubs win!), a black stretch limo pulled up to the curb outside Comiskey. The limo's moon roof slid open and out popped three bikini-clad women waving dollar bills and tossing advertising flyers for "Imagination Gentlemen's Club." Riley remembered watching an old-timer with what appeared to be a couple of grandkids in tow. The old man, a worn Sox cap on his head, turned away from the limo and muttered, "This used to be a place for families, you know."

Wrigley was different. Mesa was different. The Cubs drew fans, real baseball fans. Sure, there was your usual share of obnoxious beer chuggers in the outfield bank beyond left field, but all in all, the people came to the Harry Caray to see baseball. They would watch in spring, hope for the best in summer, be disappointed by early fall, find shards of hope in the winter. Such were the Cubs.

Lunch in the HoHoKam Room provided no surprises. Greasy hamburgers, two-day-old potato salad, some sort of bean soup; Riley's system was almost immune to it now.

Hill and Armour sat together at a table. Riley grabbed a Coke and joined them. Armour was in mid-story.

"So I'm walking past Campbell today and he says, 'Hey, scumbag,'" said the WMVP reporter. "So I said, 'Thanks. It means so much more coming from your peers.'"

"And?" said Hill.

"Well, he didn't laugh, if that's what you mean," Armour said. 'All he kept saying was, 'I know what you're about.'"

"You know, this burger isn't so bad today," Hill said.

"Do me a favor," Armour said.

"Name it," Hill said.

"Can you close your mouth when you eat? I'm so tired of seeing your amino acids at work."

"Hold on a second, fellas," Riley said. "What does that mean, 'I know what you're about'?" Riley asked.

"It means I got ratted on," Armour said. "I'm guessing Morris."

"How'd he know?" asked Hill.

"He doesn't," Armour said. "At least, not for sure. But he saw us watching Campbell that day, remember? And knowing Morris, he probably said you guys were in on it, too."

"Figures," said Riley.

"Don't worry," said Armour. "Campbell is just trolling right now. If he really had me, he wouldn't have been so polite."

"'Hey, scumbag' is polite?" Riley said.

"For him it is," Armour said. "You should have seen him this morning. I was there early, mostly because I had to get stuff for the early show, and there he was, half passed out on the clubhouse floor. He reeked of Guinness. I didn't say a word and he never saw me come in. So I'm over in the corner, waiting for Kasparovich—he was gonna be there by 6:30—when a couple of other players started to come in. Campbell heard them walking down the hallway, pulled a towel out of his locker, and started doing sit-ups as fast as he could. He didn't know that I'm watching this from across the room. The guys come in, see Campbell doing these sit-ups, and they think he's a pro's pro, that he's been there for hours working out or something. The guys walked to the equipment room to get some new sannies, which gave Campbell just enough time to puke into the towel, wipe his face, and sneak out."

"Why'd he do that?" Hill said.

"Because he ain't the biggest stud in the hardware store anymore," Armour said.

"By the way," Hill said, "did anybody watch the Weather Channel last night?"

Riley and Armour exchanged looks.

"No, I mean it," Hill said. "Do you ever watch the Weather Channel?"

"Not on purpose," Riley said.

"I do," said Armour, "but only if there's a rerun on the French Pastry Channel."

"I'm serious," Hill said. "I've watched it ever since we got to Mesa and I swear, there isn't an anchorwoman on that station who isn't pregnant. And I'm talking like eight-and-a-half months pregnant; so big they're wearing slipcovers for clothes."

"Maybe you've got it mixed up with the Maternity Channel," Armour said.

"Or the Shawn Kemp Channel," Riley said.

"Never mind," said Hill, head down, spoon pawing at the bean soup. "It was just an observation."

"Yes, and not much of one," said Armour, piling his lunch garbage on his tray.

"Sorry, Mr. Chat Room Groupie," Hill said.

"At least I'm not a Doppler groupie," Armour said.

"He's got you there," Riley said.

"Okay, how 'bout this?" Hill said. "Are you an athlete if you can wear a watch?"

"I don't follow," Armour said.

"I contend that no person wearing a watch while playing professional sports is a true athlete," Hill said. "Boxers don't wear watches. Football players don't wear watches. Baseball players don't wear watches. Michael Jordan didn't wear a watch."

"But Phil Mickelson does," Riley said.

"You got it," Hill said. "But Jeff Gordon doesn't. Understand my point?"

"What about Michael Johnson? He wears a watch," Armour said.

"Track stars don't count," Hill said.

"Why not?" Riley said.

"Because their whole world revolves around time," Hill said. "But Phil Mickelson . . . what the hell does he need a watch for? What, he's gonna get to the fourteenth hole at Augusta, look at his watch, and say, 'Damn, I've got a pot roast to cook. I'm outta here'?"

"Goodbye," said Riley.

"Wait, I'm not done," said Hill as Riley walked out the dining-room door. "What about this two-months'-salary thing for engagement rings? Whose idea was that? It wasn't *my* idea."

Riley made his way up the stadium stairs. He could hear the National Anthem in the background, meaning the game was about to begin. As usual, the press box was packed with the daily collection of HoHos, Cubs personnel, TV crews, radio crews, visiting writers, Cubs writers, security people, the public address announcer, and the medical emergency crew. Riley took his seat and glanced to his left to see one of the San Diego writers take a swig from a small bottle of green mouthwash.

Riley motioned to Hoffman. "What's with the mouthwash?" he said.

Hoffman leaned toward Riley's right ear and lowered his voice. "It isn't mouthwash. It's vodka with green food coloring."

"You're kidding," Riley said.

"Mitchell told me," Hoffman said. "Needs it to calm his nerves. Guess he's not what he used to be on deadline."

"Who is it?" Riley asked.

"Jack Redmond," Hoffman said.

"*That's* Jack Redmond?" Riley said. "I grew up reading his notes column in *The Sporting News*. He was one of my favorite baseball columnists. What the hell happened?"

"He got old," Hoffman said. "The Padres people told me his paper offered him a retirement buyout but that he wasn't interested. They can't fire him because he's a San Diego institution. The publicity would be terrible. He's been there thirty-eight years and his wife died last July, so baseball and newspapering are all he has left. Kind of sad."

"Jesus," Riley said. "So now he sits in press boxes and chugs spiked Listerine? What kind of life is that?"

"Better than sitting in an empty house looking at wedding pictures."

"I guess so."

Riley remembered some of the stories about Redmond. According to Mitchell, Redmond came back to the Astrodome press box one time after an extra-inning game, only to find his paper's columnist, Buster Orwell, slumped over his Tele-ram. Redmond slapped him on the back, only to discover that Buster was as dead as Dickens' Jacob Marley. Redmond looked at his watch . . . looked at Buster . . . looked at his watch, and then started typing furiously on his own Tele-ram. Redmond made deadline, filed his story, and then—after making sure the desk had his copy—alerted Astrodome authorities to the condition of his former colleague.

Riley decided it was time to introduce himself to his boyhood writing hero.

"Excuse me, Mr. Redmond?" Riley said.

Redmond turned the wrong way at first. Riley could see a tan hearing aid in each of his ears. Despite the Arizona spring heat,

Redmond wore a plaid sportcoat, frayed slightly at the collar, over a white golf shirt. He had a full head of gray hair and a nose that shot out like the front of a fighter jet. But his green eyes were warm and his smile was even quicker than his handshake.

"Please, call me Jack," Redmond said. "How can I help you?"

"Just by letting me say hello and telling you how much I enjoyed reading your stuff in *The Sporting News*. I'm Joe Riley. I'm with the *Sentinel* in Chicago."

"A fine paper," said Redmond. "Sorry to hear about your labor troubles. Never had to worry about union shops in San Diego."

"They come in handy whenever management decides to downsize, which is happening about every other year at our place," Riley said.

Redmond's eyes flared ever so slightly at the mention of downsizing. Riley winced at the reaction. How stupid to have mentioned it.

"I understand," said Redmond, his voice softening. "How can I be of service, young man?"

"Oh, I don't need anything," said Riley. "I just wanted to say hello."

"You know, young man, I'm an old fart, and I wear two hearing aids, and my prostate is giving me trouble, but I've still got a few contacts in this business," he said. "Baseball is a closed community, so don't get too frustrated."

"You've heard?" Riley said.

"A few things here and there," said Redmond, double-checking the lineup on his scorebook to the just-amended lineup issued by the Cubs' PR staff. "There aren't many secrets in our business, you know that."

"I'll be fine," said Riley, embarrassed that apparently the entire Cactus League knew of his struggles. "I'm guessing it was probably more fun to do this job thirty-five years ago, eh?"

"Don't kid yourself," Redmond said. "Ted Williams could be as prickly as an Arizona cactus. And Tommy Lasorda could sweet talk the visiting sisters of Saint Mary's Convent and then ten seconds later mother-*f* you until your ears needed ice packs."

"Lasorda did that?"

"That's just the way he was. Big heart, small vocabulary."

For some reason Riley trusted Redmond. "Any advice? This beat is wearing me down," he said.

"I'm not Ann Landers," said the old man. "All I can tell you is that you'll never get rich doing this job. You'll never get a weekend off. You'll never have a flat stomach. You'll never find a player who will accept you as a true equal. Being on the road is a pain in the ass. Press-box coffee tastes like motor oil. There's no overtime pay, and most of these young reporters would rather go back to their hotel room after a game and log on to AOL than find a good bar. And you know what? I wouldn't trade a single second of my working life for Albert Belle's weekly paycheck. That answer your question?"

"Not really," Riley said. "How do you do this day after day?"

"Because I still find the purity in it," Redmond said. "For every hundred Reggie Jacksons, there's one Cal Ripken. And that's enough for me. I saw Nolan Ryan pitch two no-hitters. His fastball left contrails. I saw Koufax, Gibson, Mantle, Aaron, and Maris. I was there when McGwire broke the home run record. It took an hour for my goosebumps to recede. Every time I think about retiring, I think about the moments I'd miss. I guess I'm being selfish."

"I'm not exactly planning on doing this for thirty-eight years," Riley said.

"Doesn't matter," Redmond said. "You want my advice? Here's what I'm going to tell you: I'm seventy-one and I'm hoping to make it long enough to see Junior break Hank's record. Live for the moments."

Then he tugged at Riley's shirt, pulling him closer. Redmond's breath was raw. Vodka left no odor.

"Morris is a son of a bitch," Redmond said. "I know it. You know it. He knows it. Give him a taste of his own medicine."

"Easier said than done," Riley said.

"Easier said, absolutely delicious when done," said Redmond, smiling.

"I'll keep that in mind."

Redmond started coughing. It went on for minutes. Riley tapped him lightly on the back.

"I'm fine," Redmond said. "Thanks for introducing yourself. Not many of the youngsters do that anymore."

"It was an honor," Riley said.

"To talk to me?" said Redmond, the cough now gone. "Nah. Now, talking to Jim Murray, bless his soul, *that* was an honor. But me? I'm just trying to make it to Opening Day."

Riley returned to his seat. Later, he caught Redmond taking another nip. By the sixth inning of the dreadful exhibition game (Cubs 14, Padres 4 . . . 12 different pitchers), Redmond was nodding off.

At game's end, Riley helped Redmond to the elevator and walked him to the Padres' clubhouse. "I'm going there anyway," Riley said.

"Bullshit, young man," Redmond said. "But I appreciate the straight face."

Riley smiled.

After dropping Redmond off, Riley jogged to the Cubs' clubhouse, listened to Braswell for a few minutes, talked to Gesser, Gonzalez, and Willingham (another scoreless inning of relief), sprinted up the stairs to the press box, wrote several forgettable stories, filed, and then reported to Hightower's office.

Hightower's secretary was gone by then. So Riley knocked lightly on the office door.

"I'm busy," Hightower said. "Just empty the trash can under my secretary's desk and make sure the floors are vacuumed tomorrow. Thank you."

Great, thought Riley. Hightower had forgotten about the appointment. Actually, Hightower knew exactly who was knocking on the door. This was a test. Hightower was a big believer in personality profiles. Would Riley slink away, too embarrassed to say anything? Would Riley react angrily? Would Riley regain his composure and knock again?

Riley stood in front of the door and considered tiptoeing his way out of the office. He'd make another appointment. But something told him to knock again. Perhaps this was one of those moments Redmond was talking about.

"Mr. Hightower, this is Joe Riley of the *Sentinel*. I was told to be here at 6:15."

Hightower glanced at his desk clock—6:15 on the dot. At least the guy was punctual. And he didn't ding-dong ditch, did he?

"Come in," Hightower said dryly.

Riley opened the door and found an office rich in walnut-paneled walls. On the credenza behind Hightower's impressive Victorian desk was a row of three 13-inch televisions. Another wall held a steel-framed whiteboard that featured small magnetic strips—for every name of every player on every big league roster. Major leaguers were in red, minor leaguers in blue. Righthanded pitchers in black, lefthanders in yellow.

Two bookshelves held the media guides of every team in both the American and National leagues. There were also a dozen or so thick, blue, three-ring folders, each featuring a single Cubs decal on the spine. Riley figured they were some sort of organizational scouting reports. Next to the bookshelves was a trio of detailed maps, one of North America, another of Central America, another of South America. Pins and notations marked various cities. There was a smaller, less detailed map of Japan and South Korea.

"Through looking?" Hightower said.

"Oh," said Riley, startled by the comment. "I'm sorry. Somebody told me you could tell a lot about a person by the office they keep."

"Who told you that?" said Hightower, instantly suspicious. "Somebody in this organization?"

"No, I think I read it in our Lifestyle section," Riley said. "Something about the decorating traits of the world's most successful businesspeople."

"And the conclusion was what?" Hightower said, suddenly interested.

"Semigloss over flat."

"Was that a joke?"

"Apparently not much of one," Riley said.

Hightower frowned. *A ballsy entrance, I'll give him that. Paint line actually not too bad. I like the lack of patronizing. Hoffman said not to underestimate him.*

"How can I help you, Mr. Riley?"

"You can call me Joe, sir." Riley waited for Hightower to offer a similar first-name arrangement. It never came. "I'm basically here to introduce myself. I should have done it weeks ago, but frankly, I've been struggling to keep my head above water."

"So I've heard," Hightower said. "How does any of this relate to me?"

"Well, you're the keeper of the information," Riley said.

"And that's where it will stay, too," said Hightower, pretending to look at the day's pitching chart. "I'm not in the habit of sharing details of this organization with members of the media."

This was true. Hightower had a reputation for saying as little as possible. He had played small forward for Dean Smith at North Carolina, where he learned Dean's secretive ways: speak only when necessary, reveal nothing to outsiders, keep everything within the family. He had been a serviceable hoops player, but it was in baseball that he excelled. Blessed with a curveball that defied physics, he led the Tar Heels to the College World Series in 1977 and was picked by the Cubs in the second round of the June draft. He was later traded to the Mets, then to the Rangers, then back to the Cubs, where he promptly blew out his arm. His eight-year record was 47–54, with a 4.09 earned run average. It was said that you never crept too close to the plate against Hightower, unless of course you wanted your beard trimmed. Problem was, the curveball turned his right arm into mush. It was also said that no player knew the game better than Hightower. And Hightower—who negotiated his own contracts—earned the grudging respect of management for his knowledge of the business of the game.

After he retired, Hightower went to law school in his home state at the University of Florida, earned his degree, passed the Florida bar, and was ready to join a small law firm in Coral Gables when he got a call from the Cubs. Would he be interested in becoming the team's director of minor leagues? Hightower figured he could practice copyright law some other time. So he took the Cubs' offer and four years later was promoted to vice president/general manager. He was no dummy, this James Edward Hightower. At least, that's what the clips said. Riley had read every one of them twice.

"I'm not asking for any favors, just an even playing field," Riley said.

"I don't understand your point," Hightower said.

Riley took a deep breath. "Well, I know I'm new here, but I was hoping . . ."

"Are you saying I play favorites?" Hightower said, leaning forward in his high-back leather chair.

"Not favorites, exactly," said Riley. "But Morris does seem to have a knack of getting scoops on this beat."

"Are you suggesting what I think you're suggesting?"

Uh-oh. Riley had overplayed his thin hand. "This is coming out wrong," he said.

"Let me detail my philosophy concerning the media: I do not offer information," Hightower said sternly. "I do not speak off the record. I do not gossip. I do not criticize players or staff. I do not socialize with reporters."

"But Morris is always at your office," Riley said.

"Yes, but there is a difference between being 'at' my office and being 'in' it," Hightower said. "That is a distinction you need to appreciate if you wish to better understand my relationship with the media."

"But can you see how I might think he has an unfair advantage?"

"Mr. Morris is here every day," Hightower said. "And every day I give him the same information I've given you this evening."

"But you haven't given me any information," Riley said.

"You appear to be catching on, Mr. Riley," said Hightower, resuming his fake reading of the pitching report.

Wait a second, thought Riley. *Why the daily show of force from Morris?* Was it for effect, or did he have other sources in the office?

"But if I have a story, you'll confirm it, won't you?" Riley said.

"If you truly have the story, yes, I will serve as a confirming source," Hightower said. "That's always been my policy."

"But Morris . . ."

"Mr. Riley, perhaps you should speak to Mr. Morris about your concerns," Hightower said. "I have a baseball team to run. You'll receive no extra consideration from me, which is how I also deal with Mr. Morris and the rest of the media contingent. There are no ethical dilemmas that way, no double standards, and no mixed messages. Now, if you'll excuse me, I'm expecting an important phone call."

"Mind if I listen in?" Riley said.

Hightower began to glare, but caught himself.

"Another joke, I presume?" he said.

"Another joke, sir," said Riley, closing the office door behind him.

This time Hightower allowed himself a grin. *Better than the paint joke.*

Riley was back at the condo by 6:45. He left a message for Mitchell at the hotel and then changed into shorts and a T-shirt. He did 100 sit-ups, 50 push-ups, and lasted 30 minutes on the rented Stairmaster, all the time listening to one of the mail-order CDs. The beer gut was now manageable, the love handles no longer the size of water balloons. He was getting there.

He took a shower and then had a chicken-salad sandwich. The Old Style was dessert.

"Damn. Forgot to check the mail."

He put on a pair of Top Siders and walked out to the end of the driveway where the building's mailbox was located. There were 10 separate compartments, one for each unit in the building. There it was, 101-A. Pinched into the edge of his box was a small manila envelope, similar to the one he had recently found outside his door.

Joe Riley, it read.

Riley looked around, took the envelope, unlocked the box, and retrieved a cable and electric bill. Then he half-jogged back to the condo. Once inside, he opened the envelope.

The note obviously had been typed on a computer and printed with an ink jet printer. There were three lines.

Harris won't pitch tomorrow.
Wonder why?
Won't be for reasons they say.

Riley read the note again. And again. And another time before going to sleep. Despite giving him the cold shoulder for being "scab material," Harris had pitched spectacularly during his five spring training relief appearances. The Cubs hadn't had much luck with free agent signings in the past, but Harris looked like he was worth every bit of the three-year, $24.6 million deal (with a player's option for a fourth year). His fastball was a white blur, and he had a changeup that left hitters lunging at the ball as if they had no equilibrium. Harris was also working on a split-finger pitch. And wouldn't that be a bitch to hit if he mastered it?

But why wouldn't he pitch tomorrow? And who was sending Riley these notes?

Riley put the note on the bedside table and then placed the headphones on his ears. He would fall asleep to the soothing, monotonous sounds of his new instructor.

Fourteen

MORRIS WAS ALREADY IN THE CLUBHOUSE when Riley arrived at 7:10.

"Late again," smirked Morris, who spat a grotesque stream of spittle and tobacco juice into his McDonald's coffee cup and made his way toward LeMott's locker.

Riley ignored him. He had more important things to do than spar with Morris.

As casually as possible, Riley glanced at Harris's locker. His street clothes were on hangers, but no Harris. There was a cup of orange juice on his chair, and a container of strawberry-banana yogurt.

Riley looked around the room. Little San Juan was subdued. Strickland was reading the sports section. Mormoa was thumbing through *The New York Times*' Week in Review section from Sunday's paper. Campbell was trying to pop a zit on his right shoulder.

"Hey, Rook," Campbell said to Kasparovich, "how 'bout a little help on this?"

"How 'bout you find another pus popper?" said Kasparovich, recoiling at the sight of Campbell's shoulder. "No rookie has to do that kind of stuff."

"One good squeeze, that's all I need," said Campbell, trying to reach back with his left hand. "I'll give you twenty bucks."

"No way," Kasparovich said. "Get one of the clubbies."

"I already asked," Campbell said. "They want fifty."

Blair, Hill, and Armour were in the clubhouse by 7:30. Nadel and Danger had a live shoot at 8:15 on the field with Braswell.

At exactly 7:55, five minutes before the players were supposed to be on the field for stretching, Harris emerged from a small room just off the free-weight room. The area around his left elbow was pinkish-red, which is what happens when you keep your arm in a bucket of ice for an extended period of time.

Nobody else saw Harris as he hurriedly put on a long-sleeve warm-up shirt, and then a Mizuno windbreaker. Riley thought about approaching him, but thought better of it. Morris was still in the clubhouse and Blair was lurking nearby, talking to Delagotti. Better to sit back and observe.

Harris stretched but didn't play any long toss with the other pitchers. In fact, Riley didn't see Harris throw the ball overhand once during the brief workout. He took part in the first base cover drill (Hurlock had botched the play a day earlier, prompting Braswell to schedule a remedial session) and then reported to the batting cages for bunting drills.

None of this meant a whole lot. Pitchers routinely got their arms iced. And so what if Harris hadn't done much in the morning session? With a game scheduled that afternoon at Harry Caray, it wasn't uncommon for the players—especially pitchers—to take it easy.

Harris hadn't pitched in Monday's blowout win, but with the regular season fast approaching, he no doubt would be on Braswell's Tuesday list of pitchers who needed work. The ninth inning—save time—would belong to Harris.

Sure enough, the Cubs led the Mariners 3–2 going into the eighth inning. Riley looked over to the Cubs' bullpen, only to see Willingham, not Harris, warming up for the ninth. Riley said nothing, but Armour couldn't help himself.

"Hey, our boy Harris isn't budging," Armour said to no one in particular. "That's two days in a row."

Riley saw Morris instantly look at the bullpen.

"Great," muttered Riley.

"What?" said Hill.

"Nothing."

"Armour's right," Hill said. "It isn't like Braswell to go easy on relievers. He likes them to get lots of work in the spring."

"He probably wants to see Willingham one more time before he cuts him," Nadel said.

"Probably," said Armour. "But still . . . two days in a row?"

Willingham pitched the ninth, gave up a single, got a double play, and then coaxed a fly ball out of Jay Buhner to end the game. Nobody cared. The first postgame question to Braswell came from Morris.

"Skip, is something wrong with Harris? That's the second straight day you haven't used him."

Braswell stood near the dugout, took his hat off, wiped his brow with his sleeve, and then aimed a sunflower shell at a patch of browning bermuda grass. It was the first time Riley had seen the manager stall for time.

"Nah, nothing wrong with Harris," he said. "I just wanted to take another look-see at that Willingham kid. I know what Harris can do."

"Harris didn't seem like he did much this morning, either," said Nadel.

Damn, thought Riley. *Nadel had noticed that, too?*

"Campbell didn't do much, either, fellas," Braswell said. "I'm trying to go a little easier on the vets, that's all. We've got some big cuts coming up and I want to make sure I give the borderline guys a couple of extra chances."

"So nothing's wrong with Harris?" Morris said.

Braswell paused. "Okay, there's a little something wrong, but you guys got to promise me it stays out of the papers, off the radio, and off TV."

"I don't know if we can do that," Hill said.

"Look, y'all got jobs to do, I understand that," Braswell said. "But Harris has some personal matters to deal with. Now he asked me to tell you that if you'll give him a couple of days, he'll talk to you about it. All he wants is a couple of days."

"Does he have a drug problem?" Blair said.

"Son, you just used up your stupid-question allotment for the year," Braswell said. "Next."

"So you're asking us to sit on a story? I can't do that, Braz," Armour said.

"You got to do what you got to do," Braswell said. "But *I* don't even know what's going on."

"Can you at least tell us if he has a physical condition?" Hill said.

"Can't do it," Braswell said.

"Will he pitch tomorrow?" asked Hill.

"Don't know. But I do know Harris said he'll give you the full story in a day or two, but only if you don't write anything about it until then. Those are his conditions, not mine, fellas."

"Braz, my station will never agree to that," Armour said. "You're talking about an all-star reliever, a big-time free agent signing, and the key guy in your bullpen. He's not pitching, and we're supposed to keep quiet?"

"I didn't say it was a perfect situation," Braswell said. "How the hell do you think I feel? I'm caught in the middle of this shit. But I can guarantee you this: Harris ain't talking, and nobody else knows what the hell is going on."

Riley kept quiet, but he already knew what he had to do. There was no way he could ignore the story. Armour was right: They couldn't agree to Harris's conditions. Plus, there was no guarantee that Morris or the others wouldn't try breaking the story. And that's all Riley needed, another big story without his byline.

Whoever had written that note had inside information. Harris didn't pitch. And for the moment, Harris was hiding behind "personal reasons." The note said to disregard the official explanation.

Riley decided there was only one person who could help him. After working the clubhouse—Harris was long gone—Riley slipped outside and around the corner of the building. He remembered the secret knock sequence and tapped away. Two knocks. Then four knocks. Then two knocks. A few moments later came four knocks from inside.

Riley paused and knocked once. The door opened. Max stood at the doorway, an unlit chewed cigar hanging from his mouth.

"Is that one of the Macanudos?"

"The last one," Max said. "How'd you remember the sequence?"

"Morse code is my second language."

Max gestured for Riley to come in. "You must have a good reason for coming here," Dewitt said. "Or did you want a cup? Nothing worse than getting your balls banged at the batting cage."

"Very funny, Craig Kilborn," Riley said.

"Who?" said Dewitt, unfamiliar with any TV personality who worked after 10 P.M.

"Craig Kilborn. On late at night."

"The infomercial guy with the big teeth and helicopter? The guy looks like Mr. Ed."

"Yeah," said Riley, giving up, "that's him, the infomercial guy. By the way, do you own a television?"

"Black-and-white Philco," Dewitt said. "Solid-state circuitry. Aluminum-foil antenna. Works fine."

"Ever hear of cable?"

"She that wrestling woman?"

"No, that's *Sable*. Cable is . . . never mind."

"Look, Riley, I'd love to sit here and chat about TV with you, but I've got work to do," Dewitt said. "State your business."

"You said if I got stuck on a story, you might help me," Riley said. "Well, I'm stuck."

"I said I might point you in the right direction, nothing else."

"I need pointing."

"Then tell me what you got," said Dewitt, sitting on the corner of his desk.

"And this stays between you and me, right?" Riley said.

"Do I look like the kind of guy who talks?" Dewitt said. "Now, what do you have?"

"Okay, Harris has an injured left elbow," Riley said excitedly. "He can't throw. He didn't pitch today because of so-called personal reasons. That's what he's telling Braswell. I don't believe Harris. I saw him come out of the training room today after taking some treatment on the elbow. He didn't want anyone to see him. He also didn't throw a thing during morning drills, and he certainly didn't warm up in the ninth. So I've got something here, but I'm not a hundred percent sure."

"Why don't you ask Hightower?"

"Braswell said nobody knows anything. Harris isn't saying a word about it. But I bet you know."

Dewitt spun the gnarled cigar in his mouth. He was deciding.

"Max, this doesn't hurt the team," Riley said. "I've got the story. I just need confirmation."

"All right, you did your homework on this one," said Dewitt.

"You mean he blew his arm out?" Riley could hardly contain his excitement.

"Don't go sounding happy about it," Dewitt said. "Harris might be a prick, but he's our prick and a damn good reliever. And we need him."

"Sorry, Max. I didn't mean to sound so pleased," Riley said. "It's just that this is the first story I've broken since I got here."

"I don't give a damn about your story," Dewitt said. "But if you're gonna write it, I want to make sure it's right. Harris didn't blow out his arm, yet. He's gonna get an MRI first thing in the morning. Then we'll know for sure. That's probably why he wants to wait to talk to you guys."

"How'd you know about that?" Riley said. "Braswell just told us a few minutes ago."

Dewitt rolled his eyes.

"Sorry, I forgot. You know all, see all, hear all."

"Now you've got it."

"So I can go with this?"

"Just be careful," Dewitt said. "Don't even think about quoting me. And don't get too ambitious with your analysis. The MRI might show nothing more than a strained tendon or something. Let's hope so."

"Fair enough."

"Okay, my turn," Dewitt said.

"Anything you want," Riley said. "More Macanudos?"

"Nope," said Dewitt. "But I want to know why you followed Harris this morning."

"Just a hunch," Riley said.

"A hunch, huh? You sure that's all?"

"I might have had a little help. Why?"

"Just wondering," said Dewitt. "Now get out of here. I've got some new inventory coming in. Somebody has to check it."

"Max, thanks again," said Riley as he opened the door.

"Didn't do a thing," said Dewitt. "You did all the heavy lifting."

Riley tried walking toward the press box, but his heart was racing too fast. He broke into a measured jog. For the first time in weeks, Riley felt like an actual reporter. He had a story. *His* story. This is how Rat must have felt when he was breaking stories on the Hawks.

Riley turned the corner, jogged past the clubhouse and up the stairs to the press box. He never saw Morris hiding behind one of the field-level concession stands.

About 80 Percent Luck

The first few paragraphs:

By Joe Riley
Sentinel Staff Writer

MESA, Ariz.—*Newly acquired all-star reliever Casey Harris will undergo an MRI today to determine the extent of an injury to his $24.6 million left arm, the Sentinel has learned.*

Harris was unavailable for comment and team officials declined to speculate on his condition, mostly because the 28-year-old closer scheduled the test on his own and without notifying Cubs management of the injury. Harris suffered tendinitis in his pitching elbow three years ago while with the Atlanta Braves, resulting in his first and only career stay on the 15-day disabled list. Since then, Harris has led the major leagues in saves. His offseason signing with the Cubs was supposed to fill a glaring need in the team's battered bullpen.

That was the gist of the story as it appeared in the paper. Butler held the story out of the early edition—no reason to give anybody a chance to catch up, right?—and ran it in the final. WMVP got it at 12:30, called Hightower at his Mesa condo (answering machine), and credited Riley and the *Sentinel* with the scoop.

"You finally did it," said Butler, after the final edit.

"You sound disappointed," said Riley, ignoring the backhanded compliment.

Butler was disappointed, mostly in himself. He had been thinking about it for days. How had he become such a company stooge? Why hadn't he stood up to Jarrett? No more of that. Time to be a sports editor again. Time to support his staff, or what was left of it.

"Any more from where that one came from?" asked Butler.

"I'm trying," Riley said.

Screw Jarrett, thought Butler, surprising himself with his sudden display of nerve.

"You keep knocking 'em dead, Snapper," said Butler. "Talk to you later."

Riley hung up the phone and let out a small whoop. What a high he was on. He couldn't wait to see Morris's face in the morning. It was about time that Morris munched on a breakfast of whup-ass. And what was the deal with Butler calling him 'Snapper'? He hadn't called him that in years, since his first year at the *Sentinel*.

Riley felt like celebrating, but it would have been in poor taste to call Hill, Nadel, or Armour. It would have seemed like gloating, especially since they'd be chasing the story. Megan had left her number on his machine about a week ago, but after seeing her with Strickland that night, maybe it was best to steer clear. What was that bumper sticker Riley had seen earlier in the day? WANTED: MEANINGFUL OVERNIGHT RELATIONSHIP. That's what Riley wanted.

Or was it?

Riley found Megan's hotel number in the white pages. What the hell, he thought.

"The Phoenician Hotel. How can I help you?" said the voice.

Riley still couldn't believe the paper's advertising people stayed at the Phoenician, while he was stuck in a retiree's one-bedroom condo with orange shag carpeting overlooking a Safeway parking lot. "Uh, yes, can you ring Megan Donahue's room, please?"

"My pleasure," said the hotel operator.

Six rings, no answer. Riley hung up when the hotel message system began its recording. He looked at the microwave clock. It was almost 11. The girl kept late hours.

There were two Old Styles in the fridge. Riley pulled out a frosted mug, poured the beer just so (only a hint of foam), and toasted himself.

"To your first scoop, Woodward," he said, clanging mug with bottle.

"Right back at you, Bernstein," he said.

He took a long swig and considered his situation. Max had come through big time, but he wouldn't be able to use that card very often. He now knew Hightower was like Switzerland: absolutely neutral when it came to Morris and the other writers. But Riley didn't have a clue who his mystery informant was. It wasn't Max, that much was clear. Max was too loyal to the Cubs to leave breadcrumbs for Riley. That left everybody else in the Valley of the Sun.

For the moment, Riley didn't care. He'd try solving that puzzle some other time. He took another swig of Chicago's finest and picked up the phone again. Speed dial. Same operator. Same hotel message.

Riley popped the hat off the second beer, sank into the couch, and caught the late edition of *SportsCenter*.

There was a Cubs highlight from the exhibition win and then a mug shot of Harris. Riley fumbled for the remote control and turned up the volume.

"In other baseball news, the *Chicago Sentinel* is reporting in its morning edition that star reliever Casey Harris will have an MRI on his left pitching elbow. Harris isn't talking about the situation, and neither are the Cubs."

Riley was on a scoop high. His first *SportsCenter* mention. The phone rang. *Bless her heart*, thought Riley; Mom had stayed up to watch in Chicago.

"Nice job, bunny boy," said the voice.

Mom never called him "bunny boy." It was Megan.

"You saw it?"

"Yeah, they've got cable and running water and sheets and everything here at the hotel," she said.

"I've read about the Phoenician," Riley said. "Very expensive."

"We've got a tradeout deal with them," she said. "We cut them a price for ads in the Sunday travel section and they do the same for us."

"Tell them they need to advertise in the sports section," Riley said. "I've got the only condo in America decorated in Early Doily."

"Sounds romantic."

There was an awkward silence. Riley couldn't help himself.

"So, how'd it go with Strickland the other night?"

"Oh, Brett? Good guy," she said. "We had a wonderful time. I think he's going to do the deal."

"Was that before or after the palm reading?"

"Both," she said, her tone turning justifiably icy. "Not that it's any of your business. I was just calling to tell you congratulations, but I should have known better. I thought your scoop might have taken some of the edge off your woe-is-me routine."

"I was just curious," Riley said.

"No, you were just jealous," she said. "Anyway, you really shouldn't spend this kind of time on the phone. You're depriving some poor village of its idiot."

"I deserved that."

"No kidding."

"I tried calling a little while ago," he said. "I thought maybe if I got my stuff done in time, and you're not too busy, and no stories break, and . . ."

"Are you asking me out?" said Megan, her voice playful again.

"No, I figured we'd go straight to getting lavaliered, then pinned," he said.

"Why are you so fluent in Greek? You weren't a frat rat, were you?"

"No, GDI."

"GDI?"

"Goddamn Independent," he said. "But I dated a Tri-Delt for four years. I know all the terms."

"You still haven't answered my question," she said.

"You're going to make me work for this, aren't you."

"Absolutely," she said. "I like it when a man has to get in touch with his feminine side."

Riley took a deep breath. "Yes, I'm asking you out. There, I said it. Tomorrow night. I'll pick you up in my Aston-Martin, equipped with the latest gadgets from Q. Then we'll fly to Rio for Carnival. Either that, or we'll go to Tempe and get a couple of top-shelf margaritas at Chili's."

"Tomorrow night?"

"Problem?"

"Kind of," she said. "We're hosting a dinner and cocktail party for some heavy hitters out of Chicago. They're here for a few days to watch some Cubs games, play some golf. We need their ad dollars, so we're wining and dining them. I've got to be at this thing tomorrow night."

"If I had a nickel for every time I've heard that one," said Riley.

"Why don't you come?"

"To the dinner thing?" Riley said. "I'm not a business-dinner type of guy. I'll use the wrong fork or something. I'd be like Tom Hanks in *Big* and eat those little corn-on-the-cob things with my fingers. You'd be embarrassed."

"No, really, I want you to come," she said. "You can skip the dinner part if you want. That might work out better since I'll be busy schmoozing with the clients then. But I can only be shallow and charming to these people for so long. Come for the free after-dinner booze. I'll make sure there's lots of rancid Old Style."

"Deal," said Riley. "What time?"

"About seven," she said. "The reception room will be posted at the concierge desk."

"See you then," Riley said. "I'll be the one wearing blue-jean cut-offs and a 'Dy-no-mite!' tank top."

"Perfect," Megan said. "I'll be the one instructing hotel security to escort you off the premises. 'Night. And congratulations on the story."

Riley hung up the phone. He was nervous. Excited. Proud of himself. Some of it was the beer talking, some of it was the rush of breaking a story, of asking the honorary cheesehead out on a date. Better yet, she had been the one to invite Riley to the reception. That had to be a good sign.

He'd have to get his one pair of khakis pressed, and it probably wouldn't hurt to get his aged blue blazer cleaned and pressed, too. The last time he wore the sportcoat was almost 14 months ago, the night of his ill-fated blind date with Helen, the former homecoming queen at Flossmoor High who now worked at the Beverly Area Planning Association. Who knew that she was also a voodoo priestess? Riley didn't until she invited him into her apartment at date's end and—as she was making a couple cups of decaf—casually explained why there was dried chicken blood on the Blair Witch posters on her kitchen walls. The date ended moments later.

This was different . . . Megan was different. Maybe he ought to buy a new blazer. A mock turtleneck might not be a bad idea, either. Riley hoisted his beer mug a final time.

"Here's to romance," he said.

Hill's Grand Am was already in the stadium parking lot when Riley pulled in the next morning at 7:15. Nearby were Blair's Geo, Nadel's WGN van, and Armour's Lumina. Nobody knew where Morris parked his car.

Riley dropped his laptop off at the media workroom and then

reported to the clubhouse. Armour saw him first.

"Asshole. But I mean it in a good way," Armour said.

"You know what they say . . . Even a blind acorn finds a squirrel," Riley said.

"Yeah, Yogi Berra says that," Armour said. "Anyway, Hightower's pissed because I called him so late. And he's really pissed because he can't figure out how you got the story."

Hoffman and Hill joined the conversation.

"I nurture you, look after you, shower you with wisdom that would cost big bucks on the open market, and this is how you reward me?" Hill said. "You beat my ass on a story?"

"It was about eighty percent luck," Riley said.

"Whatever it was, Hightower is trying to find the leak," Hoffman said. "He takes leaks very seriously."

"All he'll get from me is name, rank, and Macintosh serial number," Riley said.

"I'm not kidding," Hoffman said. "Hightower didn't even know about the MRI."

"Then how the hell did Halberstam here get it?" said Armour.

"Just good old-fashioned American journalism, that's all," said Riley, enjoying the moment.

"Any word on Harris?" asked Hill.

"We might have something by the end of the day," Hoffman said. "Harris has told me to tell you that he won't be available for interviews."

"He said that?" Armour said.

"Not counting the F-bombs, yeah," said Hoffman.

"Anybody seen Morris or Blair?" Nadel asked.

"They're lurking around," Hoffman said. "Morris looked more mad than Hightower. Morris doesn't like to get beaten on stories."

"He didn't talk to me for three months when I got the salary figures before he did," Hill said.

"Lucky you," Riley said.

"You don't understand," Nadel said. "This is personal to him. He won't rest until he humbles you."

"Crushes you," Hill said.

"Grinds you into ash," Armour said.

"And speak of the grinder . . ." Hoffman said.

Morris strode into the room with Blair trailing at a respectful five feet. He saw Riley and made a beeline for the group.

"Good morning, R.J.," Hoffman said.

Morris ignored him. Instead, he stared at Riley.

"Something wrong, R.J.? My sideburns aren't even?" Riley said.

"You think you've got me, but you don't," Morris said. "One story, that's all it was. But I'm on to you."

"This sounds like a scene from *Chinatown*," Riley said.

"Or *One Flew Over the Cuckoo's Nest*," Hill said.

"Shut up," Morris said. "This is between Riley and me."

"You're not taking your Ritalin anymore, are you?" said Riley. "Look, you want to make this into something, fine, go ahead. I'm not going anywhere."

"That's not what I hear," Morris said, smiling. "Bye, bye."

"Gawd, he's a strange agent," said Riley, as Morris left the clubhouse.

"What'd he mean by the 'That's not what I hear' line?" Armour said.

"I think it has something to do with our lockout," Riley said. "I think I'm on the job bubble."

"Not after today, you aren't," Nadel said.

"Don't be so sure," Riley said. "Butler has been dropping some weird hints to me. I can't figure out if he's trying to help me or backstab me. But I needed this one, believe me."

"They can't fire you from a job you never wanted, can they?" Hoffman said.

"According to them, they can do just about anything they want," Riley said. "If I didn't take the Cubs, I was a goner. If I took the Cubs, but didn't do what they told me, I was a goner. Now Morris says I might be a goner anyway."

"He's just trying to mess with your mind," Nadel said. "He's done it with all of us."

"And what happened?" Riley asked.

"I was in therapy for months," said Armour. "I'm still haunted by him. The facial tic is gone, though."

"And with that, I've got to go back to work," Hoffman said. "I'll let you know if we release something about Harris. See you at the game."

The Cubs played the Anaheim Angels at Tempe's Diablo Stadium. Depending on traffic, you could get from Mesa to Tempe in about 30 minutes. Riley got there moments before the team charter bus pulled into the gated parking lot. Braswell was always the first person off the bus, mostly because he had the first two rows to himself. The coaching staff was next, followed by Strickland, Little San Juan, the remainder of the veterans, whatever non-roster players remained, and then Kasparovich.

As the other players made their way to the visitors' clubhouse, Kasparovich waited near the side of the bus. He was wearing a WCW T-shirt, his game pants, and a pair of Griffey cross-trainers.

"Kaspo, whatcha doing?" said Riley, who had begun to talk in baseball-speak. Baseball-speak is when you add an *i-e* or an *o* to the end of every name on the roster.

"Aw, Lakie [Bob Lake] said I had to carry his bats to the clubhouse," Kasparovich said. "Says he doesn't trust anybody else. You know, more hazing shit."

"Only a few more days and you're free," Riley said.

"Nah, they say it's just as bad during the regular season," Kasparovich said. "That's okay. I'd rather be somebody's bellhop in the big leagues than spend another year in Triple A. You think I've made the team? I mean, I've had my share of at-'ems and I've been on the wrong end of the highlight tape."

That's how ballplayers are—always paranoid. Kasparovich was hitting .311 and had three home runs, including one that needed radar clearance for landing. The "at-'ems" were line drives hit directly at someone. No shame in that. And in something of a surprise, the oafish-looking rookie fielded the position with remarkable agility. He was no Eddie Coffey—the former Cubs all-star and annual Gold Glove winner who had retired a season earlier—but he wasn't a defensive liability like the Sox's Frank Thomas. Kasparovich was an Opening Day starter if there ever was one.

"I think you can probably put a deposit down on an apartment in Chicago," Riley said. "Hammler has had a good spring, but I think you're safe."

"I hope you're right," he said, pulling Lake's bag from the storage area in the bus's midsection. "With my luck, I'll break my leg or something."

Kasparovich broke his ankle in the third inning. Darin Erstad pulled a sharp grounder down the line, which Kasparovich fielded cleanly. Kasparovich waved off Campbell, who was sprinting from the pitcher's mound to cover first. But Campbell didn't see the rookie's gesture, and all three players—Erstad, Campbell, and Kasparovich—arrived at first base at exactly the same time. There was a sickening thud, the kind of noise made by dropping a five-pound bag of flour from a rooftop. Campbell caromed off Erstad; Erstad bounced toward the first base coaching box; and Kasparovich was sandwiched between the two, his left foot catching the bottom of the bag, his ankle snapping almost in two.

As Erstad and Campbell staggered to their feet, Kasparovich lay on the ground, his body twitching as if he were connected to an electroshock machine. Stevie D gently rolled him over on his back and instantly noticed the left foot pointed at a grotesque angle. Kasparovich covered his eyes with his left hand, but the pain was too much. As the Cubs' trainer gingerly placed an inflatable cast around the ankle, Kasparovich pulled clumps of turf out of the ground with his right hand.

Strickland and the other infielders stood nearby. Braswell knelt next to the rookie as the stretcher was brought on the field. An ambulance was summoned. Minutes later, Kasparovich was carefully loaded into the back of the white-and-lime-yellow ambulance and taken to the hospital.

"There goes twenty-five dingers and a hundred RBIs," said Armour.

"I just talked to him this morning," Riley said. "He made a joke about breaking his leg."

"Can I use that?" Hill said.

"Sure, as long as you attribute it to me," Riley said.

"Never mind."

The Cubs lost, 3–1, and didn't linger in the clubhouse. Rather than talk to players in Tempe, Riley and the other writers drove back to Mesa. Morris hadn't been at the game—he liked to say that he was so far ahead of everyone else that he could afford to stay home and work the phones—but he was at Harry Caray Stadium when the bus returned.

"Skip, pretend I wasn't even at the game today," Morris said. "Describe to me exactly what you saw."

"Pretend?" said Nadel. "You *weren't* at the game today."

"Fellas, I don't have time for your shit," Braswell said. "I want to get over to the hospital and see how the kid is doing. Now, do you want to have your little chickenshit cat fight, or do you want to ask some goddamn questions?"

"What did Stevie D tell you?" Riley asked.

"Said it's bad," Braswell said. "Out for the year. Rehab's going to be a bitch. But Kaspo is a strong kid. It's just a shame this had to happen to him, and to this ballclub. I think it was pretty obvious he was going to be our first baseman for a long, long time."

"What's next?" asked Blair.

"Goddamn, son, the boy just broke his ankle two hours ago," Braswell snapped. "Ah, hell, I'm sorry about that. I'm just disappointed for the kid. I'm sure I'll talk to Jim about our next move. But I'd say Hammler is our guy until further notice."

Hoffman interrupted.

"Jim is going to be busy later, so he said he'd do a group thing right now if you're interested," Hoffman said.

Braswell waved them away. "Go, go. I want to shower and go see Kaspo, anyway. Y'all got my number if you need me."

Hightower was waiting in his office. He barely looked up as the reporters walked in.

"I've just spoken with Dr. Jon Skillings, who said Lance's ankle was indeed broken and will require surgery," Hightower began. He hadn't bothered to say hello. "A pair of pins will be inserted to facilitate the recovery process. The procedure will be done as soon as the swelling decreases to an acceptable level. The prognosis for a return next season is favorable. Questions."

"So he's definitely out for this year?" Nadel said.

"The prognosis for a return *next season* is favorable," Hightower repeated.

"Skip said Hammler will take Kasparovich's spot in the lineup," Morris said. "Will you explore any trade options?"

"No comment," said Hightower.

"No comment on Hammler in the lineup, or no comment on trade options?" Hill said.

"No comment on the 'no comment,'" said Hightower, who then looked at Hoffman.

About 80 Percent Luck

"Uh, that's about it, guys," Hoffman said. "I think Mr. Hightower has some things he has to take care of."

Hightower began to shuffle several papers on his desk. Everyone started filing out of the room—except Morris. Riley could hear him say, "Jim, if I could talk to you privately for a minute"—and then the door shut.

"What do you think that's about?" Riley asked Nadel.

"Nothing good," said the WGN man.

Riley went to Hammler first, who tried unsuccessfully to hide his excitement.

"Hey, I feel real bad for Kaspie, but that's how the breaks go," said Hammler, too stupid to recognize the pun. "This means I have to go in and do the job. That's what they pay me for. You hate to win a job because of injury, but I think I was having a pretty productive spring myself."

"You're hitting .278 with one homer and three RBIs," Riley said.

"See what I mean?" Hammler said.

Riley walked past Little San Juan and nodded at Valdez, who snickered. Riley offered a self-conscious "*Hola*" to Omar, who looked at him as one looks at a chunk of roadkill—with mildly disgusted indifference. Better to try the always-talkative Strickland. Strickland had a can of Bud in his right hand and a new first baseman's mitt in his left.

"You heard, didn't you?" said Riley.

"Yeah, not that you had to be on *ER* to figure out the kid was hurt," said Strickland, before taking a long guzzle of the Bud. "See this? Coffey sent me this a couple of days ago. Told me to give it to Kaspie right before we broke camp. Look at this."

Riley leaned forward. "I don't see anything."

"See how the leather is a little darker in the pocket?"

Riley could see a faint difference. "Right, darker."

"Coffs already put a coat of Vaseline there to soften it up," Strickland said. "He liked Kaspie's potential. And trust me, Coffs doesn't send gloves very often."

"Hammler will do okay, won't he?" Riley said.

Strickland put Coffey's glove away. Then he asked a clubby to fetch him another beer.

Riley thought Strickland had missed the question, so he repeated it.

"I heard what you said the first time," Strickland said. "On the record, I know Hammie will do a damn good job for us. He's a veteran. Off the record"—Strickland looked up.

"Off the record," said Riley, closing his notebook and clicking off his recorder.

"Off the record, we're in trouble," said Strickland, lowering his voice ever so slightly. "Hammie might surprise me, but he doesn't exactly flash a lot of leather and he hits for shit whenever he plays on an everyday basis. Some guys can handle six hundred at bats, some guys can't. Hammie never has. But like I said, maybe he'll surprise me. If he does, then the wine will taste better, the air will smell fresher, and the women will look prettier."

"What would you do?" Riley said.

"I'd turn back the clock and have Erstad hit a foul ball instead of a grounder, but I can't do that," Strickland said. "So instead, I'm going to take a shower, get dressed, pay my respects to Kaspie, call me up a lady friend in town, have a few beverages, and see where the evening takes us."

"Oh," said Riley.

By the time Riley returned to the workroom, Hoffman had posted a release about Kasparovich's condition, as well as a statement regarding Harris and his MRI. The tests were negative. No structural damage. Harris would rest his arm for at least five days, and if all went well make several appearances before camp broke on April 4. It had not been a wonderful day for the Cubs, though Harris's MRI results were at least some consolation.

Copies of the two press releases were stacked next to Riley's computer, which once again was pushed slightly to the side. The cord from the electrical outlet to the PowerBook was partially disconnected. "Damn interns," said Riley, as he plugged in the power cord.

Hill and Blair were already tapping away, while Armour was busy cueing up sound bites for an update at the quarter hour. Morris sat motionless in his chair, a slight smile on his face.

Riley nudged Hill.

"R.J., you thinking about the first and only time you got laid?" Hill said.

Morris rocked back and forth.

"We give up," Hill said. "Why are we writing and you're not?"

"I'm going to write in a few minutes," said Morris, his eyes still closed. "But first I wanted to put myself in your place. It must be incredibly depressing to have to compete against me day in, day out. I bring my work ethic, my contacts, my expertise, my writing ability..."

"Your humility, your sparkling sense of humor, your Dharma-like attitude," Riley said.

Morris didn't acknowledge Riley. "In fact, I'm almost positive I'll be smiling soon," said Morris in a mocking tone. "Call it a reporter's intuition."

"Call it delusional thinking," said Armour. "I'm just hoping psychiatric care is covered under your health plan."

"If it isn't, maybe he can talk to Varsity," said Hill.

"Laugh away," Morris said. "Life returns to normal tomorrow."

"You're back to wearing women's underwear?" Armour said.

"You'll see," Morris said.

Riley whispered to Hill. "Any idea where all this came from?"

"If I were a betting man," Hill said, "I'd say it had something to do with his one-on-one with Hightower."

"But Hightower told me he doesn't play favorites," Riley said.

"He doesn't, but I can't think of any other reason why Morris is acting like this," Hill said.

"It's not polite to whisper," said Morris from across the room. "But I don't blame you. I'd be scared, too."

The envelope was wedged in the same place as the last one. Riley looked around the mailbox area, saw no one, retrieved the rest of his mail (a pizza discount coupon, a Circuit City sales flyer), and then returned to the condo. He plopped his workbag and dry cleaning on the kitchen table and then tore open the envelope. It was the same person, all right. Same envelope, same paper, same computer, same printer, different message.

"You are frickin' kidding me," said Riley as he read the note.

Hammler out.
Coffey in—if deal can be worked out.
Coffey here tomorrow. Staying at Ritz Carlton.

Riley placed the note on the dining-room table. *There was no way this could be true*, he thought. Coffey had been retired for more than a year, leaving at age 37, seemingly knowing the exact time to call it quits. His game hadn't suffered much. His last season with the Cubs saw him hit .291 with 18 homers and 86 RBIs. He had finished second in the Gold Glove balloting and everybody assumed—including Cubs management—that he would return for at least one more season. But that was before Fox had an opening on its number one baseball telecast team. They went after Coffey first and made it very simple: "If you turn us down, you'll never get another chance like this." And then they offered him a four-year, $10 million deal—outrageous money for someone who had never been a professional broadcaster. But then again, Rupert Murdoch, the ruler of Fox, had never been afraid to take chances. Coffey considered his age, the multiyear deal (versus an option year with the Cubs), the six-month broadcasting schedule, and the fact that the Cubs were sweet on Kasparovich . . . and he took the Fox deal.

At his retirement ceremony at Wrigley, Coffey was asked about the chances of his pulling a Jordan or a Sandberg—that is, come back from retirement. Coffey had laughed, but his eyes, Riley remembered, betrayed him.

"You never know what a big kid like me might do," he had said that day. "I might get bored and join NASA."

The thing was, Coffey was fast becoming one of the best, if not *the* best, baseball analyst in the business. He could criticize without demeaning a player or manager, he was funnier than the Sunday comics, and he almost always knew what was going to happen before it happened. Coffey had unlocked the great broadcasting secret: pretend you're sitting at a bar watching a game with a buddy. Talk to the audience the same way you'd talk to him. Without the mouthful of pork rinds, of course.

Riley considered the numerous reasons why the note had to be wrong. One, nobody—including Coffey—could just pick up a bat and glove, report to the tail end of spring training, and be ready for the season. Two, Coffey wouldn't come cheap. The Cubs had a habit of offering Coffey one-year deals with an option, rather than multiyear deals for market-value money. Coffey loved Chicago, so much so that he had swallowed his pride and played for less. But now Coffey might exact financial revenge. Three, considering Coffey's rising TV status, Murdoch and Fox weren't likely to be excited about the last-minute switch of careers. Coffey did sign a TV contract, though there were rumors of an escape clause if he chose to return to baseball. Four, it was too damn goofy to be true.

Which is why Riley began to believe every word of the note. That, and the fact that his mystery informant was two-for-two in tips.

Riley turned on his PowerBook, pulled out his Phoenix phone book, and called 555-0700, the Ritz Carlton. No luck. Either Coffey wasn't there, or he was using an assumed name. Riley tried Anthony Katz, Coffey's agent (as well as Campbell's). All he got was a recording. Riley left a message.

He checked his watch. Almost 8:15. He had time before the cocktail party to see if Dewitt might still be around.

Only two cars remained in the parking lot when Riley, his workbag on the passenger seat, pulled up in the Volvo. Riley used the secret knock and waited. Nothing. He tried again. Nothing. He was in the middle of a third try when the door was flung open, nearly hitting Riley in the face.

"What the hell do you want?" said the man, easily in his late forties and with a gut that cascaded over his worn Wranglers.

"You're not Max," said Riley, surprised by the new man.

"And you're not Ed McMahon with my million-dollar check," said the man. "Look, I'm busy in here. Whattaya want?"

"I was looking for Max Dewitt."

"He's not here," said the man.

"Know when he'll be back?"

"I don't think anytime soon."

"Oh, he's off?"

"I guess you could say that."

"Well, could you tell him Joe Riley stopped by? Or I could come by later."

"I wouldn't waste your time," said the man. "Considering that his office is all cleaned out, I don't think Max is here no more."

"They already sent him back to Chicago?" Riley said. "That doesn't make any sense."

"Hey, I don't know what's going on," said the man. "I got here about two hours ago and all Mr. Hightower told me was to start organizing things for the trip back home. So that's what I'm doing, organizing."

"This doesn't make any sense."

"He left during the game," said the man. "I'll tell you what, though, the guy had everything down to the last jockstrap. I don't know why they fired him. It sure wasn't because of how he ran an equipment room. I spent six years working the equipment room in the Pioneer, nine in the Southern, and four in the International—with a cup of coffee with the Braves in Atlanta—and never saw a system better than the one they got here."

"They fired Max? That's impossible," Riley said.

"Whatever you say. Sorry, but I can't talk no more. In fact, Mr. Hightower told me not to talk to anyone. You're not a reporter, are you?"

"Yeah, I was trying..."

The equipment man slammed the door shut. Riley could even hear the deadbolt lock click in.

"Shit," said Riley. Then it made sense: Morris.

Rather than drive back to the condo, Riley decided to save a little time and write in the media workroom. Blair's workbag was still there, as was a set of National League media guides where Morris usually sat. Riley closed the door and pulled out the list of emergency phone numbers Mitchell had given him.

There were five names on the list: Ed Maloney, on the Cubs' board of directors; Alan Florita, National League associate president; Beverly Blake, Cubs legal counsel; Dr. Kellen Sasserman, team orthopedic surgeon; and Hines Bradley, the Cubs' longtime superscout. Each name featured a work phone, home phone, cell phone, and beeper number.

But the Coffey story would have to wait for a few minutes. Riley first wanted to know what had happened to Dewitt. Maloney didn't answer at home or on his cell, so Riley left the workroom and condo numbers on each one. He did the same with Dr. Sasserman. Then he tried Bradley, figuring that after a combined 51 years in the organization the two men might be friends or, better yet, share secrets.

"Hello?" said the voice after four rings. It was a man's voice, and it sounded groggy.

"Mr. Bradley?" Riley said.

"Yes, it is," Bradley said. "What time is it?"

Riley looked at the clock in the upper right-hand corner of his PowerBook. "A little after nine, sir."

"In the morning?"

"No, sir. At night."

"Like hell," Bradley said. "My clock says eleven."

"Where am I calling, sir?" Riley asked.

"Athens, Georgia," said Bradley. But Georgia came out *Jo-juh*. "Eastern Standard Time, just so you know." He was awake now. And he wasn't happy.

"Sir, my name is Joe Riley. I'm with the *Chicago Sentinel*. Phil Mitchell said to give you a call if I really got stuck on a story. Said you might help."

"Joe Riley? Did Mitchell tell y'all to call me in the middle of the damn night?" Bradley said. "If I'm not on the road, I go to bed at 8:30 *pee-emmm* sharp. Phil knows that."

"No, sir," Riley said. "he didn't tell me."

"Well, now you know," Bradley said. "Call back at a decent hour!"

Riley could almost see Bradley slamming down the phone, so he quickly said, "I just wanted to ask you about Max Dewitt getting fired."

Riley didn't hear a click.

"How'd you hear about Max?" said Bradley, his voice subdued. "He only called me a couple of hours ago. But he didn't say much."

Bingo. "I just met his replacement," Riley said. "I cover the Cubs. I'm calling from Mesa."

"Fired, you say?"

"Office completely cleared out."

"Doesn't make sense . . . but then Hightower can be a pistol," Bradley said. "Threatened me a couple of times, but I told him he didn't scare me, being that I scouted him when he was a little shit at Carolina."

"Do you know how I could reach Max?"

"Got no earthly clue how you get ahold of that man," Bradley said. "Max likes to be on his own. He drives a Winnebago and lives wherever he wants to live. Used to park it right off Waveland in a special driveway he rented. I reckon he'll find you if he wants to talk."

"Did he say why Hightower fired him?"

Another long pause. "This ain't going in the *news-pap-uh*, is it?" Bradley said. "'Cause if it is, this conversation is over. That was always my deal with Mitchell."

"No, sir, it's not going in the paper," Riley said. "I just wanted to know for myself. Max is sort of a friend."

"What he said was Hightower wanted to 'try something different,' as if an equipment man is gonna make the difference in us winning the *penn-uhnt*," Bradley said. "But Max didn't say anything else, and I didn't ask."

"Did he mention a guy named R.J. Morris?"

"Don't believe he did. Is he one of Max's assistants?"

"No, sir," Riley said. "Did he say anything about Eddie Coffey?"

"He always talks about Eddie," Bradley said. "Eddie was his favorite player."

"Did he say he was coming back to the Cubs?"

"Didn't say a word. Just said he was going on a long trip. I didn't ask where."

"You know, I should let you get back to sleep," Riley said. "Do you mind if I call you back if I hear anything else?"

"Just as long as it ain't tonight," Bradley said. "I'll be in town till the weekend, if you need me."

Riley couldn't prove it, but somehow Morris must have seen him at Max's office. When the Harris story broke, Morris ratted on Max. That's what the one-on-one with Hightower must have been about. And that's why Morris had been so cocky.

It was almost 9:20, which meant 10:20 in Chicago, which meant he had about 40 minutes to make the city edition with the Coffey story. He called Florita, who just happened to be walking in from a late dinner date. Riley dropped Mitchell's name and wondered if maybe the Cubs had recently inquired about the latest rules regarding the un-retirement of a player.

"I can't comment on specific players," Florita said.

"But they have called?"

"Yes, but again, I can't name names."

"How about initials?" Riley said. "That way you're not technically divulging a name."

Riley knew it was a weak play.

"You've watched *All the President's Men* one too many times," Florita said.

"What can I say, I've got an hour until our final deadline," Riley said. "If you can't depend on Hoffman and Redford, who can you depend on?"

There was a long pause. Finally...

"Albert Einstein. But think initials," Florita said.

"What?"

"Albert Einstein. Initials. Got it?"

"No."

"You're not trying hard enough," Florita said.

"I've got no idea what you're talking about," Riley said.

"You wanted Redford and Hoffman," said Florita, his voice playful. "This is the best I can do for you."

Riley heard a woman's voice in the background. "I've got to go," said Florita. "Good luck with your story."

Albert Einstein? What the hell did Albert Einstein have to do with Eddie Coffey? Initials. Riley kept repeating the phrase. He began doodling on his notepad. *Albert. Einstein. A.E. German physicist.* Nothing. Deadline was inching closer.

"Shit," he said.

More doodling. *What could Eddie Coffey possibly have in common with Albert Einstein?* Then it clicked. Riley reached for his Cubs media guide and hurriedly thumbed through it until he found the pages marked "Cubs All-Time Roster, 1876–2000." To the Cs he went, where he found Coffey's full name.

"Alan Florita, I hope you get laid tonight!" said Riley, as he stared at his notepad.

Think initials, Florita had said.

Albert Einstein. Not Einstein's initials, but Einstein's theory of relativity: E=mc *squared. E. M. C.*

Riley stared at the alphabetical player list. And there it was: *Coffey, Edward Matthew.* Initials—E.M.C.

Blair walked in just as the workroom phone rang. Blair got to it first.

"And who's calling, please?" Blair said. "Oh, Mr. Maloney. Yes, he's right here."

Blair handed him the phone and stood nearby.

"Andy, nothing personal, but this one's private," Riley said. "Can you give me five minutes?"

"I'm working, too," Blair said.

"Give me a break, will you?" Riley said.

"I've got as much right to work here as you do."

"Hello?" It was Maloney.

"Mr. Maloney, thanks for calling," Riley said. "This is Joe Riley. Could you hold on two more seconds?"

"I suppose," Maloney said, clearly irritated.

Riley turned to Blair.

"Andy, I'm asking a small favor here," Riley said. "Just give me a couple of minutes."

"Oooh, you finally break a story and now you need some private time with one of the board members," Blair said.

Riley covered the phone. "Andy, get the hell out of here or I'll kick your ass back to Downers Grove!"

Blair looked hard at Riley, who had undergone a noticeable transformation since his arrival that first week of March. Gone was most of the beer gut, and Riley's arms had some definition to them. Whatever workout program he was on, the results were obvious. For the first time in years, Riley looked a little bit like an all-state wrestler again.

"You've got five minutes," Blair said. "And I'm informing the Cubs of your threats."

"How you going to do that with a crushed larynx?" Riley said. "I can do that, you know."

Blair ran from the room.

"Mr. Maloney, I apologize for the delay," said Riley, lowering his voice, just in case Blair had his ear to the closed door. "Phil Mitchell said to contact you in an emergency. I'm working on a story that will essentially say that Eddie Coffey is returning to the Cubs, that talks have been ongoing since Kasparovich's injury, that the National League has been contacted by the Cubs, and that Coffey is already here in the Phoenix area, ready to go as soon as a contract is completed."

"And you want what from me?" Maloney said.

"Confirmation," said Riley. "You'd be my second source on the story."

"Does Hightower know that you're working on this?"

"He will," said Riley. "I'm calling him next."

"Well, I suppose this isn't going to stay a secret for long," Maloney said. "As long as this isn't for attribution, yes, your information is correct. However, I'm not in a position to add any facts to the story. As far as specifics, you'll have to get those from Hightower."

Riley clenched his fist. "Thank you, sir."

Riley called Hightower's condo. No answer. He also tried Hoffman. Again no answer. He'd insert a line in the story stating that Hightower couldn't be reached for comment. Then Riley called the office. Butler was still there.

"Start hacking," said Butler, feeling a bit like a sports editor again rather than a corporate geek. "I'll clear out some space on the front. Give me twenty inches, and not a word more. You've got thirty minutes before you've got to push the button, maybe thirty-five if I sweet-talk some people."

Blair knocked, returned to his desk, packed his things, and left. He said nothing, though he looked scared. Riley would have to remember that the next time.

The story was done with eight minutes to spare. It was 22 inches, but Riley figured he'd let Butler worry about the extra two graphs. Riley unplugged the phone cord so he could insert the tip into the computer modem.

"Aw, Christ," Riley said. No connector piece. Riley searched his computer bag. Six minutes to deadline. He looked under his desk, and again fumbled through the computer bag. He glanced at Blair's computer. It was a Gateway; different modem jack. "Damn," he muttered.

Riley grabbed his car keys and sprinted to the Volvo. There was the connector cord on the front floor, just below the passenger's side seat. The cord must have fallen out when he had grabbed the bag. Riley ran back to the room, plugged in the modem cord and phone cord, and sent the story two minutes late.

"Cutting it pretty close," Butler said.

"Technical problems," Riley said.

"We'll get it in," Butler said. "Anyway, way to go. You're doing a super-great job."

Riley was surprised by the sincerity. "You mean that? I didn't know you had a soft side."

"That's because you've been listening to Sheila too much."

"You have to admit she does have a unique view of life."

"That's why she's been my assistant for eight years," Butler said. "Anyway, I'll talk to you tomorrow."

Riley took his time driving home. As he closed the car door in the garage, he heard the faint sound of the phone. He caught it on the third ring.

"Don't hang up. This is Joe Riley," he said, slightly out of breath.

"Kellen Sasserman."

"Oh, Dr. Sasserman," said Riley. "I was trying to get you for a story I was working on."

"Eddie Coffey?"

"Yeah, how'd you know?" said Riley, concerned.

"I've just spent the last ten minutes on the phone with another reporter," Sasserman said. "You people are quite persistent."

"Another reporter?" Riley had a queasy feeling in his stomach.

"R.J. Morris," said the doctor. "I'm afraid I wasn't much help, as I'm sure I won't be with you. Mr. Hightower is rather specific on those issues."

Good, thought Riley. Maybe Morris didn't have the story.

"Well, I could give you the broad strokes of the story," Riley said. "I've already sent it in, but I wouldn't mind asking you a couple of questions about Coffey's physical condition."

"Relative to what?" Sasserman said. The doctor was being coy.

"Relative to him returning to the Cubs," Riley said. "That's what my story is about."

"I don't know what the protocol is in your profession, but I should tell you that Morris's questions centered around that very subject," Sasserman said. "I wouldn't offer any comments to him, nor will I to you. I returned your call as a matter of courtesy."

"But you said you were on the phone with Morris for ten minutes."

"As I said, he's very persistent," said Sasserman. "But it made no difference."

Riley thanked Sasserman. Then he sulked. Hightower must have fed Morris this very nice-sized crumb. *Morris does Hightower a favor by telling him about the rendezvous with Max, and Hightower feeds him a scoop.* That was the last time Riley would believe a word Hightower said. "Switzerland, my ass," muttered Riley.

At the very worst, though, Riley had a tie on the story. It would be his second hard news story of the week, which was worth something. But Riley had become greedy. The first scoop had awakened something dormant. For the first time in years, Riley cared.

He tossed his wallet on the table. It cartwheeled across the cellophane covering of his dry-cleaned jacket and pants.

"Jesus Mary and Joseph!" said Riley, looking first at the wall clock—10:24—and then at his laundered clothes. "The party."

He dressed in five minutes, brushed his teeth, and ran his hand across his stubbled face. No time for a shave. To reach the Phoenician in the shortest amount of time, Riley ran at least seven lights and never let the Volvo come to a complete stop. When he got to the luxury hotel Riley tossed his keys to the valet, not even waiting for a receipt. He'd worry about that later.

The concierge pointed him to the Casa Grande Room, where Riley almost collided with a busboy carrying a large tray of wine and drink glasses. It took a few seconds for Riley's eyes to adjust to the room's dim lights. There were two long dinner tables, 16 chairs to a table. There were five people left at one of the tables; the other table was empty, except for a pair of dessert plates, each with a half-eaten slice of carrot cake. One of the slices featured a cigar stub stuck in the icing.

Against the far wall was a temporary bar, complete with 12 stools, all of them occupied. That's where Riley found Megan, sitting next to Strickland. Harris was there, too, as was Gerry Palmer, a second-year Cubs scout who had played with Harris in the minors. Harris and Palmer were hitting hard on a pair of brunettes, while Strickland and Megan were listening to (Riley presumed) one of the potential TSNE clients. Riley inched forward, not wanting to interrupt his story.

"So I'm thinking, straight change or bust him with heat," said the man, in his late thirties, maybe early forties, a hint of gray at his temples. "I don't throw the breaking stuff too good, and the last thing I want to do is hang something over the plate for Bo to mash."

"What year was he then?" asked Strickland, stirring a scotch and ice with a thin straw.

"Let's see," said the man, "that was 1984, so he must have been a sophomore at Auburn. No, wait. That was my senior year at 'Bama, so he must have been a junior. That's right, 'cause he won the Heisman in '85. That's what I tell my kids: that I pitched to the great Bo Jackson."

"So, what happened?" asked Megan.

"Wasn't pretty," said the former Crimson Tide pitcher. "I threw him the heater—tight, too—and he turned on that sucker so fast that I swear I feared for the ball. He hit it flush on the label and it still nearly cleared the left field light pole. That was four hundred eighty-three feet, on the fly. One of their engineering students figured it out the next day. That swing right there is why I got into the home building business. I thought I might be able to sneak into pro ball, but when you see a man hit a ball that hard—and he was just doing it on pure athletic instinct, nothing else—then you've got to reassess your future, know what I mean?"

"And now you're Chicago's most successful custom homebuilder," Megan said. "Sounds like you did very well."

"Oh, I'm not complaining, but Brett here would understand," said the man, nodding to the bartender for another Chivas. "It's hard to give it up. Deep down I knew I probably wasn't good enough to pitch professionally. It took Bo to convince me."

"Don't feel bad," said Strickland. "I had a couple of buddies who played for the Royals. Not long after they signed him, Bo came to Kansas City and took BP. He hit so many bombs—and I mean the kind you see on PlayStation—that the Royals and the Red Sox came out of their clubhouses to watch. I got a tape of it. Even the older guys, like Frank White, couldn't believe it. The vets didn't even pretend they weren't impressed. He was a stud."

"I'll drink to that," said the man, clinking his glass with Strickland's glass of Dewars.

Strickland caught Riley out of the corner of his eye. "Well, well," said the third baseman, "if it isn't Mr. Fashionably Late." Megan turned around. The homebuilder, not sure what to do, introduced himself.

"Mike Konraddi," he said. "Megan here trying to sign you up for the real-estate section, too?"

"Joe Riley," said Riley, shaking his hand, "and no, she charges more for one full-page ad than I probably make in a year."

"You're not part of the group?" said Konraddi.

"No," said Megan, interrupting, "he's part of the product. He writes for the *Sentinel*. In fact, he covers the Cubs."

"So you know Brett, here?" said Konraddi.

"We've dated a few times, but we agreed to see other people," Riley said. "I don't want to get locked into anything."

"He's a laugh riot, isn't he?" said Strickland. "But he's really grown close to the team, isn't that right . . . what's your name again?"

"See?" said Konraddi. "This is what I miss about sports. Instead, I've got to spend my days going over spec sheets with clients, or bitching with inspectors over building code."

"They're precious, aren't they?" said Megan. She turned to Riley. "You're lucky we're still here. The hotel wanted to close down the bar an hour ago, but Brett slipped the manager some jingle and told Harris and the other guy there to take care of the bartenders. So here we are, barely. And how are you doing?"

"The details of my life are quite inconsequential," Riley said.

"Yeah, yeah, I know," said Megan. "You had a typical childhood. Summers in Rangoon. Luge lessons. Meat helmets."

"Damn, you know your *Austin Powers*," Riley said.

"Like I said, I don't know what it is about men and movies," she said. "So why were you late?"

"I'm sorry," said Riley. "Something broke at the last minute."

"You gonna keep us in suspense?" Strickland said.

Riley had to be careful. What if Strickland told Morris or one of the other writers? Riley liked Strickland, but he wasn't sure about his allegiances. And what the hell was he doing here with Megan? And Riley definitely didn't want Harris to hear this.

"I'm not sure I can say right now," Riley said.

"Must be big," said Strickland. "We getting different-color stirrups this season?"

"All I can say is that you're getting something different tomorrow, and it isn't new stirrups," Riley said.

"Am I getting traded?"

"No," said Riley.

"Then whatever it is, I can wait ten hours to find out," Strickland said.

"You tease," said Megan. "Now if you gentlemen will excuse me for a moment . . ."

And off she went to the restroom. Konraddi also excused himself and joined a conversation with a handful of car dealers at the end of the bar. One of them was a Mercedes dealer that Konraddi had met earlier that night. Konraddi wanted a deal on the new S500.

"You drinking tonight?" asked Strickland.

"Yeah, what is that?" Riley said.

"Dewars and a drop."

"Same thing, but with a splash or two," Riley said. Strickland told the bartender.

"So," said Riley, not sure how to bring up the subject, "you fellas in the neighborhood or on TSNE retainer?"

"I'm thinking about doing something with your company," Strickland said. "Megan asked if I'd stop by, so I brought Harris, and Harris brought Palmer. Megan's going to throw Harris a five-hundred-dollar bone for mixing with these people. They do love their Cubs."

Riley looked down the bar to where Harris and Palmer were stationed. Harris and the first brunette had their arms around each other. Palmer wasn't having similar success. The second brunette looked bored as she sipped her gin and tonic. A moment later she tapped her friend on the shoulder and asked for a cigarette lighter.

As she leaned over for a light, Riley saw Palmer drop something into the woman's drink. It was done with the speed of a Vegas blackjack dealer. Then he quickly twirled the ice cubes with his finger.

"Did you see that?" Riley said.

"See what?" Strickland said.

Riley looked again. The woman sipped at the drink, took a drag from the cigarette, and then took another full sip of the gin and tonic.

"I'm back," said Megan, placing her purse on top of the bar. "And I'm thirsty."

As Strickland ordered her a drink, Riley watched the second brunette a few feet away. Her glass was half empty and Riley could see her head bob ever so slightly.

"Who are they?" asked Riley, nodding toward the brunettes.

"Sisters," said Megan. "They do most of the buying for Nordstrom and Marshall Field's. We definitely need them on our side."

Riley saw Palmer whisper something in the second brunette's ear. She shook her head no, grabbed her purse, balanced herself against the stool, and began to walk away. "I'll be right back," Riley heard her say. Palmer began to help her, but she waved him off. She made her way around the corner and into the corridor that ran toward the front lobby of the hotel.

Riley took a gulp of his scotch and decided to follow her.

"Where you going?" asked Megan.

"The little journalists' room," Riley said.

"Hurry up," said Megan. "It's almost last call."

Riley stepped into the hallway just in time to see the brunette open a door to one of the private phone booths at the lobby's edge. He walked slowly past the glass door. There she was trying, unsuccessfully, to slip a quarter into the pay-phone coin slot.

Riley tapped on the door. Nothing. He opened the door and leaned in.

"Need some help?" he said.

"I don't even know why I'm doing this," she said. "I've got a cell phone. I feel funny."

"Why don't you let me get your sister back at the party?" Riley said.

"No, no, no," she said. "She likes the Cub. My Cub was barely a Cub. And he has brown stains on his teeth. Why do I feel funny?"

"I'm not sure," Riley said. "I'm going to talk to the hotel people about contacting a doctor. How about if we do that?"

"No doctors," she said, trying to shut the door. "I hate doctors."

"Can I get you a cab?" Riley said. "You don't look too good."

"I'm staying here," she said.

"You can't stay here," Riley said. "It's too small."

"No, here at the hotel," she said, her words slightly slurred.

"Tell you what," said Riley. "Let me walk you to your room. Then I'll tell your sister where you are. That way she won't worry."

"Who are you?" she said.

"Joe Riley. I was at the party. I'm a friend of Megan's."

"Your teeth aren't brown."

"I floss a lot."

"You have nice teeth, Joe Riley."

"Thank you," he said. "Ready to walk?"

"Ready to walk, Joe Riley."

It didn't take long. Down the rest of the hallway, a right at the lobby, to the bank of elevators, three floors, and there it was, room 382. She fumbled for her keycard, and then had difficulty inserting it into the slot.

"Let me help," said Riley.

The green light flashed on the door handle. Riley opened the door, and then reached in and turned on the light.

"Okay?" said Riley.

"I think I'm going to throw up," she said, raising her hands to her mouth.

Riley stepped inside. Jesus, the room was huge. It wasn't a room, it was a suite. Bigger than his apartment back in Chicago. He fumbled for more light switches.

"Here," he said, finally able to see what had to be the door to the bathroom.

She staggered past him and reached the sink just in time. There was another vomit spasm a few moments later. Riley stood around the corner.

"Need some help?"

"Yes," she said weakly.

He found her sitting on the marble floor. The sink and mirror were splattered. Riley grabbed a bath towel, stuck it under the showerhead and soaked it with lukewarm water. He wrung it out and then dabbed at the woman's mouth and chin. He helped her to a chair and then wiped down the mess in the bathroom.

"You sure you don't want me to call the hotel doctor?" he said.

"No doctors," she said. "I'm feeling a little better. Is there a washcloth?"

"Right away," Riley said, soaking it in cold water.

"Here," he said, "put this on your forehead."

"Coffee would be nice," she said.

Riley remembered the wet bar area when he first walked in. There was a coffee maker and a couple of bags of Starbucks. He opened up a packet, poured in the water, and clicked on the machine. A few minutes later she was sipping on double mocha something-or-other.

"Better?" he asked.

"Better than seeing double," she said. "I'm still a little woozy. I don't know what kind of gin that was, but it packed a punch."

Riley thought about telling her what he had seen. But short of doing a chemical analysis on the glass, he could prove nothing.

"I'm going to head out," he said. "I'll let your sister know you're up here."

"You haven't even told me your name," she said.

"Yeah, I did. Joe Riley. Remember?"

"Was that pre-barf?"

"Uh-huh."

"That explains it."

"And you never told me your name," Riley said.

"Dawna Anderson," she said, "with a W."

"Interesting."

"I lucked out," she said. "My sister is Debeee, with three *E*'s. My mom had a mean streak."

"Well, Dawna-with-a-W," said Riley, "it was a pleasure meeting you. I'll send word of your recovery to Debeee-with-three-*E*'s."

"Can I ask one more favor?"

"Sure," he said.

"Can you give me ten minutes? I was with that creepy Cubs coach the whole night. I just want to talk to an actual person. Does that sound weird?"

"Well, no, not weird," Riley stammered.

"Good," she said. "The coffee helped. I just need to take a shower, change clothes. You can tell me what it is you do, Joe Riley."

Before he could answer she was down the short hallway and into the bathroom. He heard the shower water seconds later.

This was an unexpected development. Dawna-with-a-*W* was a striking woman; Riley had known that much when he first saw her at the bar. Thick brown hair. A blouse that revealed probably more than intended. Or maybe exactly what was intended. She wore a thin black leather coat that ran the length of her short black leather skirt. Riley remembered a glimpse of those legs in the phone booth.

Talk? What did she mean by that? Riley began to panic. Visions of voodoo priestesses appeared.

No, he decided, *stay calm*. He had helped a woman in distress. It was an honorable gesture. He had behaved as a gentleman and he would do so now. Talk? Sure, he could do that. He talked all the time. Move your lips, words come out. Talk.

He listened for the water. Nothing.

"Joe Riley?" she called from the bathroom. "You still there?"

"As requested," he said.

"There's a CD player in the armoire," she said. "I brought a few CDs. Pick out something you like."

Riley looked around the living room suite. No armoire.

"Don't see it," Riley yelled back.

"It's in the bedroom," she said, just before turning on the blow dryer.

The bedroom? This was getting too interesting. Or maybe she just wanted to listen to music. He found the CD player and thumbed through her small collection of discs. 10,000 Maniacs. Not bad. Cranberries. Okay. Radiohead. The woman had taste. Ella Fitzgerald. You could never go wrong with Ella. He slipped the CD into the drawer.

"There you are," she said.

Riley turned around. Dawna was barefoot and wearing nothing more than a Phoenician terrycloth bathrobe, held closed by a loosely tied knot. Riley didn't have to look hard to see that Dawna Anderson was nicely endowed. Or, how did Teri Hatcher put it in the *Seinfeld* episode? *"They're real and they're spectacular!"*

"You need to get dressed," said Riley, fumbling for words. "I'll wait in the other room."

"No, please, I'm fine," she said, standing near the doorway. "It feels good to relax. I don't mean to make you feel uncomfortable, but it's been quite a night."

"No argument there," said Riley, trying not to stare.

"Look, I'm going to get a glass of ice water," she said. "Can I get you anything?"

"Water's good," he gulped.

"Think we could kill the lights? I hate halogen," she said. "There's a book of matches on the dresser and candles on the nightstand. Do you mind?"

About 80 Percent Luck

"Uh, yeah, sure," said Riley.

"I'm going to sneak down the hall for a bucket of ice," she said. "I'll be right back."

Riley didn't know what to do. Should he leave? No, that would be impolite. Dawna *had* been through an ordeal. What was the harm of staying 10 more minutes?

The matchbook was from the Kyoto Sushi Bar. Riley wasn't a big fan of raw fish, especially in nugget form. He scraped the match across the back of the cover and held the flame to the first of three candlewicks. The candles were set at the edge of the nightstand.

There was just enough light to illuminate the room in a soft golden glow. Ella sang in the background. Riley settled in a chair next to the nightstand.

"Very nice," said Dawna, as she entered the room carrying two glasses of ice water. "This is perfect."

Dawna handed Riley a glass and then propped herself against the cushioned headboard.

"You're not a Cub, are you?" she said.

"No, I'm a reporter," said Riley. He liked the sound of that. "I cover the Cubs, at least, temporarily, for the *Sentinel*."

"Temporarily?"

"It's lockout related. I'm filling in."

"I hear it's not going well for your paper."

"You'd know better than me. I'm not in the loop."

Dawna took another sip of water and moved toward Riley. "You know, I think I owe you a little something for saving me from that creep," she said, now on her knees next to the chair. Riley squirmed.

"I'm cool," he said, his mind in shock. "I'm just glad you're okay."

"I don't believe in good deeds going unrewarded," she purred, moving closer, the terry cloth belt coming undone as she put her arms around his neck.

"You think this is such a good idea?" said Riley. "I mean, I didn't come up here for this."

"I know," she said, kissing him lightly on the neck. "That's why I'm doing it."

Riley's right hand was pinned against the side of the chair. He tried to slowly free it, but instead there was less resistance than he thought and his forearm hit the side of the nightstand.

"Relax," she purred again, this time moving her lips toward Riley's.

If this wasn't heaven, it was close. Her skin smelled of Camay and her breath was as fresh as the newly opened bottle of Listermint. Riley didn't even notice the candle had slipped from the stand.

The kiss lasted several long seconds, long enough for the flames of the fallen candle to lick the edges of the curtains. Long enough to create a small trail of smoke.

Dawna saw the beginnings of the fire and began to scream. She jumped to her feet, tried to run from the room, but instead stubbed her toe on the corner of the bed, tumbled forward, struck her head on the base of a dresser and stayed on the carpeted floor moaning in pain.

Riley reached for the ice water, but could only douse the bottom section of the curtains. By now the flames had crawled up the thin linen. There was more smoke. Riley pulled off the bed cover and began slapping it against the curtains. It worked. One more swing and the fire would be gone. Just as he swung the fickle flame caught a breath of air and kissed the bottom of the state-mandated ceiling sprinkler head. The heat triggered the watering mechanism and in moments a stream of cold water shot from the nozzle. Also activated was an in-house fire alarm, which alerted the local firehouse, as well as the hotel security personnel. The shriek of the alarm filled the room and hotel hallways.

Riley could barely make out Dawna in the darkness. He dragged her from the room, stopped long enough to turn on a living room light, and then helped her to the hallway. Security people were shooing guests down the stairs.

"Can you walk?" asked Riley.

"I'll try," she said.

Dawna took three steps before her legs buckled. She had a nasty bump on her forehead. Riley carried her piggyback down the three flights. As they emerged from the stairway door Riley saw two fire trucks, an ambulance, two satellite vans from the local stations, and then, a flash of light.

The *Arizona Republic* would have the best photograph. There on the front page—along with a brief description of a room fire that caused $9,281 worth of damage and the evacuation of an entire luxury hotel—was the picture of Riley and Dawna stepping from the emergency exit. Riley's mock turtleneck was slightly torn and his hair was disheveled and wet. His face had the look of a hero. On his back was Dawna-with-a-W, her hair soaked, a knot on her forehead, her open bathrobe flapping like Superman's cape.

"Can leap tall buildings, too," read the caption.

The newspaper photo was the talk of the Phoenician the next day. Everybody saw it, including Megan Donahue.

Fifteen

THE LOCKOUT WASN'T GOING WELL—for either side. Each day Mac-Cauley was having a more difficult time keeping his union, with its many fickle constituencies, focused on the idea of outlasting the *Sentinel* management tactics. It had been nearly six weeks, and the angry excitement that had first greeted the news of the lockout had long since been replaced by skepticism, genuine worry, and the real possibility of long-term unemployment. There was talk—quickly quelled, of course—of Guild members crossing the picket line. Mac-Cauley had anticipated the reaction. It happened all the time, especially when families were staring at a second month of no income and a second month of unpaid bills.

MacCauley instructed Moss to dip further into the strike fund. People had to eat, didn't they? But beyond that, MacCauley could do little but preach patience.

There had been a movement among some of the rank and file to approach management with a new proposal. MacCauley agreed to "ponder" the idea but did nothing of the sort. Didn't the poor bastards understand that power had to be fought with power, even if it was imagined power? If the union came crawling back, management would see that as a sign of weakness and go in for the kill. That's how these things worked. No mercy. No compassion. It was the closest thing to one of those ridiculous celebrity death matches that Mac-Cauley's grandchildren enjoyed watching on MTV. "Let's get it on!"—isn't that what the ring referee said?

MacCauley wasn't afraid of a fight. He had been a brawler all his life, first on the playgrounds of Bridgeport—Daley's old neighborhood—then at Leo High School, where the Irish priests preached God, discipline, and the merits of a good right jab. MacCauley wasn't the brightest in his class at DePaul, but his single-mindedness soon compensated for his grade point average. He worked his way through school as a bouncer at several Lincoln Park bars and was no less subtle in the business world. He was a man's man, but in an era when such things were revered. Now, in the age of political correctness, MacCauley was feeling Paleozoic.

In his office den was a sepia photograph of MacCauley's great-great-great-grandfather, who had come from Dublin to Chicago in 1865 just in time to work in the newly opened and foul-smelling 400-acre Union Stock Yards, which were located just south of Bridgeport. The somber young man posed for the portrait in a threadbare pinstripe suit and a smallish top hat. But what MacCauley loved most about the photograph was that Seamus Patrick MacCauley had his arms slightly extended and his fists clenched—a brawler's pose.

The MacCauleys would fight their way into the closed circles of Bridgeport's Irish machine politics. And they would stay there, thanks in part to their ability to get the votes. It was no accident that from the death of Anton Cermak in 1933 to the 1979 election of Jane Byrne, a Bridgeport man ruled the city of broad shoulders. And a Bridgeport man never forgot his roots. When the massive Stevenson Expressway project threatened the existence of Bridgeport's St. Bridget's Church, Daley and the MacCauleys used their political strength to alter the plans. Engineers eventually had to build the highway behind St. Bridget's.

MacCauley alternately adored and despised old man Daley, but he always respected him. Adversary or strange bedfellow, you always knew where you stood with him. Daley himself had once whispered to him the secrets of negotiating: confuse, divide, conquer. Compromise only when compromise favors you. MacCauley's staff, sprinkled with MBAs, begged him to read something called *The Art of War*. The book, based on the observations of an ancient Chinese warlord named Sun Tzu, was required reading at most business schools and standard fare in most corporate libraries. MacCauley thumbed through the pages, laughed out loud, and tossed the book in his office garbage can.

"Like I need some Chinese guy telling me it's better the arrows are aimed at my enemies than at myself," bellowed MacCauley to his staff that day. "You want wisdom? Read about the Boss."

Several years earlier MacCauley had used Daley's time-tested principles to embarrass *Sentinel* management. But the preppie Lawrence had learned from the first encounter. Now MacCauley was Frazier and Lawrence was Ali, dancing and prancing about with the confidence of someone who knew he had the advantage. MacCauley would lunge; Lawrence would smirk and dart away. It was maddening, and there was little MacCauley could do.

Deep in his gut—and MacCauley heeded such primal feelings—the union boss knew his Guild members were ready to crack. And if they did, the *Sentinel* would win the labor war and MacCauley would be back hawking votes for aspiring aldermen in Marquette Park. He'd be lucky if he got a decent table at Gene & Georgetti.

"I need information, damnit," MacCauley told Moss as they stood at the Men's Bar at the Berghoff, sipping freshly poured house beers. MacCauley liked the no-frills Loop bar on Adams Street because you could get a carved beef sandwich, pickle, and beer for less than $10. Of course, he'd liked it a lot better 30 years ago, when women weren't allowed.

"Don't we have any moles over there?"

"There" was the *Sentinel*.

"Not a single asset," said Moss, who had read one too many spy novels. "Management did a much better job this time. It has kept its inner circle tight and quiet."

"Go figure, a newspaper that doesn't leak," MacCauley said. "Just my luck."

"We're still attempting to infiltrate," said the assistant. "But Lawrence has done a good job masking his intentions."

"Where's Hoover when we need him?" MacCauley said. "A wiretap would come in handy right about now."

"Those are illegal, sir."

"And your point is?" glared MacCauley.

"Director Hoover is dead, sir," said Moss. "And anyway, these aren't the old days."

"Well, I wish they were," said MacCauley, a thin line of beer foam covering his upper lip. "Jesus-Joseph-and-Mary, we need some information. I've got to know if they're hurting over there."

"They're probably wondering the same thing," Moss said.

"For our sake they'd better be. I want us locked up tighter than the communion hosts at Holy Name Cathedral."

"I've seen to it personally, sir," Moss said.

The *Sentinel was* hurting. So was Lawrence, who had just banged his knee for the millionth time against the inside of his block-and-shell kneehole desk. Lawrence hated the antique desk, but Veronica said it added a grace and elegance to his office. His wife had purchased it at a Sotheby's auction of "Americana Masterpieces" in New York. She never bothered looking at the provenance. Instead, Veronica kept bidding up the piece until no other numbered paddle except her own was raised. Sotheby's was thrilled, mostly because the hammer price was far higher than anyone had ever expected. Then again, Veronica wasn't concerned about cost containment.

As the knee pain subsided, Lawrence stared at the daily assessment sheet and cringed. How could he be winning the war against the union—and in spectacular fashion, at that—and yet be losing ground? The numbers had to be wrong. Daily subscriptions were off slightly, which was to be expected. But it was the decline in Sunday sales that earned Lawrence's immediate attention. Down nine percent and falling. Sunday was where the *Sentinel* laid its weekly golden egg. It was where the paper could gouge its advertisers, where its circulation numbers dwarfed all others in the Midwest. At this pace Lawrence would have to consider drastic measures, such as reducing price per unit.

Even more disturbing was the call he had received from his contact at Danielson & Sons. Carefully shaded in pleasantries was a subtle warning: remedy the situation or the takeover is history. D&S wanted sure things. Lawrence's guess was that D&S had heard whispers about the Sunday section. But the contact didn't push the subject, and Lawrence treated the passing remark as if it had never been uttered. Inside, though, his mind was racing.

Nobody, not even the board of directors, had this latest information; Lawrence had seen to that. Coming so late in the first quarter, it was unlikely that the lockout's effects would have significant impact on the upcoming TSNE financial report. But if the numbers continued their present pace, the second-quarter earnings would be disastrous. If that happened, then Lawrence would be up to his suspenders in trouble.

Even with the part-time work force in place, and a handful of forced retirements and convenient firings, the *Sentinel* had the look of a paper in danger of reduced dividends (or none at all) for the first time since 1981, when newsprint prices skyrocketed. The shocking spike had left management with an outdated contingency plan. It was like trying to stop a gaping leak with fishnet stockings.

The problem this time had nothing to do with newsprint costs (TSNE had purchased its own Canadian paper mill to avert future shortages) but everything to do with Lawrence's lockout-effect model. In short, it didn't allow enough for the peripheral damage that came with such labor disputes. Chicago was still a blue-collar town, and the lockout had angered subscribers with a soft spot for unions. They still remembered the last time the *Sentinel* had tried to bust the Guild. Now they were canceling subscriptions, forming picket lines, and encouraging people to shop at businesses that didn't advertise in the *Sentinel*.

Several large advertisers—mostly the auto and department store goons—had done their own independent research and were making noise about "make-goods." Make-goods were death in the newspaper business.

Here's how it worked: Newspapers with large circulations such as the *Sentinel* could demand and receive premium dollars from advertisers. Advertisers, especially the auto dealers and department stores, wanted saturation. The larger the circulation, the more people who saw their ads. It cost a lot of money to buy that kind of saturation, but with the *Sentinel* having a near-monopoly on Chicagoland circulation (a fact hammered home by the newspaper's smug account executives), local advertisers didn't have much of a choice. So they paid.

But if circulation dipped enough, as was fast becoming the case at the *Sentinel*, then a refund of sorts was in order. A "make-good," where the newspaper ran, say, a full-page ad, at a later date for free. At the *Sentinel, free* was the foulest of four-letter words. Equally foul was the possibility that some advertisers might not renew their deals for the following year.

Lawrence had instructed the paper's ad execs to remind all customers of their binding contracts. That might work for another week, perhaps two, before the department store lawyers began demanding the make-goods. The circulation numbers weren't low enough—yet—to require a change, but that was of little consolation to Lawrence.

But this wasn't merely about financial ramifications. This was about the perception of power and the upper hand. If the union could continue to hold out, Lawrence's bargaining position would slowly erode. These latest figures, part of an internal study, would be similar to the numbers released in early April by the Audit Bureau of Circulation. And when the ABC figures were made public, MacCauley would have an unexpected bargaining chip.

The pisser of it all was that TSNE should have been part of a nationwide surge in share prices of newspaper stocks. Knight Ridder was up; so was Washington Post Company, Gannett, and Tribune Company. The Bears Stearns Newspaper Index was easily outperforming the S&P 500. Everybody was enjoying the recent resurgence except TSNE. Lawrence heard the rumblings: Investors were worried about the price-to-earnings multiples for TSNE. Never mind that he had painstakingly reduced payroll.

Of course, the *Sentinel* was still in better shape than MacCauley's Guild members. But God help Lawrence if the dividends took it in the shorts. Spoiled by years of high returns, the shareholders would be furious. They would have little patience for explanations concerning Lawrence's grand plan, which, quite simply, was to neuter the Guild once and for all.

"Claire, cancel my appointment for the afternoon manicure," he said with a punch of a button on his desk intercom system. "And please call my wife and tell her I won't be able to join her for the Lyric Opera this evening. Also, schedule a meeting of our esteemed senior editors and department heads for eight tomorrow morning."

"Trouble, sir?"

Oh, how he loved her clipped Miss Hathaway voice.

"Of course not," he said. "Just time for a strategic planning session."

And here was the strategy: To help counter the likely red ink, more weight had to be cut loose from the mother ship TSNE. He had pored over the numbers and found lots of soft spots in the newspaper's general ledgers, as well as in the comparative report of expenses. No department or service would be safe from his fiscal reductions. He would start with the big-ticket departments such as Foreign, Features, and National, and then work his way down to lowly Edit Support Services. He would question every expense, from catering services to auto allowances. Lawrence needed time. Not much—he could see signs of union discord—but enough to bluff MacCauley, that Jabba the Hut of negotiators, into a settlement. The timing had to be just right—after the takeover deal was done, and just before the ABC figures were released, and definitely before the second-quarter report in June. Once a settlement was reached, stock prices would roar back, thanks to a lean, mean TSNE financial machine. Lawrence would be proclaimed a management genius, the master of manipulation, the man who not only broke the union but broke the grip of MacCauley. Lawrence could see an autobiography, maybe a Trump-like how-to book, but with panache. The seven-figure advance and accompanying royalties would bump him up from the Range-Rover, Westmoreland-Country-Club set to the Gulfstream-IV, membership-at-Augusta-and-Pine-Valley class. Rich-rich. Maybe then he'd take a jaunty little run at Miss Beecher and take his chances with the Collagen Queen's divorce barracudas.

Sixteen

SASSERMAN WAS RIGHT; Morris had the story about Coffey's return. So did Blair, although not with the same amount of detail. Armour, Hill, and Nadel once again were left scrambling for second-day follow-ups. Hill tossed the clip file at Riley.

"Thanks a lot," said Hill, trying his best to sound indignant. "You know, my parents were going to fly in for Senior Night, but now I'm not sure it's worth it. Thanks to you, I don't know if I'm going to get my letter jacket. You've ruined everything, though I did enjoy the front page of the *Republic*. Care to explain?"

"No," Riley snapped. "And hey, it wasn't just me on this one," said Riley, gesturing to the empty workroom seats usually occupied by Morris and Blair.

"Yeah, it didn't take long for Morris to stick it to us," Hill said. "I knew he'd come back strong after your initial scoop. He probably threw Blair a little puppy biscuit for being his faithful companion."

"Nice ethics," Riley said.

"Believe me, they've been ham-and-egging it for years," Hill said. "And are you sure you don't want to come clean on the photo?"

Nadel and Armour joined in.

"Talk now or we spread rumors," said Nadel.

"Lots of rumors," said Armour.

"The short version is this," said Riley, realizing it was futile to resist. "I went to a party at the Phoenician. I think I saw someone slip a woman one of those date-rape pills. I tried to help. She tried to thank me. A candle got knocked over. The rest is front-page history."

"You're lucky," said Nadel. "None of the players read the front page of the paper. They go right to sports or the business section."

"I wish," said Riley. "Word will get out. I'm screwed."

The Cubs had yet to issue a statement concerning the Coffey situation. Hoffman had poked his head in the workroom after the players were gone, shot a good-natured bird at Riley, and then disappeared down the hall for what would likely be an unpleasant meeting with Hightower about leaks.

Riley reached Coffey's agent later that morning, only to learn that everyone else, including Hill, had called earlier for comment. There would be none until a 10 A.M. teleconference call, when Coffey would be available to discuss his plans.

"By the way," said John Kammes, who had represented Coffey since the first baseman had left San Diego State, "how'd you catch wind of this thing?"

"I have a secret admirer," Riley said coyly.

"You must," said Kammes. "This thing was covert, baby. I'm not mad or anything—it happens—but Eddie was surprised it got out this fast. There couldn't have been more than a half-dozen people with knowledge of the negotiations. I know Hightower wouldn't say a thing, and I know Eddie and I were buttoned up."

"Beginner's luck, I guess," Riley said. He couldn't divulge sources. Truth is, he didn't know who his mailbox source was.

"That's cool," said Kammes, who was going to make a commission killing on the new deal. "Anyway, call the 1-800 number at 9:55, give the operator our code, and they'll hook you right in."

"Got it," Riley said.

With an hour to kill before the conference call, Riley pulled out the floppy-disk cartridge in his PowerBook and replaced it with a CD unit. He plugged in his headphones and then, shielding the CD from Hill's sight, inserted a shiny disc into the laptop. Hill couldn't help himself.

"Hey, Mr. Secret . . . whatcha listening to?"

"What? I can't hear you."

"Yes, you can," Hill said. "What is it?"

"Some romance stuff," said Riley, not altogether lying.

"What, like Celine Dion?" Hill said. "I'm telling you, that woman looks like a pretzel stick with a nose. She can sing, though."

"Absolutely," said Riley, who began humming the theme from *Titanic*.

"Mind if I borrow it when you're done?"

"What?" said Riley, stalling for time.

"I said . . . ah, forget it," Hill said. "Listen to your music. At my place you're lucky to get a laptop with a working hard drive."

"Oh, your laptop works?" said Armour, who had been reading the daily clip file. "I've got a Desk King, which is like the Yugo of computers. I'm almost positive it came from a cereal box."

"Yeah, give me a Tandy 200 any day of the week," Hill said. "Those things are indestructible. And they're light. The only thing I'd change is the screen size, and maybe put in a screen saver, like what Riley and Nadel have on their computers. Just once, I'd like the latest technology at my disposal."

"This PC Computing minute has been brought to you by Paul Hill, cyber-nerd," Armour said. "Join Paul tomorrow when he discusses the exciting world of benchmarks and RAM."

"What?" said Hill, his feelings hurt. "I was just making conversation."

Riley's back was to Hill and Armour. They hadn't seen him turn off the CD the moment Hill mentioned screen savers and the latest technologies.

"You son of a bitch," Riley said.

"Huh?" Hill said. "What'd I do?"

"What?" Riley said.

"What'd I do? You had the headphones on, and . . ."

"I'm sorry, man," said Riley. "You didn't say anything wrong. In fact, you said everything right."

"I did?" Hill said.

"Perfect," Riley said.

"Well, would you mind calling my editor?" Hill said. "We've got merit raises coming up and I could really use a bump, if you know what I mean."

"If this turns out the way I hope it does, I'll give you something better than a merit raise," said Riley, as he grabbed his notebook and tape recorder.

"Better than cash money?" Hill said. "What is it?"

"Revenge," said Riley, as he bolted from the room.

Hill looked at Armour. "Well," he said, "I guess this means I can fly my parents in after all."

The secretary, in her mid-fifties by now, wasn't prepared for Riley's power-burst past her desk and toward Hightower's office door. Nobody did that, not even Braswell. There was protocol to be observed. If you were a member of the media (gag), you first contacted Hoffman and made a formal request for an interview. Then Hoffman would forward the request to the secretary, Alice Hodge, faithful Cubs employee for 19 years, who would conveniently "misplace" the memo. If Hoffman made a follow-up request, then Hodge would submit it to Hightower on official Cubs letterhead but slip the single sheet of paper beneath the daily mail pile.

Hodge was protective of Hightower, especially when it came to the media. The man had enough to do without having to talk to reporters. And pity the sports talk-show producer who tried an end run around Hoffman and called Hightower's office directly. Hodge loved dealing with those people. First, she would cheerfully explain the team policy concerning interview requests. The producer would then lie, telling her that Hoffman had told him to call the GM's private extension, that Hightower had already agreed to come on the air with who knows who, probably some dreadful-sounding dweeb like "Mad Max in the Morning." Of course this was impossible, since Hightower hated sports talk shows, thanks to an ugly incident the previous season when the show's host had asked the GM to list his 10 worst personnel decisions "week by week." Hodge would then listen to the producer's lie and apologize profusely for the misunderstanding. Why, of course, she'd put Mr. Hightower right on the line.

Meanwhile, back at the studio, the smarmy producer would inform the show's cohosts—say, "The Heavy Turd Crew" (they all had the same ridiculous names)—and cue up a half-dozen sound effects for the blindside interview. For instance, if Hightower mentioned injuries as a reason for the Cubs' struggles, then some slick studio engineer with a smirk on his pimpled face would insert a cartridge and out would come a baby's wail. Or maybe they'd have Bob from Barrington or the Weasel from Wheaton on hold, both of them ready to tear into Hightower for past Cubs mistakes.

About 80 Percent Luck

But what none of them realized was that sweet Alice Hodge had lied, too. As they waited on hold, Hodge casually thumbed through the greater Phoenix phone book until she found an appropriate number. Then she'd pick up the receiver and tell the anxious producer, "Transferring you now." And the producer would feel an adrenaline rush because they were already on the air and besides, the Weasel had been on hold for nearly 45 minutes, which meant he was pissed, which meant they were moments away from an angry confrontation and really good radio.

Except that Hodge never transferred them to Hightower. Instead, she would send them to Lung Hiu's Chinese Emporium in Tempe, or to Scottsdale Bible College. Or, if she was feeling especially playful, to the Federal Communications Commission in Washington.

Hodge recognized Riley as he strode by. He was the one whose interview request she had misplaced, not once, but twice. Served him right; he hadn't gone through the proper channels. It wasn't until Hoffman became involved that she grudgingly presented the memo to Hightower. Didn't they know the man worked himself to the bone? Running the Cubs wasn't an easy job. This was her ninth general manager. She had seen what the pressures could do to a man, especially when the press was leading the charge. Flip Henderson, the Cubs' fourth GM during her tenure, quit the business altogether and became a harpist for the Fresno Philharmonic Orchestra. Larry Crider, number six, was currently serving 12 to 18 months in a minimum-security facility for sending threatening mail to player agents and several Chicago columnists. All of which explained why Hodge considered it her duty to institute a more stringent, albeit secretive, media screening process. Hightower would never know.

But this time she was too late. Riley already had his hand on Hightower's office doorknob by the time she could move.

"Sir, you cannot go in there!" she said.

Riley ignored her. Hodge followed him into Hightower's office. Her boss wasn't going to like this, though Hodge thought Hightower looked William Holden–like when he was mad.

Hightower glanced up from the waiver wire sheet he was scanning, removed his reading glasses, and leaned back in his leather chair.

"I was wondering why it took you so long," Hightower said to Riley. Then he turned to Hodge. "Alice, there's no need to be alarmed.

I called Mr. Riley to my office. That's my fault. I should have had him check in with you first."

Riley, surprised by the size of the lie, said nothing.

"It's just that he didn't stop at my desk," Hodge said. "Usually they stop. They stop right at my desk and then I buzz you. But this time he didn't stop."

"Yes, you're right," said Hightower in a soothing tone. "I didn't mean to cause you any distress. Now if you'll excuse Mr. Riley and me. I believe he came here for a specific purpose—didn't you, Mr. Riley?"

Riley nodded. Hodge slowly closed the door behind her. Hightower had an amused look on his face.

"No jokes, Mr. Riley?"

"No jokes," he said.

"No witty one-liners?"

"No one-liners."

"Then what?" said Hightower, happy to play the game.

"An apology," said Riley. "Supersized."

"An apology will do nicely, Mr. Riley, though I must admit, I was expecting to see you this morning, say, about the same time you read the clip file containing the Coffey stories by Mr. Morris and Mr. Blair," Hightower said.

"I figured I'd come here after the game," Riley said.

"So what changed your mind?"

"I know you didn't feed Morris the story."

"The Coffey story," Hightower said.

"Right, the Coffey story," Riley said. "I thought you were helping Morris stick it to me."

"Why would I do that?" Hightower said. "I told you I don't play favorites."

"Because Morris told you I talked to Max Dewitt."

"What else did you think?"

"That you fired Max because we talked," Riley said. "That you and Morris had some sort of quid pro quo thing going when it came to information."

"And now you've changed your opinion?" Hightower said.

"Well, I still think you fired Max because of what Morris told you, but I'm pretty certain you didn't help Morris out," Riley said.

"Pretty certain?" Hightower said. "You're not completely certain?"

"I will be soon enough," Riley said.

"Mr. Riley, I detailed my policies regarding the media in simple terms," Hightower said. "I do not grant special favors to certain media members. Yes, Morris did come to me and offer certain information relative to you and Dewitt. Yes, Dewitt is no longer on-site. Yes, Morris did have the Coffey story, as did Blair. And, considering the *prima facie* evidence against me, I wouldn't have totally blamed you for reaching what seemed to be a logical conclusion."

"So you're saying you didn't can Max?"

"Max has been temporarily reassigned."

"To where, the unemployment line?"

"What happened to the joke moratorium, Mr. Riley?"

"Sorry," Riley said.

"To answer your question," said Hightower, "Dewitt is presently in the Land of the Rising Sun, where he will be accompanying our very expensive emergency first baseman home to San Diego in about a week's time."

"Max is a babysitter?" Riley said. "He wasn't fired?"

"Dewitt and Coffey are like father and son, if you must know," said Hightower. "And that's off the record. I needed Max to sell the idea of un-retiring to Coffey."

"But I thought Coffey wanted to come back?"

"I'm not going to get into the details, Mr. Riley. Suffice to say that Dewitt was an integral part of the negotiation process."

"You mean Coffey didn't want to play for you?"

"We've had our differences," Hightower said simply.

"So Max did some rehab on your image," Riley said.

"Again, let's just say Max was a useful tool," Hightower said. "I wanted to try something different. I'm pragmatic enough to put personal differences aside when it comes to the betterment of this ballclub."

"A long trip." So that's what Max meant when he talked to Bradley. "What about Morris?" Riley said. "He must have thought you fired the guy."

"Mr. Morris can think whatever he'd like to think," Hightower said. "But again, I assure you there were no extra favors bestowed because of his disclosure."

"Aren't you curious what Max and I talked about?"

"Curious, yes. Obsessed, no. Mr. Riley, a certain amount of secrecy is necessary to run a baseball club, especially one with a $64 million payroll. I will do whatever is needed to safeguard that secrecy. But in this particular case, I'm not aware of any secrets betrayed by Mr. Dewitt."

"You talked to him?"

"Of course I did," Hightower said. "He told me the nature of your conversation."

"And you didn't have a problem with that?" Riley said.

"I would have preferred a box of Macanudos, and that the confirmation had come from me, but it appears you had the essential facts correct in your story," said Hightower, a rare grin crossing his face. "Dewitt has always put the best interests of this team ahead of anything and anyone else. If he chose to confirm your story, then I can live with that, this one time."

"So he's not fired?"

"Hardly. In fact, with the completion of the Coffey negotiations, I've recommended he receive a significant raise. Now, you said something about an apology."

"Name the form," Riley said.

"A simple 'sorry' will do," Hightower said. "We all make miscalculations. Yours, given the equation, wasn't altogether far-fetched. If anything, I've been mildly impressed by your persistence and passion. I didn't see those same qualities during your first few weeks in Mesa."

"You noticed?"

"If it sets foot on Cubs property, I notice," Hightower said. "I'm paid to notice. In addition, Dewitt was rather helpful in his appraisals."

"I knew I shouldn't have spent so much on the vodka," Riley said. "It loosened his tongue."

"One last question, Mr. Riley," Hightower said.

"Sure, what?" Riley said. "I owe you."

"You'll tell me when I've been completely vindicated regarding Mr. Morris, won't you?" said the general manager, again smiling.

"As soon as I figure out how to do this, you'll be the first to know."

About 80 Percent Luck

"If that's the case, then be careful tonight," Hightower said. "As I understand it, some of our office personnel are quite talented."

"I'm not sure I follow," Riley said.

"The annual spring basketball game. Hoffman asked if the staff could leave thirty minutes early tonight for a brief pregame practice session."

"Practice?" Riley said. "I didn't even know the game was tonight."

"Mesa High School, 7:30," Hightower said. "Mrs. Hodge will provide you with directions."

"You're playing, too?"

"If my schedule allows," said Hightower, who never missed the game. He wasn't against flaring an elbow now and again. "Now, is there anything else to discuss?"

"No," Riley said.

"Then perhaps I'll see you in a short while," said Hightower, picking up his reading glasses from the desk. "And Mr. Riley . . ."

"Yeah."

"Please don't bring any matches or candles."

Hightower was there. So was Hoffman, two interns, the assistant ticket manager, the traveling secretary, the stadium operations director, and the publications manager. They had professional-quality jerseys, complete with stenciled names and numbers. Hightower—the former Carolina letterman for Deano—was standing only a few feet from the backboard. Exhibiting perfect form, he shot the ball against the glass. Then he moved a few feet back and started shooting short jumpers. Then he moved near the free throw line and made several more jumpers. The he slowly worked his way around the perimeter. Even at 48, Hightower still had a shooter's touch: arm extended, elbow under his shot, picture-perfect follow-through, as if he were waving goodbye to the ball. And in the Carolina tradition, he was methodical in his routine. Before long, he had the Fronties running lay-up drills and practicing what looked like a motion offense.

Riley glanced at his own team. The five-six Armour wore the latest in basketball attire, from Air Jordan mid-tops, to Air Jordan warm-up shirt, to Air Jordan knee-length shorts and Air Jordan socks, complete with the Jump Man logo on each side. If nothing else, he looked like a player. A little one, but a player nonetheless.

"Are these hot, or what?" said Armour, pointing to his fresh-from-the-box sneakers.

"Roasty-toasty," Riley said. "But can you play?"

"Watch this," Armour said.

Armour clumsily dribbled behind the three-point line and unleashed a shot that nearly bruised the rim. It caromed off the court and bounced loudly into the bleachers.

"Damn," Armour said. "Just a little more arc."

"And a little less spasm," Riley said. "You looked like you were having an epileptic seizure. Is that how you always shoot?"

"I'm not warm yet," he said. "Anyway, don't worry about me. Look at Hill."

"Do I have to?" Riley said.

Hill wore cutoff jeans, an old pair of New Balance running shoes, and a Jack Straw's of Wichita T-shirt. Like most sportswriters, his body was muscle intolerant.

"Were one of you guys going to tell me about the game?" said Riley. "If Hightower hadn't said anything, I would have never known."

"Hoffman said he told you," said Hill, who tried touching his toes in a feeble attempt at stretching. He reached his shins, grimaced, and stopped.

"This is going to be a disaster, isn't it?" Riley said.

"Pretty much," Hill said. "Nadel tried a layup, but it wedged between the rim and backboard. None of us could jump that high, so we had to get a broom to poke it out."

"That's encouraging," Riley said. "Where's Nadel?"

"Getting some water," Armour said. "He said he was exhausted."

"After one layup?" Riley said.

"That, and all the jumping trying to get the ball unwedged," Hill said.

"What about the Happy Twins, Morris and Blair?" Riley said.

"Morris said he had to break down stats of the Southern League, and, oh yeah, to fuck off," Hill said. "Blair was cleaning wax out of his ears with a rental car key."

"So none of this matters," Riley said. "We've only got four anyway."

"No, Hoffman said he found a fifth for us," Hill said. "Supposed to be here any minute."

"Great," Riley said. "The Spaz Five."

"Speak for yourself, Fireman Bob."

It was Megan Donahue.

Riley turned around. Megan had on a pair of Reeboks, some Champion shorts, and an "F 'em Bucky" T-shirt. At five-eleven, she looked every bit a former Big Ten star.

"*You're* our ringer?" Riley said.

"You sound disappointed," Megan said. "Worried that I'll break a nail? Worried Dawna won't approve?" Her tone was glacial.

"That's not it," said Riley, ignoring the cheap shot. "It's just that it's a little different playing against guys."

"Yeah, I know," Megan said. "We used to scrimmage against the guy walk-ons at Wisconsin. They weren't bad. And by the way, I won't take that as the sexist insult that it was."

"You played the men's team?" Hill said.

"Like I said, just the non-scholarship guys."

"And?" Hill said.

"We won a few games," Megan said. "Hey, if you don't want me to play, no big deal. I can go work out over at Gold's."

Hoffman jogged up to the group.

"I see you've met your fifth," Hoffman said. "Ready to start, or does Riley here have fire hose practice?"

"Hilarious," said Riley.

"So, you ready to go?" said Hoffman.

"Are we?" said Megan, looking at Riley.

"I guess," Riley said. "Give us a minute."

"No problem," Hoffman said. "By the way, we'll play to fifty by ones. Two timeouts. Got to win by two."

"Can't we just tap the keg right now and get it over with?" Riley said.

"Your competitive spirit is giving me goosebumps," Megan said. "Now, where's the rest of our team?"

"Well, this is Paul Hill," Riley said. Hill nodded hello. "The mini-Jordan is Greg Armour. Over there, gasping for breath, is Alan Nadel. And then there's me, your charming basketball host for the evening."

"The mini-Jordan . . . is he any good?" asked Megan, as she watched Armour adjust his wristbands.

"Do you mean 'good' in the fashion sense, or in the athletic-ability sense?" Riley said.

"I understand," Megan said. "What about Hoffman's team?"

"Other than depth, size, stamina, and really nice uniforms, they've got nothing on us," Hill said. "Hightower is pushing fifty, but he played for Carolina, so he'll know what to do. Hoffman played baseball at Arizona State, so he's got to be an athlete. I don't know much about the others, but they look like they can run."

"What about you?" Megan said. "You in shape?"

"For H-O-R-S-E, yes," Riley said. "I suggest we run the four corners."

"Won't work," said Hill, his game face on. "Hightower will know how to break it."

"Nadel," said Riley, "I was kidding. We'll be lucky if we score."

It was 16–0 before Armour, of all people, ended the Hacks' scoring drought. While trying to feed a pass inside to Megan, the ball was tipped by Hightower and it fell quietly through the net. By then Nadel had all but quit running up and down the court. Instead, he went as far as half court before deciding if it was worth the trouble to jog/shuffle the remaining distance. Riley had missed all six of his field-goal attempts. Hill had missed two long bombs. Megan, curiously enough, had yet to take a shot.

The margin grew to 25–1 before Megan called a timeout. Nadel collapsed on the bench, his chest heaving.

"Christ, Nadel, you're not gonna die on us, are you?" Armour said.

Nadel shook his head no, and then barfed into a towel.

"That's it," Riley said. "Let's forfeit this thing and leave with our dignity."

"Forfeit?" Hill said. "We've still got half a game left."

"We're getting killed," Riley said. "What's the point?"

"Quitter," Megan said. She was serious.

"I'm not quitting," Riley said. "I'm escaping with my dignity. And, speaking of quitting, you haven't taken a shot, Miss Wisconsin."

"It's early," she said.

"Early?" said Riley, glancing at the scoreboard, which was manned by Mrs. Hodge. "We're down by twenty-four. When were you going to get interested, at 49–1? Plus, my man Nadel here only has the use of one lung. Right, Nadel?"

Nadel wiped his mouth and in between gasps for air said, "I'll . . . be . . . okay. I'm . . . with . . . Megan. Let's . . . play."

"Well, quitter?" said Megan.

"Fine," said Riley, annoyed with the 27-year-old blonde. "I predict we'll double our score before it's done."

"Marquette wrestling . . . the *Sentinel* . . . me . . . now this. You've got the giving-up stuff down perfect," Megan said. "About the only thing you don't quit on is a babe in a bathrobe."

"Watch it," Riley said.

Hill and Armour edged away. Nadel pulled himself from the bench. "Are we going to play, or not?" Nadel said.

"We're playing," said Megan, glaring at Riley. "To help Nadel here, we're going to play a two-three zone. It will give him a chance to conserve his energy and let us collapse around that Hightower guy. If we do this right, they'll have to beat us with longer jumpers. Hoffman can drive, so can the young kid, number nine. Just try to stay in front of them. By the way, who fell into a vat of cologne?"

"That's me," said Armour. "I sprayed on a little Jordan during the water break."

"Well, go wipe it off," Megan said. "Okay, on offense, we're going to take our time. Let's try running a little screen-and-roll stuff. Riley, if you're still up to it, I want you to stand at the left corner of the foul line. I'll be at the foul line extended. Hill, you'll have the ball at the top of the key. Armour and Nadel, you guys find a spot in the corner, just in case we want to try a jumper."

"Just like M.J.," Armour said.

"Yeah, just like M.J.," Megan said, "except that you're a last resort. Okay, I'm going to V-cut to the ball—"

"What's a V cut?" Riley said.

"I'll run about four feet to the basket and then cut back to the ball at a forty-five-degree angle," she said, tracing the move on the palm of her hand.

"Is that what you and Brett were doing at Don & Charlie's, drawing up V cuts on your palms?" said Riley, instantly regretting the words.

"You are a such an ass," said Megan, her voice softening. "I really thought . . . never mind."

"What about the play, Megan?" Armour said.

"Okay, the play," she said. "When I get the ball from Hill, Riley needs to set a front screen on whoever's guarding me. Hill, you move to the right side of the court and set a screen. I'll drive wide toward the top of the key. If this works the way it should, my defender will get caught up in the screen, Riley will roll to the basket—try to use your left hand as the target hand—and we'll get an easy shot. If they cover the roll, then I'll either go hard to the hoop, pull up for a jumper, or hit Armour or Nadel in the corner. Everybody understand what's going on? It's an easy play and it gives us some options."

Somehow the Hacks began to whittle away at the lead. Hightower recognized the two-three zone immediately but couldn't convince Hoffman or the intern to dribble-drive hard to the basket. Instead, they settled for jump shots and made precious few. Meanwhile, Megan's simple pick-and-roll play was causing all sorts of problems for the Fronties. Again, Hightower was the first to understand Megan's strategy, but it didn't matter since the other four Fronties kept slamming into screens, overcompensating on Riley's roll move to the basket, or leaving Nadel and Armour open in the corners. Despite his lack of conditioning, Nadel could make three-point set shots. And Armour was right: Once he warmed up, he wasn't a bad shooter.

When the Hacks closed the lead to 36–24, Hightower called for a timeout. Megan turned in time to see several of the Fronties arguing with each other. Hightower looked winded. And she had long figured out that Hoffman couldn't go to his left and was a step slow guarding anyone who could go to their right.

"How bad do you guys want to win this?" Megan said.

"Are you kidding?" said Armour. "I'm 1–6 against them. I'm tired of buying the beer and food."

"What he said, but add an extra loss," Nadel said.

"Ditto," said Hill.

"Riley?" Megan said.

Riley said nothing. Thoroughly embarrassed by his earlier comments, humiliated by the success of Megan's strategy, Riley wasn't about to say much.

About 80 Percent Luck

"You're the boss," he said.

"Okay, I can take Hightower," Megan said. "You were right about him; he has great technique and he knows the game, but he's also getting tired. I'm going to run him around."

"Don't you ever get tired?" Nadel said. "You're hardly sweating."

"I still play in a couple of leagues," she said. "I'm in decent shape."

"What do you want us to do?" Hill said.

"Try to set some screens," she said. "Keep moving. If they double me, I'll find you. If we get stuck, we can always run the pick and roll again."

"Let's kick some ass," Armour said.

"Sounds good," Megan said. "You going to pout or play, Riley?"

Riley took a sip of water, wiped his forehead with the back of his hand, and made a half-hearted thumbs-up sign. Megan rolled her eyes in disgust.

Megan was right: Hightower had the will but not the legs. She used a step-back move that had the Cubs' GM lunging at air. She'd dribble hard toward the basket, take a big step forward with her lead foot, wait for Hightower to commit, and then step back to create space for a short jumper. When Hoffman came to double, Megan whistled passes to Riley posting low, or to the wings, where Nadel and Armour were camped. Once, in between points, Megan whispered to Riley to try a drop-step move. "Give him a hard fake to the lane, then drop with your right shoulder and leg," she said. "He won't have a clue."

Riley grunted but did as he was told. An easy basket.

Megan was spectacular. She was shorter than her defenders but knew how to create space for her shot with subtle fakes. And as the Hacks closed the score to 45–40, she began to chirp away.

"Go get that," she said to Hoffman as a jumper left her fingertips. Swish.

"Listen for the snap," she said. Swish.

"String music." Swish.

An exhausted Hightower called the Fronties' final timeout with the score tied 48–48. A three-pointer, which would count for two in this game, would win it.

"No threes, fellas," Megan said. "Extend the zone, get in their chests, hands up. On offense, let's run the pick and roll and see what happens. It's been a little while since they've had to defend it. Maybe we can catch them sleeping."

Sure enough, one of the interns jacked up a three . . . and missed. Armour grabbed the long rebound, passed it to Nadel, who passed it to Hill, who set up the pick and roll and passed it to Megan, who faked the pass to Riley, stepped behind the line and, with Hightower desperately trying to wave a hand in her face, hit the winning shot.

Armour, Hill, and Nadel enveloped her in a group hug. Riley stood nearby. Hoffman was the first to extend his hand.

"Bastard," he said. "When she told me she played at Wisconsin, I thought she meant intramurals, not varsity. We couldn't stop her."

"Yeah, I was there," Riley said.

"Hey, you weren't bad, for a wrestler," Hoffman said. "You're in a hell of a lot better shape than when you got to Mesa."

"That's because I couldn't have been in worse shape," Riley said.

"Must be the conditioning from the hotel steps," said Hoffman, before turning to shake Hill's hand.

"Mr. Riley." It was Hightower. He patted Riley on the back. "A fine effort by your team. Ms. Donahue has been well coached."

Before Riley could say anything, both Hoffman and Hightower had moved past him and congratulated Megan. Once again, Riley felt a flash of jealousy.

Riley gathered his things and drove to Hoffman's condo, where the victors enjoyed the spoils: cold Corona on tap, hot pizza in a box. Hightower didn't attend. Megan stopped by for about an hour, long enough for Riley to run out of reasons not to talk to her. She had caught him stealing glances at her during the party but immediately looked the other way. When he finally made his way toward her, Megan said a quick goodbye to everyone and left . . . with the stadium operations manager at her side.

Riley made a beeline to the pony keg.

"More grog, sir," he said to Hoffman, who filled the plastic cup to the brim. Hoffman banged his cup against Riley's.

"You know, it's none of my business, but what we have here is a failure to communicate," Hoffman said. "She's a keeper."

"You're right," Riley said.

"I thought so," Hoffman said.

"No, I meant about it being none of your business," Riley said. "You are Grog Master, not Dr. Joyce Brothers."

"Just trying to help," Hoffman said. "She said she's heading back to Chicago in a few days."

"I appreciate the effort," Riley said, "but I think I'm a permanent member of the Megan Donahue waiver wire."

"Too bad," Hoffman said. "Hell of a hoops player. And I like her style."

"It's the chicane," Riley said.

"The what?"

"Never mind," Riley said. "It doesn't matter anymore."

Seventeen

THE TELECONFERENCE WENT WELL ENOUGH. Coffey said Kammes was putting the finishing touches on a one-year deal with the Cubs. The base salary would be relatively modest, something in the $3 million range; but the contract had lots of easy-to-reach incentives, enough to push the deal to $6 million if Coffey stayed healthy. Not bad for one season. Coffey sounded pleased, mostly because the Cubs had been forced to beg.

The timetable for his Cubs return was still undetermined. He was in Japan on the tail end of a three-week barnstorming tour with 25 other former big league stars. His hands were callused—Coffey didn't wear batting gloves—from two weeks' worth of hitting, and his defensive skills were as sharp as ever. Coffey had put on about 10 pounds during the year in the TV booth, but it wasn't anything he couldn't lose once he returned to the States.

Spring training wasn't an option. Coffey had an ironclad deal with the promoters of the barnstorming tour, but he would be back in time for the Cubs' season opener in San Diego, which, when you thought about it, would be a perfect homecoming for the first baseman. As for Fox, the network had agreed to the one-year sabbatical, on the condition Coffey allow a film crew to follow him during the first week of his return. Total access. They'd turn the footage around in a few days' time and run it as an "exclusive" Fox special. Hightower hadn't been happy with the arrangement, but he didn't have much choice.

Everyone asked a handful of questions, including Morris, who wanted to know about Kishimi Mishigawa, a lefthanded reliever for the Tokyo Giants. Of course, nobody knew a thing about Mishigawa until Morris offered the information.

"I saw him on tape from last year's Japanese World Series," Morris said. "Coffs, does he still throw that piece-of-shit cutter, or does he go with the slurve these days?"

There was a long period of silence.

"Coffs?" Morris said.

"Yeah, I'm here," said Coffey, the overseas connection surprisingly clear. "I was just hoping you weren't."

"I was just asking about . . ." Morris began hesitantly.

"I heard you," Coffey said. "Hell's bells, R.J., I'm just trying to get used to eating squid for breakfast. I can't remember names."

"It's Ki-shi-mi Mi-shi-ga-wa," said Morris slowly and loudly, as if he were speaking to an idiot. It was the same way Americans often talked when traveling overseas.

"R.J., don't you have anything better to do, like memorize page 972 of the baseball encyclopedia?" Coffey said. "I wouldn't know Kishimi what's-his-name if he threw a poisoned Ninja star at me. But I'll say this about some of these Japanese pitchers: They could make a lot of money in our league."

"One more quickie," said Morris, trying to recover.

"Yes, R.J.," said Coffey, clearly tiring of Morris.

"The artificial grass there, is it a Monsanto brand or a Japanese hybrid?"

Another long silence.

"You know what I didn't miss about playing for the Cubs?" Coffey said.

"April in Chicago?" Morris said.

"No, I didn't miss you and your dog-ass insider questions about cutters and backdoor sliders and fake turf," Coffey said. "Man, you've got to get yourself a life, Morris."

"Baseball is my life," Morris said.

"No, baseball's *my* life," Coffey said. "For you, baseball is a story. Just because you spit into a cup and know where all the strip joints are doesn't make you a ballplayer."

The teleconference operator cut in. "I'm sorry, ladies and gentlemen, we've completed the allotted time for the interview. Thank you for participating in the ICC teleconference. You can listen to a replay of the interview anytime after 3:30 P.M. eastern by calling this same number."

Hoffman turned off the speakerphone in the media room.

"That was interesting," he said.

"Yeah, that was some probing question on the Japanese turf," Nadel said. "It will fit perfectly in our upcoming agronomy special. And, by the way Morris, thanks for letting us squeeze in a question. You knew we only had ten minutes for this thing."

"Kiss my ass," Morris said.

"Okay," said Nadel. "Should I kiss you with a cutter or a slurve?"

"You're not a baseball guy, Nadel," Morris said. "You're TV. Shouldn't you be getting Danger's makeup kit?"

"And miss your provocative questions?" Nadel said. "Not for all the Astroturf at Monsanto's world headquarters in St. Louis."

"He said, 'Kiss my ass,'" said Blair, doing his best to defend his friend.

"He speaks!" Armour said. "The mute speaks!"

"You're just jealous," said Blair, whose outburst caught everyone, including Morris, by surprise. Blair almost never asked a postgame question, and it was rare if he said anything at all. Now this. "All of you are jealous of me and R.J."

"Give it a rest, gentlemen," Hoffman said. "It's like Skipper Chuck's Playground Hour in here sometimes."

"They started it," Blair said.

"Did not," said Armour, smiling.

"Did so," hissed Blair, still not getting it.

Riley had heard enough. "I'm out of here," he said. "Time to mix with the chosen ones."

"Wait, I'll walk down there with you," Armour said. "I've got to head to the clubhouse."

They made their way to the field, where the Mariners were taking BP. Armour said hello to Lou Piniella and then disappeared down the Cubs' clubhouse tunnel.

Meanwhile, some of the Cubs, including Lake, were already sitting in the dugout. The right fielder had been hit by a pitch—"wearing it" was what the players called it—the day before and his right hand was swollen. X-rays had been taken, but the results were negative. He wore a thick protective wrap.

"The hand okay?" Riley asked.

"Perfect," Lake said. "I'm skipping the game today so I can compete in the regional arm-wrestling tournament. After that, I've got a piano competition. 'Is the hand okay?' Does it look like my hand is okay?"

Lake was touchy about his body. He had a reputation for spending too much time in the trainer's room and on the disabled list. Some of the other players joked that Lake had a "sprained vaginal muscle." In other words, he was a wuss. He jaked it. At least, that's what some of them said off the record. On the record, he was a "gamer," who seemed to have a lot of bad luck when it came to injuries.

Riley sat on the bench, but far enough away that Lake resumed his conversation with Boomer Hayes and Harris.

"So I'm trying to jerk off last night, but I can't, on account of the bad hand," he said.

"What, no bitches?" Harris said.

"Yeah, there were thirty of them there, but I decided to do it myself. What, you stupid as Mr. Dumbass Reporter over there?" said Lake, nodding at Riley.

"Go on," Hayes said.

"Well, I couldn't do it with my regular hand, so I looked at my left hand and said, 'Hello, who are you?' So I brought the lefty in for his first-ever relief appearance and he got the save, if you know what I mean," said Lake proudly.

"That's your story?" Hayes said. "I gotta sit here and listen about you jerking off?"

"Sorry, Boomer," Lake said. "Usually I tape it, but my battery was low on the Sony cam."

Riley still had 10 minutes before the clubhouse closed for a pregame team meeting. He got there just in time to see Gonzalez and Valdez showing each other the newest photos of their children. Pitching coach Ernie Gesser, who had spent the offseason managing in Venezuela, was trying to explain how he wanted Omar to handle Campbell. This would be Campbell's last start before the season opener, so the Cubs wanted to keep his pitch count at 85, and no more than 15 split-finger pitches; they were hell on Campbell's arm.

"Campbell *va a tratar de desafiar a* Olerud," he said haltingly. "*Eso es cómo es a veces.*"

Campbell is going to try to challenge Olerud. That's how he gets sometimes.

Omar stared ahead. Riley knew that blank stare all too well.

"Shit, my Spanish sucks," said Gesser. "Pedro, I need some help over here."

Gonzalez acted as an interpreter, making sure Omar understood how to put the clamps on Campbell's sizeable ego. The Cubs didn't need Campbell to be a hero in the exhibition season. He could try a few splitters to Olerud, who had hit the homer off him earlier in the spring, and to Martinez, but that was it. The rest of the lineup would get cheese, curveballs, and a little circle change Campbell had been working on.

"*Comprende?*" Gesser said.

Omar finally nodded.

Riley began to leave when he heard a low groan. There was a slight thumping noise and then another low groan. As casually as possible, Riley walked around the corner to where the clubbies had a cramped office and found Armour. The radio reporter was taped to a metal pole, with only his eyes and nose visible from beneath the white gauze tape. Armour kicked at the pole with his shoe heel.

"Jeezus, Terry, why didn't you tell me you were into bondage?" said Riley, as he gingerly pulled the tape from around Armour's face.

"That shithead Campbell got me," said Armour. "Ow! Be careful, will you?"

"I'm trying," Riley said. "I can come back later if I'm doing this wrong."

"Okay, sorry," Armour said. "I feel like a living advertisement for instant hair removal."

"And this is for the Ex-Lax thing?"

"Yeah, him and a couple of—hey, watch the arm hair, will you?" Armour said. "Anyway, our fearless Cub heroes put a towel over my head, dragged me in here and did the mummy thing. I didn't see any faces, but I'm sure Campbell was one of them."

"How you know for sure?" Riley said.

"Because he's the only one stupid enough to wear a playoff ring with his name engraved on the side. My back was to them as they taped my head, but I could see Campbell's ring every time he made a loop with the tape."

It took a few minutes, but Riley finally freed Armour.

"You going to tell Hoffman?" Riley said.

"Are you kidding?" Armour said. "This is only the beginning of our little war. Remember, I don't get mad, I get even."

"How'd he know it was you?"

"I'm sure Morris had something to do with it," Armour said. "You and Nadel are probably next on his list. Guilt by association. Plus, with you being a new guy, he's probably suspicious of you to begin with."

"Me?" said Riley. "Great. Just what I need: a millionaire reliever with a tape fetish. I guess it doesn't matter that I didn't do anything wrong?"

"I wouldn't count on it," Armour said.

Riley and Armour returned upstairs. Nadel was in a makeshift WGN booth next to the main Harry Caray press box. Danger had been scheduled to do a guest appearance on 'GN radio, but begged off. Something about losing his favorite comb. Nadel would serve as the replacement.

The WGN radio producer was awaiting his call and patched Nadel directly to the studio host who, on perfect cue, said, "And now to Alan Nadel in Mesa for a pregame report from today's Cubs–Mariners game. Alan?"

Nadel nudged his script forward just so and began reading.

"Thanks, Hank," he said, his voice relaxed and confident. "Manager Barry Braswell has some difficult decisions to make as soon as he readies this year's edition of the Cubs for Opening Day. Not that it will make a damn bit of difference."

Nadel stared at his script in disbelief. He hadn't written that line.

"Alan?" said the show's host. "Are you there?"

"Yes, Hank, I'm here." Momentarily flustered.

"Those are awfully strong words from a station that owns the rights to Cubs broadcasts, wouldn't you say?" said Hank, sure to get his point across.

"Let me explain," said Nadel, his voice rising in panic as he quickly read through the rest of the doctored script ("not a damn bit of difference . . . media to blame for past failures . . . Campbell the best pitcher on the staff"). *Wait a second. Campbell the best pitcher on the staff?* "I know who did this, Hank."

"Well, we'll certainly be anxious to hear your next report in an hour," said the studio host. "In the meantime, ladies and gentlemen, we apologize for that small glitch from Mesa and we'll try to rectify it as soon as possible. Now, let's get a traffic report from Dave and Judy on Sky One and then break for a brief commercial. Dave?"

Nadel flung down his headset and microphone. Dave and Judy's voices still could be heard from the headset. Since Nadel got the network feed, he wouldn't be subjected to the commercial for Chicago Copiers. Instead, he heard Hank's voice on the hot mike.

"Can you believe that putz?" said Hank, unaware that Nadel was still listening. "We give him one little update and he screws the pooch. No wonder he's Danger's caddy."

"I heard that!" Nadel said. "I heard that!'

Armour and Riley knocked on the press box studio door.

"Hey, could you keep it down?" Riley said. "We've got a ballgame to ignore. And Armour here needs some quiet time to recover."

"Recover from what?" Nadel said. "I've got some asshole back in Chicago thinking I can't do a two-minute radio feed for the pregame. And Terry, don't take this wrong way, but what's wrong with your face?"

"Well, Armour had some semi-permanent hair removal, thanks to Campbell and his duct tape squad," Riley said.

"He got you?" Nadel said.

"Nailed me," Armour said. "I almost admire the quality of it. I would have been in there for the whole game."

"In where?" Nadel said.

"In the clubbies' room," Armour said. "That's where they taped me up."

"You and me are next," Riley said.

"Wait a minute," said Nadel, waving the script. "Sorry, Riley, you're on your own. I just had my turn."

"What happened?" Riley said.

"Somehow he got a copy of my script and made some revisions," Nadel said. "I actually said one of them on the air. I wasn't paying attention."

"How bad was it?" Armour said.

"I said . . . I mean, *Campbell* said that no Cubs personnel moves would make a damn bit of difference."

"Uh-oh," Armour said.

"No kidding," Nadel said. "He must have gotten the script from the copy machine waste basket. I used the copier in Hoffman's office but threw away the first copy; too dark. He probably took the copy, had one of the interns type up a new script, and then somehow slipped it in my folder. Hightower will be thrilled when he hears about it. I won't even get a 'no comment' anymore."

"Campbell couldn't have been this clever on his own, could he?" Riley said. "I mean, this is a guy who needs instructions to eat cereal."

"Maybe that's what they mean by 'crafty lefthander,'" Armour said. "All I know is that one of us better be careful." Armour looked toward Riley.

"I didn't do anything," Riley said. "You were the one who decided to play intestinal chemist. I just watched."

"Apparently that's enough for Campbell," Armour said. "Good luck. And do me a favor, stay away from me."

Hammler got the start at first, but he was as nervous as a 17-year-old rookie. He booted two grounders, struck out three times, and then sulked in the corner of the dugout before Braswell pulled him in the eighth with the Cubs up 8–3. Mormoa played well, as did Delagotti and Valdez. Strickland had a grand slam, driving the ball just over Buhner's outstretched glove, but lost another homer when Mike Cameron made a leaping catch at the center field fence. Lake kept an ice pack on his wrist the whole game.

"That Cameron is a bitch," said Strickland afterward, pulling hard on a cigarette. He hadn't bothered to wipe the black shoe polish from under his eyes. "Didn't anybody tell him it's just an exhibition game? Damn the kid."

"I could do without the big-ass lid," Garrison said from across the room. "Shows no respect for the game. Showboat."

"Who gives a shit?" Strickland said. "If the guy wants to wear his hat four sizes too big, who cares?"

"Ain't right," Garrison said. "In the old days, we'd bust his ass."

"That what they'd do in Syracuse, is it?" Strickland said.

"I've got a right to my opinion," Garrison said.

"The kid plays his ass off," Strickland said. "If the worst thing he does is wear his lid goofy during pregame, I can live with that."

"Pisses me off, that's all," Garrison said.

"I can see why," said Strickland, tugging on the aluminum tab of his Budweiser. "Someone's going to paint his glove gold one of these days."

"At least I play the game the right way," Garrison said.

"Sure you do, when you play."

"What the hell does that mean?" said Garrison, standing up.

"It means you got a hard-on against any young player who has talent," said Strickland, glancing toward Omar, who was walking toward the shower room. "It means you haven't done dick to pop off about Cameron. The back of your bubble gum cards reads like Jim Otto's jersey number and here you are ripping on a guy who busts his ass? Last time I looked, nobody was asking you to make a PlayStation game."

"You, either," Garrison shot back.

"Damn right," Strickland said. "And they won't. But at least I'm man enough to say the kid made a helluva play. I wish he were on my team."

Garrison glared at Strickland, and then threw his perfectly clean uniform into the hamper before stalking toward the players' lounge. Strickland glared back and then took a long swig of his beer.

"This a bad time?" Riley asked.

"Nah," said Strickland, sitting down on his stool. "Garrison is too ignorant to be stupid. You just can't let him get away with that shit. And, by the way, none of that shit was for print."

"Fine," Riley said. "You don't mind if I use a videotape, do you?"

"You're kind of a smartass, aren't you, Riley?" said Strickland. "I kind of like that. Almost as much as I liked the photo of you and the brunette."

"Her name was Dawna," Riley said.

"I heard."

"Can we talk shop for a minute?"

"Fire away," Strickland said. "Get it?"

"Two games left, two roster spots left," said Riley. "One for a pitcher, one for a position player. What do you think happens?"

"That's up to Brazzie and Hightower and the fellas," said Strickland, pulling off his jersey. "I just play."

"But you've got to have a gut feeling," Riley said.

"And that's where it's going to stay, in my gut," Strickland said. "I learned a long time ago not to waste much time with personnel decisions, especially with you guys. Half the time I'm wrong."

"But you know who's looked good and who hasn't."

"I've got a couple of ideas, but I'm going to keep them to myself," said the third baseman. "I do think it will be interesting. With Coffs coming in, they could go a lot of different ways."

"Never thought of it that way," Riley said.

"Maybe that's why I'm the millionaire and you're not," Strickland said, smiling. "By the way, Hoffman told me you used to cover college basketball. I've got one team left in the pool. How good is Georgia? They play Michigan State in the semifinal."

"I covered hoops a long time ago, and I wasn't exactly a success story," Riley said.

"I heard that, too," said Strickland. "So I'll take what you say with a lump of salt."

"Well, Harrick is an underrated coach," Riley said. "He's already won one of these things at UCLA, so he'll know what to do in a Final Four game. I like your chances. Who has the Spartans?"

"Hurlock," said Strickland. "I hate to do it to him, but I've got to root for those hairy dogs. I'll buy him dinner if I win it."

"Who has Arizona and Tennessee?"

"If you can believe it, Hurlock has Tennessee, too," said Strickland, staring at his pool sheet. "What are the chances, right? But it was a blind draw—Brazzie did the picking for Hurlock—so I know the thing wasn't fixed. Kaspo has Lute and the boys."

"Good luck," Riley said.

"No, man, good luck to *you*," Strickland said. "Watch out for Campbell. You didn't hear it from me, but he has some spare time on his hands, so he's trying to even scores. You're on his list."

"Shit," Riley said.

"Yeah," Strickland said, "that's what got you fellas in trouble in the first place."

"What about Hill?" Riley said.

"He didn't know about Hill," Strickland said. "Hill skates."

"Hey, scribe!" came the voice.

"Well, speak of the devil," muttered Strickland. "You better run along and get it over with."

"Hey, scribe!" It was Campbell. "You got a minute? I just wanted to talk to you for a second."

"Adios," said Strickland.

"Wish me luck," said Riley, tucking his notebook in his back pocket.

Campbell stood near his locker, his arm in a small sling.

"What happened to you?" Riley said.

"Oh, this?" he said, tapping the sling. "Habit, more than anything. I like to immobilize the arm after a start. Been doing it since I pitched in the Little League World Series. The trainers say it doesn't do shit, but you know how us ballplayers are about superstitions. Anyway, thanks for asking. How are you doing?"

"Good," said Riley, taken aback by Campbell's friendly tone. "You called."

"Look, I just wanted to clear the air about the Ex-Lax thing," he said.

"What Ex-Lax thing?" Riley said.

"C'mon, scribe," Campbell said. "I know all about it. Hey, if it hadn't happened to me, I would have laughed my ass off, too. It was a funny gag. Armour got me and I got him back. Tit for tat."

"So what does this have to do with me?" Riley said.

"Well, you know I got the radio geek," Campbell said.

"Yeah, I heard," said Riley.

"And you probably thought you were next," Campbell said.

"That's the word on the streets," Riley said. "But I gotta tell you that I didn't know a thing about the Ex-Lax."

"You're safe, man," said Campbell, slapping him gently on the back. "Armour's the guy I really wanted. And I owed Nadel for something he said on the air a couple of years ago."

"It must have been bad," Riley said.

"It was. He said I was the worst-fielding pitcher in the big leagues," Campbell said. "He said watching me field a ground ball was 'like watching a farmer kill a snake with a blunt gardening utensil.' I remember it word for word."

"But I was looking at the Green Book and Red Book a few days ago," Riley said. "You *are* the worst-fielding pitcher in the big leagues."

"Hell, you can manipulate stats any way you want, especially fielding stats," Campbell said.

"How?" said Riley. "Either you catch it or you don't."

"You are one dumb fu—" said Campbell, before smiling. "Look, I'm not going to name names, but there was a very famous infielder here who used to have great fielding stats, but he never dove for a ball. I'll tell you why, too. One, he was a puss; and two, he didn't want his fielding percentages to suffer. If he dove for a ball and it counted as an official 'fielding chance,' then his numbers went down. There are guys in our league who still do that."

"But I've never seen you dive," Riley said.

"Who do I look like . . . Dominik Hasek? They pay me to pitch, not win Gold Gloves, right?"

Riley didn't know how to answer that one, so he changed the subject.

"So why are you letting me walk?" Riley said. "Let's say I had something to do with your 'situation' that day—which I didn't—why would you let me go?"

"We got off to a bad start," Campbell said. "My pop was a union man in Pittsburgh. Steel worker way back when. I heard you were a scab. I took exception."

"I'm not a scab," Riley said.

"Yeah, I heard the whole story," Campbell said. "I owe you an apology. Shake on it?"

Campbell stuck out his right hand. Riley shook it.

"See?" said Campbell. "That wasn't so hard. Just so you know I'm serious, I want you to come out for a couple of beers with me, Garrison, and Hammler. You're over at that shithole near Safeway, right?"

"How'd you know?"

"One of the clubbies told me. We'll pick you up at 8:30. Sound good?"

"I guess," Riley said.

"Okay, see you at 8:30," said Campbell, smiling much too sweetly for Riley's taste.

Riley wrote his stories, including an analysis of the possible options for the Cubs' final cut, which was two days away. The Cubs had one last exhibition game in Arizona, would break camp, and then would travel to Anaheim for a final exhibition game. Then on to San Diego for the season opener against the Padres. Barring injuries, the final roster cut would be made before the Cubs left Mesa. Braswell wanted his team in place for the final dress rehearsal of sorts in Anaheim.

Riley didn't know what to make of this Campbell thing. It wasn't like Campbell to be this nice, especially after Strickland had warned of retaliation. But maybe Strickland was wrong. Maybe Campbell had heard the real story behind Riley's forced Cubs career, as well as his nonparticipation in the Ex-Lax moment. Maybe Campbell wasn't such a prick, after all.

The horn honked at exactly 8:30. Riley walked outside and found Hammler behind the wheel of a Ford pickup truck. It had an extended cab, but the only way in and out was through the passenger- or driver-side door.

"Hop in," said Campbell, who moved from the passenger side, allowing Riley to squeeze into one of the two jump seats in the back. Garrison was already in the other seat, his knees pressed lightly against the front.

"Kind of cozy," Riley said.

"It's a rental," said Hammler. "I like being above everybody, but I hate those faggy mom SUVs. So I go with the old dependable, the F-150."

Hammler hit the automatic door lock.

"What's the plan?" Riley said.

"Oh, I thought we'd just drive around for awhile," Campbell said. "Be spontaneous, if you know what I mean."

Garrison turned away as he tried to suppress a chuckle.

"Am I missing something?" Riley said.

"Not a thing," Hammler said. "This is just a chance for everybody to be real friendly. There's no media–player thing going on. We're just four guys out for a drive. Isn't that right, Mr. Garrison?"

"That is so right, Hammie," said Garrison. "Just people being people."

Riley squirmed a little bit. "Mind cranking up the AC just a little bit? Opening the window a crack? It's kind of stuffy back here."

"I don't think so," said Hammler. "The power windows don't work so good on this rental."

Riley leaned forward. "I think that's because you've got the lock control on the windows. If you click that knob to OFF, the windows will go right down."

"Yeah, they might," said Hammler, "but I haven't read the entire vehicle-owner's manual yet, so I don't feel comfortable messing with the instrument panel."

"How about the AC?" said Riley, sensing something was terribly wrong. "Press AC and turn the knob to the right."

"On a beautiful evening like tonight?" Campbell said. "Nah."

"We're not going out for a couple beers, are we, guys?"

"That depends on your staying power," Campbell said. "You see, we just got back from eating a big dinner. Hammie, you had the Mexican grande with the extra bowl of black beans, didn't you?"

"Big bowl," said Hammler. "And before that, a big can of delicious Bush's Best baked beans. You know, Bush's has been making fine baked-bean products since 1908."

"Very informative," Campbell said. "And Barry, you couldn't seem to quit eating that real spicy salsa dip with your chips, right?"

"Ate two full baskets of the chips and salsa," said Garrison. "Mm-mm good."

"And I had the fajitas with the extra green peppers, which, I hate to tell you, makes me kind of gassy," said Campbell.

With that, Campbell released a fart for the ages.

"Ah, much better," Campbell said.

Riley coughed.

"A little rank back there?" Campbell said. "Believe me, it's gonna get worse. Payback is a bitch, isn't it? Time for yours, scab."

Garrison let loose with a long, loud fart that could have been conducted by Leonard Bernstein.

"Whooh, that was a good one, Barry," Campbell said. "Wasn't that something else, scab?"

"Yeah, it ought to be on *Baseball Tonight*," Riley said.

"That'd be pretty funny," said Hammler. "Peter Gammons breaking down our fart sequence."

"Fellas," said Riley, "why don't you just drop me off at the corner. I'll walk back."

"Not that easy, scab," Campbell said. "What we're going to do is this: We're going to drive and fart, and fart and drive. First one who hits the window switch or throws up loses. If it's you, you become Mummy Two, just like Armour. If it's one of us—which it won't be—we'll give you five hundred dollars."

"Jesus," said Hammler. "Five hundred bucks, Case?"

"He's a scribe scab," Campbell said. "He'll be begging for an oxygen mask in five minutes."

Hammler released some sort of toxic gas that nearly clouded the windshield. Riley's eyes began to water.

"Now, that was a fart," Garrison said. "If you could hit as good as you fart, you'd be an all-star."

"Why, thank you, Mr. Garrison," Hammler said. "I take that as a compliment."

They took turns in the bizarre fart-off. Garrison . . . Campbell . . . Hammler. Hammler . . . Campbell . . . Garrison. Light a match in the truck cab and it would have burst into a Ford fireball. The whole thing had a *Blazing Saddles* campfire-scene feel to it. Riley's stomach was doing backflips.

"Give up, scribe?" Campbell said.

Riley's seared nostrils begged him to say yes. So did his stomach. He began to reach forward, his hand beginning to make its way toward the window switch when he caught Hammler's face looking at him in the rearview mirror. Hammler wasn't smiling anymore. The first baseman's face was a pinkish blue. He looked as if he'd swallowed a wad of chaw. Riley suddenly felt empowered.

"Give up?" said Riley, pulling his hand back. "Actually, I was going to ask if you'd turn the heat on. Nothing better than a fart with the heat on high." And then—from where it came, Riley had no idea—he produced a release of bodily gas that sounded worse than it smelled. It was loud and angry, almost intimidating in nature. Hammler winced. Garrison turned away. Campbell said nothing.

A half hour turned into 45 minutes, which turned into an hour, which turned into 90 minutes, when Hammler, his face drawn and pale, said, "Hey, Travvy, I might have to stop for some gas. You know, the real kind. I'm on red." There was a certain hope in Hammler's tone.

"We're not stopping for anything," Campbell said, his voice now with a harder edge.

"But we're on E," Hammler pleaded. "E, as in *empty*."

"No stopping," Campbell said.

"Too bad it's not driven by natural gases, eh?" said Riley. "We could drive to Vegas."

"Shut up, scribe," Campbell shot back.

"I think I'm gonna puke," said Garrison.

"Like hell you are," Campbell said.

"No, I really think he's going to puke," said Riley, somehow summoning enough strength to drop another gas bomb. "I'm sitting back here and he doesn't look too good."

"Didn't I tell you to shut up, scribe?" Campbell said.

"Sorry, I couldn't hear you through the haze," Riley said. "Anyway, we're just four guys out for a drive."

"The engine's sputtering, Travvy," Hammler said. "The F-150 only gets about nine miles to the gallon. We've got to pull over."

"All I know is that if you pull over and open that door, I'm five hundred flush," Riley said.

"Keep driving," Campbell said.

Hammler rolled his reddened eyes and steered the Ford down University Drive to 143 North. As he tried to accelerate, the truck heaved forward one last time and then fell silent. There was a moment when the engine clucked like a chicken as the last wisps of fossil fuel worked through the system. And then, nothing.

Riley was nauseous. Campbell was outraged. Hammler was too scared to disobey Campbell. Garrison swayed back and forth in the back seat. No pine tree–scented odor eater would ever rid the truck cab of the horrifying smells burnt into its interior.

Campbell squeezed off a tiny fart, but it meant nothing to Riley, who now breathed through his mouth. Hammler gagged. Garrison buried his head in his knees.

"Don't you do it, Barry!" Campbell said. "The scribe's gonna crack any minute."

"I don't know, Trav," said Hammler, again staring into the rearview mirror at Riley. "He don't look like he's gonna crack."

"I'm feeling real friendly right now," Riley said. "I'm feeling the love. By the way, Barry, whatever you do, don't think of septic tanks, dog food, rotting cabbage, dead fish on a sidewalk, Spam, or anything involving chunks."

"Urghhhhh," said Garrison.

"Hang on, Barry!" Campbell said. "I'll give you five hundred bucks if you don't puke."

"That's right, Barry," said Riley. "Do you know how much mushroom compost you could buy with five hundred dollars? Fresh stuff, too. The really smelly stuff. Or you could splurge and get a real high-grade manure mixture. Just curious, Barry, but have you ever seen maggots in the bottom of a garbage can during the heat of summer?"

That did it. Garrison puked on his snakeskin cowboy boots. He hadn't lied about the salsa and chips, either.

Hammler unlocked the door and staggered out into the night air. Garrison pushed the seat forward and spilled onto the asphalt. Campbell turned and looked at Riley, and then opened his door and stepped out in disgust. Riley climbed over the seat and then took a deep, full breath of wonderful fresh air.

"I'm sorry, Trav," said Garrison.

"Wipe your mouth, will you?" Campbell said.

"Sorry," Garrison said.

"There's a gas station two blocks back," Hammler said. "I'll be back in a few minutes."

"Here's a twenty spot," said Riley. "At least let me pay for a gallon of gas and a twelve-pack of beer."

"A beer might taste real good right about now," Hammler said.

Riley unlatched the tailgate and sat on its edge.

"Hey, scribe," Campbell said.

"I prefer 'scab scribe,'" Riley said.

"I forgot," Campbell said. "Anyway, you got balls. Or lungs of steel. Whatever you got, it worked."

"I almost bought it about an hour ago," Riley said. "The neutron bomb you dropped at the corner of Center and University nearly killed me."

"Yeah, that was a good one," Campbell said, laughing. "Anyway, a deal's a deal." Campbell peeled off five hundred-dollar bills from his All-Star Game money clip. "You earned it."

"Thank you, sir. You're a ballplayer and a gentleman." Riley offered a handshake. "This time for real?"

"Fair enough," Campbell said.

Hammler came back with the gasoline and a case of Genuine Draft.

"Here's your twenty back," Hammler said. "The guy was a huge Cubs fan. The power of the meaningless autograph."

"Not totally meaningless," Campbell said. "It was worth the $1.59 for the gas, and the eleven for the beer."

"Good point," Hammler said.

They sat in the truck bed drinking MGDs as Hammler fed the F-150 the unleaded.

"Hey, scribe, how'd you know about Harris's elbow?" Campbell said. "Nobody else did."

"I saw him come out of the training room that day," Riley said. "He didn't look so good."

"Yeah, but what about the MRI and stuff?" Campbell said. "He said he barely told anybody."

"Sorry, I can't reveal sources."

"So that's what Morris always bitches about," said Campbell. "I didn't know that shit was for real. I thought, you know, that only happened at Watergate."

"Morris?" Riley said.

"Look, the guy's okay with me—a little high strung, but he treats me okay, if you're into groveling, which I am," said Campbell, crushing an empty can with his left hand and pulling out a fresh Miller with his right. "He said he knew all about your sources, and that I shouldn't trust you. Told Harris the same thing."

"He ever say how he knew about the sources?" Riley said.

"Just said he had a brand new system," Campbell said. "Foolproof."

"A system?" Riley said.

"Says he used the old system for years and just updated it a few weeks ago," Campbell said. "Beats the shit out of me what he's talking about. But he's good for a laugh. All that seamhead shit."

"The Morris Reign of Terror ends tomorrow," Riley said. "His 'system' is going to take it in the shorts."

"You gonna fart him to death?" Garrison said.

"Worse," said Riley. "But do me a favor, don't say a word, will you? I need the element of surprise."

"It'll cost you five hundred dollars," Campbell said. "I gotta get my money back somehow."

"I'll make you a deal," said Riley, popping open another beer for Garrison. "I'll give you half back. The other half I need for a special project. Believe me, it will be money well spent."

"You'll tell me what it went for?" Campbell said.

"I won't need to tell you," Riley said. "You'll know."

"You got yourself a deal," said Campbell.

Eighteen

"AND YOUR NAME IS . . . ?"

"Terry Butler," said the nervous sports editor.

"And explain to me once more why we need the services of four layout people and three different baseball writers?" said Lawrence, folding his hands ever so correctly. "In fact, could you tell me—and I mean this in a hypothetical manner, of course—why we need a sports editor? After all, the department generally runs itself, doesn't it? For instance, everyone knows the schedules of the local teams, the worthwhile events, and such. I'm not suggesting you're not necessary . . . well, come to think of it, perhaps I am."

Butler stared at his notebook. In so many words, he had just been threatened with termination if his next answer wasn't the one E. Benson Lawrence wanted to hear.

"I suppose we could get by with three layout people and—"

"Two will do," said Lawrence abruptly. "Offer the other two buyouts. Next."

"Sir, you're not serious, are you?" Butler said. "I can't ask one person to lay out the section every day. You're talking about an eighty-hour week."

"These are difficult times, Butler," said Lawrence. "Difficult times require the crust to be trimmed from the white bread. Every department is making similar sacrifices."

Lawrence glanced at his watch. His seaweed hydro-bath wrap was scheduled in his private anteroom for 8:30 A.M. Lawrence liked the wraps early in the morning. So refreshing, and only $225.

"I'll see what I can do, sir," Butler said.

"And what about the baseball writers?" Lawrence said. "Do we really need a national baseball writer, as well as one each for the Cubs and the White Sox?"

"They're three separate entities, sir," said Butler.

"Not anymore, they aren't," said Lawrence, crossing out a line on his checklist. Oh, did Lawrence love to micromanage. "Whittle it to two. We'll cover the locals, but we'll do the national beat with wire copy. That's what we pay AP for anyway—for emergencies, for things we can't always cover. Right?"

"What do I do with our national guy?" Butler said.

"I'm feeling charitable today," Lawrence said. "Train him as a layout person."

"Can we do that?" Butler said. "I mean, is it legal?"

"Find a reason," Lawrence said. "And find it within the next forty-eight hours, or you'll be joining him."

Butler looked at Jarrett and Storen, the once-proud journalists turned company yes-men. They said nothing.

The envelope was tucked inside the morning *Arizona Republic*. It was the same make of envelope Riley had received the previous times. Riley's mystery Deep Throat was at it again, and this time he or she had an end-of-camp gift: the names of the last two players to make the Cubs.

No matter what happens today, it read.

"I don't believe this," said Riley, as he stared at the two names and the brief message.

Riley packed his workbag, grabbed the keys to the Volvo, and drove over to Harry Caray Stadium. Hill, Morris, and Blair were already working the clubhouse. Armour and Nadel were in Braswell's office. Riley found Hoffman.

"When will Hightower announce the final cuts, after the game today or tomorrow?" Riley asked.

"Tomorrow," said Hoffman, sipping coffee from his Arizona State mug. "Hightower doesn't like to embarrass anybody. He'll meet with the two players sometime tonight. We'll release the names first thing in the morning."

"So we don't get a chance to talk to them?"

"Sure, if they decide to clear out their stuff in the morning, which they usually do," Hoffman said. "They'll want to say some goodbyes. It's a tough scene, but they usually talk to the media."

"Sorry, I didn't mean to sound so ghoulish," Riley said.

"No problem," Hoffman said. "I know it isn't the most media-friendly policy, but at least it gives the players a little dignity."

"But there's no way you'll release the names tonight?" Riley said.

"No way. We won't fax the league office the names until seven A.M. That's always been the way Hightower does it."

"No leaks, eh?"

"I think one of the GMs in the NL West used to feed Morris some info, but that was before the league office cracked down on leaks," Hoffman said. "It's a $15,000 fine. So Morris waits like the rest of you guys."

Riley spent the morning in the workroom. He propped his notebook next to his Mac and typed away. Hill did the same at an adjoining table.

Blair walked in. Morris followed a few minutes later. With each entrance, Riley leaned forward ever so slightly, just enough to shield the computer screen from their sight. After all, he had golden information.

"Look at them work their little fingers to the bone," Morris said. "If they only knew what I know."

"That you buy Rogaine in bulk?" Hill said.

"Shut up!" said Morris, absentmindedly touching his scalp, site of the painful and useless hair plugs. "No, I was thinking more along the lines of me kicking your asses the whole season. How sad."

"I'm surprised Northwestern hasn't hired you at Medill," Hill said.

"They couldn't afford me as a lecturer," replied Morris.

"I meant as a janitor."

"You talk a lot for someone who has broken—I've got it right here in my files—exactly four stories in five seasons," said Morris, thumbing through a manila folder. "You see, I keep track. I barely consider you a threat."

It was true, Hill thought to himself. Scoops were scarce on this beat. Every time Hill thought he had one to himself, Morris, and sometimes Blair, beat him to the punch or tied him. Now Riley, the new guy, had surpassed him on the beat.

"I thought that would zipper you up," said Morris, putting away the file.

"Good to see you took your asshole pills today," Riley said. "They're working fine, as usual."

"How sweet," Morris said. "Riley coming to the aid of Hill. I'm surprised you could take time from your very important story to talk to us."

"We'll see if you're popping off tomorrow, Morris," Riley said.

"I'm terrified. I figure one more good scoop and you'll be delivering papers, not writing in them."

Riley said nothing. Instead, he typed his byline and began the lead for his story.

> By Joe Riley
> Sentinel Staff Writer
>   MESA, Ariz.—With their season opener only five days away, the Cubs will announce a pair of daring personnel moves Thursday that will drastically reshape their roster, the Sentinel has learned. The moves, so secret that not even the players or their agents have been notified, include the trading of veteran third baseman Brett Strickland, second baseman Tim LeMott, and minor league invitee Dwight Willingham, whose surprising performance during the spring had all but guaranteed him a place on the 25-man roster.
>   In return, the Cubs will receive a package of highly touted prospects from the talent-rich Atlanta Braves system, including 17-year-old Alonzo Garcia, whose fastball has been clocked at 98 mph, and Mitch Downey, a power-hitting third baseman from Sherman Oaks (Calif.) High School, the second player chosen in the 1997 draft.
>   The impending departure of Strickland and LeMott means the Cubs' Opening Day roster will feature Varsity Mormoa at second and Jason Hammler at third. Hammler, a converted first baseman, began his career as a third baseman. With two roster spots still open, the Cubs will immediately insert Garcia into the rotation as their fifth starter and add Downey to the bench for

lefthanded pinch-hitting duties. Downey will be sent to the Cubs' Triple-A affiliate in Des Moines as soon as star relief pitcher Casey Harris returns from an expected 15-day stay on the disabled list for an injured elbow.

The remainder of the story, inspired by the names in his envelope, fell quickly into place. The Cubs needed a jolt, wrote Riley. Hightower, sensing an opportunity to make a bold statement, had traded two very good players for two amazing prospects. The Braves had a need for veterans (Ted Turner wanted to make another World Series run—now), and their minor league system was stocked like trout in a fish farm. The deal, while audacious, made sense.

Strickland was a year away from becoming a 5-and-10 guy, which would complicate matters if the Cubs wanted to deal him the following season. A 5-and-10 player was anybody who had spent 10 years in the big leagues, five with the same team. A 5-and-10 guy could veto any trade proposal involving him.

LeMott was a solid player; a little high-maintenance, but an asset. Willingham was gravy. A surprise. Who knew how good he'd be? Maybe something, maybe a one-spring wonder. But for now he had value, which is why he was included in the deal. That's the way Riley wrote it.

Riley reached into his workbag, pulled out his modem cords, typed in a computer number at the *Sentinel*, and sent the story.

"You're already sending?" Hill said.

"Had to get something done early," Riley said quietly.

"Before noon?" Hill said. "That has to be a record around here."

"What can I say? I'm a worker bee."

"I'm not going to be ill when I read tomorrow's clips file, am I?" Hill said.

"Define 'ill.'" Riley said.

"I don't like the sound of that."

"Anybody want a decent lunch today?" Riley said. "Hey, Morris, I'll even buy something for you and Igor there."

"Yeah, right," Morris said. "Keep your money. You'll need it during unemployment."

"Why don't you give the guy a break?" Armour said.

"I will . . . when he's off the beat and out of the scab business," Morris said. "Until then, he can go to hell. All of you can."

"What'd he mean by 'Igor'?" Blair said.

"I'll tell you later," Morris said.

Riley closed the laptop, dug out his car keys from his workbag, and then drove to a nearby Subway. He ordered the six-inch tuna with chips and a watery lemonade. He read *USA Today*, which didn't take long, and the national edition of *The New York Times*. Then he stopped at Circuit City. He was gone 90 minutes.

When he returned, the Giants were already taking BP and the Cubs were back in the clubhouse. According to Braswell's pitching sheet, Hurlock would start, followed by Willingham, middle reliever King Armstrong, and set-up man Ken Reed. Hurlock and Willingham were considered to be on the bubble, while Armstrong and Reed were locks. In fact, Armstrong had won an unexpected $9.1 million arbitration deal during the offseason. Hightower hadn't been happy about losing that one (ending his 8–0 record in arbitration cases), but it was hard to argue with Armstrong's pitching numbers. He led the league in "holds" and could go as many as three innings if he had to. His right arm never got tired. The players called him "Gumby."

Riley didn't watch much of the game. Hurlock gave up two runs in six innings, including a homer by J.T. Snow and an RBI double by Barry Bonds. Otherwise, it was a very respectable performance. Willingham pitched an inning, allowed a walk, wild-pitched Bonds to second, and then settled down. His line: no hits, two strikeouts, that wild pitch, one walk, and a soft chopper to second.

Armstrong pitched the eighth and struggled. Two more runs. King pitched the ninth and recorded a save as the Cubs won, 7–4, thanks to a bases-clearing double by Omar, a homer by LeMott, and four unsightly errors by the Giants.

The reporters made the customary trip to Braswell's office, only to find the door shut and locked.

Very unusual.

Riley could hear muffled voices in the room, but nothing more. Morris casually leaned against the door and pressed his ear to the wood.

"Hard to believe the public questions the integrity of the media when you see something like this," said Nadel, gesturing toward Morris.

"No," said Riley, "it's right there, in the small print of the First Amendment: 'Peeping through keyholes and straining to hear private conversations are inalienable rights.'"

"Shhhh," said Morris, annoyed.

Riley looked at Nadel, who looked at Armour. "All together now," Riley said.

On cue, Riley, Nadel, Hill, and Armour began a slow circular dance, all the time chanting, "Hare Krishna, Hare Krishna." Morris pressed his right ear harder against the door, but finally gave up.

"Assholes," he growled.

"We Krishnas believe in everlasting love," Armour said. "Join our peaceful group. Radiate from within. Here, take my hand and luxuriate in our communal understanding."

"Keep your fucking hands off me," Morris snapped, recoiling as Armour's hands reached toward him. "You're all nuts."

"Yes, we are," said Riley, moving closer. "Sing with us, gentle one."

The foursome began their chant again. That's when Braswell's office door flung open.

"What in sweet Jesus's name is going on out here?" said Braswell, wearing a pair of sannies, a pair of Hanes, and a three-quarter-sleeve jersey. Standing near Braswell's desk was Hightower. "Believe it or not, fellas, we've got a ballclub to choose here. I ain't got time for this nonsense."

"It was my fault," Riley said. "I didn't realize you were in a meeting."

"Thought I was taking a dump or something?" Braswell said. "Hell's bells, I keep the door open for that. You know me better than that. So if my door is closed, it's for a damned good reason."

"I tried to tell them," Morris said.

"Hell, R.J., you probably had a stethoscope plastered to the wall," Braswell said. "You've done it before."

"That was never proven," Morris said.

Braswell grinned. He'd made his point. "Now y'all leave me alone. I'll send for you when I'm done in here."

Braswell pulled the door shut.

"Clubhouse," Nadel said.

There is no stranger place to be than a training camp clubhouse the day before final cuts are announced. The veterans who knew they had made the team, either by performance or by virtue of their guaranteed big-money contracts, walked through the room with an air of confidence, even invincibility. Their survival had never been in question. Valdez strutted. Gonzalez was less obvious. "I like many of these players very much," he said. "But only twenty-five jobs. Someone must leave."

It wasn't going to be Gonzalez, who still had four years left on his big-ticket deal. Plus, Gonzo was leaving Mesa with a .411 batting average and nine dingers.

Strickland motioned for Riley.

"What am I, your bitch?" Riley said.

Strickland didn't smile back. "I hear there's something going on with me," the third baseman said.

"Uh . . ."

"Don't give me any of that 'uh' shit," Strickland said. "I've treated you fairly when nobody else here would give you a thimble to pee in. The least you can do is return the favor."

"You're putting me in a hell of a situation," Riley said.

"I'll make it worth your while," Strickland said. "I've got some information that will give you a woody for weeks."

Riley thought about the ethics of it all. Should he disclose his information? What if it got out prematurely, then what? What about journalistic professionalism and integrity?

Well, you've crossed that line already, haven't you?

"All right, I'll tell you what I know, but you've got to swear you don't say a peep to anybody—not Coffey, your mom . . . anybody," Riley said.

"Your secret is safer than balls in a protective cup."

"Nice imagery."

"Thanks," Strickland said.

Riley leaned forward and whispered everything he knew, including the contents of a certain explosive roster story.

"You're shitting me?" said Strickland, when told the news. "I can't fucking believe it!"

"Why don't you say it a little louder, Brett," Riley said. "I think there were some people in Tucson who didn't hear you."

"Shit, I'm sorry," he said. "I just can't believe that's the story. You sure about this?"

"My source hasn't missed one yet," Riley said.

"Yeah, I know," Strickland said. "That's why I called you over."

"The media-savvy Brett Strickland," Riley said.

"You've got to know how to play the game," Strickland said. "And I'm not just talking about baseball."

"I'm learning that all the time."

"Well, here's something else you should know," said Strickland, cupping his hands to whisper in Riley's ear.

Riley listened and then staggered backwards. "You're ten of the worst liars I've ever met," he finally said.

"I wouldn't lie about something like that, man. That's what I was told."

"This isn't another one of those clever ballplayer jokes, is it?"

"I'm not that cruel," Strickland said.

"You're me: What would you do with that kind of information?" Riley said.

Strickland leaned back in his chair. "First of all, I'd rather have a severe case of scrotal itch than be you," he said. "But if I were you, I wouldn't sit on that kind of info very long. You never know how fast things can change."

"A rare moment of lucid advice," Riley said.

"My pleasure. Now what?"

"I've got to peel back to Braswell's office and then write another story. After that, events will dictate my future."

"Well, whatever happens, you showed me something during the last month or so," Strickland said. "You've got some balls, I'll say that for you. You ever need anything, you let me know."

"I survived the Code, eh?" Riley said.

"Screw the Code," Strickland said. "Us ballplayers aren't the smartest species, but we respect someone who doesn't make excuses and who doesn't show somebody else up unless they deserve it. You did a pretty good job of that. And I wasn't the only guy who noticed."

"Thanks."

"Aw, shit, now look at me. I'm all warm and fuzzy. Get out of here before I start singing show tunes."

Riley walked into Braswell's office as Morris was walking out. Neither reporter would give way.

"Late again," Morris said.

"Maybe I was just waiting for you to leave," Riley said.

"Aw, Christ almighty, fellas, give it a rest," Braswell said. "Morris, move your fat ass out of there so the boy can come in. And Riley, enough with all of them wisecracker answers. Damn, I need this like I need a performing ulcer."

"You mean 'perforated'?" Nadel said.

"Yes, doc, perforated," Braswell said. "That's what I meant to say. Can't a man make a mistake around here without someone correcting him? Hell, the season hasn't even started yet and I've got Webster's dictionary here critiquing my every word."

"Sorry," said Nadel.

"Aw, I'm just a little edgy, fellas," Braswell said. "Final cuts are tough."

And he meant it. Unlike some managers in the big leagues, Braswell considered players something more than a magnetic strip on an organizational chart. The players had parents, friends, families, wives, maybe a mistress or two. He hated the idea of telling someone they weren't good enough.

"So you've made your decisions?" Riley said.

"We'll announce them first thing in the morning, so don't bother calling me later at the condo, okay?" Braswell said. "I'm not saying now, and I won't say anything then, either."

Morris snickered.

"What, R.J.?" Braswell said.

"Nothing, Skip," Morris said.

"Let me guess: You already know who we cut?" Braswell said.

"I'm not saying a word, Skip," Morris said. "I was just leaving."

Braswell watched as Morris left the room. He lit a cigarette, inhaled, and then sent a beam of gray-blue smoke toward the ceiling. "Two years I've endured that guy," he said. "Two years. Every Sunday I ask the good Lord, 'What did I do to deserve R.J. Morris?' And every Sunday I get no answer. It's like that feller Nielsen said,

'Whatever doesn't kill your ass makes you stronger.'"

"It's Nietzche," Nadel said.

"Nietzche, Nielsen, who the fuck cares, son?" Braswell said. "You going for your doctorate? Goddamn, can't a man have a private moment without you ruining it? Perforated . . . Nietzche . . . son, you've been watching too much Alex Tripod on *Jeopardy*."

"It's Tre— never mind," Nadel said.

"Damn right, never mind," Braswell said. "All right, gentlemen, anybody got anything else for me? If not, I'm leaving. I'll be back bright and early in the morning. We can talk about the roster then."

Riley returned to the workroom. Morris and Hill quit talking the moment he walked in. They giggled like school children.

"Showing your baby pictures again?" Riley said.

"Oh, I get it: That's a joke," Morris said. "No, I'm just writing a story that will ruin your day tomorrow."

"What, you've tracked down the newest phenom from Luxembourg?"

"Always the funny man," Morris said. "We'll see how hard you're laughing tomorrow."

Good, thought Riley. *The game is on.*

Riley placed his Mac in the padded couch of his workbag and smiled at Morris.

"See you guys tomorrow," Riley said.

"Done for the day?" Armour said.

"Almost."

Riley drove to a local trophy store, picked out the appropriate hardware, and had a plate engraved. He dropped the trophy off at a Mail-Pak, where it would be overnighted. Before the box was sealed, Riley taped the handwritten note to the bubble wrap.

Once back at the condo, Riley pulled out Deep Throat's most recent manila envelope and reread its contents. Then he poured himself an Old Style, clicked on the laptop, and wrote one last story.

Nineteen

A LICE HODGE, EVER THE FAITHFUL CUBS EMPLOYEE, glanced at the wall clock in her modest outer office. It was 6:56 A.M. Hightower always arrived by seven. He'd usually work out in the team weight room, spend 20 minutes on a StairMaster, shower in Braswell's office, dress in slacks, short-sleeve shirt (light starch), and a lightweight Cubs windbreaker. And when his hair was wet, which it was in the early morning, he would absent-mindedly flip a lock of the blond stuff around his forefinger. So adorable.

But with this being the last day of spring camp, the weight room machines and free weights had already been loaded in a leased truck for the trip back to Wrigley Field. All that remained was an ancient exercise bike, which was owned by the Ho-Hos. Hightower wouldn't be caught dead on it.

Instead, the Cubs' GM was spending an hour at a local Gold's Gym, where for $10 he could get a one-day membership. Hodge had driven to the gym the day before to arrange the workout. She had even mentioned Hightower's name at the counter—hoping they might give him a free pass—but the creatine-laced kid behind the counter didn't pick up on the hint. Didn't matter. She'd expense the Cubs for it.

Hightower walked in exactly at seven. He went directly to Braswell's office but was back in his own office by 7:17. By then, Hodge had a cup of coffee waiting for him (light cream, a sprinkling of brown sugar), the list of player cuts from each major league team, assorted Cubs administrative forms that required his attention, and the daily newspaper clip file. So intent was Hodge in getting the clip file done that she hadn't even glanced at the stories.

"Alice!"

Hightower yell? Hodge had never heard him yell before. At least, not at her.

"Yes, Mr. Hightower?" she said, rushing into his office. She hadn't seen her boss this mad since the arbitration loss to Arrnstrong.

"Find Braswell immediately!" he said. "Get Hoffman in here, too! Now! And I want to see Morris and Riley the moment they walk in."

"Yes, Mr. Hightower," Hodge said nervously. "Is there a problem?"

"There's going to be," Hightower said.

Dewitt, a cup of coffee in one hand and the clip file in another, sat on the last equipment trunk to be loaded into the semi. Back from Japan, his body clock completely screwed up, he had been awake since three, overseeing the final preparations for the Chicago trip. In the old days, he'd make the drive from Mesa to Wrigley. But that was before his knees went to hell and his back started hurting him. Now he'd catch a United flight back to O'Hare, but only after sweet-talking the ticket agent into a first-class upgrade (it was amazing what a dozen new baseballs could do). The uniforms, training-room equipment, video equipment, and playing equipment were being shipped to Anaheim for the final exhibition game. But Dewitt would miss that game and instead spend the day in Chicago getting his own clubhouse ready. Then he'd fly to San Diego for the season opener.

"Whatcha reading, Max?" said one of the clubbies.

Dewitt sipped his coffee, looked at the story headlines of Morris's *Standard* and Riley's *Sentinel*, and shook his head in disbelief.

"I'm reading about a train wreck," Dewitt said. "One fatality."

"But those are the sports pages," the clubby said.

"Doesn't matter," Dewitt said. "A certain sportswriter is about to have a very bad day. And I think I know which one."

Terry Butler arrived in his office and found the five newspapers arranged just so on his desk. One of the interns dropped them off each morning. There was a *USA Today*, a *New York Times*, a *Standard*, a *Herald Democrat*, and, of course, the final edition of the *Sentinel*.

Butler reread Riley's story and then opened the *Standard*.

"How the hell did he get this?" Butler said, as he turned to the jump of Morris's story.

But there it was in *Standard* black-and-white: The impending trade of Strickland, LeMott, and Willing-something . . . the acquisition of two minor league prospects from the Braves . . . the roster moves . . . the new Opening Day lineup for the Cubs. It was all there, in sickeningly readable black-and-white.

Butler glanced at Riley's story again and shook his head. *You just can't catch a break, can you, Riley?*

The news of the two stories swept through the Cubs clubhouse like a brushfire. Strickland sat in front of his locker stall and smiled. LeMott took turns frantically reading each account, as did Hammler, Garrison, and Hurlock. Willingham tried to contain his excitement.

In Little San Juan, Valdez translated the stories for Omar. Gonzalez leaned over Valdez's shoulder, nearly knocking the little shortstop unconscious with his five-pound gold chain and crucifix.

Hightower and Braswell walked into the clubhouse. Conversation ceased.

"Close the doors," Hightower told the clubbies. "Then leave. You have my instructions."

Braswell leaned against a wall. He took a drag on his cigarette and flicked the ash into his now-empty coffee cup.

"What goes, Braz?" said LeMott. "I mean, this is brutal."

"The man here is going to explain it all," said Braswell, nodding toward Hightower.

"About fucking time," LeMott said. "My wife is back at the condo crying her eyeballs out."

"You're married?" whispered Campbell.

"Yeah, four years," LeMott whispered back, "but don't tell any of the Annies, okay?"

Hightower stepped forward. "Men, there has been a mistake made," he said. "I don't know how it happened, but it happened."

"You can say that again," Lake said.

"Shut the hell up, son," Braswell said.

"Sorry, Braz," said the right fielder.

Hightower continued. "While you might not agree with my

personnel decisions, or even understand the reasons for those decisions, I have always tried to keep the team's best interests at heart. I have also done my utmost to keep the business of this team out of the media's reach." Hightower paused as Valdez translated for Hernandez. "The media has its job to do, but my first allegiance is to this organization and to you players."

"But the stories," LeMott said. "You told me last night—"

"I know what I told you," said Hightower, irritated at the interruptions. "And if you'll let me continue, I'll—"

There was a knock at the door. Braswell turned the deadbolt, cracked the door open, and then looked at Hightower.

"Is it them?" Hightower asked.

"Woodwind and Birnbaum?" Braswell said. "They're here."

"Let them in," Hightower said.

Morris walked into the room wearing a triumphant look. He had barely entered the parking lot when Hodge had rushed up to him and nearly dragged him to the clubhouse. The old bag was strong. A few minutes later, Hodge had delivered Riley.

This wasn't the first time Hightower had tried to intimidate him. But Morris wasn't scared. He enjoyed the confrontations, fed off them. Morris knew why he was here. He had broken a story about a huge trade and Hightower was pissed. Well, he hadn't actually broken it, but he had tied Riley for it, which, in a weird way, was just as enjoyable. So screw Hightower. And screw Riley, too. Morris had a system and once again it had worked to perfection. Long live the king.

"Hey, Strickie," said Morris, seeing Strickland sitting in front of his cubicle, "I'm sick about this trade to the Braves. You deserved better, bro."

"Thanks," Strickland said.

"And Mottie, what can I say?" Morris said. "I'll come into Atlanta a day early and we'll hit some titty bars. How's that sound?"

LeMott said nothing.

"Yeah, well, maybe not," said Morris. He turned to Hightower. "So what's with the command performance? I was just doing what I'm paid to do. I broke a story. I've done it before, I'll do it again. You guys know how it works."

"But this was different, Mr. Morris," Hightower said.

"Sure it was different," Morris said breezily. "You didn't want the trade made public until tomorrow. You know, Jim, I've got all the respect in the world for you, but you can't control the news. If they can't do it at the White House, they sure as hell can't do it here. Am I right, Lakie?"

Lake ignored him.

Morris, sensing something was wrong, pointed at Riley. "Hey, I'm not the only one who had the story," he said. "Riley here had the same thing."

"Not exactly," Hightower said.

"Doesn't surprise me," Morris said. "I've been telling you guys he's a scab. He's a washout. He can't carry my computer cord. His own newspaper wants to fire him."

"Really?" said Hightower.

"Could happen any day," Morris said smugly.

"Interesting," Hightower said. "And what do you have to say for yourself, Mr. Riley?"

"I'm speechless," Riley said.

"You should be," Hightower said.

"I'll second that," Morris said. "You never belonged here in the first place."

Morris winked at Delagotti. These were his guys. His team. His beat. If only he had a little pinch of Copenhagen.

"Uh, Mr. Morris, you said you weren't the only one with the story," Hightower said.

"Well, I'm not crazy about that, but Riley lucked into it somehow," Morris said. "But I'm sure I probably developed the trade story first. I've got lots of contacts, as you well know."

"Yes, you do," Hightower said. "But I'm curious about one thing."

"Sorry, Jim, but I can't reveal sources," Morris said. "Learned that the first day of junior college."

"Of course you can't," Hightower said. "But you haven't seen today's clip file, have you?"

"How could I?" Morris said. "Fraulein Hodge nearly snapped my neck getting me here."

"So, then," said Hightower, "how did you know Riley had the same story?"

Morris felt a flash of heat pass over his face. "Well, uh . . . I, uh . . .

I read it on the *Sentinel's* website first thing in the morning," he said. "They don't post their stories on there until 1 A.M., after everybody's late deadline. I read it when I got up."

"You read the whole story?" Hightower said.

"Every word," he said. "I didn't like the lead and he had some factual errors, but what can you expect from a rookie?"

"I see," Hightower said. "Mr. Riley, any response?"

"Just one," Riley said. "We don't have an Internet site."

"Mr. Morris here says you do," Hightower said.

"Mr. Morris is wrong," Riley said. "We did have a website, until three days ago. That's when our publisher pulled the plug on the information superhighway. Apparently he thought cyberspace cost too much. So he shut it down, all in the name of saving money."

"Mr. Morris?" Hightower said.

Morris could feel the perspiration form under his armpits. Soon the sweat would trickle down the side of his rib cage. "This is stupid," he said. "I don't have to explain myself. I saw it on the Internet. Maybe it wasn't on the *Sentinel's* site—I can't remember for sure. Now that I think of it, it was on AOL's baseball page. Must have been an AP story that credited me and the *Sentinel* on the story. That was definitely it."

Morris felt his pulse subside. He had survived.

"You're certain about that, Mr. Morris?" Hightower said.

"Yeah, it was something like that," Morris said. "Not that it matters. The story is the story. I'm sorry you're mad about it, but that's the breaks. Now if you don't mind, I've got some work to do."

"Mr. Morris, perhaps you'd like to see this before you leave," said Hightower, handing him the clip file.

Morris took the stapled file. His story detailing the trade was the first story.

"Yeah, there's my story," he said. "Right on top, like it should be."

"Read on, Mr. Morris," Hightower said.

Morris turned the page. There was Riley's story. The headline and subhead screamed at him.

CUBS PLAY IT SAFE
Opt for pitching; place rookie on 15-day disabled list

"What?" Morris said. He read the story out loud.

By Joe Riley
Sentinel Staff Writer
    MESA, Ariz.—Rather than make a trade, the Cubs decided to make a statement: They think they have enough pitching within the organization.
    The Sentinel has learned that righthanded starter Tyler Hurlock, who has spent the bulk of his five professional seasons in the Cubs' farm system, and non-roster invitee Randy Willingham, a lefthanded middle reliever, will be on the Opening Day roster. The Cubs also will announce that rookie catcher Omar Hernandez, who would have begun the season in the starting lineup, has a strained quadriceps muscle and will be placed on the 15-day disabled list. Until his return, the Cubs will use the switch-hitting Barry Garrison in Hernandez's place, as well as utility man Varsity Mormoa, who was drafted as a catcher.
    With all-star reliever Casey Harris also on the disabled list, the Cubs needed another arm in the bullpen. Hurlock struggled as spring training came to a close, but not enough for the Cubs to explore other options. Willingham, given almost no chance to make the team at camp's beginning, quietly established himself as one of the team's most dependable middle relievers during the spring.

Morris's hands began to shake. The clip file fell to the carpeted clubhouse floor.
"Mr. Morris, would you like to amend your version of events?" Hightower said. "It seems as if there's a discrepancy."
"I stand by my story," Morris said defiantly.
"That is most unfortunate," Hightower said. "Other than the correct spellings of the names involved, your story contains not one accurate fact. I am now at liberty to tell you that there was no trade and that, indeed, Hurlock and young Willingham will be in San Diego for our first game."
Hurlock and Willingham pumped their fists at each other. As soon as the paperwork was filed, the two players would begin earn-

ing the major league minimum of $200,000. For Hurlock, who made $54,000 in Triple A (plus whatever he made during the occasional call-up to the big club), and Willingham, who received $21,000 in Single A, the news was the equivalent of winning baseball's lotto.

"You want the NCAA pool ticket back?" Willingham whispered. "I think I'm going to be okay, money-wise."

"Keep it," Hurlock said. "You've got a family."

"But—"

"Think of it as my welcome-to-the-bigs gift," said Hurlock. "Now be quiet."

Hightower continued. "I'm not sure where you got your information, but it certainly wasn't from anyone within this organization. And to be quite honest, I anticipate that your ability to generate stories will be severely hampered in the future, given this most grievous mistake. I plan on contacting your publisher, editor, and sports editor immediately following our meeting here."

"This is impossible!" Morris said, his voice cracking in desperation. "I know Riley had the same story!"

"How would you know that, R.J.?" Riley said.

"Because I just know," Morris stammered.

"You looked, didn't you?" Riley said.

"Looked at what? I don't know what you're talking about."

"You're right. 'Downloaded' is a better word," said Riley.

"You're crazy," said Morris, stalling for time as he tried to find a friendly face. "Braz, c'mon . . . you know me. Would I do something like that?"

Braswell said nothing.

"Not all the time," Riley said. "Your lap dog Blair did it most of the time, didn't he? It took me a while to figure out, but only because I didn't think anyone would stoop that low."

"Don't flatter yourself," Morris said.

"And don't embarrass yourself," Riley said. "I made some calls. You're the same guy who used to spy on other writers by listening through the air conditioning vents of the adjoining room. When you used to cover the Bears, your nickname was 'Sneaks,' because you always tried to sneak a peek at everyone's computer screens."

"What do you expect them to say, that I beat them on stories fair and square?" Morris said. "That they weren't good enough? People always have excuses." Morris's face brightened. "Hey, Casey, remember that time in Chicago when Braz here told the umpires to check your glove for sandpaper? You were throwing hummingbirds up there—wild shit—and they couldn't hit a thing. So Braz thought you were cheating. Same thing as this."

Morris stared triumphantly at Riley and Hightower.

"I *was* cheating," said Harris, smiling. "I slipped the strip of sandpaper in my mouth when LaRussa came out of the dugout."

"Goddamn, I knew it," Braswell said.

"We're getting off-point here," Hightower said. "Continue, Mr. Riley."

"R.J.'s 'system' was simple," Riley said. "I'd leave the workroom and either he or Blair would pop open my Mac, press a key—because they knew that activated the screen—and then call up whatever I was working on that day. You had to find the right icon, but once you did, you were in."

"You're full of shit," Morris said. "You're making this up as you go along."

Riley ignored him. "Of course, it's risky sitting at someone else's desk, opening someone else's computer, scrolling through the icons, finding the right one, and then reading an entire story," he said. "It takes time. Sometimes too much time. That's how R.J. used to do it during the old days with the other Cubs beat guys. But the system wasn't quite safe enough. I'm guessing he almost got caught a few times, right, R.J.?"

"I hope you have a good lawyer," Morris said. "Defamation of character can be expensive. By the way, do you own or rent?"

"By the way," said Riley, reaching into his workbag, "does this look familiar?"

Riley pulled out a 3Com Palm Pilot VIIx, a hand-held wireless organizer with a small antenna, web access, and wireless radio. Morris angrily reached for it, but not before Riley dropped it back into his bag.

"R.J., where are your manners?" Riley said.

"That's not yours, you son of a bitch!" Morris said angrily. "You had no right!"

"Son, you had better settle down," Braswell said to Morris. "And Riley, you had better wrap this up."

"They're called Palms," Riley said. "This one's a Palm VIIx and it was R.J.'s answer to his time problem. They're fast and they're compatible with my Mac, and Nadel's computer, and Armour's computer, and Hill's computer, and even your computer, Jim."

Hightower shuddered. He'd have the security utilities program upgraded later in the day for the office Dells.

Riley continued. "All R.J. had to do was connect the 'hotsync' cable from his Palm VIIx to one of our computers, call up a story, and download it. Instead of spending five, ten minutes reading each story on each screen—like he used to do—he could download the information in thirty, forty seconds. What used to be a dangerous proposition was suddenly a lot less risky."

"Surely it couldn't have been that easy," Hightower said.

"The only tricky part was downloading the Palm software programs into our computers," Riley said. "That takes about ten minutes apiece. But you only have to do that once, and after that he was home free."

"Mr. Morris?" Hightower said.

"This is a hell of an operation you're running here, Jim," Morris said. "You pull me into a clubhouse, make accusations. Maybe you've forgotten I've won a few writing awards, that I've got some juice in Chicago. I've got a reputation. This guy here has nothing."

"You're right," Riley said. "You're a hell of a baseball writer. You worked your ass off, but you also cheated it off, too."

"I don't have to sit here and take this," Morris said.

"If I have anything to say about it," Hightower said, "your Baseball Writers card will be revoked, as will your Wrigley Field privileges. In other words, we won't have to take you."

"You're going to listen to this . . . this fiction?" said Morris, fumbling for words. "He's reaching. I've been on this beat for years. I don't need to cheat."

"You apparently didn't need your ethics, either," Hightower said. "Several of our interns corroborated Mr. Riley's suspicions. You and Mr. Blair were seen on numerous occasions sitting at or very near the other reporters' work areas."

"That proves nothing," Morris said.

"It proves everything, as far as I'm concerned. In addition, we do have this Palm VIIx," said Hightower, patting Riley's workbag.

Morris stared at Hightower, then turned to Braswell, then to Strickland. His eyes finally settled on Riley.

"You think you've won, don't you?" Morris said. "But I'm gonna have a job tomorrow, and every day after that. You think the Guild is going to let management fire me over some fantasy allegations? Okay, so I don't cover the Cubs. I was getting tired of them anyway—sorry, Strickie, sorry, Skip. But you're the one in deep shit. You're the one who should be worried about having a job."

Riley leaned down and retrieved the clip file. If nothing else, he would always have the photocopy of Morris's bogus story. Maybe he'd frame it. It would be a nice memento. On slow days, Riley's mom could show the bridge club.

"Yeah, R.J., you're probably right. But I'll always have this," he said, waving the file in a "bye-bye" motion.

"And you'll always have this," said Strickland to Morris, squeezing off a shot from a camera borrowed from one of the clubbies. "Say 'cheat.'"

Morris covered his face and ran from the room.

"Hmm. Camera shy," said Strickland.

Hightower actually giggled.

Riley moved toward the clubhouse door. Braswell opened it for him and grinned. "Son, you're welcome in my office any ol' day. No need to knock, either."

"Thanks, Braz," said Riley, suddenly exhausted. He looked at his wristwatch. It wasn't even 8:15 yet.

By noon, Morris had been relieved of his Cubs duties; Hightower had seen to that. A new beat man would meet the team in Anaheim. But true to Morris's prediction, the Guild was already arguing that the evidence against their union brother was entirely circumstantial. A terrible coincidence, nothing more. Morris was immediately reassigned to the Bulls. Nonetheless, the embarrassed *Standard* executives promised to issue a retraction regarding the trade story the next day.

Riley returned to his condo and packed his suitcase and garment bag. He arranged for a maid service to clean the place and left the

Sentinel's address with the condo manager, just in case there was anything left of the security deposit. He was going to miss the Volvo, but not the condo, and certainly not Mesa.

Riley tried calling Butler, but Sheila said he was in another meeting. "Something big is going on here," she said. "Call back in a couple of hours. I'll have all the gossip by then."

"Thanks, Sheila," Riley said. "I'll be over at the Harry if you need me."

"I've got the number," she said. "You run along."

The players wouldn't be available until 2 P.M. Hightower had scheduled the team photo for one o'clock and Hoffman had dovetailed that with the baseball-card people. Photographers from Topps, Upper Deck, and Fleer were in attendance. If everything went as planned, the players would start trickling into the clubhouse by early afternoon—plenty of time for the beat guys to get whatever they needed. At four the team would leave on a chartered bus for the Phoenix airport. From there, on to John Wayne Airport in Orange County, home of the Anaheim Angels.

Riley needed to write a follow-up story to the roster moves and also file some notes. It wouldn't take too long.

The light was off in the media workroom. Riley searched clumsily for the switch against the wall. The fluorescent tubes popped to life, revealing Hill, Nadel, Armour, Hoffman, Phil Mitchell, and a perfectly coifed Gary Danger. They began applauding.

"Your first and last standing o," said Hill.

"Don't tell Hightower I was here," said Hoffman.

Riley bowed his head and pinched the bridge of his nose. "Today . . . day . . . day," said Riley, "I consider myself . . . self . . . self . . . the luckiest man in the world . . . world . . . world."

"You should," said Armour. "You killed the Wicked Witch of the West, Dorothy."

"You guys helped," Riley said.

"How?" said Nadel.

"It was Hill, really," Riley said. "Remember when you were talking about laptops, and Hill said he liked the Mac because of the screensaver?"

"Yeah, so what?" Armour said.

"Well, Columbo, I'll explain it to you," Riley said. "The screensaver kicks in automatically after the keypad has been left alone for five minutes. Then it'll run for five more minutes before the computer switches to 'sleep' mode. That shuts off the screen completely. I always set it to 'sleep' when I leave the workroom, so if you saw the screensaver, that meant someone else was on my computer less than ten minutes earlier."

"Wow," Armour said. "And you're calling *me* Columbo?"

"Plus I kept noticing my computer was always a little out of place when I came in after a game or after working the clubhouse. At first I thought it was the interns who were moving it, but I asked them; they said they were under strict orders not to touch a thing on our desks."

"They are," Hoffman said.

"So, if it wasn't the interns, it had to be Morris or Blair," Riley said.

"And that's how he got the scoops?" Hill said. "It seems even too slimy for Morris."

"Ego," Riley said. "He had to feed the beast. Blair owed him, which is why either he or Blair was almost always in the workroom when the rest of us were gone. Blair did most of the weasel work and Morris would throw him a bone every so often. You don't need a phone jack to e-mail someone with the Palm, so Morris and Blair could have been trading instructions while we were in the clubhouse or press box."

"Okay, that answers that," Hill said. "But what about your story? I saw you send it in," Hill said. "Heard the modem tone and everything."

"I sent it to our Internet department," Riley said. "Nobody's there, but the computer can still receive transmissions."

"Nice touch," Hoffman said. "But the one thing I don't get is how the interns saw anything. I keep them pretty busy. Plus, they're under orders to leave you guys alone and let you work."

Riley turned away and began whistling.

"Okay, what'd you do with my interns?" Hoffman said.

"You probably don't want to know," Riley said. "Let's just say it was the best two hundred fifty dollars Travis Campbell ever spent."

"Meaning . . . ?" Hoffman said.

"Meaning interns don't make much money," Riley said. "So when someone offers them one twenty-five apiece to keep an eye on the media workroom, they tend to watch."

"But I don't get the Campbell connection," Hill said.

"And you never will," Riley said.

"How'd you get Morris's Palm VIIx?" Nadel said. "None of us ever saw it. Plus, he never lets anyone look inside that steel briefcase of his. The damn thing is usually locked."

"I never said it was *his* Palm VIIx," Riley said. "I bought it yesterday during lunch. And as soon as I can think of a good enough reason, I'm returning it for a refund."

"But how did you know Morris had one?" Nadel said. "And how did you know which model?"

"Calculated guess," Riley said. "You're the ones who told me about his thing for computer gadgets. The Palms are the best on the market, so I figured that's the way he'd go. Remember how he knew about every Marriott, had every plane fare booked, already had dinner reservations, could even tell you where the closest ATMs were?"

"Yeah, the guy is like a travel agent," Armour said.

"You can get all that stuff on the Palm VIIx," Riley said. "You can call UPS on the thing."

"Where's Blair?" Armour said.

"Gone," Hoffman said. "Even the *Herald Democrat* doesn't know where he is. He left a note saying he was resigning, effective immediately. The paper owes him all sorts of vacation and comp time, so I guess he's laying low."

"Snake," said Hill.

"So those sumbitches had been tag-teaming everybody to death," Mitchell said. "Suddenly this TV work don't feel so bad after all, Hoss."

"And the weave looks nice, too," Armour said.

"Thank you," said Mitchell and Danger simultaneously.

The phone rang at Riley's desk.

"It's probably E. Benson Lawrence himself, calling to congratulate you on a job well done," Nadel said.

Riley picked up the phone.

"Workroom," he said.

There was a long pause, followed by several "uh-huhs," followed by an "Okay, Sheila, I'll hold for him," followed by more silence, followed by a simple "thank you." Riley placed the phone back into the cradle.

"Well?" Nadel said. "I was right, wasn't I?"

"No, you were magnificently wrong," Riley said. "That was Storen. I just got canned."

"You're kidding?" Hoffman said. "On what grounds?"

"On the grounds of conduct unbecoming to a member of the *Sentinel* corporate family," Riley said. "Morris's editor called my editor to complain about my 'illegal' competitive tactics."

"But Morris was *stealing* stories from our computers," Hill said. "How can they fire you for fighting back?"

"And why didn't Butler call you first?" Armour said. "That's some chickenshit sports editor you've got there."

"Butler got canned, too," Riley said. "Actually, he resigned, but only because they were going to fire him if he didn't fire me. That's what Sheila told me between sobs."

"Butler grew a backbone," Mitchell said. "Cover me with honeydew and bury me in a red-ant pile. I've heard everything now."

"Not everything," Riley said. "It looks like both sides of the lockout are beginning to buckle. A meeting between management and the Guild is supposed to happen late tonight. This thing could be over by morning."

"I don't understand," Mitchell said.

"Sheila says Lawrence likes our new 'lean, mean machine' so much that he's only hiring back a minimum number of Guild members," Riley said. "TSNE was supposedly a target for a takeover plan, but Lawrence suddenly cooled on the idea."

"If Sheila says it, then it's gold," Mitchell said.

"That's not all," Riley said. "Circulation has dipped, but so have newsprint costs, payroll, and debt. That means more profit margin. Lawrence figures if he can make the bad publicity from the lockout go away, circulation will return to normal. Then TSNE will really be rolling in the money. Sheila said something about stock valuations catching up with 'important improvements in fundamentals.' Apparently Lawrence is going to invest big in the Internet."

"Who ever thought Sheila knew about Classical School economics?" Nadel said.

"But what about MacCauley?" Mitchell said. "He's not going to let Lawrence skate on this."

"He doesn't have much choice," Riley said. "The Guild is willing to take a chance on Lawrence, hoping he'll change his mind and take back most of Editorial. The others took the buyouts or already moved on."

"Plus, he wants to keep his job," Mitchell said.

"Survival of the fittest," Riley said.

"And what about you?" Armour said. "Even though you kicked our asses a few times, I'll hate to see you leave. Maybe if we spoke on your behalf . . ."

"Nope, I'm out of there," Riley said. "I'm taking my 401(k) and moving on."

"You could fight it," Armour said. "It doesn't make sense that Morris has a job and you don't."

"Nah, I was mini-management," he said. "Anyway, I don't want to be editing outdoors columns when I'm fifty-eight."

"What, you're gonna live with your momma in Beverly?" Mitchell said. "Maybe I can scare up something at ESPN."

"As what, your makeup man?" Riley said.

"No, research or something," Mitchell said. "They're always looking for smart help."

"You saying I have a face for radio?"

"That's exactly what I'm saying, Hoss."

"Well, fellas, since I'm now officially unemployed, I think I'll catch the next flight out of this desert hell hole," Riley said.

Twenty

THE TRAVEL AGENT BOOKED HIM on the Monday night 6:48 to Midway. Center seat. Last row. Typical TSNE efficiency. What a going-away present from his former employer.

Riley checked his mailbox—no manila envelopes today—and dropped the condo key at the front office. He loaded his bags into the trunk and then backed out of the driveway.

HONK!!!!!

Riley slammed on the brakes and craned his head out the window. Only inches from his back bumper was a late-model Jeep. Riley stuck the car in park, turned off the ignition, and hurried outside to apologize.

"I am so sorry," said Riley, paying little attention to the driver and instead marveling at how close he had come to a collision. "I wasn't paying attention and . . . well, I guess it's good you leaned on the horn. Are you okay?"

Nothing. Riley looked up. It was Omar.

"Geez, I almost barreled into your . . . Wait a second, you're the Mute Man," Riley said. "You don't understand a word I'm saying."

Omar stared at him through a pair of highway patrol–sized reflector sunglasses.

"Well, then," said Riley, "it's time to see if the Berlitz CDs really work. You laugh, I'll kill you."

Riley took a deep breath.

"*Yo voy. Yo voy a Chicago. No estoy con los Cubs. Eres un buen hombre, aunque no hables corunigo. Me gusta la manera de jugar. Tu jue-*

gas con amor por el partido. No te pierdas el amor, cómo algunos de tus compañeros del equipo."

I am leaving. I am going to Chicago. I not be around the Cubs. You are a good man, even if you don't talk to me. I like the way you play. You play with love for game. Do not lose that love like some of your teammates have.

Omar said nothing.

"Work with me here, don't work against me, Omar," Riley said. "Those CDs cost me a fortune. I spent ninety minutes a day for almost seven weeks working on the español."

Riley cleared his throat and tried again.

"*Solamente trate de hablar contigo porque tengo interés en ti, cómo persona, no solamente un jugador de béisbol. En el futuro, me llamaras? Ten cuidado con Valdez. No tengo toda confianza en él. Strickland, good hombre. El vale tú confianza. Y ojala que la pierna se sienta mejor! Un dia, dire a todas mis niños que estaba alli cuándo el gran Hernandez se hizo una liga mayor. Buena suerta a ti.*"

I only tried to talk to you because I interested in you as person, not just ballplayer. In future, you try back? Be careful with Valdez. I don't trust him all the way. Strickland good man. He is worth your trust. And I wish your leg well. One day I will tell my children I was there when the great Hernandez became a major leaguer. Good luck to you.

"Thank you," said Hernandez.

"You're welcome," Riley said.

Riley began to walk toward the Volvo when it hit him. *Thank you?*

"You sneaky Dominican . . ."

"Sumbitch?" Hernandez said.

"You speak English!"

"Quite well, actually."

"For how long?"

"Ever since the priests taught me," he said. "I was seven when I started."

"Seven," Riley said.

"*Siete.*"

"I understand," Riley said. "What I don't understand is why the silent act? Why play dumb for so long?"

"Sometimes there is wisdom in silence," he said.

"What is this, a *Kung Fu* episode?" Riley said. "You let me make an ass out of myself."

"You did it very well," the rookie said.

"And what about Valdez and some of those other guys? How did you bite your tongue when they were mocking you? I would have taken a pick ax after them."

"Anger is a useless emotion," Hernandez said. "I took their knowledge and used it to my advantage. Silence also allowed me to see everyone's true intentions."

"So you heard Valdez?"

"Valdez is a fool," Hernandez said, "but he has a pure heart."

"And Garrison?"

"Ignorant," Hernandez shrugged. "He'll make a fine backup once I'm healthy."

"About that injury," Riley said. "It wasn't until recently that I knew you were even hurt."

"Stevie D kept it a secret from the media," Hernandez said. "They wanted to see how Garrison responded to a competitive situation. The disabled list is a precautionary move more than anything else. I could play within a week."

"Why tell me any of this?" Riley said. "This would be a hell of story."

"And you would tell it to what newspaper?" Hernandez said. "You are out of work, remember?"

"Good point," said Riley.

"I tell you because you tried," Hernandez said. "No other reporter has ever tried. They treat us as if we are domestic workers. They have no understanding of what it is like to be a foreigner. Racism takes many forms. You treated me as an equal."

"But you never talked to me," Riley said.

"Yes, I did," Hernandez said.

"Oh, I forgot: the grunts," Riley said. "You're one of the most talkative grunters I've ever met."

"I spoke to you in words," Hernandez said.

"You lost me, Omar."

"I can type," he said.

"You can type," Riley said. "Congratulations. Wait a second. And I bet you had a package of manila envelopes."

"Perhaps," Hernandez said, his mouth struggling against a grin.

"Omar, I pity the poor bastard who underestimates you," Riley said.

"Me, too," Hernandez said.

"I owe you. I would have never made it without those envelopes."

"But you didn't make it. I didn't do enough."

"You did more than you'll ever know," Riley said. "You gave me back my pride. I'd lost that years ago."

The two men shook hands.

"This stays our secret," Hernandez said. "When I'm ready to talk, I will send you another envelope."

"I'll keep my mailbox light on for you," Riley said. "And by the way, you owe me $9.99 for the translation book."

"That is one envelope you will never receive," said Hernandez, smiling, as he pulled away.

The flight home took nearly five hours. There was a delay out of Phoenix and then bad headwinds. Riley's mom picked him up at Midway, where he was greeted by the loving Gil Thorp, man's best friend. Slobber kisses for everyone.

"Happy to be home, hon?" said Riley's mom.

"More than you'll ever know," he said. "Sorry about the late flight."

"I'd do anything to get rid of this pooch," she said. "Pig in a dog's suit, that's what he is. Aren't you, Gil?"

The cocker's tail thumped against the back seat.

"Anyway, I cleaned up your house and had your car battery recharged," she said. "There's food in the fridge and Gil has a fresh bag of kibble. And if I've timed this right, the six-pack of Old Style should be cold by the time I get you home."

"Thanks, Mom."

"For you, hon, anything," she said.

"You know I got fired, don't you?"

"Yes, hon. I heard."

"And you're not upset?"

"I knew you were unhappy for years," she said. "Maybe the change will do you good."

"Mom, it's not like I have another job all lined up," Riley said.

"I've got some severance, that's it."

"The DMV is taking applications," she said, smiling.

"Very funny, Mom."

"I thought so," she said, giggling.

The drive took 25 minutes. Riley turned the radio on long enough to hear the sports update on WBBM: Tennessee had won the Final Four. Willingham would be singing "Rocky Top" for years to come, thanks to Hurlock. Hurlock had given him the winning NCAA pool ticket.

Riley had been gone for seven weeks, but it seemed like seven years. They drove past the Cork, took a left at 106th and a right on Hamilton. Riley's front porch light was on. Moths fluttered about.

"See you tomorrow, hon," said Gloria Riley. "Get some sleep. You too, Gil—pain-in-the-ass dog. Did I tell you he climbed on the dining-room table and ate a pound of tuna fish salad?"

"He's on the Scarsdale Diet," Riley said.

"Well, he's all yours," she said, patting Gil on the head.

The house looked better than he had left it. For starters, he could see his kitchen counter; Mom and her cleaning fetish. "So that's what formica looks like," he said to himself.

Riley popped open an Old Style and punched his message machine. He had checked it the night before and there was nothing. Now it rewound for a full 30 seconds.

Beep. "Riley, this is Rat. You got screwed, man. They asked me back, but after what happened to you, I don't know. Hang in there, man. I'll call you tomorrow."

Beep. "Butler, here. I tried you in Mesa, but your phone was already disconnected. I'm sorry how it all worked out. I tried to stand up for you, but, well . . . I'm sorry. If you need me, I'll be at home. I'm taking a job at my father-in-law's PR firm. There might be an opening, if you're interested. I also made a couple other calls to some people I know. Again, I'm sorry."

Mitchell was right; Butler finally had some vertebrae.

Beep. "This is Storen. Please return your ID badge at your earliest convenience. Thank you."

Beep. "Riley, my friend, this is Jack Redmond calling. I just wanted to say, way to go, young man. You put a very big smile on an old hack's face."

Beep. "Joe, my name is Bill Greer with the *Los Angeles Times*. I've spoken with Terry Butler and I'd like for you to give me a call if you get a minute. My number is 1-800-LA-Times. Just ask for my extension."

Beep. "T.L. Mann calling from the *Denver Post*. I'm the assistant managing editor for sports and I'm looking for a national baseball writer. Ours just left for the *Globe*, so we're in a hurry. Give me a call as soon as you get in."

Riley couldn't write the numbers down fast enough.

Beep. "This is Dave Smythe's administrative assistant at the *Dallas Morning News*. If convenient, could you contact us first thing in the morning? Dave would like to discuss a writing opportunity with you."

Riley knocked over his beer as he reached for a new scrap of paper. Gil began licking up the Old Style.

"Cheers," said Riley. Gil slurped away.

Beep. "Hoffman here. You're not going to believe this, but I think Hightower wants to hire you for something. Call! Soon!"

Riley had barely rewound the tape when the phone rang. He let the machine do its work as he went to retrieve a new beer from the fridge.

Beep. "This is Pappy the Pirate from the Barnberry School of Art. You've just won a scholarship. Report immediately to your driveway, where a woman with an expensive car and a crooked nose will be waiting with your admission papers." There was a pause. "Yes, stupid, it's me. I'm on my cell phone. I heard what happened. I know this will come as a shock, but your mom told me what time you were coming in tonight."

Riley looked out the front door. Megan was there leaning against the Audi. She held the trophy in her right hand.

"Hello, bunny boy," Megan said.

"Hello, Employee of the Month," Riley said.

"Still interested in pursuing a dominant girlfriend–cowering boyfriend thing?" she said.

"I can't afford you," he said. "I'm out of work."

"Good. That gives us more time to know each other," she said, moving toward him.

"How do I know you're my type?" said Riley.

"Because your mother said I was. And because I've got this trophy." Megan tilted the trophy until she could read the engraving by moonlight.

To Miss Wisconsin, Hacks–Fronties 2000 MVP.
From your adoring public.

"Sorry about the football guy," Riley said. "They didn't have chickie hoops figurines."

"I love it," she said. "But I loved your letter even more."

"I bet you say that to all the knuckleheads who grovel for forgiveness," Riley said.

"Just the cute ones."

"That's what Strickland said you'd say."

"Liar," she said.

"Told me himself yesterday," Riley said. "Said you only had eyes for me."

"That's the last time I drink champagne with him," she said. "I'll kill him."

"The Cubs wouldn't be pleased."

"Brett told me a few things, too," said Megan.

"This should be rich," said Riley. "Like . . . ?"

"Like he thinks he saw that asshole Cubs scout drop a tablet into poor Dawna's drink," she said. "He also saw Dawna today at the Harry Caray. She was looking for you. She told Brett the whole story. And Brett, our new TSNE business partner—ta-da—told me."

"So I'm forgiven?"

"Totally," she said.

Megan slipped her arms around his waist.

"I love a man who can do ten push-ups."

"When you say ten, does that mean in a row?"

"You can work up to it," she said. "In the meantime, how about a kiss?"

"With lips?" Riley said. "I'm a little rusty."

"I'll be the judge of that," she said, pulling him toward her.